Carolina Rain

Nancy B. Brewer

Nancy B Brewer
2011

Carolina Rain

Nancy B. Brewer

Cover Design by: Sean Snakenberg, Brentwood
Cover Photography by: Vernon A. Brewer, Jr.

PUBLISHED BY:
BRENTWOOD CHRISTIAN PRESS
4000 BEALLWOOD AVENUE
COLUMBUS, GEORGIA 31904

Dedication and Acknowledgments

Carolina Rain

is dedicated to my husband and best friend, Vernon.

To JoAnn Rish, I wish to express my sincere appreciation
for her support and encouragement.
Without her this book would not be possible.

A word from the author

Writing *Carolina Rain* was a labor of love, which led to discoveries that have changed my life. For over four years I traveled across North and South Carolina collecting stories, old letters, visiting cemeteries and researching the history of not only my own ancestors, but also others whose stories politely presented themselves to me. Some remain famous with their names forever recorded on the pages of history. Still others left this world in a splash of color without acknowledgment of glory or honor.

As you turn the pages of *Carolina Rain* you will find yourself traveling in time; your journey will take you from Charleston, South Carolina to Stanly County, North Carolina.

Although *Carolina Rain* is written from a woman's point of view, it is certain to appeal to everyone. In 1860, the fast approaching conflict between the North and South was fearful and overwhelming for Theodosia Elizabeth (Lizzie) Sanders. Yet, underneath the layers of lace and petticoats, you will discover *Lizzie* to be a strong-willed and determined young woman.

Nancy B. Brewer
June 2010

The story content of Carolina Rain and its characters are fiction. Any resemblance to persons living or dead is purely coincidental.

CHAPTER 1

Sandy Ridge

We were all born on that plantation just north of Charleston. The oldest being my sister, Sara Dianne or "Sallie," and the youngest was Annabelle. Sallie would be described for the most part as agreeable, quiet and reserved; nothing could be further from that description in regard to dear Annabelle. Mother claimed she had the same temperament as the thunderstorm the night she was born, but Papa said she brought a sense of humor to our family.

A perfect little blue-eyed boy was born after Annabelle; sadly, he was not to live. The angels knew he was too good for this world and took him before we scarcely had a chance to know him.

"Baby, baby brother, seldom a day passes that I do not think of thee."

I was born on Tuesday, October 6, 1842 and I am the middle child, Theodosia Elizabeth Sanders or "Lizzie" as Papa called me. Mother was not too fond of the name Lizzie. She said it sounded like a slave name. Even so, I liked having two Z's in my name and it made me feel special. Papa said all his girls were special. Sallie was steady like the earth, Annabelle ever changing like the wind and I was his fiery one.

My father and mother are Jacob Sanders and Temperance Morris. When they were married in 1838, my father leased a little house with enough land to take up farming. He was following the same path as his father and his father before him, for not much ever changed in Montgomery County, North Carolina.

Just two weeks after they were married, fate revealed a different path before the young couple. Papa's uncle of questionable character, had met with an untimely end. Even though there were some strange circumstances regarding his death, he was kind enough to leave Papa this plot of land. My grandparents were sure the property was just a worthless six hundred acres of crawling timbers and soggy soil that was good for nothing more than breeding mosquitoes and Negroes.

My father was young and opportunities of any kind were rare; therefore, he and his new bride set their sights on the road to South Carolina. Papa had never been out of Montgomery County in his life. Yet, he declared it was his keen navigational skills that led him right to the most beautiful place on earth. Mother argued it was the fine map his Uncle George laid out.

Father told us many times about their trip to South Carolina. It was Mother's expressions that led us to believe Papa had a tendency to exaggerate, especially the part about fighting off wild animals and Indians. One thing for sure, it was hard to imagine my mother riding across the country in a homemade wagon pulled by a pair of broken down old mules. In fact, it is hard to imagine my mother anywhere except on this plantation.

One part of the story that was always consistent was how this place got its name. At the end of the journey they both climbed out of the wagon and ran through the fields like children. When they got to the top of the ridge, Mother caught her breath, turned to Papa, and said, sandy ridge. Tears came to Papa's eyes because "Sandy" was his nickname. Although he was touched, her reference was not toward him, but the ridge of soft sandy soil. They had a good laugh but both decided "Sandy Ridge" was a fitting name.

At first, they set up housekeeping in the old frame farmhouse that was there from the beginning. Papa swore he would never tear down that old house as a reminder that God rewards the faithful and hardworking. Papa was faithful and hardworking but most of all he was a dreamer. His spirit was unbeatable and in less than ten years, the house I grew up in was built.

We raised tobacco, corn, and flax. At times a bit of gold rice was harvested but cotton was the main cash crop. In addition to the cash crops, we raised all the other essentials for our existence. It was a year round process of growing, harvesting, preserving and putting up enough food to feed the slaves and ourselves.

All the slaves, even the children, had a job as a weaver, spinner, seamstress, cook, housekeeper, field worker, nursemaid or blacksmith. Papa treated the slaves fairly, but occasionally one would be hard to manage or stubborn. "It's time to put that one in my pocket," Papa would say. I learned later that this meant he was going to sell that slave and put the money in his pocket.

Many folks discouraged teaching Negroes to read, even the Bible. Papa taught some of our slaves to read and Mother had a little church building built in the slave quarters for the slaves to worship freely. Although Papa sometimes lost count of how many slaves we had, Mother never did. She kept excellent records on all of them, right down to every birth, marriage and death.

Since I was only three years of age when we moved into the big house, it was there most of my memories began. The big house was built in the midst of a welcoming grove of live oak trees and looked as if it had always sat on that very spot.

At the entrance way leading up to the house were two large stone pillars with modern gas lanterns. On a clear night, the lamps would completely illuminate the front lawn. Sometimes, I would imagine seeing ghosts tip-toeing in the rose garden or fairies playing in the daffodils and irises.

I have many pleasant memories of Sandy Ridge, all of which are forever imbedded in my mind like raindrops dripping off the fingertips of the trees, the grounds glistening in the morning dew and sunsets down by the duck pond.

If you were a guest arriving at Sandy Ridge, first you might stop and comment on its impressive shadow, the wrap around porches or the carved white columns. Before you entered through the large oak doors, you were sure to stop to admire the ornate railings or the sparkling tabby stone drive. Yet, most guests were speechless once they stepped inside the foyer. It was here Mother's finest treasure hung, the Austrian crystal chandelier.

Lastly, you would be invited to hang your coat on the large hall tree, adjust your petticoat or bow tie in the mirror and take a seat in one of the four French chairs. There you would wait for Cato or Mammy to make the announcement of your arrival. This was nearly a daily occurrence at our house. In those days, Mother was quite the social butterfly.

The first floor was adapted for entertaining small intimate gatherings or large functions and balls. Pocket doors on one side of the hall separated the music room and parlor. On the opposite side of the hall was Father's study and the library set up the same. Even the front windows converted into doors; giving way to nice breezes and strolls in the garden on hot summer nights.

We had two dining rooms, one for formal entertaining and the other for informal family meals. In the center of the house was the great sitting room with two marble fireplaces and Italian moldings. Toward the rear of the house were the butler's pantry and a large laundry room for sewing and spinning.

Leading up to the second floor was an impressive walnut stair railing which was hand-carved by the oldest slave on our plantation. He could still remember his African name and coming over on the slave ship. My sisters and I named him "The Wizard" or "Wiz". He could fix anything, but it was his magic that amazed us the most. His greatest trick was throwing his voice and seemingly making words come right out of the mouth of our old Billy goat.

Up the walnut staircase were eight bedrooms or nine if you count the nursery. At the top of the stairs was a cozy room with a fireplace and bookshelves filled with hundreds of books. This was where our family would gather on rainy days to spend the afternoon. In the corner, underneath the large oval window was the spot I called my studio. The light was good, even in the winter and I could spread out on the pine floor and work on my scrapbook and secret poems. Once the weather broke, I found the fresh air on the veranda more inspirational. Our upstairs porch was well used in the summer for entertaining and providing a cool place to sleep on hot humid nights.

The third floor was mainly used for storage and occasionally as temporary quarters for servants when someone was sick, like the time all three of us had the measles. Sallie and I responded quickly to the doctor's medicine, but not little Annabelle. Her poor little body was drenched in sweat and for days she lay helplessly jerking in horrible pain. The doctor said there was nothing else he could do.

It is very possible Annabelle would have died if Mother had not given Mammy permission to tend to her. After just one day of Mammy's strange medicine of herbs and boiled sheep manure, her fever broke. Mother said that boney little woman was a Godsend, but the doctor claimed it to be nothing short of a miracle. In time, Annabelle did recover, but the illness left her with a weak heart.

As the years passed, we were changing and the house evolved around us. This brings me to the time Papa returned from abroad, telling us about a most respectable home where he was an honored guest. Mother's eyes glistened as he told of the private room called the water closet, designed solely for nature's necessities. It was decided the nursery would be transformed into our very own water closet. First ordered from England was an oak washstand with a matching washbowl and chamber pot. After the piping was completed came my favorite, the white enamel bathing tub. I cannot tell you what a luxury it was to soak in that big tub by the fireplace. My sisters and I would often fight over whose turn it was in the private room. Papa made many threats to dismantle the whole room to restore the peace. We all knew it was just talk. Papa enjoyed spending his money and spoiling us all too well.

Although Mother was from a humble background, she had the most elegant manners. To most she was not a raving beauty, but Papa's eyes saw differently and he commissioned an artist to paint a portrait of her. I think I was about ten years old when Mr. Devoe came to do the painting. He was the smallest grown man I had ever seen. He swished around like a woman and spoke like someone suffering with the vapors. He was of great curiosity and we tried to hide behind the curtains and watch him work. When he discovered us, he threw down his brushes, ran out of the room and demanded to see our father at once. The whole household heard the ruckus and came out to see what was going on. Papa very calmly assured him the children would bother him no longer. Then Mr. Devoe flipped around and pranced back upstairs to his easel.

Once the door closed, Cato put his hands on his hips and began to parade around and mock Mr. Devoe. Old Cato, our manservant, was just as round as he was tall. He was giving us an entertaining show until Mammy scolded us for making fun of folks and told Cato, *"To gets his black ass back to work."*

For over three weeks we had to tiptoe around to make sure we did not disturb the artist at work. I was very glad the morning he announced he was ready to unveil the completed painting. Mother's portrait was extremely flattering and Papa said it was a masterpiece.

Almost as quickly as Mr. Devoe could get his money, he packed up and left. That very day before the sunset, the portrait was hung over the mantel gazing out the window into the rose garden.

Just beyond the rose gardens was where the second kitchen was built. On New Years Day 1858, the original kitchen went up in flames. All efforts were made to save the kitchen, but by evening all that remained was a flickering pile of embers. Papa insisted on building the new kitchen further from the house. From then on, the slaves moaned about how far they had to carry the food and Mother complained that the food was always cold.

Perhaps I have been descriptive enough that you might find your way around Sandy Ridge, still there is one more room. It is the place that separates me from the rest of the world, my room. Everything about that room was as familiar to me as the back of my hand. I used to lie in bed and count the yellow roses on the wallpaper. Over by the window was my writing desk and in the second drawer were my secret poems and letters. I kept the key to the drawer in a wooden box underneath my bed. This little box held some of my most precious treasures, a blue lace handkerchief, a feather an Indian gave me, a couple of my baby teeth, the little collar that belonged to my beloved little dog and the tear vial with the tears I shed when my baby brother died.

Sandy Ridge was not just our home, it was who we were. Papa used to say he could not tell where he stopped and the land began. Just like Papa, I loved that plantation, too. I can still remember the sweet aroma of freshly mowed hay and the musty smell of the boxwoods after a summer rain. Nor will ever I forget listening from my window to the soft muffled voices of the Negroes working in the fields.

A huge magnolia tree grew just outside my bedroom window; I used to call its white blossoms the angels of the garden. Yet, it was its strong branches that I cherished the most. I escaped countless noon naps by climbing those old limbs. Never had I experienced so much freedom as those secret afternoons in the company of my best friend, Lottie, Mammy's oldest girl.

Sometimes we went down to the cotton fields and picked a watermelon or "August ham" as the slaves called them. They were planted out in the fields so the slaves could refresh themselves while picking cotton. Lottie and I would enjoy our treat and then see who could spit the seeds the greater distance.

I was clever enough to be back in my room before anyone knew the better, except for one day. Lottie and I were skipping stones down by the creek and I fell in headfirst. I was dripping in mud as I stepped though the window only to find Mammy sitting by the window waiting. She had planned to surprise me but it was she who was surprised. I will never forget the look on her face when she jerked me up under her arm. She hauled me down the hall to the washtub scolding me all the way. *"Yous Mama iz sho' gonna raise torment if she ketches yous in des shape. I's mights have to scrub de hide off and cut yous hair down to da the ruts to get its clean."*

I did not think she would do it; still she nearly scared me to death. What would Mother say if I came down to supper with chopped off hair? She did not scrub the hide off me, but I was plenty pink until the next morning. By the time it was all over, Mammy's black face was greasy with sweat and her white apron was as muddy as that old creek. Poor Lottie had to spend all evening scrubbing and mopping up the trail of mud we left. I often wondered if she got a whipping to boot. If she did, she never told me.

Mammy agreed to stay shut-mouthed if we promised not to go back down to the creek. She reinforced her threat by telling us of a big old daddy king snake that laid waiting by the creek and was known to eat little children whole. Lottie and I were afraid of snakes, especially ones that could eat children whole.

Yet, to children being bored is worse than fear, so after a couple of weeks we decided to take our chances. This time I had a clever idea of how not to soil our clothes. Lottie said it was a fine idea too. She figured folks did not need to wear so many clothes in the summertime anyway. Free as little birds, we were just two skinny little girls running around buck-naked with flowers in our hair and wings made out of branches. Lottie being as black as night, was the fairy of the night and I was the fairy of the daylight. I will always remember those carefree days of swimming in the creek and lying in the sun with my best friend.

Lottie was two years older and she knew all sorts of things about grown up ladies and how babies were born, which she eagerly shared. I taught Lottie to read and write a bit and shared my pens and papers with her. She would bring me her artwork and I would paste it in my scrapbook. She was my friend and we told each other everything. I remember the time she told me about my cousin Gerald making her show him her breast. She said she was so scared that she never told. I often wished I had told and maybe someone would have beaten the stuffings out of him.

Lottie was a tender soul and sometimes if I was sick, she slept on the floor by my bed just to make sure I did not die in the night. I thought Lottie and I would be together forever, but when Lottie was just fourteen Papa traded her for a big Negro man named Samuel, who was trained to be an over-seer. I understood that Lottie would be only a few miles down the road, yet my heart was broken. Papa assured me she would be well taken care of and he would take me to visit her whenever I pleased.

I did go to see her a time or two. The first time I visited her all she talked about was her new mistress. *"My new Missus gots mo' dresses dan yo' eb'ry did see. Her drawers are full of 'fumes and fancy hankies. She wears silk stockin' an' her legs da be slick as glass with not a hair on dem.'*

When she saw I was curious, she said, *"I's tells yous her secret, she shaves her legs jes likes a man a shavin' his face. 'Missus says it'z way the French women do."*

I left feeling as ugly as a mud fence and thought about going straight home and taking a man's razor to my legs too. How dare she think so highly of this new mistress. Apparently, she had not missed me very much. Several months passed and I got a note from her begging me to pay her a visit. Fearing something was wrong, I went right away. However, I quickly found out she was happy enough to bust. She had gotten herself a husband and wanted to tell me all about him, including her private wifely duties. Just a few months ago, I would not have been the least bit embarrassed by anything Lottie said. Now, sitting there with her on that little porch, it was different. We had grown up and we were no longer children. Sadly, we discovered how very different we were. That day when we said our goodbyes there were tears in our eyes for we both knew that our friendship would exist only as a sweet childhood memory. I will always think fondly of those summer days when we were just two innocent little girls who loved each other without pride or prejudices.

About a year later Papa told me she had a baby. We sent her a nice package of food and clothes for the little one. I got this note back from her,

"Deer Lizzie, I got a big babe boy, his name iz Toby. Lov Lottie."

CHAPTER 2

Miss Georgette

Now, I hope you have come to know me well enough that I may speak to you like an old friend, just like Lottie and I used to do. I wish all I had to share with you were the joys of a privileged young girl living on a southern plantation. My friend, much has changed since those carefree days. Many of those I loved are forever silent. For their sakes, I must find the courage to tell our story. I have wasted too much time already; I must begin.

Sandy Ridge
Monday, 27 August 1860

It was a beautiful Indian summer morning and perfect for savoring a few extra minutes in bed. There was a breeze blowing through my bedroom window; the air was as crisp as a bite of a fresh red apple.

At any moment, I was expecting Mother to come through the door. Sister Sallie's debut party had been just two years ago and I was well aware of what "coming of age" was all about. I wondered if this was all there was to a girl's life, act nice, look pretty and hook some unsuspecting fool into marrying you? Mother said a whole new world was about to unfold before me and I should be happy. I felt more like a puppet on a string, with no control over my own life. No more secret adventures, no more playing in the barn and down by the creek. I suppose it was time to grow up and leave childish things behind, after all I would be eighteen soon. The finest families from Richmond to Atlanta were all invited to my debut party. Papa had even extended an open invitation to the senior cadets at the Citadel.

I was debating on just staying in bed for the rest of my life. In reality, it was already eight o'clock and I should have been up an hour ago. Mother and I had an appointment at the dress shop. Oddly enough, there was not a peep outside my door. I knew she had not forgotten. Just last night I overheard Papa tell her, "Don't worry, Tempie, even if you put Lizzie in a feed sack dress she will still be the prettiest girl in Charleston."

Papa's opinion could have been a wee bit jaded. He loved my sisters of course, but I was clearly his favorite. Papa always said I took after him, good-looking and stubborn.

Although my sisters were bonnie looking girls with big blue eyes, it was always their battle to fit into their clothing from one season to the next. Annabelle hated the fact sweets did not agree with her waistline. I, however, was blessed with the better constitution and could eat like a horse and never gain a pound. They envied me a bit and sometimes their jealously got the best of them, but our little spats were usually short-lived. My coloring was like Papa's, but sisters took after Mother with redheaded complexions and strawberry blonde hair. If the sun was up, they were sure to be fearful of sunburn.

I could have dozed back to sleep, but the sun shining in my eyes reminded me ot the time. I threw my feet over on the warm plank floors and walked out into the hall.

Something had to be wrong; the house was as quiet as a morgue. I called out, but nobody answered. Mammy came running up the stairs putting her finger to her lips, "*Hush yo's mouth, yo' Momma done gots herself one of her sick headaches.*

She dun worked herself up in a hissy and gots her nerves on de upset. Yo' Papa says iz going to take yo's to town to dat dress shop."

I peered in the door of Mother's room and I could hear moaning. Her head was rolling around on the pillow and her eyes were squeezed so tightly that her face looked like a peach pit. I walked over to take her hand and her eyes flew open in a panic.

I assured her Miss Georgette would have the good grace to see my choice was appropriate. Mother only groaned when Mammy came back in the room to close the curtains. She gave Mother a dose of laudanum and I put a cool rag on her forehead. By the time Papa came for me, the tension was lifting from her face. I slowly let go of her limp hand and left her to enjoy the twilight of her medication.

It was a hot morning for traveling and I worried about arriving at Miss Georgette's all wrinkled and soaked with perspiration. I fanned myself constantly until we arrived in town. We walked down several streets before I spotted the sign "Miss Georgette's Couturier." From the moment we walked in, Papa looked out of place. His hands and feet now looked as if they did not belong to him. He tried to balance himself on the tiny settee, but with his long legs spreading out halfway across the floor, he looked awkward and uncomfortable. Papa cleared his throat several times, as he often did when he was nervous. He claimed it was the perfumes that disagreed with him.

This was my first visit here. I found it impossible to take my eyes off the displays of parasols, gloves, bonnets and hats. In the glass cabinet were elaborate purses, feathers and beautiful point laces that I am sure were all from foreign houses. We arrived a bit early and Miss Georgette's assistant served us tea and biscuits. From where we were sitting, we could see a woman whom I assumed was Miss Georgette, fitting a fancy crimson colored dress on a lady. I asked Father if he knew the lady. He whispered back to me, "I believe her to be Miss Lucy.

I do not know her personally, but I think quite a few men in town do."

I was young, but he did not need to explain more, I understood. After a bit, Miss Lucy's fitting was over and she came to the front desk. I got a closer look at her; she was stunning in a common sort of way. With her gloved hand on the door, she stopped and looked directly at me. "Beautiful," she whispered under her breath smiling at Papa.

She turned her painted blue eyes toward the assistant and said something in French before she left. A peculiar feeling sweep over me, I felt as if I knew her somehow. Miss Georgette emerged from the fitting room gliding across the room like a tall lean cat. Her snow-white hair was neatly arranged at the back of her neck in a tight chignon. In a heavy French accent, she began to gush with compliments. Father did not seem flattered; he recognized a buttering up to get in his pocket. Papa excused himself and explained he would leave the dress selection to those more qualified. Miss Georgette tried to convince him his opinion was most valued, but he tipped his hat and said his business was pressing.

With Papa gone, Miss Georgette and her assistant turned their attention toward me. I was the customer now. I never experienced such a feeling of independence; this was a feeling I wanted to remember. The two ladies began to pull out material samples of all colors and textures. They scattered across the table for my inspection bits of satin and velvet ribbons, laces, pearls and glass beads.

"We have all the best choices for you, my little debutante," Miss Georgette said encouraging me toward the most expensive selections.

It was an easy choice for me, white silk, like a summer cloud. Miss Georgette was flabbergasted that I had made my decision so quickly. She stepped back to look at me as if she was studying a painting. She gave an approving nod, took out her sketchbook, and started to draw. I stopped her, reached in my purse, and unfolded a fashion page I had taken from a Ladies Magazine. This time she had me stand up and turn around, eyeing me from head to toe. With her glasses on the end of her nose, she looked at her assistant, "Excellent taste for one so young and the low neckline is, "oui, oui."

The assistant agreed with her, "I always say enjoy what God has given you and let the gentlemen enjoy it as well!"

It was their fun to embarrass me with their suggestive remarks. Miss Georgette explained it would take several weeks for the material to arrive from England. Once the material arrived, it would be at least another week before she would be ready for a fitting. Time was short, but she promised that even if she had to work night and day it would be ready for my party on October 6th.

She had me slip into a dressing gown and she began her precise measurements from the floor up. I noticed a look of pain on her face as she braced her hand against her knee to stand. Without saying a word, her assistant helped her to her feet. Miss Georgette reached up and pinned a strand of hair that had fallen down in her face. Suddenly, for the first time I realized she was not a young woman. She carried herself in such a manner that her age was deceiving.

She stood back and looked at me, "What a pretty thing you are. I have no doubt when the other girls see you in my dress they are going to drop their petticoats and run."

Her assistant laughed, "You are going to look just like you stepped right off the streets of St. Germaine in Paris."

I knew Papa must have been getting impatient waiting outside in the heat. Miss Georgette walked over and tapped on the window and Papa came in wiping his brow with his handkerchief. The assistant had already prepared the bill and politely presented it to him. Papa looked a little taken back by the bill. Miss Georgette did not wait for him to say a word. "Now Jacob," she said taking the liberty to call him by his first name. A few words of French floated out of her mouth as if by accident, "Hors de Combant," to which Papa looked confused. "Pardon me sir," let me say again in English. "I do not have a fight in this, but surely no expense is too dear when we are talking about your daughter's entire future."

Papa cleared his throat and started to speak, but she interrupted him again, "You are aware there will be other young girls coming out in society this year, shall I dare to mention the Tudor sisters."

Papa just smiled; he was a smart man and he was not about to go to war with Miss Georgette. I had decided I liked this Miss Georgette; it was not everyday in 1860 that one ran across a woman as savvy as she was.

Before traveling home Papa and I dined at the Charleston Hotel. By the time Cato brought the carriage around it had begun to cool off. Papa helped me in and we settled into our seats. We had talked all afternoon and we were content just to listen to the horses' hoofs click along the road. I took a blanket out from under the seat and covered our legs. Papa smiled and laid his head back and before long, he was asleep. My mind began to drift as I looked out across the meadows. Today for the first time I was glad my childhood was behind me. Mother was right; a whole new world was unfolding in front of me. My destiny before me was unknown, but I did not mind. I was filled with a feeling of eagerness and excitement I had never felt before.

I must have been lost in thought for it seemed like no time before we were home. The sun had fallen behind the house and was reflecting though the windows. When we stepped on the porch, we heard the music, if you could call it that. Papa stuck his fingers in his ears and shook his head and we braved our way down the hall. Mother was giving Annabelle her piano lesson again. You see, Sallie and Mother were both accomplished pianist. I played for my own enjoyment, but Annabelle played for no one's enjoyment.

When Mother turned and looked at us, her eyes were glassy and dreamy. When she spoke her voice was soft and airy and we knew the reason why. Her speedy recovery was due to more than one dose of laudanum. She was eager to hear all about our day and the selection of the dress. Papa kissed her on the cheek good-night and left me to give the details. He knew whatever I told her tonight I would most likely have to tell her all over again in the morning.

CHAPTER 3

The Disappointment

Three long weeks had passed and my material had not arrived. It was cotton season and everyone in Charleston was busy, especially Papa. Mother said it was his duty to find out what happened to that package and she could not accept any excuses. According to her, this was nearly a matter of life and death and Papa would have to make it a priority. To assure this, one of us must speak to Papa before he left the next morning to go into town. I knew it would be me, for Mother was a late sleeper. I worked out a plan before I went to bed.

Papa never left before breakfast, which was always served at eight. I would ambush him with Mother's instructions just as soon as he finished his first cup of coffee. He was to go directly to Miss Georgette's dress shop and ask her for the shipping invoice. From there, he was to go straight to the shipyard and find out the whereabouts of the ship.

When I got up the next morning, there was plenty of time to return my cousin's letter, get dressed and be downstairs waiting for Papa. I sat down at my desk, but just as I picked up my pen, I heard the horses out front. I looked out the window and the Negroes had nearly loaded all the cotton wagons. Papa was leaving early for some strange reason.

Still in my gown-tail, I ran downstairs and was relieved to find Papa in his study packing his papers. He was extremely pre-occupied, but I wanted to make sure he understood the seriousness of this situation. I swished in and out around him every step he took and was still talking to him when he went out the front door. Cato was waiting with the carriage and Papa stopped and looked me right in the eye, "Hear this Lizzie, if I have to row a boat to England myself, I will get your material. Now for God's sake please go upstairs and get dressed."

Papa kissed me on top of the head and jumped up in the carriage. Old Cato started whistling and I could hear them both laughing as they took off. I knew he thought me to be silly, but I was glad he said he would take care of it. I watched until the carriage was out of sight.

I missed breakfast and now I was late for my riding lesson. Mammy was waiting for me and I could tell by her expression she did not approve of my behavior.

"Runin' bouts half-naked though de house 'pose somebody be a visitin'. Folks all over be a talkin' bouts yo for sho. Here it'z jes a week 'fer yo's big show. Lordy, Lordy, Miss Lizzie."

The whole time she was dressing me, she was scolding me while pulling tighter and tighter on my corset strings. Although her voice was angry, her eyes were smiling. She was the best Mammy a girl could ever have.

My sisters and I had been taking riding lessons since we were six. I had my own horse, a mare I named Coal. Today it was Mr. McCoy who came to give the lesson. Of all the riding instructors, I liked him the best. He usually just sat under the oak tree and smoked his pipe. I would ride around however I pleased, but occasionally he would shout out, "slower down there Missy."

That morning I wanted to ride, not just trot around that rink. As I walked down the path to the barn, it occurred to me I was not a child any longer and I should be able to make my own decisions. I stopped a minute to watch Mr. McCoy saddling up my horse. I quickened my step calling out to him, "Tom!" using his first name as Miss Georgette did with father. "I will be riding down by the old mill today. Would you like to join me?"

His face was blank for a moment and then he simply said, "Yes ma'am."

I learned something that day; it is better to be a leader than a follower. I was glad lunch was already on the table when I came back from my ride. I was starving and went straight to the table without changing my clothes and piled up my plate. Sallie scolded me and said I was eating like a man. Her words did not set well with me and I lashed out at her saying, "Don't worry sister, I am not going to get fat like some people we know."

Mother was not amused and ordered us both to go to our rooms. Annabelle just sat there with a big grin on her face, glad for once she was not the one in trouble. I grabbed a biscuit, stuffed it in my mouth right in front of Sallie and marched upstairs. I tried to take a nap, but my mind was going in all directions. By late afternoon, the waiting was getting unbearable. I decided to go downstairs and read by the window where I could have a clear view of the road.

Finally, I heard Papa's carriage coming. I positioned myself becomingly and tried to relax. Southern girls are taught at a young age it is important to always be in control. In addition, being too emotional spoils the complexion and is harmful to the constitution. Suddenly the door opened and before me was a hornet's nest of angry men, including Papa. I recognized none of the men except for Ransom Huneycutt who had been Papa's sidekick for the past year. His friendship with my father was honorable; still we all believed he admired my sister Sallie.

I knew at once they were businessmen by their brocade vests, fancy silk ties and tailored flock coats. They looked proper, but they were not behaving like gentlemen. They were all speaking at once and the only words I caught were taxes and tariffs. When they took note of their surroundings, they seemed embarrassed to find me among their company. Quickly they began to offer up apologies for the harshness of their language. I was not at all bruised by their words, but to make them feel better I tried to blush.

After waiting all day for Papa, I was hurt he was planning to have another one of his meetings, which always lasted half the night. When Papa saw me, he pulled his gold watch out and checked the time. He took me by the arm and asked his colleagues to excuse him for a few minutes. We went into his study, but before

27

he could close the door, Ransom slipped in behind us. I could tell by Papa's approach that something was wrong. He started with, "darling, sweetheart and my dear. Please try to understand."

Explaining the taxes were unreasonable and the merchants were refusing to buy or ship anything until something could be resolved. Papa had never disappointed me before and the tears just started pouring from my eyes. Papa was at a loss for words and looked up at Ransom as if to say, "Help me."

Ransom tried to make amends, "Elizabeth, I suspect before all this is over you are going to see a lot of belles in homespun cotton dresses."

It angered me that he would suggest I wear a homespun rag on the most important day of my life. Ransom was always acting so high and mighty. Well to me he was nothing more than some Tarheel from North Carolina. Just because his family owned a dry goods store certainly did not qualify him to be a fashion expert. I was madder than a wet hen when I stomped up the steps telling Papa to call off the party. You could have heard a pin drop as the men's eyes followed me up the stairs. The last thing they heard of my thunder was the slam of my bedroom door. So much for being a lady in control of her emotions. I did not leave my room the rest of the night and no one dared to come in. Mammy made a feeble attempt to offer me a plate of supper. I made it clear I was **not** going to eat a bite and to take it back downstairs. She left it anyway, saying that along about midnight I might change my mind.

I was mortified at the thought of ever having to face any of those men ever again. I could only hope Papa had made amends for my sour behavior. Why should he after I had acted like such a child? I felt so ashamed for hurting Papa's feelings. It was almost midnight and I was considering going to him; but I was not sure he would accept my apology. When I was a little girl, he would always say apologies bear very little weight once the deed is done. I could suggest he call off the party and save his money; after all who would marry a girl who makes such a public displays of herself? I might as well become a nun instead of a debutant.

After reading my Bible for a while an inspiration came, I would write him a letter and slide it under his door. He would see it first thing in morning, providing he was not in such a hurry he stepped right over it. I had to take a chance. Jumping out of bed in the dim light, I stubbed my toe on the corner of my dressing table. The pain was intense and I felt as though I deserved it. Hobbling over to my desk, I began my composition. My first thought was to blame Ransom and claim his interferences pushed me to anger. Yet, shifting the blame to him would make me guilty of another sin. It was clear I had to accept responsibility for my own actions. I read over my letter again, dipped my seal in the wax, and embossed my initials on the envelope.

My Dearest Father,

I hope you will find it in your heart to forgive me for my most unpardonable behavior. I am painfully aware my misconduct is a reflection upon your good name and a mark against my precious Mother's ability to properly rear me up. I understand your disappointment and I am fully prepared to suffer the consequences if you feel it no longer necessary to present me to society.

I wish it were in my power to turn back time, but it is not. It is only in my power to offer my sincere apology and assure you a lesson has been so sorrowfully learned.

Faithfully yours,
Lizzie

It was after two o'clock when I returned to my room after tip-toeing down the hall and slipping the letter under his door. I was hungry now and my eyes fell on the plate wrapped neatly in a white linen cloth. I uncovered the plate and before me were two honey biscuits, a piece of chicken and a serving of peach cobbler. I could have easily eaten every bite, but a hardy appetite would appear as if I was not mournful of my sins.

So, I only took a few bites forcing myself to wrap up the plate. When I blew out the light, I laid in bed listening to my stomach growl until I finally drifted off to sleep.

The next morning I was prepared for the worst when I came down for breakfast. Father was alone at the table and I could see the letter was open lying by his plate. I sat down and poured myself a cup of coffee. He was reading a newspaper with his head tilted to the side balancing his spectacles on the end of his nose. I took several sips of my coffee before he laid his paper down. "Oh, Good morning, Lizzie," he said, as if he had not heard me come in.

We exchanged a few comments about the weather and he remarked that the eggs were especially nice this morning. Then he looked at me and took a deep breath, took off his glasses and closed his eyes for few seconds. "Little lady," he began. "Lizzie, have no doubt your behavior was unacceptable by my standards. However, when all those men saw a young woman so heartbroken, they felt even more reason to protest. Those fellows were here until way after midnight discussing plans to take action against the Union and this tax situation." Papa smiled at me and leaned forward a bit, "Mr. Isley's comment was well accepted about how much he admired a woman with the courage to speak her mind. It was agreed upon a little fire in a woman now a days was not such a bad thing at all. So it seems, what you have deemed as the worst night of your life, has worked in your favor. I would not be at all surprised if you have all the young men fighting over you at your party."

I was speechless, but I could not help smiling. Papa folded the letter and slipped it in his coat pocket. "This being said, I suggest you not press your luck and the less your mother knows of this the better."

He started to say more but Mother came in the room. He patted my hand and asked me to pass the butter. When Mother said good morning, Papa nervously cleared his throat. Mother was looking at us with great suspicion when Annabelle burst into the room talking a mile a minute. By the time Sallie came in, Mother completely forgot something seemed odd earlier.

As for Papa, he chose never to speak of it again. That was often his way with unpleasant things. I was not sure if he truly forgot about it, but I was sure he forgave me. For this, I was forever grateful.

CHAPTER 4

The Blue Silk

Within a few days, that old rawboned red headed Ransom Huneycutt was back in Charleston. Sallie saw him ride up and sent Cato to the door. Cato was pretty much a coward and he certainly did not want to be the one to break the news to Sallie that Ransom had come to call on me, not her.

I was just coming up from the barn from my ride. When I saw Cato flying up the hill on the dandy horse, or bicycle, as it was also called. I suspected something was wrong because he hated to ride that thing, even though Papa had gotten it especially for him.

As soon as he saw me he stopped, but only after almost hitting me broadside and landing himself on the ground. Lifting the bicycle upright he began to stutter and spit, *"Mr. Ransom iz heres to see you's!"* Before I could ask any questions he went on, *"Ain't no good gonn' come of dez. Miss Lizzie, if yo' goes to a courtin' Miss Sallie's beau."*

I told him to hush up with that kind of talk and go tell Mr. Ransom I would be down as soon as I changed.

He hopped back on his ride saying, *"Miss Sallie gonn' pulls your har right out yo' head."*

I was completely out of breath when I got upstairs to freshen up. I saw Sallie in the hall and she was dressed and ready to go downstairs. I paused for a moment trying carefully to pick my words. I told her for some reason I was unaware of, Ransom had come to speak to me today. Her face flamed and I was afraid she might hit me. She pushed her hair off her face and said, "You don't think that..." and she started to cry.

I reached for her arm, but she jerked away hard enough to injure herself. She was still crying when she ran down the hall to her room. I knew it would be rude to keep Ransom waiting much longer so I quickly changed into a plain dark gray dress. I looked in the mirror and thought it unbecoming. Good; maybe Ransom will think so too. Hurrying downstairs, I stopped briefly outside the parlor door to collect myself before I walked into the room. Papa was leaning against the fireplace and Ransom was talking to him in a whisper. Papa gestured me into the room, "Come in Lizzie, Ransom is here to see you." Father patted Ransom on the back. "When you and Lizzie have had your visit, join me in my study for a brandy, my boy."

Ransom and I stood looking at each other and I offered him a seat. It was awkward to say the least, but I felt it best I come right out with it. "Mr. Ransom, if the nature of your visit is to pay a social call on me, I must say I think it is very bold. For the past year, you have given my family and my dear sister Sallie every indication it is her you favor. Given the reason our Sallie is also fond of you, I find it appalling you are now here to seek my affections. Furthermore, I am alarmed it appears my father approves of your intentions."

Ransom dropped his head and I thought by the way he was shaking he was truly heartbroken until I realized he was laughing. When he regained his composer, he said, "My dear Lizzie you are indeed a jewel, but if you will allow me to explain. I have come here today to win your affection, but only as pure brotherly love. I apologize if I have given you the wrong impression."

He went on to say he knew how badly he had upset me the last time he was here. The reason for his visit today was to bring me an early birthday present. I was undeniably embarrassed thinking how vain I had appeared. However, at the same time I was a tiny bit wounded that he had made it so clear he was not interested in me in the least. I paused for a second to recover from the blow. My voice was tight and tense when I spoke, "Well this is very kind of you, but I am not sure if my father would approve."

"On the contraire Lizzie, your father has already given his permission for you to accept my gift," he responded.

Ransom had put me on the spot and all I could say was, "Well if my Father approves then I should be gracious enough to accept your gift."

Ransom jumped up and clapped his hands, which made him look ridiculous because he was so tall and gangling. He was wearing an ill-fitting pinstriped suit, which was too broad for his body, and the sleeves and pants were noticeable too short. He was smiling so big he looked like he swallowed a pie plate. Before I could say another word, he retrieved from behind his chair a large bundle wrapped in brown paper and tied with a red ribbon. He flopped the package on my lap and the weight of it caused my chair to tilt back on just two legs. I could see myself splattered on the floor smothered to death by this package in my lap. Fortunately, Ransom reacted quickly and caught the back of my chair allowing me to regain my balance. Before I realized it, we were both laughing and I was seeing Ransom in a different light. He was not as confident as I had assumed. In fact, quite the opposite, shy and unsure of himself. He could hardly wait for me to unwrap his gift. He reached into his pocket for a small pearl handled knife and cut the ribbon. When the brown paper fell open, I saw yards of gorgeous light blue silk.

I gently stroked the fine material thinking it too expensive. I wrapped it back up. Ransom must have read my mind and said, "You must accept it, my dear, or it will simply go to waste."

I knew he was teasing me, but there was nothing more to say except, "thank you."

"I only wished I had a bolt for Sallie too," he said sincerely.

When he said "Sallie," I tensed up. I had almost forgotten about her. I must have looked baffled and Ransom reached down and touched my shoulder.

"Lizzie," he asked. "Do you really think your sister Sallie is fond of me?"

"Oh yes, we all are," I replied, fearing I had already said too much.

He then pressed his lips together and squeezed out a more direct question, "Do you think Miss Sallie is fond of me in a friendly sort of way or in a more romantic sort of way?"

It was hard not to laugh at his sudden serious mannerisms. Before I caught myself I said, "Good Lord, don't you know she is crying her eyes out right now because she thinks you came to see me?"

"How wonderful!" he said and quickly popped a kiss right upon my forehead.

He paced back and forth across the room as if he did not know what to do. "I must go right this minute and speak with him, your father, you know, Mr. Sanders. Lizzie, will you please go tell Sallie I would like very much to speak to her shortly?"

I knew what he meant and I assured him I would do just that. He was so nervous that he fumbled with the door handle trying to get out and popped himself in the nose with the door. I was still laughing when I knocked on Sallie's door. She did not answer and I found Mother and Annabelle sitting on the porch playing cards. I asked if they had seen Sallie. Mother calmly replied that about an hour ago Cato had taken her over to spend a couple of days with Aunt Sara. I stomped my foot, "Mother how could you just let her leave at a time like this!"

Mother looked shocked at my reaction, "Well you know Aunt Sara is not well and is in need of company. She wrote Sallie last week and asked her to come. Honestly, Lizzie," she said and turned around to finish the card game.

I walked slowly back downstairs, knowing that Sallie had run away so she would not have to face Ransom or me. The last time Sallie visited Aunt Sara she stayed over two weeks. I was afraid she would stay even longer this time for spite. If Mother would not send for her, then I would just jump on Coal and go after her myself.

Ransom took the news much better than I thought. He and Father walked out in the garden and talked for a while until a carriage arrived to take Ransom back to town. Papa made me give my word that I would not hint to Sallie of Ransom's intentions.

That night I wrote to Sallie only telling her Ransom regretted not seeing her before he left. When I blew out the light, I must have gone to sleep as soon as my head hit the pillow, but I did not sleep well. I recall having the strangest dream. *It was night, but the sky was lit up as if it were on fire. My carriage was traveling so fast that I lost control and it flipped over. I was then forced to travel on horseback, and at last, I came to our house. The house was pitch dark except for a light coming from the dining room. I walked down the hall and found the slaves all dressed up in our clothes. They were having a fancy dinner and drinking wine out of Mother's crystal glasses. Mammy was sitting at the head of the table and I begged her to tell me what was going on. She did not even turn her head; no matter how loud I screamed they all acted as if they could not hear or see me. I ran upstairs and was shocked to see all the rooms were completely empty except for a broken down chair in the middle of my room. When I tried to go back down the stairs, the slaves were coming up after me. They were dressed like slaves again and weeping. They began to pull on my arms and legs and rip my clothes.* I was struggling to get free when Mother woke me up; saying she had heard me screaming from across the hall. She told me I must have had a nightmare and to go back to sleep.

The next morning I was haunted by the visions in my dream. I knew I had to find Mammy because she knew about things like this. I found her in the kitchen and told her about my dreadful dream. Her black eyes never left my face as I spoke and she wanted to know if I had seen a mirror in the dream. I told her yes, the one in the dining room.

She raised herself from her chair and asked to see my hands. Taking them in hers; she turned them over and spit in each of my palms. Then she drew an "x" in each one with her finger and folded them shut. When I opened them, my palms were on fire and bright red streaks were running out to the tips of my fingers. She dipped my hands into a bucket of water, sat back down, and stared out the window. I knew Mammy believed in Voodoo, but this was the first time I had ever seen any evidence it was real. "Mammy, what does this mean?" I asked.

She took a deep breath before she spoke, *"Dreams 'bout fire pose' to mean anger an' great conflict is a brewin'. When yo's see a mirror in a dream, iz means iz will be reflectin' back on yo's"*.

"Mammy," I said feeling relieved. "I know the reason for that silly old dream; it is Sallie who is mad at me."

Mammy walked over and picked up her basket of potatoes, *"I's sho hopes yo's iz right but I am mighty 'fraid this be a warnin' to us all"*. She stood frozen by the table with a potato in one hand and one hand gripped tightly around her knife.

"Now Mammy, lets not get all worked up over this. It is as plain as the nose on your face; Sallie thinks I am trying to

36

steal her beau. It will all be fine, just as soon as Ransom comes back."

Mammy asked if I had my breakfast and I told her no. She told me to hush up; dreams come true if you tell them before breakfast. Even if Mammy was uneasy, I realized I was starving. I had her fix me two fresh eggs, a nice big slice of streaked meat and a biscuit. I was happy to forget about that dream.

CHAPTER 5

The Fire Eaters

Mother was pleased with the silk Ransom gifted me, but she said there was little time to waste. The very next day she instructed Papa to take the silk to Miss Georgette's, along with a pair of my slippers to be dyed. Without doubt, Papa would be going into town, for nearly everyday he attended meetings in the morning and later a group would meet at our house for more discussions.

Most of my life I had heard all this political talk, but this was more than talk. I was older now and I understood the reasons. I was not the only one worried; Mother had become increasingly cautious of our household expenses. Among the women, the conversations about fashion and recipes had turned to discussions on the economy and the increasing hostilities from the North.

Everything you read was distressing. A few of the ladies had read Harriett Beecher Stowe's book, *Uncle Tom's Cabin* and claimed it to be nothing more than fiction. They all agreed this little book was the very reason the South was losing their support from England. The newspapers spread even more fears, with alarming news stories like John Brown's raid on Harpers Ferry, Virginia. Thankfully, Brown and his men were captured before he could confiscate the weapons and arm a band of angry slaves.

Our slaves appeared content and it was hard to believe any of them would be capable of such violence. Still, Papa warned us the news about the Underground Railroad was traveling fast among the slave communities. Two days ago he found a map down by the barn, which proved we were not immune to the trouble that was brewing. Many of the Negroes were being misled on a quest for freedom only to end up as slaves somewhere else, murdered or starving to death out in the wilds.

I had heard Papa say it was becoming impractical to run a plantation on slave labor now anyway. It was almost impossible to keep your head above water, paying taxes on every bale of cotton you sold and property tax on every single slave you owned. "Them damn Yankees will get their greedy hands in our pockets, even if they have to turn us upside down and shake us."

He predicted modern machines would replace us all someday and the Negroes would be the first to go. When I heard him talk like that it was not hard to miss the hint of melancholy in his words. He sounded so downtrodden, like a man accepting defeat. I feared what would happen if Papa would give up and crumble.

Papa was our strength and the very fiber that wove our family together. He was our foundation and our rock, but even rocks, break, given enough stress.

Thankfully, these phases were short lived and he was once again a Democrat "Fire Eater" and a force to be reckoned with.

Papa came home from town early and was in an exceptionally good mood. He was singing silly songs and whistling as he set out the chairs for another meeting that evening. He had not even taken a break for lunch. At two o'clock Mammy was ready to clear the table. She kept checking the window until finally she lost her patience and stomped out to get him. Papa came in fussing and sat down at the lunch table.

"*There now, da will put some meat on yo's bones an'iz mights jes soak up some of dat brandy in yo's belly too,*" Mammy said as she set down a big plate of what she called drizzle bread, which was brown bread fried in the bacon grease left over from breakfast.

Mammy was wise to a lot of things, including Papa's occasional overindulgences. She liked taking care of us and she was not going to let anything stand in her way. I can still see her standing in the kitchen with a butcher knife in her hand telling us, *"I's lik' to see one of dem Yankees try to drag me away from here. I's might be little, but I's as mean as a bobcat with a toothache."*

Papa ate and went upstairs to take a nap. He was a lot calmer by the time the people started arriving around four o'clock. I watched the anticipation growing as the crowd gathered out on the front lawn.

The speaker was to be a young lawyer and politician by the name of Matthew Cooper or "MC" as Papa called him. When MC arrived, Papa had to calm the crowd for him to speak. After MC's opening remarks the crowd exploded with applause.

We as Southerners are a unique people; we possess a purity, honor and chivalry that is just not found above the Mason Dixon Line.

When the crowd settled back down he continued:

"As you all know we are approaching the most important election of our time.

Many good Democrats are still split on which candidate should run on the Democratic ticket.

We must come together and pick the best candidate. If we fail, the Republican Party could be successful in electing Abraham Lincoln as President of the United States, a fate that will devastate our Southland.

With Lincoln as President, our economy will be under greater attack. Higher tariffs and taxes will completely eliminate all foreign trade for the South. We will be forced to do all our business with the North, giving them more and more control over us.

Let it be known, these tariffs are benefiting only the North and without question are increasing international tensions. Private businesses are already collapsing and the cost of living is rising.

The Union and their antislavery campaigners who preach about the evils of slavery have succeeded in splitting up both the Methodist and the Baptist Churches.

Perhaps they should study the Ten Commandments, 'Thou shall not steal,' for that is exactly what the Union is trying to do to us.

Whether or not to own slaves is not our greatest issue here at hand. We are all aware that soon machines will replace the need for slave labor. Yet, to release 200,000 Negroes at one time would inevitably lead to not only their destruction, but ours as well.

These issues have been brewing for over the past twenty years and the time has come for us to take action. We must exercise our Constitutional right and withdraw from the Union. This is not an act of discord, but a means to an end of this crisis once and for all in a diplomatic and peaceful manner.

When Mr. Cooper's speech came to a close there were a number of the men eager to contribute their point of view. MC was still up front, but he was now speaking on a more personal level with a select few men. The rest of the crowd had begun to break up into smaller groups and their conversations were low and private. Papa was weaving in and out of the groups when Mr. Cooper flagged him down. I watched the two men step aside to speak and they turned and looked directly at me. Papa nodded and took Mr. Cooper's arm and started walking toward me. Suddenly, I felt self-conscious and turned quickly to go look for Mother. Papa called my name and I was forced to wait for Papa to introduce us. Mr. Cooper seemed nice enough, but he had trouble keeping his eyes on my face and not my bosom. In the distance I could hear the rumble of thunder and within seconds a streak of angry lightening cracked just above the tree lines. The meeting was adjourned and I was relieved to escape Mr. Cooper's wandering eyes.

Father encouraged a few men, including MC, to stay and continue the debating. About five men followed him in the house to his study. Out on the lawn there were people darting around everywhere, hurrying off to get to their wagons and carriages before the rain hit.

Mother and I were the last ones left standing on the lawn and we began to gather up some of the pamphlets the wind had blown off the porch. Mother ran her hand over her head as a few large drops of rain splattered across her head. She turned and went inside, saying only *Carolina Rain.*

I knew what she meant; sometimes our storms just came out of nowhere, with big pellets of rain that sting the skin like bees. Mother used to say if you stood out in a rain like that; it would wash away your sins.

I did not follow Mother inside. I liked storms; something about them was exciting and made me feel alive. It had been an unseasonably warm day and now the cool breeze caught my hair and my dress set sail in the wind. It was a welcomed change and I closed my eyes and took a deep breath. I could faintly smell the ocean and I imagined being one of the old oak trees standing there swaying in the wind and braving all sorts of weather. I pondered what they had seen in the past and what they might see in the future.

When I opened my eyes, it was getting dark. The first few stars were twinkling against the sapphire sky. *The sky was calm and it appeared the storm had passed over us, well at least for now.*

CHAPTER 6

Time for Sallie
to come home

It had been two weeks since Papa took the material to Miss Georgette's and Sallie was still at Aunt Sara's. Papa was taking us to town on Wednesday for a fitting. Although we had all written several letters to Sallie, she had not written back to any of us, including Ransom. I was afraid she was still angry, but Mother was worried that Aunt Sara may have taken ill.

"What ever the reason, it is time for Sallie to come home," Mother said.

The plan was to pick up Sallie on Wednesday on our way to Miss Georgette's. Even if it was the most sensible thing to do, I didn't like the idea. Without a doubt, when we got to Aunt Sara's house we would be forced to stay and visit. This would mean it would be well up in the afternoon before we got to Miss Georgette's.

I was glad when Wednesday came; the weather was nice. I found Mother downstairs dressed in a quaint print dress with a pale pink collar and under sleeves. She looked tired and her hands were trembling as she placed her bonnet on her head. We sat down together in the foyer to wait for Papa. Mother gave an approving nod to my choice of attire. I was wearing my blue linen dress with the hand-painted roses and matching bonnet.

Papa was going from room to room talking to himself; he had lost his watch again. Mother told him if he was not in such a hurry all the time he would not misplace things so often. No matter where we went this was always the drill. At last, he discovered his watch under a stack of papers in his study. He passed us by as if nothing had happened and went to get the carriage. Now, it was as if he was waiting on us.

It was still early when we got on the road, but already the cotton fields were dark with Negroes. Their long white sacks on their backs blowing in the wind looked almost like wings. I thought of them as butterflies fluttering over the fields. Papa brought the carriage to a stop at the top of the hill and gazed down across the field. After a few minutes he leaned out of the window, put his fingers to his lips and whistled. Every dark head recognized the sound and stood up and looked our way. Papa's eyes carefully searched the field before he yelled out, "Samuel."

Mother scolded, "Jacob, you are going to burst our eardrums."

Papa told us to cover our ears and once again he yelled, "Sam!"

It was sometimes hard for me to tell the slaves apart, but I spotted Samuel because of his size. He dropped his bag and started to meander up the hill. Papa said he was the strongest and smartest Negro on this plantation. He claimed he could read and write as well as most white men, but I didn't like him and it was not just because Papa traded Lottie for him. The others never looked up when you walked by or looked you in the eye. Samuel was bold and would stare a hole right through you. I was going to have to tell Papa about this.

I was invisible to him sitting in the back of the carriage, but he was in my clear view. He was shirtless and his cut off trousers hung loosely around his hips. The veins in his arms were tightly stretched over his bulging muscles and his skin looked like black velvet glistening in the sun. When he got to the top of the hill he stopped and took off his straw hat and wiped his face with a rag. He then spit on the ground and pulled his pants up a bit and started toward the carriage. I could clearly see his face; he was very African looking with broad features and deep set dark eyes. He disappeared from view and then all of a sudden he reached up and grabbed the side of the carriage to steady himself. It startled me so I quickly sat back in my seat and gasped. He was so close I could hear how heavy he was breathing and his thick fingers were on the door next to my face. I could smell him.

Papa motioned for him to step back so he could get out of the carriage. The encounter was brief and Samuel said very little as Papa gave him instructions to oversee the workers while we were away. Papa jumped back in the carriage and I watched Samuel on his way back to the field as we rode away.

There is something about a fall morning in the country that heals the soul. The freshness of the dew on the grass, birds singing and the morning sun on your face is healthy and agreeable. Mother slept most of the way and by the time we arrived at Aunt Sara's she was in an encouragingly good mood.

The road to Aunt Sara's house was overgrown with johnston grass and rag weed. Fields once planted with beans and corn, now grew only bachelor buttons and black eyed susans. When I was a little girl I thought Aunt Sara and Uncle Charles lived in a fairy-tale castle, but now it looked more like a run down medieval dungeon. Five or more of the lead glass panes were broken and the elaborately carved gables were crumbling and badly in need of painting. The white wicker porch furniture was now gray and the weather beaten planters were empty except for a few dead plants spilling over to the ground.

Aunt Sara was alone since Uncle Charles O'Connor died. He was an Irish immigrant claiming to have made his fortune as a sea captain, but Papa says his story did not hold water. He always suspected he was smuggler or a pirate before he showed up in Charleston and married Aunt Sara who was at least ten years his senior. Actually Charles and Sara were not truly blood relatives to us at all. Sara's first husband Ben was a business associate of Papa's and a dear friend of our family. They never had children and they affectionately encouraged us to call them Aunt and Uncle.

When Uncle Ben died and Sara married Charles, he became Uncle Charlie. Papa finally accepted him, but he never trusted him. It was hard not to like Uncle Charlie; he was always laughing and singing and telling grand stories. He loved horses and was known for raising the finest in the South. Sadly, the thing he loved the most was to be the cause of his death. They found him dead down at the barn, kicked in the head by a high-spirited stallion.

As we approached the house I could see the fences were broken down and the pastures were grown over. It was sad to think those once fancy stables were home only to feral cats and mice now. Papa pulled the carriage under the portico and Mother looked around and simply said, "Good Lord."

We all knew what she meant. The house looked all but abandoned except for a few chickens scratching around on the front lawn and a puff of smoke coming from the stone chimney. Papa secured the horses as we stepped out of the carriage. Mother reached down to adjust her cage crinoline and again out of her mouth came, "Good Lord!"

Galloping up from the across the field were two riders. One was clearly Sallie, bare headed with her blonde hair hanging loose and blowing behind her. Papa patted Mother's arm signaling her to wait there. He stepped out so the riders could see him in plain view. Sallie dismounted first and her companion, a young gentleman, shyly slipped off his horse.

"Hello Papa, I was not expecting you today," she said trying to hide her embarrassment.

"I see that," Papa said in an inquisitive tone.

"Allow me to introduce Mr. Grady O'Connor," she said, watching our reactions.

46

"Grady is Uncle Charles's nephew from Boston; he is staying with Aunt Sara and will be attending the Citadel."

The young man reached out and shook Papa's hand. Mother left her post and introduced us to the new Mr. O'Connor. Sallie kissed Mother on the cheek and in a voice unlike hers she addressed me, "How are you dear sister?"

"Fine, thank you," I said, as if we were strangers.

Sallie had been gone less than two weeks and now she was out alone with a strange man none of us knew. Mother asked Sallie where she might find Aunt Sara. I could tell Mother was disturbed by this exhibition. She was not going to cause a scene, not here at least and not until she knew the whole story.

"Oh, she is alive and well," Sallie said, trying to break the ice. "Come let us go in, I know she will be excited to see you all." She motioned us toward the door and took hold of my arm as if I needed assistance. "Lizzie, you look pale, are you well?" she poked my way.

Before I could answer, the double doors opened and a brittle little Negro woman stepped out on the front stoop. She was dressed in a starched white apron and large mop hat that nearly covered her whole head. This made me wonder if she had any hair under there at all.

"*Hellos, Misses Sallie*," she quivered out. "*Yo's folks is come, has they?*"

"Yes, Effie, they have and will you please set up tea in the drawing room and let Aunt Sara know they are here," Sallie said, sounding like mistress of the household.

We were all clumped up together like Sunday late comers trying to squeeze through the church doors. Sallie's new peculiar manners were perplexing, but we followed her in the drawing room as if nothing was out of the ordinary. Mr. Grady O'Connor sat down in a small wooden chair by the fireplace. I think it was an effort to sit as far away from us as possible. However, he had unintentionally placed himself on display and now was the focal point of all our views. It was one of those uncomfortable times when you do not wish to look directly at someone but you just can't help yourself. The young man nervously kept trying to cross his short stubby legs and finally resorted to clasping his hands over his knee to hold it in place. He leaned back and released a satisfied little sigh and jiggled his head from side to side in a proud and arrogant manner. Once he was stationary his round face revealed a set of queer colored eyes and a rather large hooked nose. He was by no means a handsome man but his immaculate hygiene saved him from being offensive to the eye.

Papa was the first to speak, "So, Mr. O'Connor, how do you find Charleston so far?"

Mr. O'Connor said he was not accustomed to such hot humid weather, but he was beginning to adjust. We all tried to keep the conversation alive, but after a few lines exchanged about the Citadel it went as limp as a dish rag. To add to the awkwardness of the situation, Mother, Sallie and I were all perched on the edge of a small settee like three little birds. Mother fretfully kept looking over at Sallie to see if there were any outward clues as to why she was acting so strange. I could not help but wonder if Uncle Charlie's nephew was the reason Sallie had not returned our letters.

The little old Effie came into the drawing room pushing a tea cart which seemed to cost her a great effort. Her little hands were shaking as she began to arrange the cups. Following behind her was Aunt Sara, wearing the same dress I had seen her in the last time we were there. Even her hair was styled the same old fashioned way. After Uncle Charles's death Aunt Sara withdrew, even though she once loved to socialize. Now she rarely left her estate and insisted on everything being kept in the same antediluvian way.

Papa jumped up at once and offered Aunt Sara his seat, but instead she turned and looked out at us as if she was preparing to recite a poem. Aunt Sara seemed to overpower the room, towering over Papa by at least a foot. "Oh how wonderful to see you all," Aunt Sara exclaimed, reaching out her hand to Papa.

She then turned to embrace Mother and upset the vase of flowers on the coffee table. The crash awakened Effie from her tea duties and she came running with a rag to sop up the water. She quietly reset the vase on the table and went back to her duties. Aunt Sara acted as if she hadn't noticed anything happening around her, but Sallie giggled and Mr. O'Connor followed in response. After she kissed us both she stepped back and caught her heel on the rug fringe. If Papa had not braced her fall, she would have been spread out all over the floor.

This incident was too eventful for her not to pass comment, "Well, well, it seems I am losing my grace. It happens to the best of us doesn't it Tempie?" she said looking at Mother as if she shared her feelings. Mother nodded her head politely even though there was no comparison between the two ladies.

"Do say you have not come to collect my dear Sallie so soon. We have *all* had such a delightful time," Aunt Sara said and winked at Mr. O'Connor rather mysteriously.

"I am sorry to say we have," Mother said rather bluntly. "She has well over-extended her welcome and I am in such need of her company," Mother softened the tone of her voice and looked at Sallie.

"Oh yes," Papa agreed. "Her Mother needs her help with all the preparations for Lizzie's party. Lord knows, I am not much help," he added and flashed a boyish little grin.

I thought I might hurry our visit along, "Aunt Sara, we are on our way to pick up my dress at Miss Georgette's today. Sallie has always been my best critic and I could not possibly do without her input," I said hoping to make Sallie feel important.

"Ah, Georgette! We used to be the best of friends," Aunt Sara said, with reflection in her voice. "I was one of her best customers when Charles was still living," Aunt Sara's voice dropped off almost to a whisper and it appeared as if she might start to cry.

"Sara, why don't you ride with us to Georgette's?" Mother asked, surprising us. "Maybe we could pick up a few novelties for ourselves while Lizzie gets her fitting. We can sup at the hotel just like old times and return you on our way home."

Aunt Sara stood still for a moment as though she was contemplating some great decision. She turned to look at her nephew who was still sitting humped up like a hoppy toad on a little stool. "Now, Aunt Sara, don't you worry about me, I have a bundle of things to do before I leave for the Citadel. Now go on, get out of my hair for a while," he said in a playful tone. He jumped to his feet, "Now, if all of you will excuse me, I must tend to the horses before I get too deeply involved with my studies." He paused briefly to kiss Sallie's hand, "It has been a delight being in your company, Miss Sallie. I hope we shall see each other again very soon." He left the room abruptly in a grand fashion almost as if he was already practicing to be a military man.

The whole time Sallie had been quietly bouncing her eyes from person to person following the conversation. When Grady left she dropped her eyes and blushed. Aunt Sara then looked at me now, "You sure you don't mind, Lizzie?"

What could I say but, "We would be delighted for you to come with us."

I had been holding my breath hoping she would decline the invitation; after all she had not been into town in years. What a circus this was going to be with Sallie acting so odd and now Aunt Sara tagging along too.

Father suggested I go with Sallie to help speed up her packing. I followed her through the door and down the hall. I waited until we were out of sight before I grabbed her arm and made her stop and look at me. She tried to pull away, but I held on tighter.

"Listen to me, Miss High and Mighty. I can understand why you never returned any of my letters, but not returning Ransom's is a disgrace," I said and let go of her arm.

She rubbed her arm as if I had hurt her and whimpered, "I never got any old letters."

I told her I must have sent at least a half dozen and God only knows how many Ransom sent.

"Well then where are they?" she asked in an angry high pitched tone.

Again I took her arm but this time she did not pull away as I pressed my lips close to her ear, "Do you think Aunt Sara hid them from you?"

At this she gasped, "Oh my, you don't think she would do such a thing?"

"Yes I do, and just what is going on with you and this Grady O'Connor," I spit out.

"Nothing" she said on the defense.

"Well nothing is going on between me and Ransom either," I said right back to her in the same tone.

"Really?" she asked.

"Really" I said and we both started laughing.

I knew the old Sallie was back. Now, I could ease my way into asking, "Sallie, if Aunt Sara did hide those letters, where do you think she might have hid them?"

Sallie hesitated a few seconds and then took a couple of steps back to peek into the drawing room. "Wait here," she whispered.

She went back into the drawing room and told Mother she simply could not leave without seeing Aunt Sara's prized roses. Aunt Sara was easily flattered and Sallie had hit just the right note. Papa said, "Well I suppose so, if it does not take too terribly long."

Sallie met me in the hall and I followed her upstairs until she stopped and said loudly, "Here we are Lizzie, this is my room."

We ducked inside and she pulled out her trunk and instructed me to start packing while she slipped into Aunt Sara's room to see if she could find the letters. "Hurry," I urged.

She shut the door quietly and I began to rush around and gather all her belongings.

Sallie had left in a hurry the day she got mad and had taken very little with her. In a short time my work was done. After I double checked the room, I sat down on the bed to wait for Sallie to return. For the first time I took note of the room. At one time this was a beautiful room, but now the blue silk drapes were fading, the wall paper peeling and the furniture was in need of repair. Everything was dusty and unkempt and even the pictures on the wall were all hanging askew. Still, there was a certain romance about the room. Maybe it was the big window that looked out over the front lawn, the fireplace or the faint musky smell of lavender. I had gotten up early that morning and I lay back on the iron bed, closed my eyes and listened to the birds singing outside. I must have drifted off to sleep and lost track of time. I jumped up in a panic when I heard voices outside and I ran to the window and saw them walking back from the garden. I was afraid Sallie was going to get caught in Aunt Sara's room. I peeked out the door and saw Sallie running up the hall clutching something to her breast.

"Hurry," I whispered opening the door wider to let her in. Before we could close the door we heard the front door open.

Trying to catch her breath, she reached under her blouse and produced two unopened letters and one empty envelope addressed to her from Ransom.

"See," I said, knowing now she believed me.

Sallie looked at me and it was clear she was hurt, "Why would she do such a thing?"

"Wise up Sallie, don't be stupid. She was trying to keep you here hoping you would fall for her nephew." I said, standing there with my hands on my hips.

"Grady," she smirked as she started to tear into a letter.

Before she could read the first line Aunt Sara called up to us, "Girls are you ready?"

Sallie ran out to the top of the stairs and said we would be right down. She still had not combed her hair or changed her clothes, the letters had to wait.

"Go on downstairs and ask for Henry to come up for my trunk in a few minutes," she said with bobby pins in her teeth and both hands in her hair. As soon as I stepped into the hall I was startled by a well dressed Negro boy.

"Good morning, I'm Henry. Aunt Sara sent me up to bring down Miss Sallie's things."

I told him Sallie would be ready in a few minutes and he sat down on the floor in front of her door. I found it a little peculiar he had referred to Sara as his aunt too and I stopped midways on the stairs to take a look at him. He was not a full Negro at all, perhaps a Mulatto or Indian with long hair hanging in a braid half-way down his back.

It was nearly one o'clock before we took off again. Now we had Sallie and her things in addition to the very large Aunt Sara to crowd in. Papa drove and sitting beside him was Henry. Aunt Sara had insisted on bringing him along in case Papa needed any assistance.

We had not been traveling long when Papa stopped by a creek to water the horses. I was glad Effie had packed a nice picnic of ham biscuits, cold potatoes and fried apple pies. Sallie and I stepped into the woods to find a spot out of the open. Sallie was also hoping to gain a minute of privacy to look over the letters she had stuffed down the bosom of her dress. Just past the tree line I saw a nice flat rock.

"Here, this will work for me." I said as I pulled up my skirt and dropped my pantaloons down to the ground.

"Me too," Sallie said, "I am about to burst."

We braced ourselves against the rock and enjoyed the sweet relief. I had barely finished when I heard someone coming. Sallie jerked up her skirt and stepped out in front of me.

Aunt Sara's voiced called out, "Hello, is this the girl's private spot?"

"Guess so," I said, trying to make a joke.

We were still trying to put ourselves back together when she hiked up her skirt and squatted down right there in front of us. We had to step aside to keep her from wetting our shoes. I must have looked shocked at the embarrassing flatulence noises she made as she struggled to get up.

Aunt Sara looked at me and simply said, "Oh Lizzie, aren't we all common?"

I suppose she was right, but I could have done without a nature lesson today. Aunt Sara went on ahead of us adjusting her hat and humming under her breath as if nothing had happened at all. When I turned around, Sallie was nearly doubled over laughing.

"She does that all the time. She says she has a "condition," choked out Sallie.

"Condition, my foot! She is full of hot air," I replied.

Sallie agreed and started to open one of the letters, but before she could get it out of the envelope Papa called out, "Daylight is burning."

"Damn," said Sallie and stuffed the letters back down the front of her blouse. We ran back to the carriage holding hands.

When we arrived at Miss Georgette's, Henry opened the door and I stepped out of the carriage which had felt more like a jail cell. I tried to dust off my dress, but what did it matter? The wind had blow my hair all to pieces. The curtains were closed across the front window of Miss Georgette's shop and I was glad she was not watching. I opened my purse and pulled out a small mirror and tried to arrange my hair back and dabbed a little perfume behind my ears.

Aunt Sara gave Henry a list to give to Mr. Edwards at the dry goods store. He took off on foot, leaving the four of us standing under the awning. Before Papa could make arrangements what time to come back for us, the front door flew open and Miss Georgette stood in the doorway.

"Sara," she shouted with her arms wide open.

Sara trotted over to her and the two of them stood hugging each other like two little girls in the school yard. I could not help but think how out of character this seemed for Miss Georgette. The last time I saw her she was so reserved and sophisticated.

The fitting went wonderfully and the dress fit perfectly. So, the lovely blue silk dress with the velvet trim was wrapped up along with the dyed slippers, a purse and a matching fan. The whole process took less than thirty minutes. Mother and Sallie picked out some accessories, but it was Aunt Sara who kept us there three more hours. She decided it was time for a whole new wardrobe for herself. We had to turn Papa away twice and it was nearly dark when we finally got to the hotel for supper. Papa suggested we stay at the hotel for the night, but Aunt Sara said there was no need for concern. Henry could find his way through hell and back.

After supper we all crammed back in the carriage. Aunt Sara insisted Henry drive us home so Papa could rest. At first Papa seemed uneasy, but after a while, he relaxed. Soon everyone was asleep, awakening now and then by a bump in the road or Aunt Sara's "condition" occurring as she slept. I was not sure how long we had traveled, but it seemed to be a very long time. I woke Papa and asked him to check his watch. Papa pulled out his pocket watch and held it up in the moonlight. He was alarmed to find it was three o'clock in the morning.

"Hey, hold up there Henry!" he shouted up front. The carriage just kept right on rolling, so Papa knocked on the back of the carriage with his fist and slowly we came to a stop. Papa jumped out and asked Henry where the hell we were. By this time we were all awake and wondering what was going on.

Aunt Sara jumped out of the carriage, "Henry!" She shouted up to him. He still did not respond and I was afraid he was dead. Papa reached up and shook him and a whiskey bottle tumbled to the ground.

"Now ain't this a fine turn of events," Papa said looking at Aunt Sara. "We are lost out here in the middle of nowhere and your boy is as drunk as a skunk." Papa pulled Henry down out of the seat and slapped him across the face.

Sara shouted, "Don't Jacob, I promised!"

Papa screamed right back at her, "You promised what?"

Aunt Sara was crying and trying to help the boy off the ground. "He is Charles's boy and I promised I would take care of him," she said quietly. "Even if his mother was a slave, I have raised him like my own. Jacob please don't judge, I have grown to love the boy."

Papa pulled the boy to his feet and helped him back to his seat. "It is not for me to judge, Sara. That is God's job," Papa said apologizing.

We all stood there in the moonlight, waiting for someone to say something.

Mother was the first to speak, "Let's get back in the carriage; it is too cool out here."

"It will be morning soon and we will be able to get this thing turned around," Papa said encouragingly.

Aunt Sara reached in the back of the carriage and got a blanket to cover up Henry.

She was still crying when she got in the carriage. Shortly everyone was asleep again. I tried to sleep too, but I began to have familiar pains and cramps in my stomach. I had not come prepared for this. I sat quietly in my seat and prayed it would hold off until we got home, if we got home.

Before the sun came up the carriage was rolling and this time it was Papa driving. The others were still sleeping until they heard Papa's voice. A hay wagon was ahead and he stopped to talk to the gentleman driving. Papa threw up his hands in the air as he walked back to us. We had been less than a mile away from Aunt Sara's, but in the dark it might as well have been a hundred.

When we arrived at Aunt Sara's, Effie came to the door showing great concern about our whereabouts. Mr. O'Connor was nowhere in sight and I was glad. It would have been most embarrassing, for as soon as I stepped out Mother informed me my skirt was soiled.

By now I was not feeling well at all, my head was hurting and my belly was cramping. She told us to go inside and she would speak to Sara. Sallie took me upstairs to lie down and Aunt Sara came right up with a cup of Cinnamon tea. I drank it and the warmth helped calm the cramping.

"We have all been there," Aunt Sara said and left the room.

Shortly the knock at the door was Effie. She filled the wash bowl and laid on the dresser a small cord and a cotton pad nicely folded in a long clean rag. She asked for my skirt and left. This was not exactly what I was used to, but I knew what to do. I attached the cord around my waist and placed the pad between my legs and tied up the ends. When Effie returned the skirt was stain free. I got dressed and went downstairs.

Everyone was waiting in the drawing room, but nothing was said about the reason for the delay. When we got home everyone was worried about where we had been. Cato said, *"I's was a fixin' to send out a search party."*

I went straight upstairs, undressed and went to bed. I was glad to be in my own room where I could once again shut out the rest of the world. It had been an awful twenty-four hours.

CHAPTER 7

My Party

It was the week before my party and there was still much to do, which gave Mother a perfect excuse to refuse all our relatives as houseguests. She forgot one, Papa's cousin John. Five days before the party they arrived, John, his wife Kate and their two children. Mother took it in stride, but she was not delighted. John and Papa had kept in touch all through the years, even after Papa moved to Charleston. Papa went up to see John when his first wife died and again when he married Kate, a widow with a young son.

Having John visit was just like old times for Papa, but Kate was not quite as good company for Mother. Conversations with Kate either consisted of quoting the Bible or people's poor health. She was afraid of everything and anything. All her food had to be specially prepared or she claimed to suffer with dysentery. The room was either too hot or too cold and Lord forbid should she be exposed to dust or dander. Kate looked like an old leather sack of bones and her wardrobe consisted only of cotton dresses and aprons. She was not attractive, but a hairstyle that was not so tight would be an improvement. Mother was afraid Kate would be an embarrassment to all of us at the party and offered her one of her balls gowns. She refused, saying she had brought a dress and it would be perfectly fine. It was anything but fine. In fact, it was perfectly awful, dark dull and old fashioned, just like Kate. Kate was a mouthful of gloom and doom, which most likely drove her first husband to an early grave.

Mother said she was working on John and before the week was over, she might have her too.

If Kate was not enough, there was Gerald, her son from her first marriage. Gerald was twenty-one years old and a skeleton like his mother. His pasty white face was covered with pimples and he wore thick little spectacles that sat on the end of his long pointed nose. Mammy said she bet his maw still gave him the tit and wiped his butt; the way she was fretting over him every time he coughed or sneezed. I suppose he did need a keeper as he could hardly walk without tripping over his own two feet. When Kate made the casual announcement that Gerald and I would make a good match, Gerald started laughing so hard that a snorting noise came out his nose. I debated telling his Mother right then and there what he did to Lottie. I decided not, he was so precious in her sight, she would never believe he would even look at a little colored girl's breasts.

Mattie, his sister, was much more acceptable. In fact, we looked forward to her visits. She had dark curly hair and was a little on the plump side and just as silly as Annabelle. That couple of days before the party were filled with horseback riding, picnicking down by the pond and listening to Mattie and Annabelle talk about what they would do and be when they grew up. Sallie and I were both quiet. We used to talk of dreams, but it was before we understood. *"Men are free to seek their own destiny, but a woman's destiny has to be attached to a man."*

October 6, 1860

I turned eighteen that day and the house awaited my party that night. You could smell the pies and cakes baking a mile away. The cooks were making sauces and five large pigs were set to roasting. The sweet smoky aroma of pork cooking was so heavenly you could almost taste it in the air. Mother was in good form. Sallie and Annabelle were making flower arrangements and Mammy's youngest daughter, Violet, had been put to work on polishing the silver and setting the tables. It was all a work in progress and everyone in town was talking about the big party at our house that night.

The guests began to arrive shortly after breakfast. Ransom Huneycutt and his youngest brother Thomas were the first to arrive. Thomas was about Annabelle's age and we all liked his good nature and humor. As more guests began to arrive, a nice lunch was laid out on the terrace for the men. The women were escorted upstairs. Around two o'clock I heard the skeet-shooting tournament begin and men playing horseshoes. Annabelle and Mattie piled up on my bed to pull back the curtains to have a look at the men. I felt my stomach start to quiver as they claimed all the men were so handsome, even Grady O'Connor. Mattie blurted out Annabelle was sweet on Ransom's brother, Thomas. Annabelle punched Mattie and they began rolling and tumbling until they ended up on the floor with a loud thump. Giggling, they got to their feet and starting hitting each other with the pillows. Before long I was in the game too. We were all running around and laughing so hard we did not hear Mother come in the door. She broke up the party, reminded us we had guests and sent Mattie and Annabelle out of my room.

The entire upstairs was transformed into a place for the ladies to rest and prepare for the evening activities. There were dozens of little cots covered with freshly ironed sheets scented with lavender oil. The tables were set up with a fine selection of French perfumes and talcum. The basins were lined up in the hall for soaking tired feet after hours of dancing. On the way to my room, I stopped to admire the table displaying an assortment of cakes, cookies, candies and nuts. How nicely it had all come together. I wished to be a guest lying out there with the other girls, just relaxing, eating butter rum cake and inhaling the sweet lavender and perfumes.

Mammy's two daughters were appointed the duties of helping dress the ladies. Mammy described Cindy Lou as a little off in the head and Violet as smart as a whip.

I found it sad the way they both pitched a fit to be my personal attendant, but Mammy made it clear she had been dressing me since I was a babe and now was not the time to change. Violet was pleased Mammy agreed to her idea to put fresh gardenias in my hair and said, *"Miss Lizzie wills be a smellin' as sweet as she iz a lookin."*

It had begun to sound like a hen house outside my bedroom door. I peeked out of my room and there were ladies everywhere, stripped down to their corset and pantaloons. Some were stretched out on the cots and a few of the younger girls were playing cards.

Most of the older ladies were on the porch with Mother. I overheard them talking about what they had seen in the Harper's Weekly last Saturday. A strange animal was brought from Africa to England. The paper said it might be half-man and half-monkey. They were calling this creature by the name of "gorilla." I was not sure if I believed the creature even existed. Mother said she would have to see it to believe it.

I spied Annabelle and Mattie over by the food. I hissed at them and motioned them to my door. I begged them to bring me something to eat. Within a few minutes they had returned with a delicious plate of goodies. I had just bit into a little blueberry cake when Mammy came through the door with a tray of beauty mixtures.

"Lizzie!" she yelped. *"Hows in the world, do yo's spect to fit in you's dress eatin' pies an' cakes. Ain't no fine southern gentlemens gonna wantz no big fat wife,"* she warned me, looking at Mattie and Annabelle. They took the hint, stuck their bellies way out, and laughed at each other.

"Yall run 'long now; I'z gots to commenced my work on Miss Lizzie," she stood by the door and patted them on the bottom as they filed out the door.

I knew she was just teasing me and I played along. "Well, I might just have to marry me a big fat old Yankee," I said and winked at her.

"Over you's daddy's dead body you's will," she replied.

She was still rattling on while she mixed up one of her "beauty spells," as she called them. First, she scrubbed my face with cornmeal and a hot towel. Next, she mixed an egg, honey and a bit of brandy in a bowl. Then she reached in her pocket and pulled out a little leather pouch and put something else in the bowl. I smiled because I knew she would never tell us what was in those little bags. She just called it her "Mojoe." The mixture began to tingle as she smeared it over my face and chest. When the treatment was over, I put on my chemise and pantaloons and Mammy laced up my corset.

Then she set a small velvet box on the dresser. I jumped up and read the card attached.

Dear Elizabeth,

I wanted you to have these on your eighteenth birthday; I was eighteen when my Mother gave them to me. Someday I hope you will have a daughter you are just as proud of as I am of you. Please pass them down to her with love from her grandmothers.

Love, Mother

Inside the box was Mother's sapphire necklace and earrings. Mammy helped me fasten the necklace and I put on the earrings. It was almost dark and Mammy lit the oil lamp sitting on the dresser. I watched Mammy in the mirror placing the gardenias in my hair. I admired how the sapphires caught the light as I turned my head from side to side.

She put the comb down and said, *"I's almost forgets, I'z got something' for you's too. A real fancy lady called Miss Lucy, sent it to you's.* Mammy pulled a little tin can of rouge out of her pocket and laid it on the dresser. *"If yo's be in an accordance to usin' a bit tonight, donts nobody knows 'bouts itz buts me."*

She put a few finishing touches to my hair, stepped back and took a look at me.

I lifted up the tin of rouge, handed it to her and she giggled like a little girl. I closed my eyes and she patted some on my lips and cheeks. When I opened my eyes, there to my amazement, was not a girl but a woman. We both were spellbound as we looked at this strange new person in the mirror. We heard a knock at the door; it was Papa. He had come to escort me downstairs.

The moment was here. It was time for me to make my entrance. I took one last look in the mirror and took Papa's arm. Mammy had tears in her eyes, as if she knew the little girl in pigtails was gone forever. I looked at Papa as we walked down the hall. His tailored jacket emphasized he was as trim as a man half his age. His soft wavy gray hair touched the back of his collar and his skin was smooth and tanned. *He smiled at me and I felt the tenderness only a daughter could feel.*

Papa walked down the steps, steady and straight. Every eye in the room was on me. My knees felt weak and my head started to spin. Papa must have felt me stumble and took a firmer grip on my arm.

When I was half-way the down the stairs I saw "him" and our eyes met. He gave me a quick little nod, and walked out on the terrace. I wondered who he was. How dare he be so arrogant as to walk out during my entrance. It seemed like it took forever to get to the bottom of the steps, but as soon as my feet hit the bottom step everyone was upon me with compliments and introductions.

The party appeared to be a success, the band was playing; people were dancing and enjoying the food. The married woman hovered around each other and single girls lined up hoping to engage in romance. Some men were dancing, but plenty stood in groups talking politics and speculating the affairs of the Union. For the first half of the set I danced almost every dance with a different young man. Gerald was always waiting in line while his Mother looked on with an approving smile. Every time I had to dance with him, he made the oddest little noises. I could not be sure if he was clearing his throat or counting out his steps. I lost count of the number of times he stepped on my toes.

It was not surprising Annabelle and Mattie had a group of young boys from the Citadel gathered around them most of the evening. What did surprise me greatly was Sallie. She was quite the belle, flirting and giggling worse than Annabelle or Mattie. Sallie's newfound personality had made Ransom sit up and take notice. He was watching her every move, especially how many trips she made out on the dance floor.

The band ended their first set and all the ladies went upstairs to refresh. When the party started, it was cool and the fireplaces were lit. As the night progressed and bodies were crowded in the house, it became stuffy and hot. Once upstairs the ladies began dropping their dresses and kicking off their slippers to soak their feet. Mammy and Cindy Lou ran behind them collecting the fallen ball gowns. Seasoned party goers knew these parties were likely to last most of the night, so they seized the opportunity to stretch out on the cots and rest.

I had expected Sallie to be in my room waiting for me, but she was nowhere in sight. I was on my way to look for her, but before I could there was knock at the door. It was Sallie standing there, wet with perspiration and her hair falling down around her face. I pushed her through the door and closed it behind her. She was gasping for air and her eyes were so glassy I asked if she was drunk. I made her sit down on the bed and take a deep breath. Finally, her voice came to her, but I could not tell if she was laughing or crying. Mammy heard the uproar and came in the room. She went over to Sallie and shook her by the shoulders, *"What in tarnation is wrong with you's child?"* she asked.

It took Sallie a bit before she could get the story out. She said she had been dancing with Grady O'Connor and they walked out on the terrace alone together. Ransom followed them and asked Sallie to come inside. Grady started talking rough and told Ransom to mind his own business. Papa came out and told Grady to calm down or go home. Sallie said she got scared and ran upstairs.

Mammy was listening intently and fiddling with Sallie's hairstyle, patting and trying to pin up her curls, Sallie wanted to know if we thought Ransom was jealous. Mammy said, *"Yo's never can tells 'bouts dim men folks."*

The band had already started playing and the party had resumed when we came downstairs. Ransom was standing over by the fireplace talking to another man. Both men took notice of us as we walked by. I recognized the other man as the mysterious man who had walked out on me during my entrance. I warned Sallie to remain calm and we walked arm in arm toward the refreshments.

We saw Ransom's brother Thomas trapped in conversation with Verina Tudor over by the punch bowl. It was an unspoken rule a young man did not walk away from a lady leaving her unattended, even if it was Verina Tudor. Our plan was to rescue

Thomas, but before we could reach the table, Gerald intercepted our path.

"Oh, Gerald, I said, "Have you met the charming and talented, Miss Tudor?"

I took his arm and gestured him toward Verina. He pushed his glasses up on his bony nose and sniffed as if he was a dog on the trail of a rabbit. Sallie laughed; we hoped Gerald would be the keeper of Verina for the rest of the party. Better still, I would not have to dance with him again.

Papa spotted us from across the room and came trotting over. He insisted I dance with him at that very moment. I hesitated to leave Sallie, but she nodded it was all right. The dance was the Pattie-Cake-Polka and we exchanged partners so often that I could not keep my eye on Sallie. When the dance was over, Sallie was gone. In her place stood Gerald watching Verina stuff her little fat face with another plate of sweets.

Papa and I had just begun our second dance when the man I had been wondering about came and tapped Papa on the shoulder. Papa stepped aside to allow him to take his place. Papa quickly introduced the man as Mr. Joel Simpson of North Carolina and excused himself from the floor. From the moment we began to dance, I was completely at ease as though we had danced many times before. He took the lead and his hands were steady and dry. With my hand on his waist, I was aware of his trim figure. Then suddenly, as if he had asked me to, I looked up into his watery blue eyes. I wanted to look away but my eyes were frozen. I could barely hear the music or the soft rhythmic sound of petticoats swishing around us. He was smiling at me as if to question my thoughts, but it did not distract me from studying his handsome face. His dark hair and his perfectly groomed beard were speckled with gray, which had given me the impression he was older. Now, I could clearly see his face was young and firm. The hint of tobacco and brandy on his breath was almost intoxicating. My eyes fell on his soft full lips, something inside made me want to toss my head back and feel those lips upon my throat. *I had never kissed a man before.* I am not sure how long the music had stopped before we realized it.

When he escorted me off the dance floor, it was clear our dance had not gone unnoticed. It was almost as if everyone held their breath and watched as we walked off the dance floor. I was not sure if they had read my mind or my fantasy was not a dream.

Papa was standing by the door with a half-cocked smile, reached out and took my hand as we approached. He patted Joel on the back as if he approved. They exchanged a few words but my pulse was beating so rapidly and my tongue was too thick to speak. Within minutes Sallie interrupted the conversation saying she must talk to us right away. Joel excused himself and I watched as he walked away.

"Ransom has proposed," She said excitedly.

Papa looked at her and said, "And you said?"

"Yes, I said yes!" She said almost shouting.

"Well, pardon me, I must go and find my future son-in-law," Papa responded.

Sallie took my hand and said," Lizzie are you listening to me? Ransom and I are going to be married."

"We all knew it was just a manner of time," I said and gave her a hug.

After the last song, Papa announced Sallie and Ransom's engagement. Everyone was offering their congratulations except for Aunt Sara and Grady O'Connor who were wearing sour faces.

The carriages were pulling up to collect their guests and I bit back the tears and reflected on the moment that Joel took me in his arms. Foolishly, I scanned the room looking for Joel, who seemed to have disappeared. It became Sallie and Ransom's night, not mine. I was lost in the shadows. I walked out on the terrace alone and unnoticed.

"Miss Lizzie," the voice came from behind me.

"I am glad I found you," I turned and it was Joel.

"Forgive me for catching you alone, but I could not leave without saying good-bye."

He approached me and stood directly in front of me and I dropped my head. He lifted my chin so he could look directly into my eyes. "Please, turn your face to the moonlight, I would like to remember how beautiful you are," he whispered almost as though he had not wanted to.

That feeling came back over me and I closed my eyes hoping he would kiss me. Instead, he took my hand, lifted it to his lips, and kissed it very slowly. His lips were still upon my hand when we heard voices.

"Joel, there you are," Ransom said.

"I was just saying good-bye to the most beautiful belle in the South." Joel said as he released my hand, but not until he had given it a little squeeze.

"You are a smart man my friend," said Ransom.

"A man with half a brain would think the same," Joel said looking back at me.

"Lizzie, I hope to see you again soon," were his last words to me.

Ransom asked Joel if he would be taking the early train back to North Carolina. He said yes and the two men walked out together engaged in conversation.

When Ransom returned Sallie was on his arm, smiling as if she were in a dream. Ransom looked at me and began to tell me about his friend Joel from North Carolina.

"We have known each for a long time, Lizzie. He is a fine man and was my cousin's husband and..."

The word *husband* burned right through me and I was afraid Ransom had noticed how badly he had caught me off guard. I cut Ransom off in the middle of his sentence and excused myself. The party was over for me.

It was four o'clock in the morning and finally all the guests had gone. Annabelle and Mattie were already asleep on the porch and Mother went to her room. The hustle and bustle was over, with only Mammy and Cindy Lou left to restore order to the upstairs.

Sallie asked if I would sleep with her; she was too excited to be alone. I went to my room, undressed and changed into my nightgown. When I stepped out in the hall Mammy was asking Sallie if she had seen Violet. We both told Mammy no, not since she was seen emptying the last of the chamber pots. Mammy started fussing. She bet they would find her somewhere asleep in a corner.

"Itz mights be she's runs off with that boy named Harper," Cindy Lou said sounding like a jealous sister. She had a right to be, for Cindy Lou was no match to Violet in wits or looks. Pretty as a picture was Violet, with a little doll like face and big dark eyes.

Sallie and I gathered up a stack of plates to take downstairs, but as we started down the steps, Violet was creeping up. I called her name, but she did not lift up her head. When she got to the top of the stairs, she collapsed on the floor in front of me. I called out to Mammy, "Something is wrong with Violet!"

Mammy came running with a look of terror in her eyes. She dropped to her knees and scooped her up in her arms, *"What's wrong with you's child?"*

Violet's face was streaked from tears but her eyes were dry and fixed like someone in a trance. One eye was swollen and blue and her lips were bleeding. There were no words exchanged, but Mammy knew what had happened. She lifted up Violet's skirt and her petticoat was soiled with blood. I felt myself go weak and Sallie was as pale as a ghost. For once, I did not wait for Mammy to tell me what to do, I ran to get Mother.

When Mother came to the door she was alone, Papa was still downstairs. Mother grabbed her robe and followed me out in the hall. She saw Mammy folded over Violet on the floor. At once Mother, the true plantation mistress, took over. She asked Violet to tell her who had assaulted her. Violet would only say it was dark, real dark. Mother got stern and demanded she tell her if it was a white man or colored man. To this Violet only said, "white."

We all gasped at the thought that someone who had been a guest in our home could have possibly done this. Mother's voice was tender and low when she told Mammy to put Violet in Sallie's bed. She instructed Sallie to get some clean rags and water and told me to go fetch her laudanum. When we returned, they had already taken Violet to Sallie's room. I knocked on the door and Mother came out leaving the door cracked. The light was dim, but I could see Mammy examining Violet's frail naked body on the bed. Mother took the items we had brought her and closed the door.

Sallie came back with me to my room. She snuggled down next to me like a little girl. She asked me if I was afraid. I lied and said, "No, I am not afraid."

She just wanted someone to take care of her and tell her everything was going to be fine. It was easy for Sallie to go off to sleep with so much happiness in her heart. For me, with my head full of worries and fears, it was not so simple.

"Dear God, Please let me overcome the weakness of my gender. Give me the strength to face the hardships that are before me and the compassion to forgive."

Mother was a closed book the next morning about what had happened to Violet. If Papa knew, he never spoke a word. Annabelle and Mattie came down to breakfast arm in arm still teasing each other about the boys at the party. John and Kate said the party was wonderful. When their heads hit the pillow, they slept like a baby. Gerald did not come down to breakfast at all that morning. In fact, none of us saw him until the family was leaving to go home. Even then, he had very little to say and was the first one to load up the carriage.

Sallie and I talked a little about "the incident," as we would refer to it from then on. She was afraid to be alone after that and never went outside after dark. I wished I could have eased Sallie's mind and told her the assaulter was miles away in North Carolina, but of this, I could not be sure. If the incident had happened to one of us, the man would have been hunted down and hung before sunset. For those on the other side of the color line things were different. I suppose it was understood and Mammy never said a word.

My heart was scarred forever with the memory of the pain and sorrow I saw in Mammy's eyes that night. The Lord says, *'Vengeance is mine'* and for Violet's sake I hope that is true.

CHAPTER 8

The Harvest Festival

Over three weeks had passed since my party and the incident with Violet. Time had swept it under the rug and somehow now it all seemed like a bad dream.

Ransom had written to expect him and Thomas in time for the annual harvest festival. Mother was delighted and insisted they stay with us since they were practically part of the family now. They arrived on the 30th of October.

From the moment Ransom arrived, he exhibited a sense of urgency to arrange for their wedding as soon as possible. Anyone could see that Sallie's devotion for him was not likely to change. Nevertheless, the wedding date was set for the 11th of November. Sallie was happy; but Mother was disappointed and urged Papa to persuade them to reconsider until spring. Papa ended the debate with only a few words, "I think it is best they get married now; it is not a good time to put things off for better days."

The underlying meaning of Papa's words went over the top of Sallie and Annabelle's heads, but Mother and I knew it was the threat of a war that was the pressing issue.

With the wedding date set, the planning was left to Sallie and Mother, while Ransom and Papa spent the afternoon fishing. This left Annabelle happily in charge of entertaining young Thomas. I was left to be on my own, which was beginning to be a habit as of late.

I was not to spend my day in vain. The book I had long awaited for had arrived that day. Sometimes I much preferred the company of a good book to that of people. The pages of my book were calling me. As I made my way up the stairs, I heard Mother say to Sallie, "That girl suffers with the worst case of "book madness!"

It was a misty rainy day. Everything in the house was damp and I felt a chill down my spine. I lit the fireplace in my room and settled down in the wicker rocker by the window. Unwrapping my new book, I studied the portrait of the author and read her biography on the front piece. I turned the pages; a life of romance and scandal was revealed. Mary Shelley, a girl of only sixteen runs away with a married man. The lovers traveled among the upper-set in London and wrote books and poetry. Upon accepting a challenge from Lord Byron, she wrote her story, called *Frankenstein.*

I closed the book and rested it against my breast. I was eighteen, two years older than this Mary Shelley. Yet, of what travels or adventures could I speak? Innocent I might be, but I understood passion and a burning desire for romance. I tried to read, but my thoughts keep returning to Mary Shelley. I found it peculiar to be reading her book on the eve of Halloween or "All Hallowtide." Perhaps Mary's book was prompted by the old folklores told this time of year. Mammy used to say, *"Ain't but one way to hide under dat' big old harvest moon from dem' evil spirits, but to pretends to be one of dem.' Even den,' if you iz wise you will put out some treats for da' devil or else he mights tak' yous soul."*

The Negroes took these superstitions seriously, but most white people considered it just child's play. I laughed thinking what Mammy would say if she heard about this Frankenstein monster.

That night's dinner conversation was centered on the wedding plans. The wedding was to be small and intimate, just family and close friends. Mother would play the wedding march and I was to recite, "How do I love thee" by Elizabeth Barrett Browning.

Ransom turned to Sallie and muttered, "Let me count the ways."

I was sure I would most likely go insane if I had to listen to this for three more weeks. As soon as dinner was over, I excused myself and went upstairs. I was awakened several times during the night by a dog howling in the woods. Mammy and Cato were jumpy the next morning over hearing the howling dog during the night. Mammy stopped Cato in the hall, *"Reckon it was a Banshee we hears wailin' last night?"*

"I's sees nothing, but I sur hears it," Cato replied.

"If it be a Banshee she be callin'out somebody soul befo' long," Mammy's voice was low, hoping the rest of us did not hear them talking.

Sisters and I spent the afternoon preparing for the evening festival. Mother's tradition was to make each of us a good luck apron to wear to the festival. We decorated them ourselves and stitched our names and date on the pocket. We kept them from year to year. It was fun to see how much we had grown and how we decorated them in the past. Mother forgot about the aprons this year. We were forced to change the date and reuse last year's aprons. "An entire year will be missing from the apron collection. Why is Mother forgetting so many things lately?" Annabelle whined as she ripped out the stitches of her apron.

"She has a lot on her mind and she just forgot, that's all," Sallie answered shortly.

I suspected the real reason was in the little bottle she kept by her bed. Our aprons were pressed and we were ready to leave shortly after three o'clock. Cato had already brought the carriage around and Mother and Sallie were loading up their pies. Ransom and Thomas looked out of place standing on the front stoop. It was clear we would have to take two carriages. The decision was made; I would ride with Mother and Father and the others would ride in Ransom's carriage. We made our way into town like a band of gypsies. It made me angry to hear the laughter and singing coming from their carriage.

Once we arrived in town amidst the excitement of the festival, I felt my mood lifting. There were people going in all directions and the porches were glowing with Jack O' Lanterns. Annabelle smiled at me. We began playfully kicking up the multicolored leaves at each other. Even Ransom and Sallie, walking ahead arm in arm, were beginning to seem natural now.

Thomas was confident he could catch the greased pig and win the prize. Annabelle said she would like to see him try as they ran off together hand in hand. Mother and Sallie looked at the time and realized the pie contest would be starting soon; they took off down the street with their baskets held high. Strolling along behind them, enjoying their conversation, was Papa and Ransom.

Was I expected to just run along behind them like a poor little puppy dog? Feeling hurt, I lagged behind. From where I stood, I could hear the music down the street and smell the sausages cooking in the open air. The sun had gone down and it was getting cooler; I pulled my wool cape out of my bag and tossed it over my shoulders.

Standing there in the shadows, I watched the people pass by. I felt invisible. Directly in front of me, crossing the street, I saw a woman laughing and walking arm in arm with two men. When she came to the curb, she lifted her skirt with both hands and vulgarly displayed a pair of indigo stockings. After she passed by, it occurred to me it was Miss Lucy.

I would have enjoyed lingering along the side roads to view wares the vendors had on display, but I had pondered too long already. I knew it was not respectable or safe for a woman to be alone on the streets at night. As soon as I started across the way, I saw Sallie and Annabelle bent over talking to a withered looking little woman sitting on the steps. As soon as they saw me, Sallie called out in a stern voice, "Just where have you been, young lady?"

Before I could answer, her face lit up and I realized she was teasing me. When I joined them, the woman turned her head toward me. Her streaked gray hair practically touched the ground. Even in the dim light, I could see her worn expression. She wore a ragged frock and her feet and hands were dirty, but I did not pull away when she reached out and took my hand. Her hands were soft as butter. She spoke to me in a low voice. She said she could pare an apple for me and as the peeling fell to the ground, it would reveal the initial of my future husband. Sallie had already had a try and the peelings had fallen in the shape of a perfect 'R'. Sallie begged me to take a turn. I told her and the apple peeler I most certainly did not believe in such things.

"My dear, some things one does not see with the eyes but with the heart," whispered the peculiar little old woman.

I did not give my permission, but she began to peel and let the peeling drop to the ground. Its curled up position meant nothing to me, but Annabelle declared it was a 'J'. The old woman slowly nodded her head. Annabelle clinched my hand and her voice was shaky when she asked if she could have a turn. The old woman was silent when the apple she peeled fell to the ground and split in two pieces.

Annabelle questioned, "What does this mean? Am I not to have a husband?"

The woman asked Annabelle, "Shall I peel for you again?"

"No!" Annabelle said in a determined voice, "This is all non-sense."

I poked Annabelle and pointed to her purse. She nodded and the three of us turned around long enough to sort out some change to pay the woman for her romantic predictions. Oddly enough, when we turned back around, the step was empty.

Annabelle called out, "Hello," but no one answered.

Sallie suggested the old woman might be a witch. We huddled up and quickly made our way down the street to find the others. Mother and Papa were enjoying the music in front of Market Hall. Ransom and Thomas were almost in a panic when they saw us. Ransom took hold of Sallie's arm and in a stern controlling voice he asked, "Where have you girls been?" Sallie drew back and started to cry. Ransom realized his tone was too harsh and he rephrased his words, "We were all worried dear."

Mother looked over at me as if I had been the one to lead the group astray. I remained with my family the rest of the night. The streets were spinning with people dancing, laughing, and having a good time. I watched my sisters with envy as they danced by me. Sallie lit up in love and Annabelle in the arms of her new sweetheart.

Ever since I was a little girl, people warned Papa that all the young men would be chasing after me. Now, it appeared even Annabelle would marry before me. Had I been mocked all my life, with nothing but lies? For the first time I felt sorry for the not so pretty girls, the unpopular ones, because tonight I was afraid I had joined their ranks. It was not like me to believe in silly superstitions, but it was beginning to seem like some evil curse had fallen upon me on the eve of my eighteenth birthday.

The festival was over and Verina Tudor's sweet potato pie won the ribbon. All night long, Cato had been waiting by the carriage to drive us home. He was wearing one of Mammies little bags of "Mojo" around his neck, most likely to protect him against evil. I am sure he was most glad to see us and be on his way home.

When we turned on the road home, I could see the fires burning down at the slave quarters. On this night, the Negroes celebrated the Harvest Moon. They tossed bones into the "Bone Fire" and asked the yellow moon to shine its protection over them. When I retired to my room, I was glad to be alone with my thoughts and feelings. The curtains were not yet drawn and with the moonlight spreading across the room, I could see clearly. I undressed and slipped a soft cotton gown over my naked body. I pulled the blanket off the foot of my bed, covered my shoulders and walked out on the balcony. The cool night air blowing through my hair served as a reminder that only a hint of summer remained in this year of 1860. In the flickering fire light in the distance, I could see the Negroes' dark bodies swaying in motion. I could hear their soft voices singing and smelled the meat roasting. I felt the beat of their drums; it was primitive and sensual.

I thought about slavery and freedom. In many ways, we were all slaves, whether owned by man or enslaved by our own inhibitions. Perhaps one day we would all be free. I watched until the fire's light began to dim.

October 31, 1860

"Tonight the harvest moon shines, but it is not me it shines upon.
I cannot see its golden glow, for I hang my head low.
Forgive me Lord, for I am gloomy and full of envy.
Where shall I dispose my heart or who shall listen to my passions?
If loneliness shall be my teacher, God let me learn quickly."

At breakfast the next morning, Ransom broke the news to Sallie he would be leaving straight away. He would be unable to visit again until the day of the wedding. Sallie started to cry. Ransom, at a loss for words, turned to Mother. "Sallie," she said. "Businessmen are much in demand and you will have to learn to be considerate of such."

We all tried to resume our conversations while Sallie sat quietly stifling her tears.

After breakfast, Thomas asked Ransom if there was time for a short ride with Annabelle before they left. Ransom reluctantly gave his permission and went to pack his things. We went out to sit on the porch with our last cup of coffee.

In a brief time, Ransom was back downstairs. Sallie did not turn her head his way and sat quietly with her eyes fixed straight ahead. Not knowing what to say, Ransom sat down beside her and gathered her hand in his. Again, he tried to make a clumsy attempt at small talk, but Sallie remained silent. I was just on the verge of telling Sallie she was just full of piss and vinegar. However, Mother took over, "Ransom, I think this is all working out beautifully. Sallie and I have so much to plan and the time will pass by quickly," she said smiling sweetly at Sallie.

The room was tense waiting for Sallie to speak. Suddenly she jumped to her feet and blurted out, "I am being childish and there is no reason for me to carry on like this!"

Ransom drew a deep breath and this time his voice was not so strained, "That's my girl. Mark my words, when I return it shall be the happiest day our lives. So, my dear, will you take a short walk with me before I leave?"

Sallie lifted herself from the chair, trembling like a person recovering from a sickness. Ransom took her hand and helped her to her feet. I rolled my eyes at Mother and she shook her head and puckered her lips warning me not to make a display. Just as Ransom had gotten the frail and helpless Miss Sallie to her dear little feet, the front door flew open and Annabelle and Thomas burst into the room. "We need to talk to Papa," Annabelle shouted.

Mother just looked at her and said, "Down at the barn!"

Out the door they ran, leaving us all to wonder their motives. Ransom and Sallie went for their walk, mother picked up her needlework and I picked up my book. In less than thirty minutes, we saw Papa coming up the hill with his arm around Annabelle and Thomas lagging behind them. The front door flew open and Annabelle came running in and told us Papa said she and Thomas could get married.

Mother was caught completely by surprise, "Jacob, she is only a baby!"

Papa smiled and looked at me and winked, "Now Tempie, there are some conditions our Annabelle has not yet told."

The excitement dropped in Annabelle's voice as she told us they had to wait until she was eighteen. Mother took a deep breath and sat back down in her chair. Annabelle looked at Papa hopefully, "But, we can tell everyone we are engaged can't we Papa?"

Sallie's long face was gone when she and Ransom came back in the house. She was thrilled with Ransom's arrangements for a six-month long honeymoon. They would be staying at the home of Mrs. Mary Cuthbert on Bay Street in Beaufort. Won't that be heavenly, Lizzie? You and Annabelle can come and visit me and we can go to the seashore."

Ransom added he felt it would be nice to keep Sallie closer to home before they moved to North Carolina. We all agreed, but I would have preferred to keep her right down the hall. Annabelle was still busting to tell her news. "Thomas and I are getting married too," she said wasting no time on the formalities.

Ransom cut his eyes at Thomas. For the first time, Thomas was the one to speak up, "Listen Ran, don't start getting excited; we are not getting married until Annabelle is eighteen."

Ransom gave Thomas a rather firm, but brotherly slap on the back and said, "Well you best get working on making your fortune pretty soon."

We all laughed, but I knew it was true. How could he support a wife with no means? Annabelle was a spoiled little daddy's girl; she would not do well on next to nothing. Ransom and Thomas left and the great departure was over. Mother and Sallie spent the rest of the afternoon planning the details of Sallie's wedding. Now her trousseau would need to be prepared for her honeymoon.

Sallie was twenty years old and her hope chest had been waiting for years. We all had a hope chest in progress, adding to it from time to time the sort of things we would need to set up our new homes. With not much time to plan, it was a good thing. Sallie wanted a simple wedding, but Mother still was insisting on a few wedding traditions. The wedding would be on Sunday for luck. There must be something old (grandmother's Bible) representing past family ties, something new (the ring) representing a new life ahead, something borrowed (Mother's pearls) symbolizing trust and lastly, something blue (lace garter) to protect against bad luck. Annabelle sat there right in the middle planning her own wedding in her head. I had heard all I could stand, closed my book and announced I was going up to take a nap. Annabelle looked at me as though I had said something wrong. So in a very condescending tone, I asked, "What do you think you are looking at?"

"Maybe I am looking at an Old Maid!" she said, returning my remark.

"Good!" I said and stomped up to my room.

When I opened the door, my hope chest seemed to be the first thing I saw. I spoke to it as if it were a person. "Are you a hope chest or a hopeless chest?" How long do you plan to just sit there patiently waiting? "Old Maid, my foot," and I kicked it as hard as I could. Now my toe was throbbing and I really did need to lie down.

I began to think about some of the old maids I had known; some were schoolteachers or governesses. Then there were two old spinsters, the Rhett sisters, Miss Eloise and Miss Gracie. Their home had once been one of the finest plantation homes in Charleston, but now it was in worse disarray than Aunt Sara's place. They had outlived all their relatives and now they lived alone like two old witches. All the Negroes were afraid to go near their house maybe due to all the tales Violet had told. On several occasions Mother would send Violet over to take them a little cake or pound of butter. She always came back claiming she had seen them attending to the devil's work. I suspect the Rhett sisters found fun in deliberately trying to scare the Negroes. Much like the mischief those two boys caused last year, running around the slave quarters with sheets over their heads.

Well, if I turn out to be an Old Maid, I will never allow myself to be a meek and helpless creature. *If nothing else, I would be powerful and rich, anything but insignificant.*

CHAPTER 9

Sallie's Wedding

November 10, 1860

By the beginning of this week, it was clear summer had its last fling. It rained most of the week and the house was shadowy and damp. The misty view from my window set a lonely stage. The trees were bare with only the memory of their beautiful leaves piled at their feet. The days of Sallie living here with us would soon be a memory, too.

Sallie would be leaving and I would be the oldest. I could not possibly take up Sallie's demeanor. She was like Mother, serene and careful with words. Sallie was humble when I was bold; she was tender when I was harsh. Her greatest desire was to be good and she loved me when I was not so good. Now, Ransom will be taking her away. Nobody understands what Sallie's leaving would do to me, or for that matter, all of us. Sallie was our ground and our earth.

I could hear Mother and Sallie across the hall packing up things for her honeymoon. I tried to read, but the pages were damp and stuck together. My hands and feet were cold and I felt hollow inside. I found myself praying Ransom would not come for her. Then I prayed God would forgive me for my selfishness.

Dear God,

Clear my heart of impending gloom and fill me with joy for my sister's happiness.

Most of all Lord, I am afraid for my Southland. Abraham Lincoln has been elected President and our fears have come to pass. Help us to accept all things are in your hands. Protect and guide us to do Thy will, Amen

I spent the entire morning in my room. I didn't even bother to get dressed. It was afternoon when I heard a knock at the door. I assumed it was either Mammy with my lunch or Mother with some task for me to do. The food would be nice, but I really did not want to see Mother. "Yes, come in," I sang out trying to sound cheerful.

The door opened and Annabelle pushed her way through carrying a bundle of clothes. She threw the pile down on the bed and started undressing herself. Within seconds, she had outfitted herself in a pair of men's breeches and an old calico shirt.

"Come on Lizzie," she coached. "There's a pair for you too." She handed me the pants and I took them slowly.

"Where on earth did you get these things?" I asked, almost afraid to touch them.

"I found them in the rag bag and Mother said I could have them." She tossed a pair at me.

"Surely she did not know you were going to actually wear them!" I replied.

"Oh yes, she does, I am going down to the creek to collect a bucket of pecans and you are coming with me," she ordered. I raised my eyebrows and she changed her tone, "Please come with me. I want to pick up some pretty leaves for my collection before they all rot away."

I was inclined to say no, but it was hard to resist her. She looked so cute standing there with her hands on her hips and dressed like a rag-a-muffin. It was true; I was beginning to feel like a hothouse plant, cooped up in my room all this time. If Mother said it was all right, then I suppose it was. I lifted up my gown and slipped on the trousers.

We spontaneously burst into laughter as the pants fell down to the floor. I jerked them back up around my waist and started digging around for something to hold them up.

Taking hold of the curtains hanging behind me, Annabelle's eyes brightened up.

"Here! This will work perfectly," she said as she took the tieback off the curtain.

It was a splendid idea and I fashioned a belt out of the rope. I buttoned up the old shirt and we found a couple of hats and some old shoes. Even though we were able to slip out of the house without being noticed, Papa caught us at the barn. Pretending that he did not know us, Papa asked, "Well, where did you boys come from?"

"*Ah, we are the McKinney boys, down around bouts' midway,*" Annabelle sputtered out, playing along with Papa. "*Sir, we'd like to borrow a couple of these here horses for a spell,*" she said trying to lower her voice and to sound like a country boy.

"You look like nice boys to me; I reckon I could spare a couple," Papa said carrying on with the dialogue. He helped us saddle the horses and we wasted no time taking off across the meadow. Papa shouted out to us, "Don't tarry too long boys!"

It finally stopped raining and the sun was breaking through the clouds. We liked to ride fast and there was no one to tell us we could not. It was miraculous what a couple of hours in the woods, a bucket of pecans and a few brilliant colored leaves did for my outlook. I even decided that Sallie getting married was not such a bad thing. Perhaps change was a good thing.

I knew Sallie would be excited to show off her wardrobe. I went straight upstairs, changed my clothes, put on a cheery face and went to Sallie's room. Everything was a work in progress. Sallie was still packing, Mother was at the sewing machine and Mammy was ironing. Even little Violet was attaching more lace on a petticoat. Time did not allow a new elaborate trousseau to be purchased for Sallie's going away. Even if there had been enough time, I am not sure Papa would have consented to pad the Union's pockets with more taxes. The talk of secession and the rising inflation had curbed many

Southerners' spending habits. Basic staples were at an all time high and even plain calico was up to $2.00 a yard. Fortunately for Sallie, Mother had saved fourteen yards of English Boars Head Cotton in her cedar chest. The fabric background was a pale blending of green and white and the foreground was sprinkled with pink and yellow roses. It may have been a bit too practical for a wedding dress and the weight a little light for the season. However, under the circumstances, it was a blessing for Sallie.

Sallie had wanted the dress to fall off the shoulders in a Juliet fashion, but Mother insisted the colors would be more flattering close to her throat. Therefore, the dress was born with bishop sleeves and a high neck with point lace trim. The skirt had twenty-two small tucks across the 180-inch sweep and was supported by a fashionable five ribbed cage crinoline. Her wedding costume would be completed by a moss-covered hairdressing of dried roses and ribbons that Mammy had made for her.

The John Sanders family received a wedding invitation, but with the uncertainty of the economy they decided only Gerald would attend. Mattie wrote she was disappointed she was not the one to come. I think I can speak for all of us when I say we were equally disappointed.

There was much to remodel and consider for Sallie's honeymoon. None of us had ever been away from home for any extended length of time and six months seemed like a lifetime. Mother fretted over Sallie's wardrobe with greater anxiety than Sallie. We were approaching the social season and there would be parties and balls she would attend. Certainly, there would be plenty of day trips and excursions, luncheons and dinner parties. All would require Sallie to be properly attired. Nothing could be neglected.

Right after dinner, Mother insisted Sallie take to the bed early to rest for her big day. Her room was not yet completed, so Mother tucked her away in my room, leaving us to finish the details. Annabelle's job was transforming Sallie's room into the honeymoon suite for the next night. She polished the furniture, set out the washbowls, dressed the bed in fresh white linens scented with rose oil, and then fell asleep on the chaise. It was shortly after midnight when Mother and I closed the lid on the last neatly packed trunk. Ready or not, Sallie was packed.

Mother lifted herself off the floor and woke Annabelle. They both staggered off to bed and Annabelle said she would leave the door open for me. Mother followed Annabelle's lead. I should have been exhausted as well, but I was not. I looked around Sallie's room, but there was not a single remnant of the little girl who once grew up here. There were no dolls, books or dirty shoes scattered across the floor. Nowhere in sight was there a bonnie blue dress or a dainty little pinafore. The room felt sad. Perhaps those walls knew tomorrow night it would witness its little girl become a woman.

I crossed the room to blow out the light when I saw a page out of Mother's notebook had fallen out on the floor.

Myrtle green traveling dress

Grey twill suit with crimson trim and matching hat

Maroon silk bonnet with black lace veil

Assortment of gloves, stockings, garters, handkerchiefs and sashes

Two evening gowns, white and blue

Brown silk tunic and skirt

Black cloak, scarf, muff and mitts

Brown beaver hat with ostrich feather

French straw hat

Headdresses, snoods, pins and combs

Four light weight frocks

Monogrammed pillow cases and robe

Two each: night dresses, pantaloons, corset covers, corsets, crinolines, slips, petticoats, undershirts and two cage hoops

Two pairs of dancing slippers, walking boots, embroidery mules and house shoes

Two umbrellas one for practical purposes and another for fancy dress

Three purses

Before turning to go to bed, I stopped and looked over the trunks. Was all this fuss a waste? Today I felt completely free just dressed in rags. Perhaps there was a lesson to learn in that somehow.

November 11, 1860

At daybreak, the house was already alive with servants and wedding preparations. Mother slept late, but was dressed and downstairs before Ransom and his family arrived. Sallie was a bundle of nerves already, even though we reassured her everything was in perfect order. Every time Mammy came in and out of the room, Sallie asked if Ransom had arrived. Poor Mammy was as patient as Job, but she finally grew tired of Sallie's inquiries. *"Miss Sallie, when 'dat boy an' his folks get here. I's gonna blows a horn so loud dat de devil himself can hears itz. So's donts axe me no moe, till you hear the horn blows!"*

Mammy left and returned with a cup of chamomile tea and told Sallie she best pull herself together. Sallie cut her eyes over at me and then at Annabelle. "Ya'll leave, I want to talk to Mammy alone. Now scat!"

I knew she was apprehensive about meeting her future in-laws, but I had a good idea there was something else. Just as I pulled the door shut behind us, I hear Mammy break out laughing. *"Lordy, Miss Sallie, donts you worry, Mr. Ransom he'll knows what to do."*

It was a long morning until we heard a carriage pull up. Sallie ran to the window and pulled back the curtain; it was Ransom. She threw her hand to her chest and gasped, "Oh my God, they are here!"

"Let's all get a look at our future in-laws," Annabelle boasted.

The carriage came to a stop and Ransom jumped out wearing a dark tailcoat and trousers that fit him perfectly, for a change. We watched as he took a comb out of his breast pocket and slicked back his hair. Thomas bounced out, looking dapper in a new suit and Annabelle starting jumping up and down and clapping her hands like a wind up toy. Next, the father steps out joining Ransom and Thomas. He was the tallest of the three but his height was somewhat exaggerated by his thinness.

Then the last traveler stuck out her head and began to clamber out of the carriage. Although Ransom was offering his assistance, it was with very little grace and much effort she was able to squeeze herself through the door. When the little robust woman stepped to the ground, the carriage gave a sigh of relief. Annabelle almost choked laughing. We told her to collect herself at once. Sallie just stood there with her hand over her mouth, not knowing what to say. Sallie would have to wait to be introduced to them until after the wedding. Tradition would not allow her to see Ransom before the wedding.

Annabelle was eager to see Thomas and meet his family, so I had to escort her downstairs. She was in such a frenzy to get downstairs she rammed into me on the stairs and caused both of us to lose our balance. Just by the grace of God, we did not wind up at the feet of our guests who were now standing at the front door witnessing the whole scene. Before we could offer up an apology, Mr. Huneycutt starting laughing and every one joined in. He was much older than Papa and was bald except for a few red hairs waxed across his forehead. In a very loud voice, he introduced himself as Reuben and his smiling wife as Cynthia. Then in a grand gesture, he bowed to us, dropping his spectacles on the floor. Before he could attempt to collect them, Thomas picked them up and placed them in his hands. Ransom began to introduce all of us to his parents. Each name Mr. Huneycutt was told he would repeat incorrectly and Ransom would have to tell him several times. Ransom told him my name was Lizzie and he looked at Ransom with a puzzled look and said, "Hizzie?"

Annabelle was standing beside me and I could feel her start to shake. I did not dare look at her because I knew how contagious her giggling was. Annabelle put her hand over her mouth and began to cough. Now everyone was laughing except Mr. Huneycutt who looked baffled.

There was still time for the Huneycutts and the Sanders to socialize before the rest of the guests arrived. Gerald and a few friends of the family were enjoying the refreshments when the minister arrived promptly at four o'clock. Mother sat down at the piano and Father went upstairs to get Sallie. He returned shortly with Sallie on his arm. She looked beautiful and the ceremony was sweet and simple. On her finger now was a handsome band of gold with three little stones spelling out Sara Dianne Sanders: *sapphire, diamond and sapphire.*

Dinner was served, the cake was cut and the champagne bottles were empty. By eleven o'clock that night, the house was quiet. Sallie and Ransom were upstairs in Sallie's honeymoon room, Thomas and Gerald roomed together, the Huneycutts were in my room and Annabelle and I were already asleep.

Following the honeymoon night, Sallie did not come down for breakfast with Ransom, but no one asked why. The Huneycutts had plans to stay in Charleston for two more weeks to visit with friends. Everyone, especially Annabelle, overwhelmingly accepted Papa's invitation for Thomas to stay with us while his parents were in town.

I watched Mammy pour Gerald's coffee. Her hands were steady and calm. I suppose I was the only one who had doubts about Gerald. Perhaps I was wrong. Right after breakfast, Gerald left to return his carriage to the livery and catch the noon train.

Ransom spoke to Mother in private while the others went up to pack. For reasons unknown to me, it was decided Sallie and Ransom would stay with us a few more days before leaving for Beaufort. Sallie did not come out of her room that afternoon even when Ransom left to drive his parents into Charleston. Mother had been in and out of Sallie's room and Mammy had taken food in to her.

With Thomas making up our foursome, we had spent the afternoon playing cards. Ransom came back from town, went straight to Papa's study and Cato came up to get Mother. Shortly, Mother called for us and I knew something was wrong. Nothing could prepare me for what I was about to learn.

Ransom was sitting by the fireplace with his head in his hands and Papa had his back to us. Thomas went directly over to Ransom and asked what was wrong, but Ransom did not answer. Papa turned around and sat down slowly. His voice began to crack when he spoke, "There is no easy way to say this; sooner or later you will have to be told. Gerald has been murdered," he said, taking a deep breath.

"Murdered!" Annabelle jumped up in disbelief.

Papa spoke directly to me when he answered, "Yes, apparently he was ambushed on his way into town; Ransom was the one that found him."

Ransom stood up and in a shaky voice tried to tell us what happened. "I saw him slumped over in his carriage about a mile from here and I stopped to see what was wrong. When I walked up to the carriage, I saw blood everywhere and realized his throat had been cut. He was already dead. There was nothing I could do but go to the authorities and ask that they telegram his folks."

Thomas looked worried when he asked, "They didn't think you did it, did they Ran?"

"No," Ransom said, but they pretty much ruled out robbery because all his personal property was intact. He had over fifty dollars in his wallet. From what they figure right now, it might be the work of a crazed fugitive slave. We may never know."

Papa and Ransom discussed going into town that night to file a report, but Mother opposed greatly to the idea of them traveling at night. Ransom agreed they should not leave the women alone tonight and asked that we not discuss this in front of Sallie.

He felt it would be a shame to upset her before they left for their honeymoon. He would tell her himself in due time. We all agreed and went upstairs to bed. Papa went out back to speak with Samuel.

CHAPTER 10

Thanksgiving 1860

It was Cindy Lou who served our breakfast the following morning. Mother gave Mammy a pass for a couple of days. She went to visit with Lottie, who just had her second baby. Sallie was out of seclusion after two days. She bounced down the stairs with Ransom looking well and in good spirits. Papa had barely taken a bite off his plate when Cato announced the sheriff was here to see him. Sallie looked stunned, but Papa was careful with his response, "Another lost shipment, I am sure."

He excused himself and Ransom made a lame excuse to follow him. Sallie looked at ease as Ransom left the room and continued to talk about their honeymoon plans. I was certain she did not know about Gerald.

We learned that arrangements had been made for Papa to accompany Gerald's body back to North Carolina. Papa would be leaving on the afternoon train and returning after the funeral. Papa was in an awkward situation as he faced leaving us at home with a murderer on the loose.

Sallie took the news better than we would have expected. Ransom explained that under the circumstances, they would not be leaving right away on the honeymoon. The delay would give Papa time to return from North Carolina. Then, if his folks could extend their visit, we could all spend Thanksgiving together.

Secretly I think Sallie was glad and I know Annabelle was delighted Thomas would be staying longer.

Papa called us together for a family meeting the day he left. It was his belief that Gerald's killer had long fled. It was highly unlikely to be one of our slaves. He had spoken to Samuel and all our slaves were accounted for the day of the murder with the exception of Mammy, who was with Lottie. Yet, he said this was a good time to start taking precautions, keeping the doors locked and permitting only the house servants in and out of the house. He stated, to his knowledge there was no reason to be fearful of our slaves. However, they were a secretive lot and we should report any suspicious activity. Mother seemed a bit tremulous when Father said he planned to teach each of us to use a firearm when he returned.

By suppertime Mammy was back and all seemed well. At the table we discussed our annual Christmas performance. For as long as I can remember, my sisters and I wrote and performed a play for our family and friends on Christmas day. This year since Sallie was going to be away, we decided to present our play on Thanksgiving. Annabelle was excited and said this would be our grandest performance, and with more actors. There would be more parts to write and more costumes to make. We would have to get started right away. Ransom and Thomas were not sure they had any acting ability, but agreed it would be fun. Directly after dinner we went in the parlor to start working on the plot. Sallie wanted it to be drama, Ransom and Thomas were in favor of a comedy, but Annabelle wanted it to be a tragic romance. When the ideas started flowing, I went to get a writing tablet and my pen. Mammy and Cindy Lou were standing in the hall next to the pantry. They did not see me. They seemed to be planning something and talking just above whisper. Papa said to keep an eye open to anything suspicious. I quietly stepped behind the curtain to listen; this did seem suspicious.

Mammy was telling Cindy Lou to boil the cotton root and add a handful of okra seeds. After it steeped for a while, she was to start giving Violet the broth until the pains started. Cindy Lou looked worried, but Mammy told her it was best to get it over with now. She will be clear by morning and the last of that man would be gone. I drew up as Cindy Lou passed by and waited until I heard Mammy go upstairs. I decided I would not report what I heard.

November 28, 1860

Papa was home and we joined our Southern friends in a day of fasting and prayer. I did my best, but I found it hard to concentrate on an empty stomach. I went to bed before dark.

Thanksgiving Day, 1860

Our performance was set to begin at 2:00 o'clock in the afternoon. Sallie and Ransom made a backdrop out of some old curtains and Thomas said it looked like a real stage. Annabelle and I worked on the costumes until the very last minute. As always, Papa was the Master of Ceremonies and read the introduction. Then he took a seat along with Mother and the Huneycutts.

Our play begins:

A young man, (Thomas) went out to seek his fortune and while on the road, he was bitten by a poisonous snake. The young man fell to the ground and was near his death. A high society lady (Sallie) came by in her fine carriage and refused to stop and help him. A robber (Ransom) came by and stole all his money.

Finally, a fair young lady (Annabelle) came across him and fell in love with him. Seeing her true love was near death, she knew she must go deep into the dangerous forest to the house of an evil witch (me) to find a magic potion to save his life.

The fair young lady traded her gold locket for a magic potion...

We had a surprise ending planned, which Annabelle was unaware. Thomas was supposed to come to life as soon as he drank the magic potion. Instead, he pretended to be dead. Annabelle knelt beside him and tried to get him to get up, but he laid there like a stump. At the end, he jumped up and ran away with the witch (me).

Annabelle was not laughing with the rest of us and remained kneeling on the floor. Everyone watched as her body begins to shake and rock back and forth. I was sure she was crying and must have taken our little joke badly. Mr. Huneycutt announced, "Dear God, I believe the girl is in some kind of distress."

Mother jumped up to offer her assistance; Annabelle whispered something in Mother's ear. Mother snickered and politely walked around to the rear of Annabelle, lifted her skirt and detached the little heels of her boots that were caught in her hoop slip. Annabelle, now released, jumped up and took her bow, which provoked an uproarious applause. Mrs. Huneycutt thought it so hilarious she nearly fell out of her chair. Papa complimented Mother's acting and said she must have been part of the script. We all agreed it to be the best play we ever performed.

After our performance, Mrs. Huneycutt insisted Mr. Huneycutt recite a new poem. Mr. Huneycutt pretended he was not fond of the idea, but she continued to encourage him to take to the stage. He lumbered back and forth for a few minutes before he cleared his throat and stepped out in front of the curtain.

"The poem I shall recite tonight tells a story of a heroic young man who sounded the alarm and warned the Americans the British were coming. "Paul Revere's Ride," by Henry Wadsworth Longfellow." He lowered his voice to a mysterious whisper and began,

"Listen my children and you shall hear
Of the midnight ride of Paul Revere,
On the eighteenth of April, in Seventy-five;
Hardly a man is now alive

Who remembers that famous day and year.
He said to his friend, "If the British march
By land or sea from the town to-night,
Hang a lantern aloft in the belfry arch
Of the North Church tower as a signal light,—
One if by land, and two if by sea;
And I on the opposite shore will be,
Ready to ride and spread the alarm'..."

My mind began to drift from his words. How odd he chose this poem. Who would warn the South if the Yankees were coming? I was brought back to consciousness when I heard clapping signaling the end.

Thomas's conclusion was that Paul Revere was almost like the Pony Express. "I just saw a notice in the newspaper wanting young, skinny, wiry fellows," he said, rather out of the blue. "The pay was $50.00 a month and I figured between that and panning for some gold out there in California, a fellow could get himself set," he added looking at Annabelle.

Annabelle asked, "Well, suppose a fellow goes to California and never comes back?"

Thomas only smiled, but gave no reply.

The Thanksgiving meal made up for the day of fasting; split pea soup, fried oysters, roast turkey with stuffing, cranberry sauce, pickled beets, deviled eggs, boiled green beans and potatoes. Dessert was pumpkin pies and apple tarts.

Mrs. Huneycutt may have enjoyed the theatrical performance, but it was clear the food was her favorite. Mr. Huneycutt started a discussion at dinner over Charles Darwin's new book, *The Origin of Species*. Papa and I both agreed we would like to read the book, but Mother said she would not waste her time. The only thing she believed was this Darwin was making a monkey out of a lot people with his theories.

The conversation carried on into the parlor and it was becoming a moot point to most of us, but Mother loved a good debate.

93

With lesser workloads the holidays were a happier time for the slaves. Cato reminded us the Negroes were roasting what they called "gubas" or goober peas.

We got our wraps and went outside with Cato. The fire was blazing and the slaves were starting to gather around. Some sat on stools and others paired up under quilts.

An old Negro took out his harmonica and started to play. As if on cue, another slave started with the call, *"Swing low, sweet chariot."* Soft voices seemed to come out of the dark, *"comin' for to carry me home, swing low, sweet chariot, comin' for to carry me home."* We all felt drawn into their circle as they encouraged us to sing with them. *"If you get there before I do, comin' for to carry me home, tell my friends, I'm comin' too, comin' for to carry me home."*

Sallie and Ransom stood with their arms around each other, Annabelle and Thomas shared a blanket and I stood alone with my back against the wind. In one of these little cabins lay Violet washing away her secret. *I held my head back and looked upward. The moon was hidden and only a lone star dared to break though the darkness. Was I part of all this, or was I just a page torn out of a book, floating off into the dark?*

CHAPTER 11

Christmas

The Huneycutts left the next morning and Sallie and Ransom the following day. It is difficult to say which was more unpleasant, Sallie leaving or living with Annabelle since Thomas left.

We all rode into Charleston to take Sallie and Ransom to the train station. Many of the storefronts were already decorated for Christmas. It was a cold day and I was glad there was time for lunch at the Safe Harbor Café. I had a nice bowl of oyster stew. I ate every drop. Sallie barely touched hers. It was evident she was dreading leaving her family.

We walked hand in hand together until she took her last step before boarding. The engineer's bell was ringing when Ransom helped her on board. She turned one more time and waved good-bye, but not before she reached in her purse and handed me a little package wrapped in blue cloth. I kissed the package and slipped it into my pocket, watching her fade into the line of travelers.

"Well, we are finally rid of them," Papa said, trying to make light of the situation.

Papa was on the board of the Charleston Merchant's Exchange, which was meeting in less than twenty minutes at the Farmer's Bank and Loan. The purpose of the meeting was to determine if the charges of selling unhealthy Negroes were founded against a Mr. Cohen, a local businessman. We bid Papa goodbye on the square and arranged to meet him back at the Cotton Warehouse at four o'clock that afternoon. We spent the afternoon doing some early Christmas shopping. Our first stop was Miss Georgette's. Much to our surprise, there was Aunt Sara on her way out. She was dressed in a most desirable fashion and was accompanied by a gentleman.

"Christmas complements to the Sanders!" Aunt Sara called out making sure we saw her. She then hustled across the street with the old gentlemen tagging along behind her. Aunt Sara just stood there smiling from ear to ear as proud as if she had won first place in a hog-calling contest. "Allow me to introduce Mr. Ottolengui," she said as the handsomely dressed gentleman bowed and tipped his top hat to us.

"Well hello there," Mother's reply was more of a question than a pleasantry.

"Tempie, we have so much to catch up on. I will call on you soon."

We said our goodbyes and went on to our shopping. I remembered the little package Sallie had given me was still in my pocket. I unwrapped the gift to find a lovely silver handled tatting shuttle. Before we left that day, I bought a bundle of red tatting thread to make Sallie a lace collar for Christmas. Mother bought Annabelle a new cloak, which cheered her up only slightly.

The entire ride home Annabelle was in debate with Father. She said he simply must give his consent to let her marry Thomas sooner. She said anything could happen in two years; it was just too long. Unexpectedly, it was Mother who turned the card. She reminded Papa she was seventeen when they married.

"Yes, but almost eighteen," Papa added.

"Still only seventeen and look how happy we are," Mother said taking Papa's hand.

Papa had no choice. Annabelle was given permission to marry Thomas as soon as she turned seventeen on March 10, 1861. Annabelle slumped down and laid her head on Mother's shoulder like a little girl. Mother seemed pleased she had been the one to restore Annabelle's happiness. Now it was clear to me I would be the old maid in the family. All I needed was a cane and a rocking chair. I was certain I was doomed. As soon as the front door opened that night, an overjoyed Annabelle ran upstairs to compose her letter to darling Thomas.

December 2, 1860

All the rain in the late fall and early winter had turned the marshes and low grounds into a breeding swamp for mosquitoes. With very few warm days left to dry out the land, it was a fearful time for yellow fever. The slaves seemed to have more immunity against the fever and malaria than the whites did. Many people took ill and died of these diseases; fortunately, we had been blessed. This was mostly due to Papa's instructions to have trenches dug to drain the marsh and burn the low grasses.

Just as Papa was precautious with our health, the same was true for the slaves.

Once the work slowed down in early December, Papa hired Dr. Walser to perform the slaves' annual examinations. They were treated for what ailed them, but every slave was treated for parasites and hookworms. Head lice were a big problem, and Lord forbid if it spread to us. Therefore, it was important that at least once a year the cabins were cleaned and smoked out. The slaves got new clothes, shoes and bed ticking and their old belongings were burned. Mother kept the medical records and the whole process lasted over a week.

The Negroes' annual outfitting was not cheap, nor was Dr. Walser's services and medicines. Some planters were not so gracious with the care of their slaves. Papa said it was just good business, but Mother said it was the just being a good Christian.

The next couple of weeks were busy ones. Papa lived up to his word and taught us all how to shoot a gun. My hand and arm were trembling. By the end of the day I was sure I could shoot something or someone dead ahead, even though I hoped the opportunity never arose. After the lesson, Papa handed me a little leather case. Inside was a small pistol he called a Philadelphia derringer. He told me to keep it in my drawer by my bed and to take it with me when I left the house. This is when I realized this was much more than a game.

It was the beginning of the social season and already our calendar was almost full. It was seldom guests arrived unannounced, especially gentlemen callers. Mother kept a silver tray on the table in the foyer where those wishing to visit could politely deposit their calling cards. The first week of December, six calling cards and three boxes of candy were left for me. They were men I met at my party, but I did not recall any of their names, except Grady O'Connor. To be sure, Aunt Sara had coached him in my direction since her efforts had failed with Sallie. I admit it was flattering, but when I thumbed through the dish, I was almost hoping to see Joel Simpson's card. Was he the kind of man who would write a note or a sweet poem? Of course not, his card was at home with his wife for the holidays.

Surely these men must be shallow minded if romance was all they had on their minds right in the middle of the South's greatest crisis. Nevertheless, they all deserved a response. It was Mr. Paul Isley who seemed most persistent, leaving at least two cards a week. Papa reminded me it was Mr. Isley who had come to my defense the night I got angry and stomped upstairs.

"Lizzie, you are not a foolish girl. Mr. Isley is a lawyer and from a very nice family," Mother pleaded with me to accept a visit from him. She was right, I was not a foolish girl and I knew it was not just about my feelings. I agreed to have him for afternoon tea and Cato delivered the message to him the next day. Mr. Isley arrived promptly at two o'clock on Tuesday and joined Papa, Mother and I in the parlor. He was handsome enough and a witty conversationalist. The afternoon passed quickly and was much more enjoyable than I expected. Before he left, he invited all of us to a *homespun-party* and charity auction for the orphan asylum. Mr. Isley, or Paul, explained that everyone would dress in homespun outfits demonstrating the South's resourcefulness and independence.

We arranged to meet Paul at the church at seven o'clock that coming Friday night. Papa was quick to say we would stay overnight at the hotel. Paul agreed that late night traveling could not be justified with the present tension in and around Charleston.

That afternoon I wrote Sallie a letter.

December 4, 1860

Dearest Sallie,

I trust you and my new brother-in-law are well and in fine form. I know you must be having a wonderful time at this most precious time of your lives. Thank you for the tatting shuttle; you will see soon that I have put it to good use. How is the weather there?

You both will be surprised to learn that Papa will be releasing Annabelle in March to marry Thomas if he will still have her. Poor boy does not know what he is getting into I am afraid. Annabelle is a big lot to handle.

I have news too; I have accepted a social call from a Mr. Paul Isley. Perhaps you or Ransom will recall him as a tall sturdy built fellow with dark hair and a mustache. Papa seems to like him and I find him agreeable too. He is an attorney in Charleston. Now, don't you two start thinking wedding bells. We have had enough of that going on...

I had not yet finished my letter when I decided to wait and complete it with the details of the homespun party.

Finding ourselves clothing that had been woven from our own looms was easy enough. The process of dressing the slaves had just begun and there were several new dresses, pants and shirts still being completed.

The day of the party, I chose a navy plaid dress and a white apron. Mammy pressed the pleats in extra nice. She said if I had to be dressed up like the colored folks, I was going to look extra fresh and clean. I pulled my hair back in a snood and covered my shoulders with a wool cloak. I liked how it felt, not fussing or cumbersome like all the laces and crinolines I was accustomed to.

Papa placed some hot bricks on the floor of the carriage to help keep our feet warm until we got into town. Just as we came out on the main road, we meet a hay wagon. Papa threw up his hand and pulled over to let them pass, "Those boys will be burning the midnight oil if they are hauling hay this late on Friday evening."

As we approached town the streets were lined with carriages and gaily dressed guests. Cheerful voices rang into the clear of the night. The evening frost made the gas lanterns look like sparkling crystal bells. I loved Charleston during the social season; there was no place on earth I would rather be. We drove along the Cooper River and passed the outdoor markets. When we crossed over to Meeting Street, we could see the gaslights burning in front of the church. Money was still flowing in Charleston that Christmas. It was evident by the elaborate Christmas trimmings and décor of the houses.

Paul was waiting for us out front and made a beeline toward us. His face was flushed and his hands were cold as he helped us out of the carriage. Mother and Annabelle walked ahead and Paul and I took the rear; leaving Papa to secure the carriage. Something caught my eye by the lamppost. It was a young girl waiting to cross the street. Her shoes were tied on with rags and her only warmth was a thin shawl across her shoulders. I paused, causing Paul to question what had caught my eye. Mother and Annabelle kept walking and did not notice the girl. She saw my stare and lowered her eyes as if she were embarrassed of her status. Her face was sweet and tender and her frail slender form so vulnerable to the night. I stepped off the wooden sidewalk and Paul impulsively took hold of my arm to restrain me. I ignored his caution and walked up to the girl. The only word I could think to say was, "Hello."

She responded with her teeth chattering, "Good evening Miss," and she turned quickly to walk down the street.

I cried out, "wait."

She did not turn around and began to walk more briskly. I realized I must have frightened the dear girl and again I called out, "Please stop."

It must have sounded like a command and she came to a complete halt. I ran over to her and realized I was towering over her. "Pray tell me, dear girl, what brings you out on such a night alone?"

"Me brother is sick and I came out to looks for papa," she said in a heavy Irish brogue.

"You must be cold and hungry?" I asked.

"Aye, but not as much as me brother," she said seeming anxious to head on her way.

I looked in my purse, but I had no money, she waved her hand as if to say no. I reached over my shoulders, took off my cloak, and covered her shoulders. Her mouth dropped opened and she stroked the fabric before she attempted to give it back to me.

"No, keep it please," I said, realizing my action had caused a crowd to gather behind me. I felt a hand on my shoulder and turned to see it was Papa. He reached in his wallet and gave the girl a fold of money. He then put his arm around my bare shoulders to lead me inside. Her little voice followed us as we walked away, *"Blessin' to you both."*

Paul was still standing there on the walk with his head tilted to the side. He gave me a crooked little smile and said, "Lizzie, you are a jewel."

"Yes indeed she is, one of kind," Papa responded squeezing me tightly next to him.

My gesture started a chain reaction and many of the others stopped to offer the girl clothing and money. I turned and took one last look at the little girl now heading on her way with a coat on her back and a pocket full of money. I wondered how many more children were left out in the cold night. I had been given so much and had so much for which to be thankful. I prayed to God that one day I could find a way to help those sad children.

It was a wonderful party and the music and the dancing were extraordinary. I was not even put off when Paul stepped on my toes during the Virginia Reel. People seemed unusually high in spirit that night. Others were a bit high on bottled spirits. It was most fitting since the auction was to raise proceeds for the orphan asylum. Everyone seemed most generous with their bids. Before the close of the auction, a young man stepped on to the platform. He began by saying his precious aunt's last request was for him to find a suitable home for her last remaining slave. He was planning to enlist in the army and regretted he could not be responsible for her. He said it had been an answer to his prayers the day the minister announced the auction for the orphanage. He knew his aunt would approve of this endeavor and it would be an opportunity to find Erma a good home.

He described her as being around eighteen or twenty, of good moral and genteel manner, an excellent cook, laundress and seamstress. She had been a faithful servant of his aunt's and had nursed her up until the time of her death. He made it clear no one other than the most kind hearted should bid.

He left the room and returned with a petite mulatto girl. She held her head high as the bidding began, almost as if she was offering herself as a tribute to her past mistress. It was a touching expression of her devotion. Many of the women had tears in their eyes, including Mother. She nudged Papa and he nodded his head. Mother politely held her card up and said, "I will start the bidding at five-hundred dollars." Then it went to six-hundred to nine-hundred and then from the back of the room a voice I recognized called out, "one thousand and five hundred dollars." It was Aunt Sara.

The crowd went hush and then someone started applauding. No one bid against her and Aunt Sara stood up and took a bow. She walked up the aisle to collect the girl. Mr. Ottolengui, who was now referred to as the fiancé toddled along behind her shaking hands of the people as if he were a politician of sort. Aunt Sara ate up the glory of everyone knowing she was rich and very generous.

Perhaps so, but we suspected she had just bought Henry a Christmas gift, a little bride. We all left the party singing Christmas carols. It was a grand night and one I will always remember.

The next morning when we returned home Samuel and two other slaves appeared to be standing guard at the front entrance. They had taken up arms, Samuel held an axe and the other two a hoe and pitch fork. Papa slowed the carriage. I watched as he reached for his pistol and slid it under his coat. I, too, slipped my hand down into my purse to feel the cold handle of my derringer pistol. Mother put her arm around Annabelle who started to cry. "Shh!" she warned. Keep your wits about you girls; this is no time to fall apart."

Papa edged the carriage forward, "Sam, what the hell is going on here?" he demanded.

Mother took a deep breath when the three men dropped their weapons and Samuel stepped forward. *"Master Sandy,"* he said in a voice tired and worn out like someone who had been weeping. *"Som' thang awful don happin' heres last night. Four white mens comes riddin' up in de dark, howlin' an' shootin'. Deys wus pullin' a wagon. Fer it wus all over de loaded up five of our colored folk an' den da kilt old Wiz."*

Papa jumped out of the carriage and pulled Samuel to the side. All I could think of was Old Wiz was dead. Then Annabelle said, "Wonder if they took Mammy or Violet?"

The color washed from Mother's face when Papa climbed back in the carriage.

Mammy, Violet, Cindy Lou, Cato and another man named Cletus had been kidnapped.

Papa pulled the carriage up to the house and within minutes, we were surrounded by the slaves, some were crying and others held makeshift weapons in their hands.

"Harper don tok off after dem on Miss Lizzie horse an' we ain't seen him since," explained Samuel.

Papa told us to go inside. We opened the door, but there was no one to greet us, the house was cold and ghostly. Mother and

Annabelle were crying. I started a fire in the parlor and we sat down waiting to see what was still in store for us. It was over an hour before Papa came in the house. I never saw him so upset; his face was red and his hands were shaking. Even though it was before noon, he went to the bar and poured himself a brandy. We learned Old Wiz was dead, but not because of the gunfire. It seemed he had fallen and hit his head on a large rock during the scuffle. Slave napping was a serious offense and Papa had no choice but to leave us alone while he went after the sheriff. He would be stopping along the way at the other plantations to see if they had any reports of what happened.

It would be dark before he returned, but he would not be taking Samuel with him. He felt it was too big a risk to leave the house unprotected. Mother said he could not leave on an empty stomach and she went out to the kitchen to prepare food and water for his trip. Samuel was waiting outside the parlor door and I heard Papa ask him if he knew how to shoot a rifle. *Yes sirs, I sur dos,"* he said in a determined manner.

Papa unlocked the gun closet and handed him his Enfield rifle. Annabelle looked at me in total disbelief. Never in our lifetime had we seen a Negro carry a gun. From the window, we could see the slaves coming down the hill where they had buried Old Wiz. It was a sad sight. He was the last of the old Africans and I felt we had lost more than we realized.

When the funeral was over Samuel came and propped himself up next to our front door to protect us until Papa got home. I had changed my mind about him. Something about him now seemed so terribly tender, almost like a lost soul looking for his way home. I felt guilty for the thoughts I used to have of him. This is the last I will speak of them.

It was after ten o'clock and Papa was still not home. Terrifying pictures of Papa lying beside the road with his throat cut wide open like Gerald raced through my mind. As the hours got later we hardly spoke at all, afraid we would not hear him drive up. Samuel opened the door around eleven o'clock and said they were coming down the road. Mother let out a shout, "Praise the Lord!"

We were anxious to see if he had Mammy and the rest of the slaves with him. There was someone with him, but it was Harper. Papa looked exhausted when he dragged himself in the door. He did not come into the parlor, but sat down in one of the French chairs in the foyer. Papa dropped his head between his legs. Harper and Samuel were standing next to him. We stood there waiting for him to speak, "Lizzie, I am sorry to tell you, your horse is dead. The men shot him out from under Harper when he took off after them. I picked up Harper on the way to town."

Harper looked at me, *"I's real sorry, Miss Lizzie, buts deys nothing' I could dos."*

I closed my eyes and took a deep breath. At first, I felt angry. Why did he have to take my horse? My Coal, why did he not take one of the other horses? Then I slowly felt my knees start to buckle and my body collapse. The next thing I was aware of was hours later. When I opened my eyes, I was in my bed and Mother was sitting next to me. Mother went to the door and called for Annabelle. Shortly, Mother came back with a tray of food. Not only had the shock of all that happened taken its toll, I had not eaten all day.

Mother acquired the assistance of a slave named Harriet to see to my needs that day. It was late afternoon the next day before I was well enough to come downstairs.

Papa was not home. I was informed he had ridden over to Aunt Sara's to see if she would lease the mulatto girl to us until Mammy and Violet could be found, if they could be found. Papa arrived back home shortly with the girl as well as Henry. Papa introduced the girl to us as Henry's wife, Erma. They would be staying on the third floor.

I did not see them again until she quietly knocked on the door to tell us dinner was served. It was not Mammy's cooking, but it was well appreciated. Over the next couple of days, Papa set about seeking the services of a white overseer. Toward the end of that same week, a man named Jones and his family moved in the old farmhouse.

I still had an unfinished letter to send to Sallie. I told her all the details of the party. I closed saying I was apprehensive that Mr. Isley was falling in love with me. Regretfully, I was not following suit. I did not tell her about the slave napping. Her wedding journey had been spoiled enough. We hoped the slaves would be returned to us soon.

December 16, 1860

Papa left that day for Columbia with Mr. Isley as his traveling companion. They were to attend the convention on the 17th of December to vote on whether South Carolina will secede from the Union.

We received a letter from Papa.

December 18, 1860

Dear all,

I regret to say there has been an outbreak of small pox in Columbia. The meeting was held for only one day and has been moved to Charleston on the 20th. However, the vote was unanimous to secede from the Union. Mr. Isley is on his way home to attend the meeting in Charleston. I have been detained and will need to remain in Columbia for another day or so. I shall make every effort to be home before Christmas Eve. Although I have the utmost confidence in Mr. Jones as overseer, I have asked Mr. Isley to check on your welfare. You will hear from me again shortly.

All my love,
Papa

Mother read the letter. We were all speechless. Why Papa did not give us the reason for his delay was a mystery. Nothing like this had ever happened and there was nothing we could do but wait.

We sent out the Christmas cards and our gifts to Sallie and Ransom. Annabelle sent her special package to Thomas. The days were clicking away until Christmas. This was the first Christmas without Sallie and I was afraid it would be the first without Papa.

On the evening of the 20th, Henry answered the door to find an excited Mr. Paul Isley at the door. Paul hardly waited to be announced, walked in and handed us a page from the Charleston Mercury. On the front-page there in bold letters: THE UNION IS DISSOLVED!

We were prepared, but seeing it in print was overwhelming. Paul said the vote was passed at 1:15 pm and by 1:30 pm the newspapers were being passed out on the streets.

When he left the city, there were celebrations everywhere. People were walking the streets singing Dixie and firecrackers were popping off in the distance. He continued to rattle on, "I tell you we have seen history unfold today. This is a mighty day for our new South." Then without warning, he stopped in the middle of his sentence. "Forgive me ladies I almost forgot the purpose of my visit. First, I must let you know your father is safe and well. Second, there is a matter in Columbia he has asked me to act on as his attorney."

Mother looked stunned and asked, "Is Jacob in some kind of trouble?"

"No, Mr. Sanders's character is not in question," he assured her. "I wish I could say more, but I hope you will understand this is a very sensitive matter. I am leaving to go back to Columbia first thing in the morning. I have full intentions your father will be returning home with me on the evening train."

Paul's visit was short and he made no reference when he might return. He did not ask that I walk him to the door and he left on his own. Now added to my fears were rejection.

December 21 and 22

There was no word from Mr. Isley or Papa. Annabelle had fallen into a mood and I was afraid Mother was back on her medicine. She hardly got out of bed on the 22nd.

The cupboards were bare and the kitchen was cold. There were no slaves having their Christmas jubilees. There were no colored children running foot races, wrestling or begging for Christmas gifts. The only clue anyone existed outback was the smoke from the chimneys.

We received a package from Sallie and Ransom and I placed it under the Christmas tree. One of us would have to make the decision soon to write Sallie and Ransom about what was happening. If we did, I was sure Ransom would consider it an emergency and reason to come home.

December 23, 1860

I awoke before sunrise. The dark curtain was lifted from my eyes and something was telling me Papa was on his way home. I rummaged through my wardrobe and threw on the ragged pants and old shirt that Annabelle and I had worn riding. I had work to do today and I was not going to waste time on frills. Taking the steps two at time, I galloped up to the third floor. I knocked loudly on Erma and Henry's door. "Get yourselves dressed; we are going to plan the grandest Christmas feast this plantation has ever seen!"

Henry leaned against the door, still half asleep. He eyed me over and I am sure he thought I had lost my wits. Erma was stirring behind him and she was smiling. I could tell she shared my excitement. Right there in front of me she commenced to jerk off her gown and dress herself. *"Henry,"* she scolded, *"Misses Lizzie iz a needin' our hep!"*

Henry turned around to see little Erma standing their bare breasted with her dress over her head. He looked a bit embarrassed, "We will be down shortly," he said and closed the door softly.

I was on a mission and it felt wonderful. I slung back the front door and ran across the front yard, my hair stringing down and the mist on my face. It was cold but I did not care. I was completely out of breath when I knocked on Mr. Jones' door. A gentle looking woman came to the door with a little girl hanging on her skirt tail.

"Is Mr. Jones here?" I asked, still trying to gulp in air.

"No, he has gone out, but he will be back in shortly," she replied pushing a hand full of curly dark hair out of her face. "You are welcome to wait here for him. Please come in out of the cold." She stepped back and motioned me in; the little girl was still attached to her legs. I was inside of the house where Mother and Papa had first lived. It was warm and cozy and the furnishings were simple and handmade. I sat down in a small cane bottom chair next to the fireplace. The smell of coffee and bacon cooking made me realize I did not have breakfast.

"Let me get you a cup of coffee," she said without waiting for a reply. She shook the little girl loose from her and poured me a cup of coffee. "I am Rose and you must be Lizzie," she said looking pleased.

"L-I-Z-Z-I-E," the little girl spelled out. Before I could even respond, she proceeded with, "A-N-N-A B-E-L-L-E."

The mother laughed, "Your Father has spoken of all of you".

Then the little girl said, "And there was Sallie, but she is dead now".

"Dead!" said the Mother. "No, No, I told you she went away, not died!" Trying to recover, she said, "This is Mary".

The child shook her head and said, "No, it is *Ladybug*."

"That is her Papa's pet name for her," Rose said looking at her daughter affectionately.

"Well, Ladybug, it is very nice to meet you," I said and extended my hand out to her.

Her big blue eyes scanned over me and she climbed up into my lap. She was as light as a feather. It was almost like holding a doll with moving parts. Rose began to tell me she believed in the importance of education. She was already teaching Ladybug to read and write. I heard the back door open. Ladybug jumped down and ran to the door.

"Papa, one of the ladies from the big house is here and she's dressed up like a man," were the first words out of Ladybug's little mouth.

Mr. Jones' expression showed he was just as shocked at my appearance as I was of his. He must have noticed my eyes fall on his blood stained shirt. "Nothing like rabbit stew on Christmas Eve," he said grabbing a rag to wipe his hands. He was a big imposing looking man with thick black hair; but the way he looked at Ladybug told me he was not too intimating. I began to tell him I needed his help to get the Negroes working on the Christmas Feast. He said he would do his best. I got up to leave, but Rose insisted I stay for breakfast. I spied the hoecakes on the table and I accepted.

When I got back to the house, I found Mother and Annabelle in the dining room. Apparently, Henry or Erma had informed them I was up to something. They were less enthusiastic, but I reminded them Papa said he would be home before Christmas Eve. He would never disappoint us. I almost bit my tongue on my words. Papa had disappointed me once, but it had all turned out well and good. I just had to pray this would too. By the nightfall the fires were going, cakes were baking and meat was roasting. Papa had not come home that day, but tomorrow was Christmas Eve. I dozed off to sleep listening to the high-pitched echo of a Negro's banjo.

December 24, 1860

We hung the red and green. We trimmed the wreaths with ribbons of blue and gold. Red for the blood of Christ, green for his everlasting love, blue for heaven above, and gold for the King of Kings. I was sure Papa would be proud of us.

Aunt Sara, Mr. Ottolengui, Grady O'Connor and his new romantic interest, Carol Sue Tudor would be coming to dinner. In addition, we had added to our guest list little Miss Ladybug and her family. It was a family tradition on Christmas Eve; Papa would dress up like Santa Claus and pass out little gifts to the slaves. There would be candy for the children, tobacco, and even whiskey for the men. The women would receive handkerchiefs or talcum. This year Mother made the announcement that gifts would be presented on Christmas Day. It was a simple announcement, but it came with great concern that even then Papa might not be home.

The day lingered on. Mother made Ladybug a cloth doll and Annabelle and I kept busy making dresses for it. No word had come and it was almost three o'clock. Aunt Sara and Mr. Otolengui sat in the parlor with Mother. This left us to entertain Grady and Carol Sue. We played charades for a while and a new game called smiles. One person got up and did silly things to try to make the others laugh. The one who was able to hold out the longest wins. It was easy for me to win that game, as I had nothing to smile about.

It was five o'clock and the Jones family had arrived. Mr. Jones made us an unusual gift; a tiny Christmas tree with branches made of goose feathers that had been dyed green. Ladybug quickly let us know that she helped with the decorations of this little tree. Her constant chatter was a welcomed distraction from our fears.

Erma came out to say dinner would be served shortly. The Negroes had a big pot cooking out back. I knew of their dish called gumbo. I liked most of their spicy dishes, especially the okra and cornbread, but I drew the line when it came to the pickled pig's feet. It was time for dinner and Mother sat down first. Her nose was red and I knew she had been crying. The table was set with boiled ham, cabbage, green beans, mashed potatoes, fried fish, deviled eggs, corn relish and wheat bread. The food was passed around and we filled our plates. It all looked wonderful, but it was almost impossible for me to swallow. We tried to make small talk to uplift Mother's spirits. Our meal was interrupted by Samuel bursting into the house in a fit of excitement, "*Santie Claus is here! He is coming right down this here road!*"

This was indeed odd and we could not even begin to imagine what he had seen. We all left the table and ran out the front door.

Coming down the road was a covered wagon pulled by what looked like reindeer. Ladybug clapped her little hands together and screamed, "Look, it is Santa!"

The wagon, drawn by four mules with tree limbs attached to their heads for antlers, pulled right up to the front door. Then out jumped a man dressed in a stocking cap wearing a long white cotton beard. He shouted, "Merry Christmas," and my heart skipped a beat. We all recognized the voice as Papa's. Mother ran out and Papa lifted her up in the air.

Mr. Isley jumped out of the wagon and cried out, "surprise!" Then out came Mammy, Cato, Violet, Cindy Lou and Cletus. By this time, the slaves had come around to see what the commotion was all about. They saw their friends and began singing and dancing for joy. The Negroes and whites embraced on this wonderful occasion. In the heat of the excitement, Mr. Isley grabbed me up and kissed me on the lips.

We all went inside and had dinner. Mammy and the rest sat right down at the table with us for the meal. Afterwards, we opened the doors for all the slaves. We sang Christmas carols around the piano. Harper and Violet were the happiest of all. Tomorrow was Christmas day and they would be married right here in the front Parlor.

Papa and Mr. Isley told us the thrilling story of how they rescued the salves. Mr. Isley started the story, "When we arrived in Columbia we had to walk a great distance to the First Baptist Church where the secession convention was to be held. As we passed by the slave market down off Main Street, Mr. Sanders happened to see a Negro girl that looked like Violet. We immediately crossed the street to find the whole lot of kidnapped slaves being held captive around back."

Papa said it was his first instinct to demand the return of his slaves. However, the bidding had already begun. He also knew he had no proof to establish that they were, in fact, his property. So, he began to bid on his own slaves while Mr. Isley went for the authorities. When the auction came to the end, Papa had secured all five of his slaves. Mr. Isley had not yet returned and Papa refused to pay up. This caused an uprising. The sheriff was sent for and Papa told him the whole story. With no way to verify the facts, Papa was taken to jail and the slaves were held for evidence. Mr. Isley came back to Charleston to secure the bill of sales on each of the five slaves. Once he returned to Columbia and presented the evidence, Papa was set free. The final leg of the story was the most intriguing. The sheriff and his posse of men went out to round up the kidnappers. When they found them, they resisted arrest and one of the men was shot and killed. The others were apprehended and questioned. Under duress, the youngest one of the three confessed he did help with the slave napping, but he had not killed that boy.

As the story unwinds, we learn Gerald had arrived a day early before Sallie's wedding. He stayed in town that night to visit some of the local taverns. At one of his stops, he ran into this crew of ne'er-do-wells. One drink led to another and Gerald began to brag about his rich uncle and all his slaves. Gerald also confessed to raping Violet the night of my party. The men plotted the kidnapping and told Gerald they would let him in on the profits. When Gerald left to go the train station, he met the men and begged them to call the whole thing off. They were afraid Gerald would go to the Sherriff so they killed him.

I was glad that Gerald's killer had been found. Secretly I had a fear Mammy killed Gerald, after all she was gone that day and she had a motive. I made up my mind, even if Gerald's killer was never found, I would never tell anyone of my suspicions.

CHAPTER 12

The New Year 1861

Our Christmas tree was down as were the decorations, but for some reason I found it difficult to move on after the season. Everyone and everything seemed to be suspended in time since South Carolina left the Union. Even the New Year's parties were jaded by the people's anticipations and fears of what 1861 might bring. Some of the men were quick to opt for war and were even being encouraged by their wives to join the fight. Others said South Carolina could stand independently and they saw no reason for a conflict.

On January 3rd, I started writing Sallie an overdue letter to thank her for the lovely miniature she sent me for Christmas. It was my dread to tell her and Ransom about the kidnappings and Gerald's murder. Even so, I knew the shock would be easier coming from home than reading about it in the papers.

Papa labored over his letter to Cousin John. After a sleepless night, he wrote John with the details and the date of the upcoming trial. He left it up to John to make the decision whether to tell Kate or not. John did make the choice to tell Kate and they decided to be here for the trial.

The day they were to arrive, it was so cold I needed my shawl and an extra pair of stockings even in the house. Annabelle had been in such a mood since Thomas left, mostly just sleeping and eating. I thought possibly that a little entertainment might take her mind off her troubles. I invited her in the parlor so that I might read to her. Reluctantly she came in and flopped herself in the rocker. I threw another log on the fire and after a bit she seemed to brighten up. Perhaps it was not my reading, but the cookies and hot chocolate that Mammy brought in for us. I read a little poetry, but she wanted me to read something else. We were making a selection when we heard a knock at the front door. Cato went to the door and I heard a man's voice, but it was not John. Within minutes, I heard Papa say, "Joel, I am glad you could make it."

I held my breath for a moment, but all I could hear were footsteps in the hall and the door to Papa's study shut. Nobody said he was coming. Wild thoughts ran though my head. I thought about running upstairs and changing into something more becoming, but Annabelle would question me. Would he be staying for dinner, or even overnight? Maybe his wife was with him. I suddenly realized I was walking back and forth across the parlor, when Annabelle took hold of my arm and said, "What is wrong with you?"

I know she must have thought I was ready for the lunatic asylum and I could not even explain. I made some excuse about being cooped up in the house all the time. She seemed to accept my reason and settled back down. The first thing I came to was Mother's new book, *Notes on Nursing*, by Florence Nightingale. I opened the cover and began to read, "First rule of nursing, to keep the air within as pure as the air outside." I continued to read at great speed trying to ease my nerves until I heard a voice.

"Lizzie, I had no idea that you were interested in nursing?" I lifted my head to see Joel smiling at me with Papa by his side.

I could not make the words come, "I don't, I was just reading, yes, I like nursing."

"Please continue. I have heard this book is most informative," Joel said.

Papa and Joel came in and sat down and I could feel my face flush and my ears burning. When I tried to read my voice would not come and I cleared my throat to make another effort. Thank God, we were interrupted when our guest arrived. Mattie bounced in the room looking unaffected even though she and her mother were both dressed in mourning costume. John looked tired, but it was Kate's haggard face that told the story. Her hair had turned gray and she was painfully thin and frail. Joel jumped up, offered his chair to her and shook John's hand.

Mother had just entered the room when the conversation had turned to Gerald. Mother thinking of Annabelle and Mattie as children, excused them until dinner. I was left to sit in with the adults and be party to the mourning. I listened to the conversation, but I was aware more of Joel. Every word he spoke vibrated in my ears. Every time he crossed his legs or folded his hands, I knew.

That night I lay in my bed and remembered the book Mother had given Sallie before she married. Sallie and I had nervously laughed at the drawings in the book and I teased her about being overtaken by those so-called "erotic passions." Now that Sallie was married, I wished I could ask if the things in the book were true. My room was warm and cozy and the sheets were soft and smooth against my bare skin. I thought of Joel in the room next to me.

Kate did not look well the next morning and Mother tried to convince her not to subject herself to the trial. Kate insisted she was going to the trial with the men that day. She wanted the killers to have to look her in the face and see what a mother looked like that had lost her only son.

After they left, Mother planned a visit to Aunt Sara and tried to convince me to go along with her and the girls. I declined. It was a clear sunny day and I had promised Ladybug to take her riding. After breakfast, I rode over to pick up Ladybug. I was on Sallie's horse now that Coal was gone. We had grown fond of the Jones family, especially little Ladybug. She was an outspoken child and spoke her mind to whomever she pleased. Mother liked her too, but complained that her mother would have her hands full one of these days. We had a nice ride and I returned home around lunchtime.

I was stabling Sallie's horse when I heard someone ride up. I walked out into the open to see a rider coming hard and fast down the drive. I had not remembered what Papa said about the pistol. In fact, all of us had dismissed extra precautions now that Gerald's killers were apprehended. Here I stood, defenseless

116

against a possible unwelcome intruder. I did not look up and slowly started walking toward the house. The rider slowed down as he approached me and called out my name.

"Lizzie, wait!" It was Joel.

My first fear was that something had happened to Papa in town or maybe the trial had gone wrong. He slid off the horse, which was black as night and stood at least fifteen hands tall. Joel was breathing hard and perspiration was dripping from the sides of his forehead. He pulled off his hat and wiped his brow with his sleeve. He was smiling.

"Whoa, some kind of ride isn't he?" he said trying to regain his breath.

"Yes, he is a beautiful horse," I replied.

Joel led the horse over to me. I slipped off my glove and stroked the animal's nose. How gentle he looked now when moments ago he was a storm of fury.

"So, you like him?" Joel said almost as if he were teasing me. I nodded, and ran my hands through the horse's mane. Joel reached up, took my hand, and said, "He is yours."

"Mine?" I said bewildered.

"Yes Lizzie, when your Father wrote and told me what happened here, all I could think of was you. Sallie's moving away, your cousin's murder, the slave napping and then the loss of Coal. I wanted to do something for you. I am just a man who raises horses; this is the best I can do."

I did not know what to say. At last, someone was thinking about me, and it was Joel. Without thought, I threw my arms around him and kissed him. I could have kissed him on the cheek or lightly pecked his lips, but I did not. I pressed my lips against his and as our lips parted, I felt his tongue touch mine. He did not resist me and pulled my body in closer to his. His hand cupped the back of my head and he pressed his lips harder against mine. My only support was his hand around my waist, for my legs were too weak to stand. I believe we were overcome by the "erotic passions" described in Sallie's book. Therefore, we did not hear the carriage drive up or Mr. Isley call out, "Miss Sanders!"

117

Mr. Isley parked his carriage and was half-way across the lawn before we saw him. He was all bundled up in a heavy wool overcoat as if it were snowing. He was walking angrily toward us and his face was flushed and red. "Have you forgotten our visit, Lizzie?" he said as if he were my father.

"Oh no, not at all," I lied.

Joel snickered, dropped his head and wiped his lips.

"Paul, this is Mr. Joel Simpson," I said trying to sound formal.

Joel turned and extended his hand, but Paul did not take his hand out of his pocket. Joel cleared his throat and looked at the ground. This was most embarrassing.

"Paul, Mr. Simpson is from North Carolina and he raises horses. I was just thanking him for his most generous gift."

"I see you were; perhaps I should disbar myself and take up a more common trade," Paul said being very sarcastic. "Lizzie, I have something important to discuss with you in private. So if your friend Joe will excuse us, it is time sensitive," Paul saying to be intimidating.

"The name is Joel, not Joe. You might want to remember that," Joel cut back at Mr. Isley.

"Lizzie, I am sure you would like to freshen up before we meet in the parlor," Paul said trying to take my hand and lead me inside.

"No, I am fine." I replied hoping to inject a subtle insult.

Joel laughed and took hold of the reins to stable my new horse.

I walked ahead of Mr. Isley toward the house. I could hear the melting ice crystals crunching under his boots behind me. Gladly, the house was mine, except for Mammy. There was no need for excuses for behavior or for my appearance. I walked directly into the parlor and sat down. Mr. Isley followed. He wasted no time telling me his plans were to go to England and take up law at his uncle's practice. He had great fears for the state of affairs in America and he did not wish to be a part of it. He wanted to offer me the opportunity to travel with him abroad. Although, he clarified, this was not a marriage proposal, it would be wise for me to say yes. My private thoughts were, "what a low-down weasel." Not only would he stick his tail between his legs and run, he expects me to compromise myself as well. Instead, I took a deep breath and voiced a more polite response, "Paul, have you spoken to my father about this?"

"No, I have not. You know your father. He is too old fashioned to understand the younger ways. This will have to be a private matter between you and me," he said trying to employ diplomacy.

"So you expect me to leave my home with a man that is promising me nothing, behind my father's back?" I answered hearing my voice grow louder.

"Lizzie, I *am* offering you something; a safe haven and possibly marriage if it is agreeable for both of us," he said still trying to justify his insults.

I walked across the room, opened the door and stood with my hand on the knob.

He remained seated as if he did not understand the invitation to leave. "Mr. Isley, for an educated man, you are a fool. What makes you think I would run off with you like a common whore?"

"Lizzie, if marriage is what it will take to convince you, then I am willing!" He said, standing up as if offering himself as the great sacrifice.

"For your records Mr. Isley, I have no interest in going to the barn with you, much less England, and as for marrying you; I would sooner jump off a cliff!"

He walked past me, hesitated and left the room. Before Mr. Isley could find his way out the front door, Papa and Joel came bursting in the foyer. They were laughing and talking like old friends and nearly ran into Mr. Isley.

"Oh, good to see you, Paul. Allow me to introduce my good friend, Mr. Joel Simpson," Papa said, patting Joel on the shoulder.

"We have met!" Paul barked.

Then without another word, he arrogantly flipped around blindly to leave. I peeked out the door in time to see him trip on the rug and nearly crash into the foyer table. Joel reached out and caught him just before he broke Mother's crystal vase. Paul jerked back his arm as if Joel had put a hot poker to it. Things became more comical when Mr. Isley grabbed hold of the doorknob, which came off in his hand. He threw the doorknob on the floor, slammed the door, and left muttering something to himself all the way out to his carriage. Papa walked over and picked up the handle, turned, and looked at us, "I have been meaning to fix that thing."

We all starting laughing and Papa winked at me. Even though he did not know exactly what happened, he knew I put Mr. Isley in his place. It seems I was getting good at that kind of thing.

John and Kate were quiet during dinner. The trial was a success if you can call it that. All four of the men were found guilty. Mattie asked if there was going to be a hanging, could she go see it? It was a most inappropriate question, but I thought it was funny. I had to put my napkin over my mouth to hide my laughter. I looked up at Joel and he was smiling too. It was strange sitting there with Joel listening to him carrying on a polite conversation with everyone. How could he, knowing we had practically committed adultery that day right out in the broad daylight? I wondered what Papa would say if he knew.

Joel left that night to catch the train back to North Carolina. Before he left, I thanked him again for the horse, but not in the same manner. He made me promise to write and let him know how "Midnight," as he called him, was adjusting to his new home. He regretted he could not stay longer and see how well we fared together. He winked at me and said maybe next time.

Before I woke the next morning, John and his family were gone. Now, with Mattie gone, Annabelle slipped back into her old mood. Things were somehow brighter for me; I had something special to do now. I was the keeper of Joel's horse, Midnight.

Later I was to tell Papa about Paul Isley. Papa said it was a bit of a surprise, but Mr. Isley was a peculiar sort and he doubted he would ever get married. I did **not** tell him or anyone else about what happen with Joel. It was not because I was sorry for what happened, even though I knew I should have been. I was glad I kissed him and I would do it again if I had the chance.

On January 26, 1861, Mother received a letter from Aunt Sara.

Dear Tempie,

I wanted to thank you for your kind visit here last week. Henry and Erma were happy to see you as well. Erma has been a good influence on Henry and they are expecting a baby.

I have decided against marrying Mr. Ottolengui. We are both too old and set in our ways. I have buried two husbands and with the looks of him, surely he would be the third. To tell you the truth I think he is relieved to be off the hook. All is well and we still plan to continue our friendship.

I am sure you do not know that Grady O'Connor was among the Cadets from the Citadel that were involved in the incident on Morris Island on January 9th. The Cadets opened fire on a Union military cargo ship, "Star of the West."

After the incident, Grady left and joined the Union army. He is a selfish young man and of bad breed, so I suppose he will most likely survive, that kind usually does. Once a Yankee, always a Yankee. I say good riddance to them all.

Hope to see you soon and give my love to all,
Sara

CHAPTER 13

Annabelle's Secret

My hobby began when I was six years old and just learning to read. I was a "clipper" as Mother teased me. I was obsessed with cutting little articles out of newspapers and magazines and gumming them into scrapbooks. Neatly pasted on the pages were invitations, cards, letters and photos. Printed under each was its own remark. If someone were of the mind to, he could almost write my life story by those little books. At a young age, my clippings consisted mostly of pictures of animals, dolls and children's stories. However, over the years my clippings expanded to include other interests, such as recipes, fashion designs and wedding or death announcements. It was February and my box of clipping was overflowing waiting to start the scrapbook for 1861. I went up to my studio, under the oval window and started pulling them out of the box. I liked to place them out on the floor and plan the page layouts. I used to pretend that I was a newspaper editor and it was my job. I was eighteen years old and I found myself still pretending just a bit as I spread them on the floor.

Seven States succeeded from Union: *South Carolina, Mississippi, Florida, Alabama, Georgia, Louisiana and Texas. More expected to pull out.*

England is in a panic over the South's Cotton!

Abe Lincoln leaves Springfield and heads for Washington.

February 18, 1861 grand day for the Confederacy! Jefferson Davis sworn in as President on the steps of Alabama State Capitol.

South anxious for peace but ready for war.

The last little clipping was folded up in the box, *"Dr. Livingston, African Explorer."*

I read over the clipping, Dr. Livingston, a world-renowned explorer had returned from the wilds of Zambezi. A place where the truth is stranger than fiction. A paradise for strong-minded women and their kind. Imagine a country where the men are submissive and the women govern. I was contemplating the idea, when I heard Mammy's voice coming out of Annabelle's room. *"I's ain't gonna keep yo secret no mor,' Miss Annie. If yo's donts tells yo Mama today, I's will."*

In minutes, Annabelle was standing over me. She hesitated as if she wanted to say something, but hurried down the stairs instead. I was curious, but not enough to leave my job. Next came a wild-eyed Mammy with Mother's medicine in her hand. *"In jus' bouts one minute, you's Mama iz gonna' be callin' up heres for dis."* She handed me the bottle and instructed I best give her a double dose.

When I walked in the parlor, Annabelle was on the settee crying. Mother was wringing her hands and pacing across the room saying repeatedly, "How could you?"

I stood there for a few minutes not knowing who to comfort. By the time Mother saw me she was talking hysterically, "Oh, Lizzie, do come in. Have you heard the good news? Annabelle is going to have a baby."

I was temporarily speechless. Now it all made sense. The moodiness, the eating and the laziness, Annabelle was pregnant. No wonder she was pushing Papa to let them get married. Surely she did not think she could have kept this a secret. I put Mother's medicine down on the table, sat down beside Annabelle and put my arm around her. She curled up in my arms, laid her head on my breast, and sobbed. I asked Annabelle if Thomas knew about the baby and she shook her head "no."

"Mother this is not that tragic, they are planning on getting married. We will just have to rush things up a bit," I said, trying to sound cheerful.

Mother picked up her medicine and drank a big dose right out of the bottle. I had never seen her do this before. Then she sat down slowly and looked at me. I could see she was pondering over my suggestion. "Furthermore," Mother begun, "I see no reason to trouble Papa with all this if we can just work it out ourselves. Right, Lizzie?"

"Exactly, that would be my thought," I said encouraging Mother.

Annabelle lifted her head off my chest, looked at us and tried to smile. Papa was at his meeting at the Masonic lodge, which gave us plenty of time to scheme. Mother was sure the only thing to do was to put Annabelle on the train to North Carolina as soon as possible. Thomas and Annabelle could get married; the baby would be born and given enough time no one would ever know the better. Annabelle asked Mother how she would get Papa to agree. Mother just laughed and said she had her ways. Her voice was steady when she told us to leave her to prepare her letter to Mrs. Huneycutt.

She walked over and opened up the secretary, smoothed out the back of her dress and sat down. She took out her writing papers and her fancy pen and did not look back up. I pulled Annabelle to her feet, "Come on dear, let's get your things packed."

Annabelle stopped dead in the middle of the room, "but Lizzie, I can't, we can't possibly…"

Mother broke in and said, "Yes, you can and you will."

Annabelle started bawling again and I was forced to lead her up the stairs like a cripple. Mammy had the wisdom to predict the outcome. She had already pulled out a couple of trunks. When we walked into the room there were clothes spread out everywhere. Annabelle saw the room in such disarray and threw herself across the bed. "Mother has cast me out into the world," she wailed, burying her face into her pillow.

Mammy looked at me, shook her head and rolled her eyes. The two of us started packing her things while Annabelle lay there moaning something about the "gates of hell." Suddenly she jumped up and ran to the window. "Dear God, he is home!" Annabelle panicked and dried her face with her sleeve and turned to me. "Oh, Lizzie, what do you suppose is going to happen to me?" she said as if I had the all the answers.

"Well," I said, stumbling for words. "I suppose *you* are going to have a baby and marry Thomas, but hopefully not in that order."

She cracked the door, but we could barely hear Mother talking to Papa in the hall. Annabelle begged me to go downstairs and see what was going on. I reluctantly gave in and crept down the stairs. Papa and Mother were in the parlor with the door closed.

Just as I pressed my ear to the door, the door flew open. I tumbled forward scarcely catching myself before my face hit the floor. Eye level to the floor I saw a pair of polished boots in front of me. I stood up slowly to find that I was face to face with Papa standing there with his hands on his hips. He was not smiling and he was not the least bit amused. "Oh, hello Papa I did not know you were home," I lied.

"Well I am, and you can just go upstairs and get Miss Annabelle for me right now!"

I was obligated to retrieve a very nervous Annabelle. Papa was sitting by the fireplace with a brandy in his hand and Mother was standing by the window gazing out across the garden. We stood at the door like two little girls. I knew I was not in trouble, but I felt guilty too. "Ladies, please sit down," Papa said and gestured to the settee.

We both sat down so close that our knees were touching. I could feel the heat coming from Annabelle's sweaty body.

Papa took a drink and started his speech, "Annabelle, your mother tells me she is fearful of your emotional health. It is her recommendations that you be sent to North Carolina to marry Thomas as soon as possible. I must admit that your Mother's plea was convincing; however, I was not born yesterday. I think there is a more delicate situation here at hand."

Mother whirled around and looked at him. Annabelle started to cry again.

"None of you need to say more," Papa said. "Here is what is to come. I will personally escort Miss Annabelle to North Carolina. Once there, I plan to have my say with Mr. Thomas and see that the marriage takes place." It was hard to hear what else Papa was saying over Annabelle's uncontrollable crying. We all knew how dramatic Annabelle could be and most of this display was for sympathy, not in remorse. I did feel sorry for her. Maybe because I knew Annabelle had little self-control. She could no more resist Thomas than a piece of Mammy's pound cake. How could I pass judgment, when I feared my own self-control? We all had our weaknesses; hers was Thomas, but mine could easily have been Joel.

On February 14th, Papa and Annabelle left for North Carolina. I walked her downstairs not knowing when I would see her again since all the arrangements were still up in the air. While the carriage was being loaded, Annabelle sat between Mother and me on the settee. She held each of our hands and stared out the window. We were trying not to show too much emotion knowing it would create a wave of tears. I spoke up hoping to lift the dark curtain a bit, "Annabelle, have you given any thought to a name for your dear baby?"

At once, I realized nobody had spoken of the baby since the night we found out and certainly not in a positive light. Annabelle turned her head toward me, her blonde curls dangling down around her face like a little girl and said, "A baby. My baby."

"Yes," Mother said. "Your baby, a sweet little baby we will all love."

Annabelle's eyes began to sparkle with tears, "I will name him, "Thomas Jacob Huneycutt."

We had not noticed Papa leaning against the door until he said, "Well, what if *he* is a girl?

We turned to see Papa smiling for the first time in the last couple of days. Annabelle jumped up and ran to him. He took her in his arms and kissed her on top of her head.

Papa had a way about him that could heal the worst of hurts. Mother jumped to her feet saying, "I hope it is a red headed little girl!"

We were all laughing and sniffling when Annabelle and Papa got in the carriage to leave.

Mammy came running out the last minute, *"Yo's ain't gonna' leaves heres outs tellin' yo old Mammy good by!"* Mammy gave them a basket of food and Annabelle gave her a big hug. Mammy's tone was serious, *"Miss Anne yo take care of you's self. If them folks donts know notin' 'bouts babies yo send fer me."*

"I will Mammy, I will," Annabelle's voice rang out as they rode off. It had began to sprinkle snow and Mother commented she hoped it did not turn off too cold. We went inside and closed the door.

The mail was delivered, but Papa in his hustle to get Annabelle off, did not sort through it before he left. Mother picked up the pile of letters and handed me the silver tray filled with cards. We sat down in hall and began to divide our piles. We had been so absorbed in Annabelle's dilemma, I forgot it was Valentine's Day. I opened a card from the Tudor sisters inviting me to their Valentine Masquerade party. The card must have been delivered on Monday and I had not even offered a response. Mother said it was too late, even though I tried to convince her to send Cato to announce that I would be attending. She refused; it would not be proper and besides I could not possibly go without an escort. I would have offered up a more sincere plea, if I had known how scarce party invites would be that year. A few cards were for

Mother and a visitation request for me, from a man by the name of Dr. Clarence Wendell Bullwinkle. We both laughed at my comment, "The poor man will have trouble finding a wife. Who would want to be Mrs. Bullwinkle?"

Mother handed me a letter from Sallie and remarked there was a letter for Annabelle from Thomas, "Oh well, she said. "He can tell her whatever he wants to in person soon. I suppose you best write Sallie and Ransom and tell them what has happened. You are better at that kind of thing than I am." She shivered and pulled her shawl up around her shoulders. It was the last I would see of her that day.

It was getting colder and the foyer offered very little warmth. The house not only felt cold; but it was hollow. Sallie was married and Annabelle would be too. I was alone now and left to float along these halls with their memories. I went upstairs to read Sallie's letter.

Dear Lizzie,

This is to let you know how fine Ransom and I have been here in Beaufort.

Isn't it something about all the states pulling out from the Union? Do you remember we met Jefferson Davis at one of Papa's meetings last spring? I remember him well; he spoke so formally and had that nervous twitch in one eye. His wife was much younger and quite lovely. Her name was Varina. Little did we know then he would become the President of these Confederate States.

I am praying it does not come down to war. I admit I am praying somewhat selfishly too. I do hope we can stay here until spring when you and Annabelle will be able to join us.

We have made many new friends during our visit. Between the eating at the cafés and the dinner invitations, I can barely lace my corset.

The suite we are leasing is not so spacious, but it is lovely and Mrs. Cuthbert tends to our every need. She is a dear widow woman and tells the most delightful stories. We enjoy her immensely and made a promise to come back again next year.

I must tell you, unbelievably my dear sister, Mrs. Cuthbert is teaching me to cook. In fact, I have enjoyed the experiment of my own recipes. Mother will be so surprised when I come back. I fully expect to bake her a cake.

The weather here has been mild and on Saturday, Ransom and I went for a carriage ride. What we saw nearly caused me to fall out from fright; an enormous apparition descended upon us from the sky. I can only try to describe it, as a huge colorful pillow of air floating above us in mid air. A basket dangling below and a man braved to be riding in it. There were crowds of people collecting to watch. Some of the men were armed and ready to shoot it right out of the sky when Ransom and I pulled over. Ransom screamed out to them to hold their fire, the flying device was a "Hot Air Balloon."

This balloon landed right down in front of us. A man leaped out claiming to have lost his way from Ohio. He convinced a man with a wagon to haul him and his balloon to the rail station.

It was quite the excitement; I wish you could have seen it too. Ransom said he would like to take a ride in that thing. I told him I would not, but I bet Lizzie would fancy it. Ransom said that he thinks the Confederates ought to get one of these balloons to spy on the Yankees.

Well I will close for now. We are going to the Smith's for dinner tonight. I miss all of you dreadfully; please write soon.

With all my love.
Sallie

PS: Lizzie, on a very personal note. You know I have suf-
fered always with my monthly sickness, but since I have
married this has stopped. In fact, I have not even been
afflicted with the sickness for almost 3 months now. Ask
Mammy about this and write me back.

I finished reading her letter and thought how silly both my
sisters were. Now it seems I will have to write Sallie about
Annabelle and explain the facts of life to her as well. Surely, she
should have a clue why she cannot lace her corset or has skipped
her monthlies. I laid down my pen and thought of Papa and
Annabelle. By now, they had boarded the Charleston Railway
and were heading full speed toward Charlotte, North Carolina. In
Charlotte, they will catch the train to Albemarle, where Papa will
lease a carriage. I had never been out of South Carolina, nor
Annabelle. I wondered what she was seeing out her window.
Papa said he knew the Huneycutt's farm; it was not far from
where he grew up. Joel's home must be near there too. I closed
my eyes and tried to focus my mind on his face. What was he
doing this very moment, caring for his horses, sitting in a favorite
chair or making love to his wife? To the latter, I let my mind drift.

For the next several days, Mother and I went in and out of
rooms barely speaking to each other. One or more of those
days she remained in bed all day and the others she took long
naps and barely ate. Poor Mother did not hold up well under
stress. When she was up, her eyes had that familiar glassy
look. Lord forbid should we run out of her medicine, I am not
sure she could cope at all. It certainly was not mine to judge
my dear Mother.

On Monday, I decided to ride over to the Jones' to see if
Ladybug would spend the day with us at our house. Mother said
the child was wayward, but she was always amused by her just
the same. I stayed longer than I had planned. Mrs. Jones, or
Rose, was so easy to talk to and we became good friends. I confessed to her the story of Annabelle and she was most

sympathetic. She assured me once Mother laid her eyes on her grandbaby all this would be forgotten. Then she lowered her head a bit said, "Mothers always do." We both looked over at Ladybug playing with her doll and I thought yes, it will.

I was going to be an aunt soon, maybe even a double aunt if Sallie was expecting too.

Then before I could enjoy my thought, my mind presented a picture of me as the Old Maid Aunt taking care and tending to other people's children. I quickly brushed away the image and we got Ladybug ready to ride out with me. The arrival of Ladybug brightened up Mother a great deal. We played cards and Mother read to her that afternoon. Mammy made a delicious pot of chicken and dumplings. The highlight of the evening was Mammy's story about the dinner. She had us all laughing so hard our bellies' were hurting. "*Hows wuz I 'pose to knows da old rooster was som kinds of a fighter. He looks like a pot roster to me. He be so poor an' wuz good fer nothin' buts broth. De boys can be mads if de wants toos. De ain't 'pose to be bettin' on no cock fightin' no ways.*"

Mother said she was not sure if she would have enjoyed the meal quite so much if she knew she was eating a prize-fighting rooster. Ladybug was tired and I took her home before dark.

The next morning we received a telegram from Papa:
Start: Mail delay. Honeycutt's surprised. Much here to resolve. We or I will return on Wed. Expect letter from Thomas, Read Love, Papa....stop

CHAPTER 14

The South Roars

Mother misplaced the letter Thomas sent; we searched the entire house upside down. It was not until the next morning that Mother found it tucked inside a book. I was the one to open the letter. I could not help but feel dishonest reading Annabelle's private mail. Nevertheless, Papa had given his instructions.

My dearest Annabelle,

I trust you and your family are well and happy. I hope you will sit yourself down before reading this letter. After I left for home, I felt guilty and wished we had run off to get married.

However, lately it has come to me that I have no means to support a wife. I am writing to tell you what I hope you will think is good news. I have been hired on for six-months with the Pony Express. By the time you get this letter I will be on my way to California. When I get back we can get married right there in your Mama's parlor. I will write to you soon.

Yours forever,
Thomas

As soon as I finished reading the letter, Mother's fingers started counting the months. I knew exactly what she was doing.

132

It looked like Thomas would be gone at least until August. With all possibility, Annabelle's baby would be born before then.

Late Wednesday afternoon, just before sundown, we heard Papa's carriage drive up.

My heart sank when I saw Papa was alone. I was secretly hoping Annabelle would come back home with him. If she were to have a baby out of wedlock, at least she would be with people who loved her.

Papa explained to us that it was arranged for Annabelle to stay with the Huneycutts. Word would be sent to Thomas to come home as soon as possible. Annabelle would assume the role of Thomas's wife and once he returned they could be privately married.

According to Papa, Annabelle got along just fine with the Huneycutts and they were delighted to have her. It was a lovely home and she would be staying in Thomas's room. Papa felt he had left her in the best possible hands. As soon as Papa got back to Charleston, he went directly to the newspapers and placed the announcement that Annabelle and Thomas had married. Mother was a little shocked, but he said it was only a white lie. The realization hit me; Sallie was not coming home and now Annabelle was gone too.

I believe February and March of 1861 were the longest months of my life. I missed my sisters, Mother was no company and Papa was tied up with all the political upsets. If not for Ladybug, I think I would have perished from boredom.

We spent most of winter at home with very few visitors and even fewer outings. Sallie and Annabelle's letters made me lonelier, serving only as a poor substitute for their company. I was never so glad for spring to break. At least I could ride Midnight out by the pond and enjoy the long awaited sunshine.

On Monday April 2nd, we received a letter from Ransom informing us they would be returning to Sandy Ridge by Friday April 12th. With ten days to wait, I was glad Mother had volunteered us to help with the church bazaar. Our work there helped to fill in the time. The topics of discussion were first the economy, then as usual, gossip over-rides politics when it comes to women. Thank God, it was not Annabelle who was the focus of their gossip. Mother was too wise to give them the slightest hint that anything about Annabelle was not exactly to her liking. It was the news of Mr. Isley's departure to England with Kaylene Tudor that took center stage. Mother and I listened as they talked about Mr. Isley. I could have sweetened the gossip pot quite a bit if I had told them Kaylene was not his first choice. Then it occurred to me perhaps I was not either.

When we returned from the church, I was surprised to come face to face with Dr. Bullwinkle, who had been leaving his calling card for me the last month. He was speaking with Papa when we came in the door. Dr. Bullwinkle claimed he and I shared a delightful conversation at the homespun party. I tried to conceal my embarrassment that I did not recall meeting him. Mother graciously extended her hand and invited him to stay for tea. At first, he declined, fearing he would be intruding. Mother quickly replied, "It would be our pleasure."

She looked at me and now all I could say was, "Yes, of course, Dr. Bullwinkle."

"Please call me Clarence," he said as Mother took his arm and escorted him into the parlor.

Papa winked at me and under his breath said, "Bullwinkle?"

We were both laughing when we walked in behind them. Mother raised her eyebrows signaling our conduct was inappropriate. I quickly excused myself to attend to the refreshments, leaving Papa to collect himself. When I returned they were in a middle of a conversation. I came in quietly and sat down. With the spotlight off me, I found myself playing a game in my head, as Sallie and I used to do. When we met someone for the first time, we would determine what kind of animal he or she most resembled. Dr. Clarence Wendell Bullwinkle was most definitely a mouse. He was thin enough, but his coat was too small to button across his middle. His grayish brown hair parted in the middle was tightly oiled to his head, displaying his large rosy ears. Next, it was his darting little dark eyes I noticed, followed by how his nose wiggled over a scraggly mustache when he talked.

I was drawn back to the room when Mother called my name, "Lizzie!" Did you hear Dr. Bullwinkle say he attended the College of Charleston?"

"Oh, yes of course, shame they don't accept women. I would love to go there myself," I replied, only to see Dr. Bullwinkle look surprised.

I could not be sure if he thought my statement alarming or perhaps he agreed by his polite comment, "Yes, it is a pity."

He was polite and well dressed. I would say it was important to be such, for a man named Bullwinkle. Before he left, he invited us to Sunday lunch at his home on East Bay Street. All eyes fell on me for a reply. I could think of only one real reason to refuse; Sallie and Ransom would be here. We could not dare cut their visit short. Dr. Bullwinkle left with a promise we would accept the invitation at a later date.

March is suppose to come in like a lion and out like a lamb, but the lion was not at rest that April. Our Southern Lion roared on April 12th. Just after daylight on Friday morning, there were men at our house to see Papa. All we knew was something was going on out in the harbor. For the balance of the morning, more men continued to show up and disappear into Papa's study. Mammy and Cato kept busy carrying food and coffee into the Papa's study. Mother, fearing the worst, insisted Mammy stay in the room long enough to hear the conversation. She looked terrified when she came out of the room, "*De say de war is started. Theys bombed da Fort Sumter and de stills bombing tills de Yankees gives in.*"

It suddenly occurred to me; where were Sallie and Ransom? Had they been caught up in the crossfire coming in from Beaufort? I did not mention my fears to Mother. She was upset enough.

It was late afternoon before the meeting was adjourned. Some of the men came out laughing and talking excitedly, while others were calm and reserved. When they left Papa called us into his study. He confirmed General Beauregard had given the orders to start the bombardment on Fort Sumter. He demanded the Union surrender Fort Sumter over to the Confederacy. Papa said Charleston residents were awaken before dawn and rushed out on their porches to watch the shells arc over the water and burst inside the fort.

Mother was the one to ask the question about Sallie and Ransom. Papa's face was calm, but his voice was shaky. "I am sure the railways are temporarily shut down. As far as I know, there is nothing more to be concerned about on the mainland. I think it is fair to say we should not expect them until this has ended."

Papa went into town the next day on Saturday, the 13th. Sallie and Ransom had not arrived. It was almost dark before Papa got home announcing the Union had surrendered. The battle would have ended without a single causality on either side, if the Union had not insisted on a 100-gun salute to the US Flag as terms of the surrender. A pile of cartridges exploded, killing one Union soldier and wounding several others. Two men were taken to Charleston Hospital.

We were all much relieved when Sallie and Ransom finally arrived on Monday the 15th. Ransom had grown a mustache and Sallie surprised us wearing a new fashionable hairstyle. We stood back to admire her becoming new style. Slowly she removed her cloak to reveal her biggest surprise; she was very much pregnant. It seemed like such a shame to spoil such a happy occasion with the talk of war or even Annabelle and Thomas's dilemma. Thankfully, everyone had the good grace not to discuss either that night. The next day was a different story. Papa and Ransom left early to go into town for meetings. Mother and Sallie discussed the arrival of the two babies.

Sallie told us Ransom had purchased a farmhouse near his parents in Stanly County. It was Sallie's understanding the home-sick Annabelle was hoping to come back to Sandy Ridge just as soon as Thomas came home. Mother seemed confused. She went to her desk and read to us the letter she received from Annabelle.

April 2, 1861

Dear Mother,

First, I must tell you just how much I miss you, Papa and Lizzie. Please do not fret; I am happy here and well. I have met many new friends and Thomas's family has been very kind to me.

The best news is Thomas is coming home on May 5th. We have a preacher who has agreed to privately marry us the very day he gets home. My only regret, it will not be a lovely wedding like Sallie's.

I can hardly wait for Sallie and Ransom to get here, and then I am sure it will feel almost like home to me. Promise me you all will come to see me when the baby is born.

Mrs. Huneycutt has taken me to see her doctor; he says the baby will come around the middle of July. I just know it is going to be a boy and I am going to name him Thomas Jacob and call him TJ. I think it will be a sweet name.

The Huneycutts have a large family. I still do not know all their names. Sallie will like them all, especially Ransom's sister, Caroline.

On the fifth of this month Mrs. Whitley, who runs the boarding house, is going to give me a baby tea and many of the ladies from the Bethel Church will be there.

Tell Lizzie she should see how fat I am getting. Well, I must close. Please write soon. Until I see you again, hold me in your hearts and prayers and I will do the same for all of you.

Love always,
Annabelle

Sallie looked stunned when Mother finished the letter. "Oh well, that is our Annabelle changing with the wind," I said, and we all laughed.

When Ransom and Papa came home, they told us what was going on in town. Since the first gun was fired, young men had begun to pour into the city from all directions to join the Confederate Army. Market Hall was now the headquarters where they were issued their orders and given supplies and weapons. I could not help but reflect back on all the balls I had attended at Market Hall. How strange it seemed that the same young men who had stood in line waiting to dance across those floors, now stood in line there waiting to go off to war.

CHAPTER 15

The Carolina Parrott

April 25, 1861

Sallie and Ransom had been home for ten days. The time had passed quickly. We all tried to block May 1st out of our minds. Even Sallie dreaded the day when Sandy Ridge would no longer be her home. With just five days left, the last of her belongings were packed. The trunks were out in the hall waiting to be sent ahead by rail. Ransom, Papa, and Mother went into town to arrange for the cargo. Even though I knew a shopping trip might be included, I felt I should stay home to keep Sallie company.

With all the present hostilities, Lincoln's threat of blocking goods in and out of the Southern ports had become a reality. Ransom feared for the stability of his business if trade came to a complete halt. Mother, like all the other women, was worried about the availability of the necessities to run her household.

While they were away, Sallie and I enjoyed a long walk. She talked about her trip and the people she met in Beaufort. Sallie was bold enough to discuss a few intimate details of her honeymoon. Apparently, men never tire of the "experience." I did not ask what she meant by the "experience." I suppose I knew, but I had not heard it referred to by that name. Sallie often had a unique way of defining things, now even sex.

We only spoke of Annabelle and Thomas in the kindest of terms. Sallie said a baby changes everything. To speak of regrets at this late date would almost be blasphemy against the innocent child she carried. Anyway, all would be set straight soon. Sallie and Ransom hoped to be there in time to witness their marriage. When we came back from our walk, Sallie looked exhausted. I told her a little nap would serve her well and she went upstairs to rest. I seized the opportunity to go for a ride. Since Sallie was home, I had neglected my duties to Midnight. I was sure he could use the exercise. As I approached the barn, I could smell the fresh load of manure the Negroes were loading into the wagon. Samuel was standing on the back of the wagon with a pitchfork. Without saying a word, he jumped down off the wagon and left to saddle up Midnight. I waited outside the barn until he returned with my horse. He handed me the reigns with his eyes lowered and went back to his work. He never looked directly at me anymore; perhaps Papa had spoken to him.

Midnight was in high spirits that afternoon and eager to stretch his legs. I leaned into him and let him take off. Sometimes I felt like Midnight and I were one in the same; this was one of those times. We ran past the newly plowed fields and several of the Negroes stopped planting and called out to me. Midnight never broke stride until we reached the lake where he stopped to take a cool drink of water. His first gulp of water went up his nose. He snarled, shook his head and showered both of us with beads of water. "Take it easy boy," I said, taking a firmer hold on the reigns to keep from sliding out of the saddle.

I was complimenting him on what a magnificent beast he was and I thought of Joel. So much had happened since I saw him last. I tried to think of the day we kissed as just something that happened. It meant nothing. We lived in different worlds. Mine was here and his was in North Carolina with his wife.

If Annabelle had seen him since she moved to North Carolina, she did not mention him in her letters. Why should she? In her mind, of what interest would Joel be to me? I wondered should I dare confide in Sallie. After all, she trusted me with her intimate details. Before I could give it much thought, I heard thunder in the distance and the sky began to gray. I turned Midnight toward the house, but he halted to my command, which earned him a slight kick of encouragement. We were still at least a half mile from the barn when large drops of rain began pelting my back. It was not the first time we were caught in a storm, but this time Midnight was acting strange. I was glad to be on the home stretch when suddenly a streak of lightning popped the ground behind us. Midnight reared up and instinctively took off for the barn. I tried to slow him, but he was wild and out of control. It began raining so hard I could barely see. The barn was just ahead of us when I saw the gate was closed. Midnight was heading full force toward that iron gate.

With all my strength, I began to pull back on the reigns, screaming at the top of my voice, "Whoa!"

Two or three of the slaves working at the barn had heard the commotion and attempted to halt the animal, but Midnight was deaf with fear. It looked like he would either crash into the gate or attempt to jump over it taking off the top of my head.

From out of nowhere, I heard Samuel shout, *"Lizzie, ducks yo head!"*

It was all like a dream from then on. Samuel somehow caught hold of the reigns and pulled Midnight to his knees, tossing me off his back into a pile of fresh manure. I was not unconscious, but still I could not move. I could only lie there watching Midnight dancing above me trying to regain his footing. A sharp hoof hit my hip and I feared he would fall and crush me to death. Next thing I remember was a firm hand on my shoulder pulling me out from under the horse. Samuel then lifted me up and carried my soaking wet body into the house. Several of the slaves followed us into the house. "Mammy!" Samuel shouted as he gently laid me on the floor in the foyer. I was concerned about Midnight and attempted to get up, but he held me down and said, *"Yous best not getz up yet."*

Mammy covered me with a blanket and Samuel carried me upstairs. I suddenly realized I was drenched in manure; even my hair was dripping. I began to vomit from the smell. After Mammy's examination concluded there were no broken bones, she bathed me and put me to bed.

When Mother and Papa came home, Mother insisted that Papa go for the doctor. I begged against it and proved to her I could walk across the room. Papa said it appeared Samuel had saved my life. A couple days of bed rest and I should be as good as new.

When Sallie came in to see me, I showed her the big rent in my new riding dress and the huge bruise on my hip. She laughed when I told her my hip would mend, but there was not much hope for my skirt. Mammy brought supper up and Sallie and I ate in my room. After we ate, Sallie helped me with my scrapbook clippings. The newspaper headlines were mostly unpleasant. We did not discuss them as we pasted them to the pages.

Washington-April 15, 1861
United States President Abraham Lincoln declares Civil War!

Lincoln *calls for 75,000 federal troops with plans to extend the forces to 200,000.*

April 17, 1861-Virginia secedes from the Union!
Joining South Carolina, Mississippi, Florida, Alabama, Georgia, Louisiana and Texas as part of the Confederate States of America.

Confederate Capitol *to move to Richmond, Virginia*
President Jefferson Davis and his wife will move into new home, along with their children, Margaret age 6, Jefferson Davis Jr., age 4 and Joseph age 2.

April 19, 1861 - President Lincoln issues Blockade against Southern ports and attempts to limit supplies to the South.

Robert E. Lee *resigns the US Military and joins the Confederate Army.*

Thomas J. Jackson, *professor at Virginia Military Institute, joins the Confederacy.*

Colonel Wade Hampton *is looking for experienced riders to join the Cavalry!*

Where *does England and France stand in War?*

The last of the clipping was from Harper's Weekly and a story of interest.

Napoleon and his bride, Eugenie De Montijo, *met with Abraham Lincoln in New York City on Monday. The beautiful Spanish Empress is well known for her splendor of dress and fashion trends. She appeared in a costume by her own personal designer, Charles Frederick Worth. All over Europe the ladies are following her trend and are now wearing the new cage-crinolines.*

It was still pouring rain when Mother came in to say good night. She smiled as she reflected back on the last thunderstorm she remembered like this. It was the night Annabelle was born. She said the wind was blowing so hard she thought the house would break apart. It was only eight o'clock, but Sallie said she too was ready to call it a night.

The thunder and lightning made it difficult for me to go to sleep. It was sometime after midnight before I finally drifted off to sleep.

I was awakened from my sleep by a strange pecking noise at my window. I was surprised to the see the sun had already risen. At my first attempt to get out of bed, I was as stiff and sore as an old woman. The noise at the window was getting louder; I hobbled over to the window to investigate. There, sitting on the windowsill, was a small green bird. I had almost forgotten about such a bird, called a

Carolina Parrot. When I was a child, the fields were often covered with these birds, feeding on the seeds, berries, fruits and vegetables. The birds had a devastating effect on the crops and the planters were forced to destroy them. When a bird was shot, the others would swoop over the fallen one with mournful screeches. They seemed to say, "Please get up and fly away with us." Sadly enough their reluctance to leave made them easy prey for the hunter's next bullet.

It was Annabelle that came to mind when I saw the bird. Old Wiz gave her one of these birds as a pet. A bullet had clipped its wings and it was unable to fly. He collected the bird and tamed it by dipping it repeatedly in water. The bird never once bit Annabelle, but Wiz claimed it must have bit him a hundred times before he finally got the wild out of it. The little bird lived for years. When it died Annabelle's heart was broken. I could only suppose the bird at the window was separated from its flock during the storm. Perhaps it came to the window seeing its reflection in the glass. I opened the window and the bird flew in. It was flying all over the room and screeching so loudly that Mammy came running in the door. Her face dropped when she saw the bird, as though she had seen a ghost. She took out her handkerchief and carefully swished the bird out the window. I asked her if she remembered Annabelle's little bird. She said yes, looking worried.

April 30, 1861

Sallie and Ransom's visit was about to come to a bittersweet end. We had planned a special dinner on the eve of their departure, but our leisure time was interrupted when a letter was delivered by special carrier. Papa answered the door himself and gave the boy a tip. Once seeing the letter was from North Carolina, he immediately asked Ransom to come with him to the study. We were all concerned about the urgency of the postage.

Mother, Sallie and I sat in the parlor fearing the worst. Something must have happened to Thomas or Ransom's parents.

It was over an hour before Mammy came in with a bottle of sherry and several glasses for us. Mother stood up and asked her, "What do you know?"

Mammy only said, *"Mr. Huneycutt says to brings dis in da parlor room."*

Mother caught Mammy's hand and stopped her from serving the sherry, "Mammy, dammit, what is going on?"

Mammy pulled back her hand and ran out of the room crying. Before Mother could call her back, Papa and Ransom entered the room. Papa's face was red and his eyes were wet. Ransom took his seat beside Sallie and took her hand. My heart started to swell up in my throat when I heard Papa try to speak. He attempted to clear his voice before he dropped his head in his hands and began to cry. Something awful had happened; Papa never cried.

Ransom walked over and put his hand on Papa's shoulder and Mother fell down on her knees in front of him. Sallie and I held hands when Ransom began to speak. "The letter is from my mother. It appears that a traveler who took up lodging at Mrs. Whitley's boarding house has died of typhoid fever. Unfortunately for the people of Stanly County, the illness spread and others have died as well." He stopped and walked across the floor and looked out the window and I knew before he could say anything else, it was Annabelle. "It is Annabelle, they did all they could do for her, but you know she has a weak heart. It was not God's will and she departed this earth at eight o'clock on the evening of April 25th."

Mother's mournful screech was reminiscent of the little bird that flew in my window just that morning. By this time, Cato and Mammy were both standing at the back of the room crying. Mammy came forward and helped Mother off the floor. Cato's trembling hands poured the sherry. We each took the drink and Papa stood and poured two more. Mother and Sallie were weeping in each other arms. I sat alone to bare my own pain. "And what about the baby?" I asked.

Papa's voice was a little stronger now, "The baby, by the most miraculous grace of God, has survived. It is weak, but the doctor believes with proper care, *she* will survive."

We all looked at Papa. Mother said, "She?"

Mother wanted to know if Thomas had arrived before Annabelle passed. Ransom shook his head, "but he was there when they buried her."

"Buried her!" Mother cried out. "Buried my child without me being there! Who could do such a thing? I want her buried here, this is her home!"

There was much weeping and sadness shared by all of us for a very long time.

At last Ransom spoke, "My dearest mother-in-law. My mother made every effort to have Annabelle's body delivered here by train so that you might properly mourn her death. However, with infectious disease, the train would not consent to freight the body. The body had to be taken by wagon down the back roads to the church. Please understand it was for the welfare of all the people."

"And what of my welfare, who cares if I die from a broken heart? Damn your mother and damn you too Ransom for bringing that boy here! It is as much your fault as anyone that my Annabelle is dead. Now she lies in the cold earth in a humble grave unattended by the ones she loved."

Papa's voice was angry when he spoke to Mother, "Tempie, there is no one here at fault for what happened. What you speak now you will regret. What is God's will is God's will. I understand you are angry, but I will not have you blame Ransom or anyone else."

Mammy offered Mother her medicine, but for once, she refused it. Papa walked over, took the bottle from Mammy's hand and poured a spoonful. He placed a firm hand on Mother's shoulder and held the spoon in front of her. She took both doses without a quarrel. Papa looked at Ransom with compassion and shook his head. Ransom returned the look, "It is alright Jacob; I know she does not mean it. I don't blame her; let her be angry if it helps. This has been a terrible shock to her. It is a terrible shock to us all."

He went back and sat down beside Sallie, taking her up in his arms like a rag doll.

An hour may have passed in silence before Sallie asked, "Where is the baby now? Who will care for it? Not Thomas, I am sure."

Ransom addressed the question, "Do you remember me speaking of my sister, Caroline? She was in the process of weaning her own child and by the grace of God was able to take over the responsibilities of nursing Annabelle's baby. She and her husband have agreed to take in the child as their own, should it be agreeable with the rest of the family."

Mother looked up and asked if the child was given a name. Ransom smiled and said, "Yes, Annabelle was sure the baby would be a boy and she wanted to name him, Thomas Jacob. When the child she delivered was a girl, they called her TJ."

"Huneycutt or Sanders?" Mother asked.

Papa said the letter stated it was Thomas's wish that Annabelle be buried Annabelle Sanders Huneycutt. However, as for the child's full name, the letter did not say.

Mother wanted to make arrangements to leave as soon as possible to go to the gravesite and see the baby. Papa drew a deep breath, "That will not be possible for quite some time. The county is still under quarantine because of typhoid."

Sallie looked at Ransom and he nodded his head knowing she had questions too, "I am sorry dear; our travels will have to be delayed as well. It is far too great a risk to your health and the baby."

"I could not agree more," Papa said as his voice cracked. "You are welcome to stay here as long as you need to."

Sallie said nothing nor did I. It was as if I was the outsider looking in, who cared about my feelings, my needs or concerns? I had no husband to comfort me and it was all Papa and Mother could do to comfort each other. That night before I went to bed, there was a soft knock at my door. Mammy entered the room carrying the little wooden cage that once housed Annabelle's little bird. She quietly sat it on the windowsill. She sat down and I threw my head in her lap and cried. I am not sure how long she held me. After awhile I was exhausted from crying, she washed my face, combed my hair and helped me into bed. She pulled over the old rocker, covered herself with a quilt, and blew out the light. *"I's gonna be's here all night, you's try to getz some sleep,"* she said stroking my hair.

"Mammy, why do you think God let this happen?" I asked once the light was out.

"God don't letz dis happen, itz just the way of this old world."

"If only God would have let me say goodbye to her," I said aloud, almost in prayer.

Mammy said, *"He did child, he did. Whys do yous thinks I brough dis cage to yous. I knows when I seen da bird it was not natural. Miss Annabelle came to tell yous goodbye before she flew off to heaven. I just knows she did and yous gots to believe it too."*

As I lay there in the dark, a warm feeling came over me. I did not just believe, I knew. Annabelle, my dear little bird, came to me that day to tell me she loved me and was watching over me from heaven. My windy little sister was born during a thunderstorm and she left this world the same. Now she would forever live in my heart.

The days of mourning began; dark drab clothing, closed windows and visitations from well meaning friends. It was a difficult time for all of us. When I was despaired, I had only to look at that precious little wooden cage.

My Dearest Annabelle,
   You danced on this earth for such a short time, too few springs that you came to know. Darling, know you

this, your tender life will not be in vain. I promise you, your child will know your sweet name and the joy and laughter you gave. Soundly I sleep knowing you are watching from above. All my love to you my little bird, until we meet again.

CHAPTER 16

A World Out Of Control

With time, grief has a way of slipping down in the crevices of your heart. It never really leaves; it just makes room for more. It was less than a month since Annabelle passed. Yet, it seemed like years since I saw her face. I prayed I would never forget how she looked, the sound of her laughter or how she used to slide down the stair rail making Mother so mad.

Ransom made the announcement that he and Sallie would be leaving by the end of the month. Papa said it was understandable they wished to be settled in before the baby was born. It was reasonable to everyone except Mother. Nothing pleased her anymore. She spent most of her time in her room, sleeping or complaining of headaches. Several of the women from church made regular visits. The Minster had been by a couple of times as well as the doctor. All of them left saying the same thing to Papa, "It will just take time."

I was beginning to think if I heard that once more, I would scream and scream I did. More than once, I rode Midnight past the fields and down to the top of the cliff and screamed out over the ridge until my voice collapsed. I had once read in a book that this was the way of the Indians. Although exhausting, it did seem beneficial. I also found it painful to see what Papa was going through. He said nothing unhandsome about Mother. Still I knew her lack of courage, especially in the face of everything else, was

149

terribly disheartening for him. Papa read the newspapers daily and talked about the war. He and Ransom went on and on about the "Flag." I could not understand just what that flag meant to them.

On the Monday before Ransom and Sallie left, a note arrived from Mary Chests saying she would like to visit Mother and me on Wednesday. I knew how Mother admired Mrs. Chests and I took the note to her right away. She was sitting in her chair staring out the window when I handed her the note. She made no attempt to read the letter until I said, "Mother, it is from Mary."

She read the note and blankly said, "Thank-you."

On Wednesday morning, Mother came downstairs bathed and dressed to receive her social call from her friend, Mary. Papa was so pleased to see her come down for breakfast there were tears in his eyes. In fact, even the servants made a fuss over her. Mammy came running out and kissed her. Mother looked up at Mammy and said, "Enough is enough, no amount of mourning will bring Annabelle back from the grave, or anyone else for that matter."

No it sho wonts, alls we can dos is be here for de living." Mammy replied as she poured Mother's coffee.

Mrs. Chests arrived around one o'clock that afternoon. The nature of her visit was to encourage us to join the "Ladies Soldiers Aid Society." She told us the women in town had put their heart and soul to the cause. Society Hall was set up as their workroom for making goods for the soldiers. She said dozens of hospital shirts and uniforms had already been made.

Mother said she was afraid she would have to decline her invitation, but perhaps Lizzie would like to join. To this, Mrs. Chests stood up and looked Mother directly in the eyes, "I understand what you are going through. Honestly Tempie, I do. However, if there is one thing that will heal the soul, it is hard work, steady and constant. We need you and you need us."

Mother did not respond, but I could tell she was contemplating the request. She had not been out of the house since we received the news of Annabelle's death. It was high time. Valiantly I answered for both of us, "Yes, we will be there."

"Excellent, we meet on Friday. Please bring all the old linens you can spare," Mrs. Chests said, as she stood up to leave. We said our goodbyes and Mother went upstairs.

Mother was back down shortly and joined us for dinner. She was almost like her old self again. She was even able to share a few fond memories of Annabelle. The mood changed when Ransom asked if he could read a letter he received from Thomas that day.

May 25, 1861

Dear Ran,

These last couple of weeks I have done some powerful growing up. The preacher up here says we are not supposed to question God. Still, everyday I ask why the sweetest thing on this earth was taken away.

I had been thinking crazy things like just going out and blowing my brains out.

Then one day I was holding my baby girl and it was as if God spoke to me. I realized I had a purpose on this earth and a reason to live.

Nothing can ever take Annabelle's place but I love this little baby with all my heart. I hope Annabelle's folks can find it in their heart to love TJ too.

All of my earnings from the Pony Express went to cover Annabelle's doctor bills and funeral expenses. What was left I gave to Caroline to help take care of TJ.

Today when I was in town looking for work, the Confederacy was rallying up troops to join the Stanly Marksmen. When they came around to me, I joined up. The pay is eleven dollars a month and I spect that will near take care of the baby.

Maw liked to have a fit when she saw me coming home with that yellow ribbon tied on my arm. Pa says since I am eighteen and North Carolina has joined the Confederacy they will be calling for me soon anyway. So, I might as well go ahead and get it over with now. Me and Pa both say it won't take long for us to whip them Yankee boys.

Well, it looks like I will be on my way to get my training before you get back home.

So you take good care of your Sallie girl and I will see you all when I get back.

Love, your brother Thomas

PS: I am taking Brownie with me. I reckon he will be a lot of company to me away from home. A couple of the other guys took their dogs too.

After Ransom finished the letter, we were frozen by our own selfishness. Papa cleared his throat and tried to speak, but Mother took the floor. "How in God's name can we ever make this right? I, we have been thinking only of ourselves, while that poor boy has been suffering as much or more than the rest of us."

"Yes," said Papa. Not once did I consider that boy's expenses, which I could have easily covered. Why didn't someone say something?"

Before Ransom could speak Mother answered, "Don't you see Jacob, the boy felt guilty? He couldn't possibly ask us for anything. Annabelle would be so ashamed of us. She loved Thomas so much and we have treated him so badly."

Sallie and Mother both were sobbing and Papa began pacing the floor.

"Well then, we will just have to make amends the best we can," I said, and everyone looked with questions. "First, we see that the child, our own flesh and blood, is well provided for. Second, we will have to repay Thomas for all his expenses. As for myself, I will be the first one there on Friday to help prepare supplies for the soldiers. It's the least I could do for Thomas."

"I'll be there too," added Mother.

Father then announced he would make arrangements for us to go to North Carolina to see the baby.

Friday May 31, 1861

It was almost mania at our house that morning. We were all going to town, Sallie and Ransom to catch their train and Mother and I to start our new job at Society Hall. I rode with Sallie and Ransom. Papa and Mother followed us. I found myself thinking about the night we all rode in for the Harvest Festival. I was so jealous that night of all of them, laughing and having fun. I laid my head back and could almost hear Annabelle singing. I was glad she was happy that night.

It was not so bad saying good-bye to Sallie and Ransom. North Carolina was not the other side of the world and Papa promised we would be visiting soon. Besides, one thing I had learned, never begrudge others their happiness. Who knows when happiness will be short lived?

Papa dropped us off at Society Hall and Mother and I went inside. We were surprised to see so many women there; I could guess at least seventy-five. A minister, John C. Butler, offered the opening prayer. I was completely caught off guard when they announced the speaker as Dr. Bullwinkle.

He gave an informative lecture, addressing the medical care of the soldiers. With the help of a young lady, Dr. Bullwinkle showed us how to prepare bandages and roll lint or *charpre* as he called it. With a pine shingle knife the girl scraped over a clean table linen until she had produced a pile of soft lint. She then rolled the lint into a small bundle. Dr. Bullwinkle explained the lint was mixed with wax to pack wounds or used as compress sponges.

Mary Chests then took the floor and committees were formed for preparing clothing, making bandages, lint scraping, and sewing. Once Mother and I were assigned to the lint scraping committee, we took our bundle and joined the group. Dr. Bullwinkle must have thought the task very complicated or perhaps he felt I was not very bright. Either way, he found it necessary to look over my shoulder and offer his very personal instructions.

It was getting late and I was glad when the meeting began to break up. My hands were tired and blisters were forming on both my thumbs. When Papa finally came busting in the room, all the ladies were gone and we were left waiting with Dr. Bullwinkle. "There you are Mr. Sanders, I hope you don't mind that I have been keeping your pretty ladies company until you arrived," Dr. Bullwinkle said and winked at me.

"I am most thankful for your attentions, Dr. Bullwinkle, and I am sorry I was delayed," Papa replied.

Dr. Bullwinkle invited us to dine with him at the hotel; Mother nodded her head to accept. Dr. Bullwinkle, who now insisted that we call him Clarence, also insisted I ride with him to the hotel.

It was just dark when we left the hotel to return home. The streets were empty except for two men walking in the middle of the street. When we attempted to cross the street, they called out ordering us to stop. Papa stepped in front of us and I saw his hand slide into his breast pocket to rest on his pistol. Mother took a firm hold of my arm. Papa's posture must have been intimidating and the men quickly grabbed him and took him to the ground. Mother screamed out for help, but there was no one to answer. All we could do was stand by watching. Once the men had gained control of Papa, they identified themselves as the Town Patrol. They recognized Papa's name and quickly released their hold.

"What in the hell are you people doing?" Papa shouted at them. "I assure you I will go straight to your superiors and tell them what idiots they have working these streets."

Mother stepped forward and started dusting off Papa's suit. One of the men eyed me and the other spoke up, "Ma'am, we are sorry for the misunderstanding; it is just so many people are coming in and out of the city these days. Our orders are not to take any chances. Surely, you know these streets are under curfew; it has been posted for weeks. We have the authority to arrest anyone white or colored on the streets after dark."

"I am sorry to say we did not. We have had a death in our family and this is our first visit into town," Papa said. He settled down a bit, but he was clearly annoyed.

The men truly looked embarrassed and one of them spoke up, "Very confidentially sir, we have reasons to believe Lincoln's Government has sent out a number of spies to Charleston. We are under strict orders to keep a watchful eye out at all the restaurants, boarding houses and hotels. The merchants are reporting these scallywags are even passing out counterfeit money."

"I see," said Papa. "But I suggest you be a little more respectful of the town folk."

"Yes indeed sir," apologized the spokesman.

Papa placed his hat back on his head, "Now if you don't mind, my family and I will be on our way."

We made quick steps back to the carriage. Papa was still wound up and before the door was closed, he began his speech, "The whole city has gone mad. I tell you, mad! I could hardly get to the bank because there were so many troops coming into the station. Boys from all over, even boys from Virginia and Maryland. I spoke to a man on the street that said President Davis wants the troops to be ready to march at a moment's notice. When I finally got to the bank, there was a mob there too. People were standing in line to withdraw their money, fearing the banks will go broke. After I left the bank, I went into a couple of gun shops trying to pick up some ammunition, with no luck. Finally, I went down to the one just off Market Street. The owner was a Yankee who had bought up all the guns and ammunition he could get his hands on. Not only had this bastard created himself a monopoly, but he tripled the prices. After my day, I decided I would pick myself up a bottle of French brandy and a couple of good cigars.

When I came out of the store, there was a temperance preacher on a platform warning against the evils of tobacco and spirits. That man has no idea how close I came to hitting him right in the nose."

Papa was upset and with due cause, but I laughed at the thought of him hitting the preacher. Mother said with all that goings on, no wonder the Town Patrol was so nervous.

Before I went up to bed that night Papa gave me a bundle of newspapers for my scrapbooking. I took the papers to my room. As I started the cutting, I realized how sore and blistered my hands were from the days work. My scissors were dull; I would have to have Cato sharpen them. I fell asleep before I finished my work. Some of the clipping were still scattered across the bed when I awoke the next morning.

Lincoln trampling the Constitution and laws under his feet.

Two opposing capitals, Washington, D.C. and Richmond, only 100 miles apart, have created a hotbed.

Southern Life Insurance Company announces all policies on Military men will be void.

No more credit, cash only policies adopted by most stores. Panic starts as prices soar on groceries and dry goods.

Free men of Color volunteer to fight against the North.

CHAPTER 17

Dog Days Of Summer

July 6, 1861

My Dearest Sister Lizzie,

It was with great thrill I received your letter of your impending visit. Tell Mother and Papa not to worry one bit; we have four bedrooms and plenty of room. Ransom said he hopes to fill them all up with children. I have not made comment since I have yet to give birth to our first.

Of course, the accommodation will not be as Sandy Ridge, but I think you will be comfortable. The baby is due around the end of September. If all goes well, you will be here when it comes. I have a nice doctor, but it is reassuring to know my family will be close by.

July in North Carolina is a little cooler than home and most evenings a nice breeze blows in from across the meadow. You can smell the honeysuckle and mimosa all through the house.

Our farm is lovely with lots of rolling hills and pastures. We have forty-five acres all together. Most people here do not have slaves nor do they have much interest in politics. Poor Ransom works at the store and takes care of the farm too. It is an awful lot of work.

I am grateful when we were in Beaufort, Mrs. Cuthbert taught me some cooking skills, but Ransom perhaps more.

My middle has gotten so big now I cannot even see my toes, much less do my household chores.

Starting next week Ransom has hired a Negro man and his wife to help us. It is a great expense, but it is only for a short time. Ransom's sister has been kind enough to help me out some. She has her hands full with her little boy, Robbie, who is just a little more than a year and Annabelle's little TJ. Speaking of TJ, she is beautiful and has the sweetest disposition. I can hardly wait for you to see her.

All my new family live close by and we often have meals together. We are worried Ransom's store will be in trouble if this war goes on much longer. He has always prided himself in giving his customers good products at a fair price. Since the war, supplies are limited and the cost has tripled. Sugar is up to 75 cents a pound and flour is $18.00 a barrel.

Mother wrote that you have met a nice doctor with an odd sort of name. I suspect since you have not mentioned him in your letters, you are not too fond of him.

I am sure we have much to talk about when you get here.

Oh, I saw Joel Simpson and I told him you would be visiting. He said he had some new horses you would like. Many of the single men are joining the army and I hope he does not go too. Well, I will close for now, please write and let me know the very day that you will arrive.

> *You are always in my prayers,*
> *Love, Sallie*

After I read the letter, I went to talk to Papa. He read the letter with concern.

"I have been wanting to talk to you, Lizzie, about what we may be facing," he said. "As much as I would like to shelter you, it is not in your best interest. I know you have read the news. Charleston is most likely to be a prime target for the North. If they can gain our harbors, it would be greatly to their advantage. You are at a prime time in your life to marry. It is disheartening many of the young men are going off to war. Make no mistake; I am not like your Mother. I certainly will not have you marry someone out of desperation. This being said, we must all take precautions. It is important that I not delay in setting aside provisions to take care of my family. Do you understand what I am saying Lizzie?"

I shook my head and said, "Yes," but it sounded like someone else's voice. Papa had never talked like this. Since the war began, he assured us we were not in great danger.

He opened a drawer, took out a small black bag, and dumped the contents onto his desk. "Do you know what this is Lizzie? Gold," he said, *solid gold*. He tossed me a nugget so that I might feel the weight of it in my hand. "I am a man of means, but if the South does not win this war, my money will not be worth much. Gold does not see North or South; it is valuable to both. I have converted a great deal of money into gold. Lizzie, I need to trust you with where it will be hidden. Can you handle this task?"

I promptly answered, "Yes Sir."

"Then, I will need you to meet me here tonight around midnight. I want to make sure all the slaves are asleep and no one sees our coming and going. Tell no one about our conversation. Not even your mother."

"Not Mother?" I asked.

"It is not that I don't trust your mother," he smiled. "It is just I have witnessed her looseness of tongue when she is taking her medications. If she would drop the slightest hint that there is gold hidden on this plantation, who knows what might happen. As for your mother, I took her to see Dr. Bullwinkle last week. He says her headaches are results of the mid-life crisis and will be self-eliminating. However, he fears she has developed dependence to the laudanum, but to stop it abruptly would be wrenching. He is weaning her off the old medication by giving her an inhalant that is safer and more effective."

When I went up to bed that night, Papa and Mother were reading in the Parlor. Papa looked up and said, "I will see you later."

It was a perfectly normal way to say goodnight.

Just before midnight, I cracked my bedroom door, Mother's lamp was still on and I saw Mammy coming out of the room. I waited until half past, but I could still hear voices outside. I would have to resort to my childhood escape route. I pulled back the curtains and lifted myself out on the roof. As I climbed down that old tree, I was reminded how hot and humid July can be. The perspiration was dripping down my face by the time I got to the bottom. All was quiet, but just as I leaped to the ground I heard footsteps. My heart skipped a beat; it was Mammy. I drew up and waited until I saw her go back into the house.

Fearing someone might mistake me for an intruder; I bypassed the front door and crept around to Papa's window. I could see him sitting at his desk. The window ledge was too high, so I began throwing stones at the window. The noise alarmed him and he quickly moved away from the window and blew out the light. Thank God, it was a full moon and he could clearly see me waving up to him.

"Wait," he whispered.

In seconds, he joined me. "Young lady that is a good way to get yourself shot, especially these days! Now, follow me before someone sees us."

We walked briskly until we reached the duck pond. I was nearly out of breath when we stepped up on the gazebo. Papa took out a hammer and lifted up a few boards. Underneath the flooring I saw only bales of straw.

"Give me a hand with this straw," he encouraged.

I was astonished to see a rope ladder dropping down into a large pit. Papa started down the ladder and lit his lantern, "Come on, but watch your step."

The pit was more like an underground room with wooden beams to support it. It was damp and musty and I could smell the earth. After my eyes had adjusted to the dim light, I saw trunks and barrels along the walls. Papa explained he had built this chamber as our safe-haven. Fresh air came in though metal pipes leading to the surface and the ceiling could be latched from the inside. There were barrels of fresh water, food, blankets, candles and matches. The gold he spoke of and other valuables were locked up in the trunks. We climbed to the surface and walked back in the house without notice.

The next morning I learned why Mother was still up after midnight. Dr. Bullwinkle had warned her that the inhalant was highly flammable. Apparently, she had spilled some on her hand. When she blew out the light, the tablecloth caught fire and she burned her hand. Fortunately, Mammy heard her, came in, and helped her put out the fire. When I saw Mammy the night before, she was coming back from the herb garden. She had gone out to get a few leaves of lamb's ear to wrap up Mother's burn.

Over the next couple of weeks it did appear Mother was improving. Now it was three to four times a week we went to work at Society Hall. She seemed tireless, although at times she was still inclined to be sad and tearful. Dr. Bullwinkle's "Ether Formula" was becoming to Mother. The only fault was the strong chemical smell it left on her breath.

Our work at Society Hall never ended; most of the young girls were assigned to taking baskets of food to the incoming soldiers. Twenty or thirty belles on a mission marching from Society Hall to the train station attracted a lot of attention. People waved and cheered, and sometimes shop owners stopped us to stuff goodies in our baskets.

Hundreds of soldiers came through every week. Some were wounded, more were sick, but all were hungry. The soldiers playfully roughhoused with each other to collect baskets from the prettiest girl. I am sure I could have put brickbats in my basket and they would have fought over it all the same.

Only once did a soldier refuse my basket. I believed him to be a Lieutenant or Captain. When I offered him the basket he responded with, "My dear, sweet as it might be, there are men here that need it more than I. But, if you don't mind, I will pause only to partake of your charms." He bowed and kissed my hand. His blue eyes flashed in the sunlight like cobalt and his smile revealed a pair of boyish dimples. My breath nearly left me and I could say nothing.

My suspicions told me he knew I was caught off guard by his striking good looks, but I was not the only one. He squared his broad shoulders and looked pleased to see the other girls looking on with envy. With a tip of his hat and a quick turn he walked away leaving the other girls giggling and whispering to each other.

I wondered how many other train stations he had made such a display. Perhaps, if the truth were known he was starving, but would rather feed his ego than his belly.

On that same day after we returned to Society Hall, we heard music and drums. All of the ladies ran out in the street to witness a parade of soldiers, mostly Zouave. The procession included a musical band and a wagon carrying four or five women known as "Vivandieres." These women were all dressed in uniforms copied from the unit, but with gaudy braids and laces. They wore knee length skirts with Turkish pantaloons and large hats with feathers. They were beating drums and singing war-songs, like Dixie. One song I remember well the words, "Ye Sons of Carolina awake from your dreaming. Lincoln's guns upon us are streaming."

Mother and I stopped to watch, she said she did not know if the women actually went into battle. She referred to them as "Hospitality Givers," ladies who provided whiskey and frolic to the men. However, we both knew of respectable woman called "Angels of Mercy" who offered their services as nurses and ministered to the men, but these women looked far too fanciful to be God's workers.

Dr. Clarence Bullwinkle was now a frequent visitor at our house, claiming Mother to be his best patient. He ate meals at our house, went fishing with Papa and brought me little gifts. Clarence had a keen mind and a clever wit; he liked the theater and enjoyed music. He loved children, was financially secure, and was even kind to animals. Lastly, he was so admiring of my every move. In so many ways, he would make someone a fine husband, just not me. I was afraid the question was eventually going to come up and I had prepared my speech.

He spent so much time with our family that people were already assuming we were a pair. When Verina Tudor sent us the invitation to her wedding, it read, Mr. and Mrs. Sanders, Elizabeth and Dr. Clarence Bullwinkle. I had little choice but to politely accept Clarence as my escort.

Verina Tudor was the last girl on earth I would have expected to be one of the first to marry, but I suppose it was time. She was already twenty and two. She had four sisters, Kaylene who ran off with Mr. Isley, Carol Sue, Dora and lastly Florence who died of smallpox around the same time as their mother.

Their father was an Englishman who claimed to be a Lord of some sort. Most people took him at his word; viewing the fact Mr. Tudor was more likely to spend money than earn it. Papa said Mr. Tudor thought way too highly of himself, but was not likely to add much to the fruits of the earth.

For most of the month of August, Verina's wedding was the topic of discussion at Society Hall. It was a welcome change to hear the Belles gossiping and talking about petticoats and frocks instead of forts and battles.

Saturday August 24, 1861

I was not the only girl that would not be wearing a new dress to the wedding. Mother had taken several of our dresses to Miss Georgette's and she had cleverly redone them in the new fashion. The wedding was planned for six o'clock in the evening. It looked as if it might rain. On a wedding day, rain was not a good omen.

It was unbearably hot that afternoon and I was afraid my shoulders would burn before we arrived at Clarence's home on East Bay. We were to have cocktails with Dr. Bullwinkle and drive together to the Tudor's home several streets over.

Papa knocked, but there was no answer. We agreed that perhaps Dr. Bullwinkle had been called out on a medical emergency. The sun spreading its rays across the porch was blinding and it became embarrassing as carriages passed by.

Mother was suggesting that we take a carriage ride and return in a half an hour when the front door opened. It was not Dr. Bullwinkle, but a young Negro woman with brassy red hair and a freckly face. "We were expecting you, please come in," she said, using perfect grammar.

We waited in the foyer while she opened the doors to the drawing room. The home was elegant, but it was badly in need of care. The wallpapers were peeling, plaster was cracking and the fine English furnishings in the hallway were covered with dust.

The servant girl led us into the parlor, Papa sat in a worn leather chair by the mantle and mother and I took a seat on a faded red velvet settee. She sat first, but as I commenced to sit, the springs gave in. My expression must have given me away and the servant girl laughed, "Master Bullwinkle has not updated this house since his Mother died. It is well in need of a woman's touch," she said, smiling sweetly at me.

Before we could say more, a Negro gentleman entered the room with a tray of drinks and refreshments. "I see you have met Millie, my wife. I am Simon," he said, speaking as eloquently as his wife. "Dr. Bullwinkle has been detained, but he should be returning shortly. If you prefer, you may wait out on the piazza. It is pleasant this time of the evening."

"Yes, speaking for myself, that would be nice," I said.

I was glad when Mother agreed; it was stuffy and dark inside. Simon lifted the tray and we followed him out on the porch. It was much cooler now. Simon set the tray down on a glass top table. Before we could sit down, he insisted we take a walk through the courtyard. It seemed a bit strange, but we followed his instructions. It was a quick walk with little to see, with the exception of the medicinal herb gardens. When we returned, Simon and Millie were busy spreading clean sheets over the wicker chairs. I understood the delay. Simon was afraid the cushions would soil our clothing. We had been waiting only briefly when Clarence arrived. By the time he had made his apologies it was time to leave.

Clarence told us his medical emergency was Aunt Sara. Apparently, she climbed on a ladder to attend to her roses, fell and hit her head. She lay unconscious for several hours until she was discovered. She had a few nasty cuts and was complaining with her hip. The biggest concern was infection, nothing heals well during the dog days of summer.

When we arrived at the Tudor's there were servants lined up to attend to the carriages. It began to sprinkle rain and I was sure the wedding would be moved inside. I was to discover that even in this troubled economy money could still buy almost anything.

Mr. Tudor was prepared and had purchased a huge canopy tent to accommodate the guests.

Brightly dressed servants with coffee colored complexions greeted us at the door.

Their speech was more like the British tongue, not at all like our African slaves. After offering us champagne, they escorted us through the house and out to the courtyard. There, we joined the other guests.

The house reflected Mr. Tudor's mysterious lifestyle. It was exotically decorated with strange and unusual furnishings. Mr. Tudor, an acclaimed world traveler, described himself as a scientist and explorer. Yet, some people claimed he made his fortune in slave trafficking. After his wife died, he was gone for extended lengths of time, leaving his daughters in the care of governesses.

The gardens were alive with tropical flowers and plants, giving one the feeling of a Caribbean island. Drinks were flowing, people were laughing and a band played happy sounding music on steel drums. There were many people we knew, soldiers in uniforms, politicians and prominent businessmen. Something about the atmosphere was freeing. Even Charleston's socialites looked less stuffy. Maybe it was the music or the wine, but I wanted to break away and mingle among the crowd.

I was well aware of the admiration I was getting from the men. Miss Georgette was right; my blue silk dress was much more sophisticated as a strapless. I had been concerned that my sapphire necklace and earrings might be an overstatement, but all was just right. In fact, I felt wonderful for the first time in many months.

Clarence was concerned about where we should sit. Mother and Papa were engaged in conversation with friends when I saw Kaylene. She came to me at once and gave me a big hug. I almost did not recognize her. It was for sure she had tinted her hair and was wearing rouge. Her gown was glamorous in an ostentatious way. She looked over my shoulder at Dr. Bullwinkle and I felt compelled to introduce him. It was an awkward moment when I had to say his name, but I recovered with, "Dr. Bullwinkle is a family friend."

"I see," said Kaylene. "Then I am sure he won't mind if I steal you for awhile, we have so much to catch up on."

Clarence looked hurt, but before he could say anything, she quickly whisked me away. "Lizzie, did you know that Paul Isley and I got married four months ago in Paris? Traveling across the world is tiresome, don't you think, Lizzie?"

Kaylene knew full well I had not traveled across the world. She was as much a braggart as her father. When her husband joined us, he looked as though we had never met. How could he have forgotten? Certainly, he remembered that day he insulted me in my own home. Unbelievable yes, but I was more shocked to see him standing next to the Lieutenant I met at the rail station.

"Lizzie you remember Paul?" Kaylene's voice seemed to echo in my head. "And Lizzie, this is Lieutenant Edmond Cook. Edmond and Paul attended the University together."

The Lieutenant bowed and kissed my hand and I was momentarily relieved thinking he had not recognized me. I knew I was wrong the moment he spoke, "My dear, once again I am honored to partake of your charms."

"Oh, so you have met?" Kaylene said being very flirtatious.

"Actually we have not, I am just an admirer of this young lady and I do not even know her name," Lieutenant Cook added.

I knew it was raw the way he was looking at me. I should have been insulted, but instead I found myself returning his flirtations. Our encounter was brief, it was almost time for the wedding to begin and Clarence came for me. I had no choice but to join my escort. We took a seat in the second row next to Mother and Papa. Lieutenant Cook waited until all the chairs had been taken except the one next to me. He sat down and smiled to my parents. We all stood as Verina walked down the aisle. The massive amounts of material in her gown upset some of the chairs as she passed. Yet, she was steady with her march to the altar as if crashing chairs were part of the ceremony.

I found I could barely concentrate on what the minister was saying. I was ill at ease trying to prevent my person from touching either Clarence or Lieutenant Cook. The wedding was lengthy and ladies were forced to fan themselves. I was afraid we might all fall out from the heat before they finally said, "I do."

At dinner, the same happened; Lieutenant Cook managed to seat himself next to me. Mr. Tudor sat across from us and immediately began to monopolize the conversation boasting of his adventures and business prospects. Mr. Tudor informed us that Verina's new husband, Henry Wickham, was also his newest business partner. They had just returned from the Amazon Rain Forest with the prospects of raising exotic trees here in Charleston. He claimed the by products produced from these new trees would be more valuable than cotton and maybe even gold. "Rubber trees and Kapok Trees," Mr. Tudor announced.

Clarence seemed to be intrigued, "I am familiar with rubber trees, Mr. Tudor, but not the Kapok tree."

Mr. Tudor leaned across the table to get closer to Clarence, "The Kapok tree produces a usable fiber, but the natives of the Rain Forest claim its real value is the medicine they make out of the pods. This may be the greatest medical discovery of our time, my boy." Clarence's eyes brightened and now Mr. Tudor had his full attention.

I was glad I was relieved of entertaining Clarence. Lieutenant Cook seized the opportunity and we spent the entire dinner talking. When dinner was over Clarence said he would like to speak with me alone. I reluctantly excused myself and followed him out into the garden.

"Lizzie, I have spoken to your father," he began.

A feeling of dread came over me because I knew where the conversation was leading.

"In times like this a man must prioritize his life and make commitments…"

"Clarence," I said, stopping him in mid-sentence.

He gently put his hand over my mouth and said, "Please let me finish. I have grown fond of you and I believe you feel the same about me. That is why I cannot wait another day to ask you something very important. Every man needs a woman to care for his household, but as you can see, I have none. I know we have not known each other long, but I would like to ask you to make a commitment to me. Would you oversee my home while I am away?"

"Away!" I said.

He looked at me as though he felt sorry for me, "My dear, the Army is badly in need of doctors. I feel it is my duty to offer my services to those poor men fighting for our rights."

"So, you are asking me to care for your home while you go off to war?" I said.

"Yes," he said. "I don't expect much and I will be happy to pay you for your services."

I was relieved but almost hurt, "Why me?" I asked.

"Because I know I can trust you and besides, who else could I ask?" he laughed.

"You can count on me Clarence, I will be happy to do what I can for you."

"Good," he replied. "I will be leaving the second week of September. I will leave you money for upkeep and to redecorate as you wish. I hope you will feel free to move in and enjoy the city while I am away.

He leaned down and gave me a brotherly kiss on the cheek and we walked hand in hand back inside. The last few guests were saying their good-byes; Mother, and Papa were waiting on us. Lieutenant Cook was gone and I was sure I would never see him again. I did not mind. I decided I did like Clarence. He was a kind man and he trusted me.

August 30, 1861

From: Private Thomas Huneycutt
Stanly County Marksman,
Company H the 14ʰ Regiment of North Carolina Troops

Dear Mr. and Mrs. Sanders and Lizzie,
I am writing to let you know I am holding up pretty good in the Army.
I guess my time in the Pony Express toughened me up a bit. A lot of the fellows are fallen out sick and some of them don't hold up to marching long ways in the heat. I think my dog, Brownie, likes being in the Army.

Our company has been in a couple of skirmishes, but they have not amounted to much. I reckon before long we are going to get in some real fighting. They sure are giving us a lot of training for something and more troops are joining us.

We are in Virginia now and I expect we are going to be around these parts most of the winter. It looks like Richmond is where the Yankees are heading.

I heard from Ransom and he says TJ is really growing and doing just fine. I hope she will take to me when I get back home. Write to me sometimes if you can.

Yours,
Thomas

After Papa had read Thomas' letter Mother said, "Cold." I could not image what she meant. The last couple of days had been so hot; Mammy said you could fry an egg without lighting a fire.

"No, I mean this winter in Virginia, that poor boy camping out in the open," Mother clarified herself.

It was decided, I would knit him a pair of gloves and Mother would knit him a Baladava helmet to keep his face warm. I would start on the gloves as soon I finished my scrapbooking. I took the bundle of newspapers Papa set aside, went up to my room, and started clipping. I was glad Cato had sharpened my scissors.

Battle of Manassas, Virginia. *Grand victory for the Confederates. Frantic Union troops left running in all directions back to Washington.*

July 21, 1861 Lincoln's Army hits "Stonewall"
Confederate Commanders Brigadier Generals Joseph Johnston and P.G.T. Beauregard are commended by President Jefferson Davis. However, it was Colonel Thomas J. Jackson that stood steady as a stonewall that possibly led to the Confederates victory at Manassas. Earning him the nickname as "Stonewall Jackson."

169

The Price of War *Over four thousand men were killed in the battle of Manassas and thousands more wounded or missing. Among the Confederate casualties were General Bernard Bee and Colonel Frances Bartow.*

85-year-old widow *and invalid killed by Union fire. Judith Carter Henry was unable to leave her bed when the battle broke out. Confused Union soldiers turned their guns on her house. Shells crashed though the walls of her bedroom blowing off the widow's foot and inflicting multiple injuries resulting in her death.*

War No Picnic, *Citizens of nearby Washington came with family and picnic baskets to watch the battle. The thrill seeking Yankees quickly learned that war is not a spectator's sport. Gunfire and the bloody reality sent the panic-stricken civilians fleeing back to their homes.*

New Flag *for the Confederacy to be carried into battle. The new flag will be more visible and clearly sets it apart from US flag.*

Old Lincoln disappointed *with General McDowell, replaced him with Major General George McClellan.*

Carolina coast *is attacked by land and sea- August 28-29, 1861 Fort Clark and Hatteras forced to surrender and fall under Union control.*

President Jefferson Davis *worried as Union blockade is strengthened.*

CHAPTER 18

The Family Bible

Mother laid the family Bible on the table in the parlor. Without saying, I knew she planned to take it to North Carolina to record the birth of Sallie and Ransom's child.

That Bible had been passed down to my mother from her great-grandmother. For over a hundred years, it had been the eye-witness to the marriages, births and deaths of my ancestors. I held the Bible in my hand and I could almost feel the joys and sorrows that connected me to the past.

In my grandmother's handwriting was Mother's birth, her marriage to Papa and all of our births. Two pages over was Mother's accounts of Sallie's wedding and lastly, written in the book for all times was Annabelle's death date. The ink was smudged where a teardrop had hit the page, but the date was clear, April 25, 1861. It was another reminder that Annabelle's death was real and she was gone. I kissed the cover of the Bible and laid it gingerly back on the table. I wondered what would be written henceforward and who would be the readers.

We would be taking the 6:45 train to North Carolina in the morning along with a gift of two slaves for Sallie and Ransom. Mammy chose Violet and Harper to be the ones to go. She said, *"Harper waz a good workin' man. The "bad thing" done messed up Violet and iz lookin' likes she wus not goin' be havin' no babies. So she might as well go and take care of Miss Sallie's chillin."*

It was a year since the 'bad thing' happened. Gerald's name was never mentioned and Papa rarely heard from Cousin John.

It was a bittersweet departure for Mammy and Violet that morning. In all Violet's seventeen odd years, she had never been more than five miles from Sandy Ridge. Now she would be hundreds of miles away. Mammy knew that Violet and Harper would have a good life with Sallie and Ransom, but still it was hard knowing they may never see each other again. We all waited patiently for Violet and Harper to say their final good-byes.

When we arrived at the station, Papa cautioned Violet and Harper to stay nearby to avoid being questioned. It was a dangerous time for colored people; the laws were strict on runaways. I was used to the hectic goings on at the train station, but Violet was petrified as she held on to my skirt. The girls from Society Hall were already at work distributing baskets to the hungry soldiers. I waved, but today I would not be joining them. Perhaps I should not have, but I felt sorry for the Yankee prisoners in handcuffs. I thought of their mothers and sweethearts as the weary soldiers marched by us. It was a sad sight. War is not a good thing.

The conductor blew the whistle. It was time to board and Violet was still holding on to my skirt. I had to explain to her that colored folks were not allowed to ride in the same car as the whites. She looked like a lost puppy when Harper came for her.

Papa made sure Mother and I found our seats and then went to take care of Harper and Violet's travel authorizations. He was back before the train pulled out. Mother and I made small talk, but Papa did not offer in on the conversation. We must have been traveling less than an hour when Papa announced he was going to check on Harper and Violet. He stood up too quickly and nearly lost his balance. It was comical watching him make his way to the back of the train swaying back and forth trying to keep from tumbling over on the other guests.

It was a cool morning and I welcomed the warm sunshine coming through my window. I snuggled down in my seat and watched an elderly gentleman across the aisle light a thin cigar.

Smoke hovered over his head and he cracked his window letting in a wisp of country air. A Negro steward dressed in a starched white jacket was serving freshly brewed coffee. I closed my eyes, inhaled the pleasant blend of aromas, and drifted off to sleep listening to the hum of the train.

The squeaky wheels of the lunch cart and rattling dishes awakened me suddenly. Mother had been asleep too, but Papa's seat was still empty. She sat up straight in her seat and attended to her hair. "Papa has been gone for hours," I said.

When I told her the time, she wrinkled her brow and looked toward the back. She looked puzzled, but after a few minutes she took out a magazine and tried to occupy her mind. Just as our trays were being served, I saw Papa at the back waiting for the aisle to clear. I told the steward to leave an extra tray.

Papa squeezed through and sat down heavily, "Damn scalawags, just what I was afraid of. I knew I did not like the looks of that crew back there. Violet was the only woman amongst the Negroes onboard and one of the crewmembers was eyeing her when I brought her in. By the time I got back there, Harper said a white man came in and roughed him up and took Violet. We took off down through those cars banging on every door until I found the conductor. Harper described the man and the conductor knew just where to find him. Sure enough, he had Violet and was preparing to do things to her too brutal to mention. Thank God, I got there in time. The conductor said he would see charges were pressed against the man. He put Harper and Violet in a private car and assured me they would be treated like first class citizens the balance of the trip."

Mother shook her head, "You can't trust anybody these days. I sure hate that poor girl had to go through that. A white girl with a sweet face is a blessing, but I reckon to a Negro girl, it is almost a curse."

Our next stop was a two-hour layover in Columbia. Papa suggested we stretch our legs and mingle though the shops at the station. I suspected he really wanted a sweet from the bakery. The

Columbia station was not as hectic as Charleston, but we noticed a crowd forming in front of a large luggage platform. An elderly Nun was addressing the crowd. She identified herself as Sister Irene and her two companions as Sisters Ann and Theresa. The three of them were there on behalf of the New York Children's Society. We listened as she told of the horrible conditions of children living on the streets of New York City. She spoke of abandoned and orphaned children, sleeping on the streets and eating out of garbage cans. Most were children of German or Irish immigrants whose families came to America in hopes of finding the *'land of milk and honey,'* only to find crowded streets, no jobs or housing.

Sister Irene offered up proof of her words as a cargo of ragged children were unloaded and put up for exhibit. Spread across the platform were over twenty children, all holding hands with only their first names pinned to their jackets. One by one, she offered the small children up for adoption and the older ones out as indentured servants. My knees weakened as I looked at their hollow faces and eyes begging for comfort.

Mother made a comment to a middle aged couple standing next to us. The lady looked at Mother, "Have you not heard of the Orphan Trains? My husband and I lost our only child. We came here today in hopes of bringing a child home with us."

Mother called out to the woman, "God bless you!" as her husband pushed her forward to the front. We stood back with tears in our eyes as we watched her admiring the line-up. Her husband very clearly made his choice and gently lifted a little girl up in his arms. He tried to hold the child, but with all her might she fought to be released, screaming, "Brother, Brother!"

Both Mother and I were crying and Papa encouraged us to walk on, but we could not leave until we saw what was to happen. From the line-up, a little redheaded boy of nine or ten came forward. We could see him motion the little girl away; he knew what was best for her.

My heart was breaking. How much he must love his little sister and now he will never see her again. The little boy bravely took his place in line and looked straight ahead. His little body was quivering as tears rolled down his face. I closed my eyes and prayed, "Go back for him; surely you have room for him too." When I opened my eyes, my prayer had been answered.

Suddenly my mind turned the page back to the night I had seen the little Irish girl standing out in the cold. I had forgotten her, but now seeing these children, I knew someday, somehow, I must find a way to end this suffering.

We had been traveling for over fifteen hours before we arrived in the town of Albemarle, North Carolina. It was too late to drive to Sallie and Ransom's house and the livery stables would be closed at this hour. We would have been stranded at the station until daylight had it not been for a kind traveler who directed us to the Stanly House Hotel. The hotel was dark, except for a lamp burning in the front room. Papa knocked several times before a man in a stocking cap peeped out the door. Papa inquired about the accommodations and the man stretched his long skinny neck out the door to take a look at us all standing on the sidewalk. "Two women, one man and two Negroes?" he asked.

"That's correct, my wife, daughter and a couple of slaves for my son-in-law, Ransom Huneycutt," Papa answered.

The door opened and the man stepped back and motioned us in. "Well then, nice to meet you, I'm Joe Marshall. Ransom's Pa and I go rabbit hunting every chance we get. Why, I have known Ransom ever since he was knee high to a grasshopper." Suddenly embarrassed of his stocking cap he jerked it off and gave us a big toothless grin. He walked behind the desk and rang a little bell, "Don't ya'll worry none, I'll send Roby over to get your luggage."

It was not the Charleston Hotel by any means and the furnishings were dull. The old musty smell hit us as we walked down the hall to our rooms. Needless to say, we were all dead dog tired and glad for a warm place to spend the night.

Papa must have been the first customer at the livery; he was back and ready to go just after daylight. Harper rode up front, but

Violet sat in the back with Mother and me. The scenes from our window might have looked natural to Mother, but for Violet and I the landscape looked strange and unfamiliar. There were rolling hills with little farmhouses, not slave quarters, but hardly plantation homes. I saw a few cotton fields, but mostly golden wheat and tobacco waiting to be harvested. I turned to mother, "Trees grow tall here in North Carolina."

Mother talked about the long leaf pines and the red maple trees. Violet silently gazed out the window pondering over her destiny in this new world, away from everything she had ever known.

I would have known Sallie's house at once. It was exactly as she described in her letters. When we pulled up, the front door flew open and there stood Sallie. It was after ten o'clock in the morning and she was still in her dressing gown and robe. Her long hair was untied and hanging loose, but her belly was her most prominent feature. Papa pulled the carriage to a halt and Sallie waddled out in her bare feet.

While Ransom took Violet and Harper to introduce them to their new cabin, Sallie gathered us inside. The house reminded me of our old farmhouse at Sandy Ridge where the Jones' now lived. It was simple and plain with cozy touches and lace curtains. In the corner by the fireplace was a cradle waiting patiently for its new owner to arrive.

We followed Sallie into the warm kitchen where we sat down around a homemade walnut table. Sallie leaned back on two legs of the chair and smiled. She looked almost impish with her full rosy cheeks. It was hard to believe, seeing Sallie here in her motherly state, that less than a year ago she was a Charleston Belle.

She appeared not the least bit embarrassed of her attire or her lack of finery. Even her dialect was noticeably different. Without doubt, Sallie had adapted well to the country folk way of living.

The hired Negro woman served us coffee, salty ham and some biscuits with jam. Sallie rattled on and I found myself almost envying her. There were no pretenses or strict rules of etiquette here. It was true Sallie had paid a price for this newfound freedom, but it was a price even I might be willing to pay.

One of the first things Mother wanted to do was visit Annabelle's grave. Second, was to see her grandchild. It was a dread to go to the grave, but a desire we all had. As soon as we were refreshed, we left to go to the church where Annabelle was buried.

When we arrived at Bethel Church, Ransom stopped to speak to the young minister, Weston Little. He felt it would be fitting for him to accompany us to the gravesite. Driving around to the gravesite, he drove slowly giving us opportunity to admire the little church, its flowerbeds and the duck pond in the back. The green grass was neatly trimmed around the tombstones, which were scattered out under the feet of some big old oak trees. It was a peaceful place, fitting as any for eternal sleep.

The pastor retold the words he delivered that day and gave us an account of his last visit with Annabelle. He knew in his heart that Annabelle was safe in the arms of the Almighty. His words began to fade in the wind as I listened to the birds singing and watched the sunlight dancing over the inscription on her tombstone, 'Annabelle Sanders Huneycutt.' Then as if it came with great strain the pastor continued, "What is marriage, but man's law. How could God, who is love, condemn a love so pure and devoted that even death cannot sever?" There were no tears. Through this young man, God had given us peace.

Our next stop was to visit TJ. From the moment we walked up on the porch where Ransom's sister Caroline sat barefooted shelling butter beans, I knew. I knew she was a good and honest woman. Her soft gray eyes illuminated with kindness. When she spoke, her voice was like a soft melody. She was a natural beauty and her simple dress almost made me feel ashamed of my finery. She seemed confident to be entertaining us right there on her front porch. One could only guess if she knew of Charleston, the plantation homes or the social elite. Even if she did, I doubt she would have received us any differently. I decided North Carolina girls are a special breed, of which I think not a bad thing.

Her husband Robert came out of the house with a baby in each arm. On one hip a little blonde boy who was kicking and squirming and TJ on the other. He lowered the little boy to the floor who began crawling around to investigate his guests. Without asking, he sat TJ on Mother's lap. Mother studied the baby's face, her clear blue eyes and a head topped with blonde curls. Her fat little hands and legs were as blushed as rose petals. "Jacob," Mother said with tears in her eyes. "I am holding an Angel."

"I do believe you are," Papa said choking back his own tears.

We spent the afternoon taking our turns holding and admiring TJ. As we prepared to leave, Caroline began to cry. "Robert and I love TJ with all our hearts and souls. We feel no less love for her than we do for our own darling boy. We are not wealthy people, but I can assure she will not go without. This being said, I can not honestly stand in the way if you feel she would be better off in your care."

Mother looked at Papa and I was afraid of what she might say. "Caroline, there is nothing in this world I would rather do than to take TJ home with us. Sadly, I must face the reality, I am well over forty years old and Jacob is my senior. We are too old to raise a baby. You have nursed and loved her as your own. The child is healthy and happy and I believe you will be a good mother to her." Mother's voice dropped and we all knew she was thinking of Annabelle.

Papa gave the final word as to the custody of the child. "Thomas made a wise decision placing the child in your care. Far be it for us to interfere with his wishes."

Caroline took a deep breath and I could see a great burden had been lifted. Papa looked at the baby and smiled, "But, she *is* our granddaughter. Robert, before I leave, I plan to set up a trust for TJ's care. I encourage you to spoil her rotten, on my behalf."

Robert looked shocked, "We can't ask you to do that sir."

"You are not asking, I am insisting," Papa replied.

Over the next couple of weeks, I would come to regard North Carolina as a sanctuary. This Stanly County was timeless, away from almost everything and especially the war. It was a place where people shared the same simple values as their ancestors that settled there before them. It was a perfect view from Sallie's front porch, where days began sipping coffee in the golden sun and ended watching the sunset. I grew to love those red dirt fields and rolling hills.

September 26th was one of those mornings. Ransom had taken Mother and Papa to see TJ. After they left Sallie and I never bothered to dress; we just sat on the porch talking for hours. It was cool enough to wrap up in a quilt, but with the sun baking down on our faces and shoulders it was glorious.

Sallie asked me to braid her hair. When I combed her hair, it fell down across her shoulders smelling of sweet lavender. The strands shown like gold and I praised her beautiful head of hair. She said Ransom hoped for a little girl with golden hair too.

She closed her eyes and was drifting off to sleep when we heard a horse approaching. The sun was in our eyes and we could not see who the rider was until he was almost upon us. "Oh my Lord, Sallie, it is Joel Simpson and just look at me!" I said before I thought.

Sallie's eyes flew open and she looked at me almost laughing. "Is there something you forgot to tell me about sister?"

Sallie was still trying to get to the bottom of my remark when Joel slid out of his saddle. I scowled at her and thankfully, she hushed. I knew it was just for now.

"Good morning ladies," Joel called out. He started up on the porch, but seeing we were in our night clothing, he halted at the steps.

Joel's eyes fell on my face as though he was studying a map. I dropped Sallie's braid and froze. Sallie looked up at me and then at Joel, not knowing what to say. At first the conversation was awkward and one sided on Joel's part. He talked about his horses, his tobacco farm and a bit about the war. Fishing for something else to say, he said, "If we have time, we should all go over to Rocky River Springs."

179

"Yes," Sallie agreed and began talking. "Lizzie, I am surprised you have not heard of Rocky River Springs. It has become a regular tourist spot, with its own hotel, restaurant and shops. People come from all over just to bathe in the mineral springs. They say the sulfur, magnesium and copper have great healing powers."

"One spot flows into what is said to be a bottomless pit. A fellow claims to have seen an alligator down there one day when he was fishing. Ever since people have been calling it Alligator Branch," Joel added.

"Do you believe that Lizzie?" Sallie asked.

"Yes, I do! Strange things happen all the time," I answered, looking directly at Joel.

"Speaking of strange things," Joel said. "I want to see this pure white colt Ransom claims was born last week from a mare as black as the ace of spades."

With a bit of effort, Sallie lifted herself from her chair. "Lizzie, why don't we go up and change and then we can all go down together to see the colt. Joel, while you are waiting on us, I bet Violet still has a few hot biscuits left with your name on them."

"Hot biscuits? You don't have to twist my arm," Joel said and headed for the kitchen.

I was not sure if it was a good idea for her to go to the barn, but she insisted. When we came back downstairs, Violet was talking Joel's ear off. A plate of biscuits sat on the table and Sallie stuffed one in her mouth. She laughed, "I suppose I am eating for two."

Violet made big eyes, but said nothing as we escaped out the back door.

Joel was delighted to see the little colt was indeed white as newly combed cotton. He unlocked the gate and went in with the mother and baby. Talking in a low gentle voice, he examined the little horse. "Fine creature," he said as he locked the gate.

On the way up the hill, Joel asked Sallie if they had selected a name for the baby.

Sallie was laughing saying it might have to be just "baby" until Ransom and she could agree on a name. Suddenly she stopped; grabbed my hand and bent over double with pain, "Oh my God Lizzie, the water has broken."

I did not know a lot about babies being born, but I understood it was now reason to panic. Joel and I helped her in the house. I called for Violet even though I did not know what I could expect from her. She did not know much more about babies than I did, but she knew enough to say we needed the doctor. Without hesitation, Joel got on his horse and took off for the doctor.

We dressed Sallie in her gown and put her to bed. Violet said we should boil some water and get some clean sheets. Why I was not sure. Mother always said, it is best to stay calm in situations like this. "Everything is going to be just fine, Sallie," I said sounding like Mother. I was not sure if she believed me, but I could tell she sure wanted to.

Words cannot express how relieved I was when I heard Ransom's carriage coming up the drive. I ran out the front door and cut in front of them, Ransom pulled the carriage to a halt and I screamed, "The baby is coming!"

Ransom and Mother jumped out and Papa took the carriage around back. They followed me into the bedroom where Sallie lay. Little Violet was frantically trying to be the nurse with her boiled water and clean sheets. I told them Joel had left around an hour ago for the doctor. Mother went to Sallie and spoke to her very softly. I was not sure if Mother knew how to deliver a baby, but she seemed to be in control. Smiling, she told Ransom not to worry and sent him and Papa to the drawing room.

Sallie called for me and then for Mother. She twisted and turned and the sweat began trickling from her brow. Mother instructed Violet to bring dry sheets and I mopped Sallie's face and stroked her hair.

Nearly three hours passed and Joel had not returned with the doctor. Mother looked out the window; I could see she was worried. She turned toward the door and then back to Sallie as if she was not sure what to do. Slowly she walked over to the bed and lifted the sheet, exposing a half-naked Sallie. With both hands, she began feeling over the baby inside Sallie's bulging belly. Violet and I watched intensely trying to read Mother's mind.

There was a soft knock at the door and I was sure it was Ransom hearing Sallie moaning and screaming. Instead, quietly entering though the door was a petite woman with long black hair. Her face was weathered and wrinkled and she wore a primitive homespun dress and leather moccasins. "Mrs. Sanders?" she asked.

Mother stepped to the back of the room to speak to the dark skinned woman. After a brief conversation, Mother shook her head and the woman left. Within moments, the woman returned carrying a small medical bag. She went directly to Sallie and spoke, "Sallie, listen to me carefully, I am Minerva. Dr. Waddell is ill and I have come in his place. It is important that you trust me and do as I say. Can you do that?"

Sallie's eyes fixed on the woman's face. There was something about her that was calming and peaceful and goodness shone though her eyes. "Yes, I will," Sallie said bravely.

"Good," said Minerva. She examined Sallie's belly and then her right hand disappeared between Sallie's legs. When she removed her hand it was covered with blood. Violet gasped, but Mother did not flinch. Minerva wiped her hand on her apron and went to her bag. "You," she said looking at Violet. "I need you to take this birth root and make a strong tea for me. Do you know how to make teas?"

"Yes'um," Violet said and scrambled out the door with the bag of herbs.

Minerva took out a small drum, held it close to Sallie's head, and began to beat a soft slow rhythm. "Sallie, if you do what I say there will be no pain," she said. "You are to concentrate only on the beat of this drum, breathe with it, let it be your heartbeat, and do not think of anything but the beat. Do you understand me?"

"I will try my best." Sallie answered, as if she was in a far away trance.

Minerva nodded and turned to me, "I need you to keep the beat. Do not stop for any reason no matter what, until I tell you it is time to stop!"

Without stopping the beat, we switched hands and I was the keeper of the drum. Violet returned and Minerva gave Sallie the tea to drink. Within minutes, Sallie's body relaxed, but her eyes fixed upon the ceiling. Her moaning slowly became synonymous to the beating of my drum. Somehow we were a team, bringing this new life into the world together.

Minerva put some sort of oil on her hands, sat at the foot of the bed and entered Sallie again. I am not sure where Mother or Violet were in the room, but I could not stop to look. Sallie screamed and Minerva called out to me, "Beat faster and louder!"

I began to beat the drum harder and Minerva called out again, "Louder, louder!"

I was beating so hard the room echoed and Sallie moaned to the rhythm. My arms were aching but I did not stop. I would not stop. No matter what, until Minerva said so.

When I saw Minerva lifting the baby from Sallie, the sight was so miraculous I dropped the beat. Minerva's dark eyes flashed at me. I was exhausted, but I obeyed and continued to beat the drum. Minerva cut the cord and handed the baby to Mother. I could not hear if the baby was crying for the beat of the drum. I could only pray softly, "Dear God please let it be crying." I was still beating when Minerva turned her attention back to Sallie. She lifted Sallie's head, gave her something to drink, and pushed on her belly until it was flat again. I was still beating the drum.

Minerva covered the baby in a blanket and laid it on Sallie's breast. I could not see the baby's face or see if it was moving. I prayed, but I kept beating. Sallie's hands were trembling as she loosened the blanket; my eyes were fixed on her face. When I saw her smiling, I lowered my head and whispered, "Thank you Lord," but I did not stop beating.

Minerva encouraged the baby to nurse. She wiped her hands on her apron and nodded at me, "Your job is over sister drummer."

It was my job to tell Ransom he had a healthy baby girl. I stood up only to realize how stiff and sore I had become. Sallie rose up and insisted on brushing her hair and changing her gown before Ransom saw her. Mother and Violet attended to Sallie and Minerva handed the baby to me. The minute they heard me coming downstairs, Ransom ran out in the hall. I took each step carefully as I carried the precious little bundle in my arms. Ransom made no attempt to come upstairs, but stood at the bottom of the stairs holding his breath. Papa and Joel were standing in the doorway of the study smiling. I handed the baby to Ransom and slowly he turned to let his friends view his newborn daughter. It was a tender sight to see three big grown men nearly in tears over a tiny little baby. It is moments like this that are not easily forgotten.

When Ransom took his daughter and went up to see Sallie, I was sure the day's excitement had finally ended. When Mother joined us downstairs it was clear she was exhausted. Papa embraced her; they were overcome with emotions. I wanted to leave them alone to enjoy their moment, but I was trapped there watching over them with Joel.

I was looking for an excuse to leave the room when I heard the soft leather soles of Minerva's moccasins coming down the stairs. She passed by the room, looked in briefly and quietly slipped out the front door. My thoughts were she was too humble to ask for compensation. I turned to Joel and it was as if he had read my mind; we both followed her out the door. When we walked outside, we saw her standing in the middle of the road with her arms stretched up to the sky. From the porch, we could hear her singing a soft and mournful chant. Joel caught my arm and suggested we take a walk and leave her to her ritual.

Joel said when he found out Dr. Waddle was ill, his only hope was to go for Minerva. Everyone around Stanly called her the "Medicine Woman." Supposedly, she was a Cherokee, but where she came from no one knew. As long as he could remember she lived alone in a little shack down by the creek.

I shook my head and agreed, "It is true; she is miracle worker."

My dress was damp from perspiration and I found myself shivering in the night air. Joel noticed and took off his coat and covered my shoulders. "Lizzie, I must know if you remember the day I brought Midnight to you?"

I was shocked that he would bring up that day but I said, "Yes."

"I think of that day often. Because of that day, I want you to know something about me," he continued. "I am not sure how much Ransom or even your Father has told you about my situation. Amanda and I were never a match and we should not have married. Her father warned me about her temper, but we were young and I thought of her as a challenge, almost like taming a wild horse. Yet, after a year or so, her fits of rage and irrational behavior were more than I could handle. I found myself looking for any excuse to be gone for weeks at a time. Finally, I took a job with the railroad and was gone a year. Ransom was the one that sent me the letter telling me she had lost all reason. I came home and took her to the best doctors I could find. They all said she was sick, but I still blamed myself. When nothing could be done, I had no choice but to take her to Black Mountain."

Joel dropped his head and I could hear how hard the words were for him to speak. What a horrible thing this must be for him. I moved closer to him and took his hand.

"Not long after I took her there, she stopped feeding herself and could not even tell you her own name, much less mine. It was her folks who insisted that I sign the papers to have the marriage annulled. They said it was not fair for a young man to devote the rest of his life to a woman who does not even know she is in this world. It has been over seven years and even though I am not legally married to her, I made a promise to myself to be responsible for her the rest of her life. I always felt like it was my duty, but not a burden I could ever expect another woman to take on."

185

Then he stopped and looked directly in my eyes, "Even if I found myself so helplessly in love that every waking moment my head was filled with thoughts of her. Even if every night I tossed and turned longing to hold her in my arms and make love to her like no man on earth could do. It would not be fair to ask a woman to share half a man. Do you understand what I am saying, Lizzie?"

I was at a loss for words. I wanted to kiss him and say half of him was more man than most. Yet, was he saying he was in love with me or warning me not to fall in love with him? It was too late; I was in love with him. One thing he made perfectly clear. There was not going to be a future for us. His words cut through me like a knife. I felt foolish and turned away from him. It was a long time before Joel had the courage to speak.

"Hear that owl, hooting in the woods?" Joel asked. "I guess he is telling me, it is getting late and I should be getting on home. Come on, let me walk you back inside."

We started walking back in silence; the only sounds were the rustling wet leaves sticking to our shoes. I stopped, "Joel, I want you to know," I said, looking directly at him now.

He looked at me, without control took me in his arms, and kissed me once again.

I knew now that he loved me. I stood there begging for more, but he gained control of himself and said, "Please Lizzie, understand you deserve more than I can offer you. If only things could be different, but they are not."

We were alarmed to see Mother and Papa standing out in the road with Minerva looking up in the sky. "Something is happening!" said Joel, and we took off running toward the others.

"The great comet!" Papa called out to us. "Look, it is in plain view tonight!"

How small and insignificant we all seemed standing there gazing up into the heavens; Mother, Papa, an Indian woman and a brokenhearted couple that will never be lovers.

"This has truly been the night of miracles and we have you to thank for one of them," Mother said, and turned to Minerva.

"The Great Spirit is to be praised for all things; it is in his time not ours that life, love and happiness is born."

"Yes, how true that is," Joel said. Joel bid us good night, Mother and Papa settled with Minerva and I went upstairs to bed.

Sometimes during the night, I woke up with chills and a sore throat. I must have caught cold from the night air. The morning brought a rainy damp day and I was glad to be sick in bed. At least if I slept the entire day, my mind could rest from thoughts of Joel. Mother came in with my evening meal and the family Bible. "Here Lizzie I want to show you something." she said, turning the pages to our family. "Elizabeth Minerva Huneycutt, born September 26, 1861."

CHAPTER 19

Unexpected Kindness

We arrived at the train station early, but the lines were long with people seemingly in a panic. We had to submit to being bumped and pushed around in order to locate our train, only to find ourselves stranded at the end of the line. After five days in bed, I still had not completely recovered from my cold. We were on the first leg of our journey and I was already weary. My bag was getting heavier by the moment. It was a cool October morning, but I was flushed and hot, most likely due to a residual bit of fever.

When the conductor finally took our tickets, it was a battle to push our way through the annoyed passengers to find our seats. We had seat reservations, but we would discover my seat was taken by a young woman with a baby. The woman showed her ticket to the conductor; it was the same as mine. Every seat on the train was taken and I could hardly make a mother and child give up their seat. The conductor looked puzzled and said he had a solution. At the very back of the car was a drop down seat. It was mainly used for the crew, but he would be happy to offer it for my use. Papa said he would take the single, but I persuaded him to stay with Mother as I was little eager for conversation. With reserve, Papa watched me as I followed the conductor to the back. I sat down on a worn leather seat that offered very little cushion and found myself staring straight at a scarred up metal door. It was best that I was companionless for much conversation would be impossible over the vibrations and sounds of the engine.

However, after a few minutes I decided in favor of the seat. There was a window and I would have a chance to catch up on my reading. In my bag was a stack of newspapers and my scissors. I would spend some of the time clipping headlines and writing in my diary. All would pass the time, but the first thing I wanted to do was read the two letters Papa had given me this morning. I opened my bag and read the envelopes. Both were addressed to me. One was delivered by post from Dr. Bullwinkle and the other, hand delivered by Joel. Dr. Bullwinkle's letter would wait while I opened Joel's letter.

October 5, 1861

Dearest Lizzie,

When I heard from Ransom, you were coming to North Carolina, I found myself in turmoil. Even though I wanted nothing more than to see you again, I wished it was not so. The ball and chain I wear is ever draining and robs me of the hope of happiness.

I want you to know I have talked to your father and he understands how fate has not been kind to me. However, we both agreed that fate has yet to unfold for you. Like your father, my only desire is your happiness.

The last thing I would ever want to do is cause you any pain, but I feel I have done just that. I wish I was a man of great words, but I am not. I fear I have fallen short in expressing myself and left you with only feelings of discord and rejection.

Lizzie, from the moment I saw you walking down the steps on your father's arm a year ago, you had me captivated. I spent the entire night trying to fight my feelings, but by the end of the night, I lost the battle. Call it what you may, I knew you felt it too.

When most men would be delighted that the woman they admired returned their favor, it was not a delight for me. I felt disgust within myself. On such an important night of a young woman's life, I was the last one on earth that should

189

be the champion of her heart. I withdrew early not to tease you, but in hopes that some dashing young man would come along and sweep you off your feet.

I tried to stay away, but when I heard of so many unfortunate things that happened, my heart bled for you. I realize now it would have been best if I had not interfered.

In these uncertain times, we cannot predict the future, but one thing I know is that a woman needs a man to protect her from the evils of this world. As much as I cherish you, I wish it could be me. It cannot be.

As hard as it is for me to say, I beg you to find love, seek it out and do not rest until you hold it in your hand. I now know that love is life's greatest treasure. I pray that God protect you and bless you in all you do.

> *With my undying love always,*
> *Joel*

PS: Please let me be the first one to say Happy Birthday.

I read the letter twice before I folded it back in the envelope. "So that is that," I found myself saying aloud.

A little antique lady in the next aisle looked over at me and said, "Were you speaking to me dear?"

"No, No, sorry," I replied. She looked perturbed, shifted in her seat and peeked at me over the rims of her glasses.

Now I understood Joel was sacrificing his own happiness for mine. I would not disappointment him; I will be happy! I will find someone and marry, but I will never stop loving Joel.

I had almost forgotten it was my birthday. It was hard to believe that just a year ago I was the center of attention. Now, it appeared, everyone had forgot except Joel. There were no gifts, cards or even a Happy Birthday blessing from Papa or Mother. I suppose at nineteen all that is foolishness.

I thought again of Joel. He said he spoke to Papa. I wondered if I dared talk to Papa about Joel. I decided I would not; nothing would change things. I took out Dr. Bullwinkle's letter and as I opened it, I whispered to myself, "Mrs. Clarence Wendell Bullwinkle." Nothing could ever make me like the sound of that.

September 30, 1861

Dear Lizzie,

I hope this letter finds you fit and well. I am sure you are delighted with the arrival of your new little niece. Your father wrote that she was named in your honor. I suspect she is just as beautiful as you are.

I am writing you to give you a few instructions on the care of my home. By the time you receive this letter I will have begun my orientation in Port Royal, South Carolina. I will room at General Thomas's plantation on Hilton Head Island for the first week or so. Then I will begin to work on organizing hospital units on Forts Beauregard and Walker.

Mr. Caldwell at Charleston First Bank will be expecting you. I have left him instructions that you shall be in charge of my affairs in my absence. I think you will find there will be ample amount of funds in my estate to maintain or make any improvements your heart should desire.

I trust you will make yourself at home as the new mistress. Simon and Millie will be cooperative to your every need. Simon and I grew up together during which time I taught him reading, writing and mathematics. He has an excellent mind, which may come in handy for you. Millie also reads and writes, but I cannot attest to what extent.

It is with a heavy heart I must leave and I know I will miss your bright smile. However, as a doctor, I took an oath to help those in need. In my lifetime, there may never be a greater need.

I will write to you soon. Please keep our soldiers and me in your prayers.

With love,
Clarence

I folded the letter and whispered to myself, "Mistress of the Bullwinkle home."

Looking around I hoped to call for coffee when I discovered I had become the focal point for the little lady across the aisle. She was spying at me over her newspaper, so I asked if she knew when lunch would be served. She quickly shook her head no and looked down at her paper. She thinks I am crazy, I laughed to myself. I thought I would tease her a bit.

"Today is my birthday," I said. She ignored me as if I were talking to myself again. Therefore, I said it a little louder. "Today is my birthday."

This time she looked up, "That's nice Mrs. Bullwinkle."

That old bird had been looking over my shoulder and reading my letter. How dare her! With the letters read, I picked up the first newspaper and took out my scissors. Under the watchful eye of my traveling companion, I began to clip the main headlines of interest.

Plot discovered to assassinate Lincoln -*Allan Pinkerton hired*

New type of canvass shoes for army, due to scarcity of shoe leather

Confederate War Tax we must fight or starve

We do not need Lincoln's Pharmacy! Lincoln stops supply of Quinine and other medicines into the South hoping the soldiers will die more rapidly. Southern Doctors are returning to the old fashion ways. Dogwood bark, boneset, wild cherry and snakeroot make excellent teas and tonics!

Salt up to $15.00 a sack. Hickory Ash and Molasses cures meat almost as well as salt.

Coffee Shortage: reuse coffee grounds several times before discarding

Keeping spirits high! Many families who have lost love ones due to war are refraining from outward displays of mourning on their house and in their attire.

NC woman fights by her husband side: *Mrs. Mary Blaylock discovered as one of the soldiers of Company F. Undetected until her husband became ill and was discharged, thus she exposed her identity and went home as well.*

Lincoln's Blood Hounds: *Sweeping up everything of value, Negroes, money, houses. Lincolnites overjoyed as fine southern cotton and trains of Negroes are unloaded in Yankee-land.*

It was late when we finally arrived home to Sandy Ridge. Cato met us at the door and the fires were burning. It was good to be back home. Mother and I went straight upstairs to bed and left Papa sorting his mail.

At breakfast the next morning Papa read us the letter he had received from the firm of Mr. Claude Winslow and Sons, Attorneys at Law.

October 1, 1861

Dear Mr. Sanders and family,
*   We have been retained by Mrs. Sara Butler O'Connor to execute the terms of her will.*

Mother grabbed her throat and gasped, "Aunt Sara has passed?" She asked looking confused.

"Yes, I am afraid so," Papa said. "I think you will find this letter will explain it all clearly." Papa cleared his throat and continued.

I am very sorry to be the bearer of the sad news of your Aunt Sara. It appears Mrs. O'Connor's fall left her immobile. Complications of a staff infection set in and shortly thereafter pneumonia claimed her life.
*   At your earliest convenience, please contact me to discuss the provision she left in her will for you and your family.*

Sincerely yours,
Claude Winslow

Papa arranged a morning appointment for me with Mr. Caldwell at Charleston First Bank on Thursday, October 11th, and our appointment with Aunt Sara's attorney that same afternoon.

Papa delivered me to the bank before taking Mother to Society Hall. I went in the bank alone and was taken directly to Mr. Caldwell's office. I knocked on the door and found Mr. Caldwell sitting at his desk. I attempted to introduce myself properly, but it was difficult with the manner in which he was eyeing up and down my frame.

"I can see now why the good doctor left you in charge," he mumbled from beneath a large handlebar mustache.

"I beg your pardon?" I asked feeling more than a little annoyed at his wrongful assumptions.

Mr. Caldwell pretended to cough to cover up the silly little smirk on his face, "Do have a seat, Miss Sanders."

I sat down slowly and looked him directly in the eyes, "Dr. Bullwinkle has employed me to be in charge of maintaining his home until he returns from his duties with our military. Under the circumstances, I could hardly refuse. Do I make myself clear, Mr. Caldwell?"

"Yes, of course, now let us get down to business," he replied, trying to hide how stunned he was that I had called him out on his coy remark.

Rightfully so, this *was* business and just because I was a woman, he had no right to treat me any differently than a man. One thing I learned from Mother was a woman must command respect. I was slowly beginning to discover what a good teacher Mother had been.

With the arrangements made, I excused myself and took a seat in the lobby to wait for Papa. There were several newspapers for reading, but I was to wait well over an hour for Papa to return. I pondered in my mind what a glory it would be to have my own carriage. I knew it was not readily accepted, but someday I might just have to challenge that rule.

Mother seemed nervous on the way to the lawyer's office. She was mournful over the loss of her dear friend, but was also concerned Mr. Ottolengui might have swindled Aunt Sara out of her entire estate. After all, she had no real family of her own. There was her second husband's nephew, Grady O'Connor. Sara seemed fond of him until he joined the Yankee army. Surely, Grady O'Connor was not on her list.

When we arrived at the attorney's office, we were greeted by a young man who offered us a seat. Within seconds, the door to Mr. Winslow's office opened and Mr. Ottolengui toddled out.

"Hello again. Pity to meet again under these most unpleasant circumstances," he quivered. He closed his eyes and shook his head. When his eyes opened he departed with a simple, "Good day."

Papa whispered to Mother, "Poor old fellow, he sure looks distraught."

Mother answered Papa, but she remained looking straight ahead, not to be accused of whispering, "Perhaps he is shaken up over the contents of the will."

"Now Tempie," Papa scolded.

Mr. Winslow appeared at the door and invited us into his office. His office smelled of pipe tobacco and was decorated in rich brown shades. Mother and I sat down in the upholstered chairs and Papa sat in a wooden chair next to the bookshelves.

"It is nice to finally meet all of you; Sara spoke of you often. I was very sorry to hear about your youngest daughter," Attorney Winslow said sincerely. There was a moment of silence before he spoke again. "Now let us begin with you, Mr. Sanders. Sara wanted very much for you to have the gold watch that belonged to her first husband, Ben. Mrs. Sanders, her diamond necklace and earrings, Elizabeth a ruby bracelet and to Sallie a cameo pin and gold chain. To the two girls she also leaves one thousand dollars each. Do you have any questions so far?" Papa looked at us and Mother shook her head, no. "Good," Mr. Winslow said. He got up and walked across the room. With a few turns and clicks, he opened a safe in the wall. He handed each of us a large envelope with our names written in Aunt Sara's handwriting. Lastly, he handed Papa Sallie's package.

Now, I would like each of you to open the envelopes and verify the contents please."

I opened my envelope to see a stunning ruby and gold bracelet and a thousand dollars in cash.

"We are almost finished here, except fulfilling Sara's last request," Mr. Winslow said, looking at Papa. "This is where you come in Mr. Sanders. Her greatest concern was the welfare of her servant boy, Henry, his wife Erma and an elderly Negro woman by the name of Effie. According to her wishes, I have drawn up the papers and each of her former slaves are now free Negroes. In addition, her wishes were to leave her entire estate to this Henry. It was against my best judgment for her to leave her money and property to the boy, unconditionally. I finally convinced her to set up a trust fund for him placing someone she trusts as the executor. Furthermore, as for the property, it should be jointly owned by the executor as well. This will give the boy full rights to the property. However, in the event he should become shiftless and not maintain the property the executor would have the full right to take ownership. Mr. Sanders, will you accept this responsibility?"

I could tell Papa had reservations, but he reluctantly agreed. Mr. Winslow looked at his watch, stood up and walked to the door indicating our time was over.

A blast of wind nearly blew off my bonnet when we stepped out in the street. The misting rain left a salty taste in my mouth and I pulled my shawl up around my neck.

Papa seemed a bit nervous as we walked toward the carriage. I knew he was thinking about the money and valuables we were carrying. His mood was serious until we had been on the road for quite awhile. At last, Mother said, "Poor Sara was always thinking of others and now this unexpected kindness. She loved children. It is a shame she never had any of her own. I wonder if Henry knows how lucky he is. Few women I know would have accepted their husband's half-Negro son, as she did."

We rode without speaking; there was much to digest that day. Mother stared out the window most likely reflecting on the life of her friend, but Papa and I were lost in thought of our new assignments. Breaking the silence Mother asked, "So, Lizzie, what do you propose to do with your money?"

I hesitated to respond knowing she would not approve and it would be very likely Papa would not either.

"Lizzie, any thought?" Mother came again.

"Yes, I am going to buy myself a carriage," I said, closing my eyes and holding my breath.

"Jacob, did you hear what Lizzie said?" Mother punched Papa on the shoulder. "Yes, Tempie, I did and I think it might be an excellent investment for Lizzie," he answered. Before Mother could say more or even I could plea my case, Papa went right on to expand his point. "Tempie, times are changing. Lizzie has a job to do for Dr. Bullwinkle. You have your work at Society Hall and I am not always readily available to run a taxi service."

"Surely you don't think she should drive herself all around the country, do you?" Mother asked, obviously upset.

"Well, we will have to see how things go, won't we Lizzie," he replied looking over his shoulder at me. "I do think, Lizzie, you should consider investing some of the money. Right now is not a good time for money to be just sitting in the bank, in bonds or stocks. I have been giving some thought to investing in the shipping business, more point blank, a Privateer."

"A Privateer, Jacob, why those men are not much more than Pirates. Lincoln has made it clear he will hang everyone that is caught!" Mother quickly responded with intense disapproval.

"Not exactly Tempie, it is true they are not actually part of the military. President Davis has signed the letter of 'Margue' giving private owned vessels the authority to run the blockade, destroy or confiscate enemy ships. Also, it is legal for them to resell the ship's cargo, whether it be sugar, coffee, iron and even gold, at a fair market price. There is already great talk of the advancement of profits. Now, as for Lincoln's intent to hang the privateers, Jefferson Davis made it clear he would retaliate by hanging Union prisoners. Nobody wants that kind of blood shed on their hands, not even Lincoln."

197

"Well Jacob, it sounds like you have already have made up your mind. Far be it for me to interfere." Mother's tone had softened and it was my guess she agreed with Papa's viewpoint.

"Yes, I believe I have; I have been offered an opportunity to invest in the 'Seagull.' It will sail right out of the Charleston Harbor. Lizzie, can I put you in for a few hundred?

I laughed, but I was not ready to commit. First, I would have to see how much the carriage would cost. Second, I had a secret desire for some of the money.

The next week Papa agreed to take me to Biddle and Sons Carriage and Buggy Factory on the east side of town down by the shipyard. When we pulled up in front of the establishment, there was a large handmade sign at the front gate that read, "*Selling low for cash. No credit or bank notes.*" Papa whispered to me as he helped me out of the carriage, "Cash talks my dear."

I was to learn quickly the price marked was not the real price; one must be savvy and bargain with the salesman in order to obtain the best price. Papa explained it is important to examine the craftsmanship and consider the vehicle's resale value. It was not at all a simple choice. Although the fancy Runabouts, Phaetons or Surreys were fashionable and sporty, they would not appeal to a family man. The two-passenger gigs were nice and light, but a parasol top did not offer much protection from the elements. A two wheel Landaulet seemed a likely choice, but Papa was concerned it was too easy to turn over.

Papa was convinced the best of the best was the English Brougham, like he owned. The downfall would be I could not drive it myself and I would have to employ a coachman. I was the one to make the final decision to have a custom-made carriage. It would be a closed cab for privacy and comfort like a Brougham, but smaller and requiring only one horse. I chose black with royal blue pin striping for the exterior and blue velvet curtains and seats with buttons and tucks. Papa was satisfied that it would have four wheels and two polished brass lamps.

Arrangements were made for it to be delivered. Now the last thing was to see how Midnight would take to pulling a carriage.

On the way home, a feeling came over me that I had almost forgotten. It was happiness.

It was time to harvest the cotton. What Papa's plans were to do with the cotton this year was a bit of a mystery. It was a well-known fact, with the blockade; it was sheer luck if a shipment made it to England. Perhaps his privateer's ship, the Seagull, was his shining star or maybe he did not have a plan. Either way we did not ask, nor did he volunteer the information.

Over the next couple of weeks, the warm Autumn sun rose and set. Mr. Jones worked along side the Negroes in the fields. Soon the slaves would begin their harvest rituals and another season would come to an end. It all seemed timeless, as if nothing had changed. I guess this is what Mammy calls, "just folks existing."

Dear God in heaven! I did not just want to exist, I wanted to live. I had to start taking care of myself. Papa was right; times were changing. Yes, I would invest in this ship, Seagull, but first I would write to Sister Irene in New York. It was high time I do something of merit. I could help the Children's Society or the homeless children wandering along the streets of Charleston. Next, I will see to it that Midnight is trained and ready to pull my carriage just as soon as it arrives.

With winter coming again, I thought of how lonely it will be without Sallie and Annabelle. I must find happiness in my pen and be thankful I can at least write to one of my sisters.

October 27, 1861

Dear Sallie,

Hello sister. Please kiss Minerva for me and tell her Aunt Lizzie is thinking of her every day. I hope you are able to see TJ often. Please tell me she is still as healthy and beautiful as the day we left. I bet she is crawling around by now.

Sallie, was it not a shock about Aunt Sara's unexpected passing? She seemed so robust and healthy. One would have never guessed she was nearly eighty years of age.

Papa wanted me tell you he has arranged for your money and cameo to be delivered to you. Your package is due to arrive on Thursday, November 5ʰ by Wells Fargo.

I am sure with little Minerva there are plenty of uses for the money, but I hope you will buy yourself something nice as well. Papa strongly suggests you turn at least a portion of your money into gold and keep it in a safe place.

I have invested some of my money and bought a carriage. Saturday I drove myself to town for the first time. I would have been content to go alone, but Mother insisted I drag along Cindy Lou.

You know that I am working on the refurbishment of Dr. Bullwinkle's home. It has not been refashioned since his mother died in 1840. I suspect it has not had a proper cleaning since then either. Anyway, he has two most agreeable servants and I have put them to work at the chore.

I am having all the sofas upholstered and buying new carpets. The old ones are hardly worth saving. The selections of goods in town are thin, but I have made out quite well. I have employed a few men for painting and carpentry work. Papa says he will bring over some of the slaves once the work at home has given out.

Sallie, it is so lonely here without you. I have decided if I am to have any social life at all this season, I am going to have to seek it myself. Therefore, as early as next week, I plan to take up residence at Dr. Bullwinkle's house at least until spring. Then who knows, I might come to North Carolina for a while if you will have me.

I thought Mother would be beside herself when I broke the news, but she is in such a mood it did not seem to matter much. Papa has endorsed the idea. He says town is as safe as anywhere, especially now with all the town patrol and military presence.

I was almost glad to hear there is not to be a harvest festival here this year. I could hardly bear the thought of going alone. Nor could I dare open that trunk where our aprons rest. I am sure I would break down at the sight of Annabelle's neatly folded as if waiting for her to return.

I have a fear that the war is not going to be so short lived. In last weeks papers they were calling for more soldiers. If more men do not volunteer, there could be a conscription. I cannot imagine how many more soldiers they could possibly need. Just last week over 2,000 came through Charleston.

Many of the men here are mustering up. I dare to ask, but has Ransom or Joel spoken of it? Thank God, Papa is too old or he would most likely be on the first train.

On October 31ˢᵗ, Jefferson Davis is calling for a day of fasting, humiliation and prayer by the people of the Confederate States. I have never really understood how starving ourselves can help the war efforts, but it is to be that day.

They are setting up hospitals here in town for the wounded and sick soldiers, mostly sick. Many have measles and fever. I am still working at least two days a week at Society Hall, but I am afraid Mother is losing interest. She is complaining of her headaches again. By the signs of things, I am worried she is taking too much medication again. Please keep us posted on Thomas. Promise you will write as often as you can.

Love,
Lizzie

November began and I was anxious to establish my new residence. I was now driving myself all over town and tongues were wagging. It was a well know fact, I would be spending this year's social season in town at Dr. Bullwinkle's home. Papa laughed and said the gossip was nothing more than jealousy. He was right; the other girls were green with envy. I dare say that most of them would have gladly taken Dr Bullwinkle up on his offer.

With our country at war, some Charlestonians had declared it unfitting to host the fancy soirees and galas as was customary of our holiday season. Instead, they would be hosting more somber events such as prayer luncheons and benefits to raise money for the war efforts. However, others felt it was important to keep the spirits high. Their doors would be open to entertain their guests as richly as their pocketbooks would allow.

Papa made good on his promise and with the additional slave labor, the house came along brilliantly. Enough so, that by November 6th, Election Day, I was ready to spend my first night at the Bullwinkle home. My belongings had been moved into the bedroom I selected for my stay, which was once Mrs. Bullwinkle's room. I chose this room because I so admired the beautiful writing desk that sat under the large window. I fancied myself writing in my journal and looking out over the city on cold rainy days.

The newly hung wallpaper in a blue willow print, white lace curtains and bed clothing gave the room new life. I was positive Mrs. Bullwinkle would have been proud of my work. In fact, the whole house, once gloomy and dull, was now bright and sunny. The stale dusty smell was now replaced with clean freshly painted walls and the fragrance of fresh flowers on the tables. If walls could speak, most certainly they would say, "Thank you." It was not just the house that had taken on new life. It was Simon and Millie too.

I noticed how crisply ironed their uniforms were now and Millie seemed delighted with her new chores.

Mother insisted Cindy Lou move in with me as my hand-maid. I would have been perfectly fine without her, but it made Mother feel better. Papa and Mother personally delivered Cindy Lou that day, partly because Papa wanted to be in town for Jefferson Davis' formal election and partly because Mother wanted to visit.

Mother and I had tea in the parlor and she remarked how pleased she was with my decorating skills. Simon laughed when he heard me tell Mother I had fallen in love with that old house. Then almost as if he was speaking with superstitions, he lowered his voice to a whisper, "Once this house casts its spell on you, you can never leave."

Mother looked around the room and folded her arms across her chest as if a chill had fallen on her. Suddenly Simon began to

202

laugh, "Miss Lizzie, perhaps you might just have to marry Master Bullwinkle."

I did not even hesitate with my reply, "Perhaps you are right, Simon." Mother raised her eyebrows in question, but I did not open the subject for conversation.

Cindy Lou sat quietly in the hall waiting, as if something ghastly was to happen to her. Each time Millie or Simon passed by Cindy Lou made no effort to speak and lowered her eyes to the floor. However, as if some secret code of the slaves had been exchanged, Millie tucked Cindy Lou under her wing. That evening she took her to the third floor and introduced Cindy Lou to a room of her own. For the first time in her life, she would spend the night alone, away from Mammy.

Dinner was over and the hour grew late. I, the new mistress of the house, attired in my best dressing robe, would relax in the parlor. I sat in the rocker by the fireplace and opened my book. Out the window, I could hear voices as people walked by, carriages traveling down the road and the ocean in the distance. This was a different life from the country. Here I was not just existing; I was a part of something.

I was still taking pleasure in my new surroundings long after the servants retired. I thought briefly about the blue bedroom where the fresh linens sheets and cozy woolen blanket waited to tuck me in. I decided this night was too special to waste much of it on sleeping.

I felt completely at peace as the silence of the house fell around me. The halls and the empty rooms seemed to be calling out to me to ponder and roam. I felt like a princess in an enchanted castle, strolling the halls with my lamp. As I stepped into the foyer there hung the two magnificent portraits I had discovered in the attic. Simon identified the paintings as the mother and father of Clarence. Apparently, Clarence had taken them down shortly after his mother died, but now they were returned to their place of honor. Oddly enough, they did not seem as strangers. I was the detective but, slowly and surely, the Bullwinkle's history manifested before me. My treasure hunt revealed a secret drawer of love letters, a box hidden under the bed with precious photos and Mrs. Bullwinkle's journal with her intimate daily thoughts. Yes, I knew these people,

Frederick Lamar Bullwinkle and his bride Anna Jane Parker Bullwinkle. He was a German immigrant who came to Charleston with only a hope and a prayer.

Among my discoveries was Mr. Bullwinkle's death notice still carefully folded in the family Bible. It read, "Mr. Bullwinkle, a wealthy merchant and pillar of the community, names the "Germany Friendly Society" as beneficiary of a large trust fund for the support of widows and orphans of German immigrants."

Yes, I knew of Mrs. Bullwinkle's secret lover, Mr. Bullwinkle's drinking and the dreadful sickness that claimed the life of little Jane and nearly cost Clarence his. Still there were stories yet to be discovered and boxes yet to open. I had braved the attic, bedrooms and study, but not yet Clarence's office or clinic. Somehow, it seemed forbidden, but tonight it was the most intriguing. I listened upstairs. All was still. I walked down the hall and laid my hand on the crystal knob leading to Clarence's domain. If the door was unlocked, I must assume it was permissible to enter.

The door was unlocked and I walked inside. Facing me was a large desk with stacks of books and scattered papers. The chemical odor in the room reminded me of Mother's breath. I held my lamp to scan over the bookshelves, seeing hundreds of books, mostly medical in nature. Framed documents hung on the walls and the file cabinets were overstuffed with patient records.

A smaller room led from the office where I saw an examination table and some medical supplies. This room was lined with windows. I am sure it was a sun porch at one time. It was sterile and cold looking with pointy medical instruments lying on a metal table. In the corner, there was a small closet; the door was partially opened inviting me to peek inside. I shined my light in the room and I was nearly taken to my knees by a full hanging skeleton. Once I came to my wits, I justified its likely existence for the purpose of medical diagnostics.

I walked back toward the door to leave. I stopped to thumb through the scattered papers on Clarence's desk. It was all of little interest, a few bills, receipts and a letter or two. In the last stack, something caught my attention. There before me was a sealed envelope with my name on the cover. Had Clarence intended to send it to me or had he changed his mind?

If I dared break the seal to read it, he would know. Perhaps I should just take the letter, leaving him to assume it had gotten lost in the clutter. I was debating the lesser of the two evils. Then suddenly, I was over taken by a gust of cold air, which extinguished my lamp. My heart fluttered and I was frightened to find myself in the dark. Quickly, I put the letter down and fumbled my way back out into the hall. I took this as an omen; it was time to go to bed. I found the bed comfortable, but just as I began to drift off to sleep, a horrid vision of the skeleton popped in my head. I was to lie there shaken for some time, wondering what other skeletons might yet be discovered.

I awoke the next morning panic struck unaware of my strange surroundings. As sleep faded, I caught hold of my fears and regained my mind. I believe that very morning, I decided if and when Clarence asked to me marry him, I would accept. He was a kind man and I could do much worse. If his mother, Anna Jane Parker could call herself a Bullwinkle, I suppose I could too.

I would write Clarence a nice progress report and let him know everything is working out fine. Afterwards, I will continue my work on the house, have lunch at the café, go to Society Hall and have tea in afternoon with Mrs. Gibson.

I must say, by the time I arrived for tea that afternoon at Mrs. Gibson's, I was feeling a bit spent. Mrs. Gibson, a widow woman, had lived in the house next to Clarence for over sixty years. She was a delight, but I quickly realized her main reason for the invite was curiosity. I found her questions harmless and I thought we would be great friends.

When I returned home, I was surprised to find Papa waiting for me. I knew at once by the look on his face something was wrong. The first word out of my mouth was, "Mother?"

"No, Lizzie, your mother is fine. Have you received the evening news?" he asked. Without waiting for my answer, he pulled the paper out of his coat pocket telling me to sit down and read. I lit the lamp and sat down in the rocker. My hands began to tremble as I read the headline.

November 7, 1861, a fleet of Union vessels attacked Forts Walker and Beauregard. As the bombarding continued and shells ripped though the fort, Confederates running out of gunpowder were forced to abandon both forts. Shortly thereafter, a storm of cheering Federal soldiers entered the forts and raised the Union flag.

Immediately following the capture of the forts, the Union forces occupied the town of Beaufort. It is feared their next move will be the St. Helena Sound and onward toward Charleston's coast.

Despite the large expenditure of shot and shell, Confederate casualties and losses were low. 11 killed, 48 wounded and 4 missing. Among those killed was a Charleston Doctor, Dr. Clarence Wendell Bullwinkle. He was killed while attending the needs of a wounded soldier. The wounded soldier is expected to recover.

I was rendered speechless and felt as if all the blood was drained from me. I did not know what was worse, the loss of poor Dr. Bullwinkle or the fear of a Union invasion.

I was too weak to speak. Papa broke the news to Simon and Millie. What was to happen to them, this house and now me? Papa said those were questions for Mr. Caldwell at the bank. Papa came prepared to spend the night and his plans were to take me to see Mr. Caldwell in the morning.

The morning found me with little sleep and despaired. I had so many mixed emotions. Over the last months, I had settled in my mind a happy life here in this house as the doctor's wife. I thought it all through, the clothes I would wear, the parties I would host, down to how many children we would have. I was ashamed that the tears I cried were over my own disappointment, not mournful tears over Clarence.

There was a faint knock at the door; Cindy Lou came to let me know Papa was waiting for me in the kitchen. I started downstairs, pausing briefly as I passed the mirror in the hall and viewed my hollow reflection.

This time walking in Mr. Caldwell's office was much different. He was not flirtatious or coy. It was with a much more serious tone that he addressed Papa and me. "Miss Sanders, I am very sorry for your loss. Clarence was a loyal customer at our bank as well as a dear friend. He will be greatly missed in the community."

"Yes he will be missed. He was good man and a fine doctor." Papa added.

Then Mr. Caldwell peered over at me, as if he was examining me for flaws or imperfections, "Did Clarence speak to you at anytime about what he planned to do with his estate if he did not return?"

"No, it was never discussed; this has been such a shock," I answered feeling as if I would really start to cry.

"This is not the best time to discuss this, but time does not stand still for financial matters. Clarence sat right there in your chair the day before he left. I helped him compose a will in the event this most unthinkable thing was to happen. I am sure you know that Clarence was an only son and that he had no living relatives. In fact, he had very few close friends. He was a private sort. He was a lucky man to have won your favor, if I do say so myself."

I started to speak up and clarify to Mr. Caldwell that Clarence and I were not engaged, but Papa patted my hand, "Please dear, let the man finish." I obeyed, looking at Papa with curiosity. His expression was blank which was characteristic of his business face. He always said it was not wise to lay all your cards on the table at one time.

Mr. Caldwell, looked at both of us for a few minutes, almost as if he was testing us or uncertain of our natures. Slowly he got up, went to file cabinet and produced a document, which he opened to read to us.

"I, Clarence Wendell Bullwinkle, on this day of October 26, 1861 being of sound mind and excellent health, do hereby proclaim that in the event of my death, that my home and its contents, slaves, horses, carriages, savings, stocks, bonds and any and all of my worldly possessions be left entirely to my fiancée, Miss Theodosia Elizabeth Sanders.

Only the following limitations shall apply:

My two slaves, Simon and Millie cannot be sold or separated. If Miss Sanders does not see fit to keep them or if the house is sold, the two said slaves are to be freed from slavery and given a sum of five thousand dollars.

If Miss Sanders can not assume the responsibility of ownership of my property, estate and monies, her father, Mr. Jacob Sanders, shall make the decision to which charity or organization it shall be donated."

Clarence W. Bullwinkle

"Miss Sanders, do you understand what this means?" Mr. Caldwell asked.

"Yes, I think so," I said looking at Papa in disbelief.

"Well let me clarify things for you a bit. Mr. Bullwinkle's father was a shrewd businessman and invested wisely. Clarence was likewise and thrifty. Miss Sanders, you are now one of the biggest stockholders in this bank. In short, Miss Sanders you are a wealthy young woman!"

CHAPTER 20

Up In Smoke

Mother and I decided it was best not to dispute the assumption that Clarence was my fiancé. After all, it would have been most likely true had he not been killed. This being said, it was only fitting that I arrange for a nice service for Clarence and contact his minister. On Sunday afternoon, we opened the home for Clarence's friends and acquaintances to pay their last respects to the good doctor. Mother brought Mammy along to help prepare food and spend time with Cindy Lou.

I was amazed at the number of people that came through the door, many of them the so-called Charleston socialites. I found it short of embarrassing that last week they scarcely had the time of day for me. Nowadays they were treating me as though I was practically one of the family. One seems to rise in popularity with a rise in financial status. Fools! Did they not think I could see past my mourning veil? Not only were the thrill seekers dropping by hoping to somehow profit by associating with my new money, but also young men hoping to lure me to their favor for the same. For all they knew, Clarence had been the love of my life. How crude to think my love could die so quickly.

The evening grew late, but the people were still trickling in. The hum of the soft conversations filled the rooms. I was trying to give it my most earnest effort, but Mother was bravely suffering with the bulk of mingling with the crowd. I observed Papa standing by the fireplace engrossed in a deep conversation with a couple of men. I recognized Paul Isley, but the other man had his back to me. As soon as Paul saw me, he lunged forward to gush out his regrets. The other man turned around to face me. It was Lieutenant Edmond Cook. Oddly, he was not wearing a military uniform.

At last, the guests were nearly gone; Mrs. Gibson was saying good-by when Papa's meeting broke up. The two men paused to say "good evening" and Papa walked them to the front door. For the first time, I realized Edmond was walking with a cane and I wondered what had happened to him. Edmond had made not a single attempt to flirt or otherwise look my direction. Perhaps it was out of respect or he was never interested in me in the first place.

Papa and Mother would stay in town with me until all the financial transfers had taken place. Papa and I spent several long days in Mr. Caldwell's office, going over all the details of Clarence's financial profile. Papa warned it was better to be safe than sorry and wind up inheriting a mountain of debt or overdue taxes.

When Papa was finally satisfied, they were ready to go back home. It was left up to me to make the decision if I wanted to stay at the Bullwinkle home. I made my decision to stay in town at least for now. Mother took my decision with little disappointment. It was somehow unnatural how little emotion she seemed to have lately.

Once again, I was the mistress of the house, slaves retired and me alone in the parlor. How different things were this time. A house that might have seemed like a ghost house to some, felt like an old friend to me. I only wished I could have thanked Clarence for his kindness.

Papa left a stack of newspapers for my scrapbooking. War news covered every page. I think at first some people were actually enjoying the excitement of the war. Since the battle at Port Royal, people were keeping close to home and talking less. Fear changes a lot of things. Papa says there is nothing good about war, especially when it is almost on your doorstep.

I chose only two headlines for my scrapbook.

New baby born at the Capitol. *Mr. and Mrs. Davis have a son, William Howell Davis.*

Prince Albert has died *of typhoid and the South has lost a powerful friend. The grief stricken Queen says she will remain in mourning the rest of her life. Prince Albert and Queen Victoria had nine children.*

The last article I pasted in my book was Clarence's death notice. Then I picked up my lap desk, took out my pen and set my hand to writing a letter to Sallie. I had composed only a word or two, when I remembered the letter in Clarence's office with my name on the cover. Nothing was stopping me from going in any room of this house. Nothing was hidden or forbidden; it all belonged to me including Clarence's private papers. With almost a feeling of defiance, I put down my pen and walked straight to Clarence's office. I went directly to his desk and recovered the letter. I hesitated only briefly before I opened the sealed envelope.

Dear Lizzie,

Over the last couple of months I have grown very fond of you, which makes this the hardest letter I have ever written. What I will share with you is so personal I had fully expected to take the details to my grave.

If I were like most men, I would have already seized the opportunity to advance toward a more intimate relationship with you. Do not think for one moment I have not dreamed of such a thing.

When a man and woman marry, the two shall become as one and from that union children are born. It is natural and all according to God's plan. However, I am not like most men. If I were to marry a woman no matter how

211

much I might love and cherish her, we could never be as one, nor would children bless a happy home.

When I was only ten years old, my little sister Jane and I both became seriously ill. My Mother sought out the care of a well-known doctor, but his medicine could not save Jane and she died at only six years old. Although I was to owe my life to the good doctor, his medicine cost me a great price, my manhood.

My belief is that God takes nothing away without a purpose or reason. Therefore, I dedicated my life to the science of medicine. If I could save the life of just one child or prevent a tragedy such as mine, perhaps my life would not be in vain.

Up until now, I have been content with my resolution. Since I have met you, I have felt the curse of my misfortune so great that it is almost more than I could bear. I have since sought medical advice from a doctor in Columbia, where again my fears were confirmed. My condition is hopeless.

If you were to marry me, all I have to offer you is brotherly love and mere possessions. Would that be fair to a vibrant young woman like you?

Yet, in the times we have been alone, I am thankful you never gave me any indication that you were seeking anything more than friendship from me. This has given me hope that you might be the sort of woman that could resolve to a life of celibacy.

I would gladly offer you all that I have and pledge to protect and honor you for the rest of my life. However, we must consider your happiness. All I ask from you is that you search the chambers of your heart to seek the answer to my question. Could you be happy as the wife of a man such as me?

Your friend forever,
Clarence

Poor Clarence had been brave enough to give his life for his fellow man, but not brave enough to give me this letter. I slowly tore the letter in bits and pieces. "My dear friend Clarence, your secret is safe with me forever," I said aloud as if he were standing next to me. I sat down in the worn leather chair and folded my arms on Clarence's desk. Through my tears, I looked around the room. How could I leave his whole life's work locked up in this room? Slowly I began to open the drawers and files; with every card or letter I read Clarence intrigued me more. I hated myself for not taking time to know him better, now this was all there was left. I found myself asking, "Why was God against me? First Annabelle, now Clarence, was I somehow to blame?" Perhaps it was best Joel had his own convictions or God would have taken him too.

As I sat there trying to put together the pieces, I looked up at the clock to find it was four o'clock in the morning. I lay my head on the desk feeling almost too tired to go to bed. I shall never know if I had drifted off to sleep or was fully awake when I heard Clarence speak to me, "God takes nothing away without a purpose or reason."

I was sure the message was from God and my whole being was suddenly empowered with a new energy. I was no longer sleepy or tired and my empty mind was possessed with new thoughts and inspirations.

At six o'clock the next morning when Millie came down to prepare breakfast, she was surprised to find me sitting at Clarence's desk. I spent the entire night working on the details of my plan. I had written a half dozen letters and was finishing my last letter to Sallie, when she stuck her head in the door. "Good morning Miss," she said with great curiosity.

"Good morning to you!" I returned with great excitement. "I could eat a whole hog for breakfast, I am starving," I teased.

She turned toward the kitchen looking as if she thought I might be intoxicated. I stacked up my letters neatly and walked out in the hall. I could not help but laugh hearing her talking to Simon, "Poor girl is nearly insane with grief; she has not slept a wink all night."

I did not wait for Simon to respond and burst into the kitchen whistling. I poured myself a cup of coffee, sat down at the table, and took up the newspaper. Simon and Millie drew up as if wondering what I might do next. "I have good news!" I said. "Last night it occurred to me, it was Clarence's only mission in life to help others, especially children. I am planning to continue his good work. It is my hope to find a new doctor and reopen the clinic. In honor of Clarence, the new clinic will be called, *The Bullwinkle Medical Clinic for Children*."

Simon smiled almost looking relieved, "Millie and I will help you in any way we can. I am sure Clarence would be most pleased."

"Well that is excellent," I said. "No child will be turned away. If they are too sick to be cared for at home, they will stay here. Simon, Clarence spoke of your sharp mind and said that I could rely on you. Millie, you, Cindy Lou and I will begin to study Clarence's books on nursing. First at hand is to ready the clinic, it must be bright and cheery for our little patients."

After breakfast, I put Millie and Cindy Lou in charge of cleaning, while Simon and I went to town to shop for paint, wallpaper and material for curtains. I was disappointed to be returning with no material, no wallpaper and only a can of red paint.

Millie and Cindy Lou, although working steadily, barely made a dent in the cleaning. The dark curtains and walls seemed even gloomier in the daylight. I was feeling depressed, overwhelmed and discouraged. Perhaps it was all just a foolish plan. I sat down on a stack of books to rest briefly. The next thing I knew, Millie was helping me up to bed, I was exhausted.

When I opened my eyes, the sunshine was beating down on my face and I was alarmed to discover it was half past noon. I was angry Cindy Lou had not come in to wake me. I threw on my clothes and went downstairs to give her a piece of my mind. The kitchen was empty and the pots were cold. A scary thought ran through my head. Did Simon act on what he might have read in some abolitionist's pamphlets? While I was weak and asleep, did they take this opportunity to run away? If so, I would have to give up hope on the children, lock the doors and go home to Sandy Ridge.

"Damn!" I said as I walked from one empty room to the next. Lastly, I walked down the hall to Clarence's clinic. The door was not locked, but it appeared to be jammed. I thrust my weight against the door.

"Hold on, I will open the door," Simon called out to me. Simon cracked the door slightly, as if trying to block my view, "Did you rest well, Miss Lizzie?"

"Yes, thank-you," I answered, looking over his shoulder. Seeing I could not be contained, he stepped back and gestured a grand sweep with his hand.

"We have been working all night to surprise you," Simon explained. "It was Cindy Lou's idea to mix the red with the left over white paint. Millie made the curtains out of tablecloths. Now mind you, there is still plenty to do, but it is a start. We can't give up, right, Miss Lizzie?" Simon's face was frozen in a smile as he waited for my response.

I looked over the room in total disbelief; the dark walls and clutter were gone. Everything was clean and polished, lace curtains hung at the window and a crystal vase with white camellias sat on the desk. The room was painted a pale shade of rose and the back wall displayed a mural of red flowers as fine as any artist's work I had ever seen.

I walked over to it and laid my hand on the wall, "Who did this?" I asked.

"Cindy Lou," Simon said.

I was so overcome with emotion that I sat down and began to weep. Cindy Lou came over and knelt down beside me, "Miss Lizzie, *ain't mad is yous?*"

I grabbed her and gave her a big hug, "No, my sweet little Cindy Lou, Miss Lizzie is not mad."

Over the next couple of weeks, I followed up with more letters to every source I could find. I was desperately hoping to find a doctor as soon as possible. I organized all Clarence's books on

215

nursing and Millie was put in charge of reading and training Cindy Lou. I wanted Papa's encouragement, but instead he warned me it would be difficult to find a doctor at this time. Over half of the doctors were already obligated to the military.

Three weeks passed with no responses to my letters and I was getting discouraged. My hopes were renewed on December 8th, when I received a letter from New York.

My Dearest Miss Sanders,

We were delighted to receive your letter. It is my understanding that you are in the process of opening a clinic in Charleston for the medical care of children. It is with great excitement that I am writing to tell you that I may have a likely candidate for you.

Forgive me for my slow response. I first wanted to write to Dr. Frances Holloway, who is a recent graduate of the Bedford College in London, England before I made the recommendation.

Just today, I have heard from Dr. Holloway who whole-heartily has agreed to meet with you. Dr. Holloway is a loyal supporter of our cause here, as well as to the suffrage of women.

Here is my proposal for you. On January 4th, three other sisters and I will be traveling through Charleston. I would like very much for you to return with us to New York. I am very sensitive to your concerns of traveling, especially as a Southern woman in Northern territory. However, your safety is assured in the company of our sisterhood.

Miss Sanders, if you are to be fully committed to our cause, which is the welfare of all children regardless of race, origin or financial status, it is important that you be the eyewitness to their suffering. Perhaps nowhere in the world are there more orphaned children than on the streets of New York.

I hope you will find it your heart to accept our offer. Please notify me as soon as possible of your decision so I can arrange an interview with Dr. Holloway while you are here.

Yours in faith and love for our Lord and Savior,
Sister Irene Maloney
The New York Children's Society

I wanted to run out in the streets with joy; at last my prayers had been answered. I had no idea what Papa or Mother would say. As far as I was concerned, I would go to New York!

I was pleased they were reasonable when I told them of my intentions. Mother admitted it would be a good experience for me, but she feared it would be too dangerous. Papa's initial opinion was I should be in safe hands traveling with the nuns, but his greatest concern was the security of the trains traveling across enemy territory. Papa was never quick to come to important decisions. If I wanted his consent, I would have to wait until he could speak to a few of his colleagues about the dangers. He felt he possibly could have an answer as early as Thursday. If not, he would wait to give his final word on Saturday, the 14th of December. Papa was not superstitions as a rule, but he was not about to make this decision on a Friday the 13th.

I would wait, after all it was just a couple of days and I had a lot to keep my mind busy. I had an invitation to lunch with Mrs. Gibson on Sunday. Monday and Tuesday there were my duties at Society Hall and a benefit concert at the Theatre on December 11th.

In my free time I spent studying Clarence's personal medical journals. His handbooks were laid out so brilliantly that even a layperson like myself could understand. First, he would list the causes and symptoms of the disease, then a detailed description of his protocol for treating the illness. He always included both pharmaceutical and herbal remedies. He left nothing to second guess, the compounds, portions, where to order supplies and exactly how to prepare the herbs.

I was particularly interested in the herbal and natural formulas since Mr. Lincoln had cut off supplies to the South. Clarence taught Simon how to maintain the herb gardens and prepare the herbs to make the medicines. We would replant as soon as the weather broke. For now, there were enough dried herbs on hand.

I spent most of the day on Wednesday studying and I had forgotten about the concert, which gave me some excuse for allowing very little time to prepare my toilet and my costume. Cindy Lou and Millie's thoughts were ahead of me and they had already taken care of most of my needs.

It was against Simon's advice and I am sure my Mother's had she known, but I took the carriage myself. It was only a couple of streets over and I wanted to leave early if I felt the need.

Once inside the theater, I found my seat next to Verina Tudor and her new husband and thus the evening began. For the entire first set, she continually talked. She made sure I heard her by raising her voice to an annoying pitch much higher than the music. Did she not know that people did not come to hear her? I was contemplating developing a headache and leaving during the first intermission.

Shortly before nine o'clock, a great disturbance was heard in the lobby and people were leaving their seats. A man in tails and a top hat went up on the stage and whispered something to the conductor. The music stopped and we were told it would be necessary to evacuate the building immediately.

The whole audience was panic stricken as they pushed and shoved their way to the doors. Women were screaming and men were shouting at each other. A massive man stepped on my foot and his wife knocked me down on the floor. I might have been trampled to death had not a kind gentleman stopped to help me to my feet.

With great effort and a torn dress, I finally made it out the door into the open street. I could hear church bells ringing and sirens going off all over the city. The streets were full of people running in all directions. I had no idea what was going on and if anyone else did, they did not stop to tell me. I was certain we were being bombarded by the Yankees.

"God help us all," I said as I jumped into my carriage and forced Midnight through the mob. At last, I was able to get onto Market Street. Suddenly I heard a huge explosion coming from the wharfs and I watched in horror as it burst into flames higher than the buildings. I realized at once the stench in the air was burning oil from the factories.

My carriage was trapped in the middle of the street as angry fires began to leap from one building to the next. I looked back through the smoke and the fumes and saw the theater from which I had just left was now enveloped in a mass of flames. Red-hot sparks were hitting the road all around me greatly spooking Midnight. This cold winter night had suddenly turned hot by a huge bonfire burning out of control. It was all I could do to manage Midnight's fury, holding tightly on the reigns I encouraged him to proceed through the crowd.

It was a horrific sight as I made my way down the street. Negroes along side of their masters both males and females were hauling out household goods and valuables into the streets. Entire families were evacuating their homes, mothers with babies in their arms and crying children clinging to them for dear life.

One of the houses was nearly lost to the foundation, leaving an elderly woman exposed in her nightgown and her servant standing on the road sobbing bitterly in each other's arms. At the foot of Hazel Street, Russell and Old's Sash and Blind Factory was ablaze and Negro laborers were attempting to salvage it.

I was afraid the excitement was too much for Midnight and I would have to lead him the rest of the way home. I was trying with all my force to bring the carriage to a halt when a fire engine manned by Negroes came out of nowhere and nearly sideswiped my carriage.

Midnight reared up and I felt the wheels under me lifting, I was sure the carriage was going to roll. Fortunately, it collapsed back on all four wheels, but the back right wheel had broken.

Now, I had no choice but to unhook Midnight and walk. I took hold of his rope but he would not budge. I put my face next to his and looked directly into his eyes, "Dammit Midnight! If we are going to die in this hell, we are going to die together. So get your ass moving. Do you hear me?" It was as if he understood me and without force he began to follow me toward East Bay Street.

Once I turned the corner, I saw Simon running toward me. He grabbed the rope out of my hand, took control of Midnight, and told me to follow him.

"Wait, I have to know what is happening! Please tell me if the house is on fire!" I begged.

"No, the house is safe for now, but for God's sake hurry Lizzie. It ain't safe for you out here!" he called back.

We both took off running toward the house dodging through people, horses and carriages. A great pain began to develop in my side and I had to stop briefly to catch my breath. Simon looked back, "Lizzie, it is not far now. Hurry, you can make it."

When we turned on East Bay Street, I saw a wagon filled to its capacity with Negroes and others were marching along carrying picks, axes and shovels.

Simon was a good ten feet ahead of me and stopped to let me catch up with him. He told me to get on Midnight and ride like hell to the house and lock the doors! I tried to question him, but with one quick sweep, he lifted me up on Midnight and gave the horse a slap on the flank. Now, all I could do was hold on and try to steer Midnight toward the house.

As I got closer to the Bullwinkle house, I could see some of the surrounding homes were on fire. For the first time I thought about Cindy Lou, Millie and poor Mrs. Gibson. Somebody has got to help them.

The Bullwinkle house was straight ahead of me and I pulled up to the porch, jumped down and secured Midnight to the front railing. The house was dark and the door was locked. I knocked on the door, but no one answered. I pounded on the door and called inside. At last, Cindy Lou opened the door to me, *"Oh, Miss Lizzie yous iz nots dead, thanks be to Jesus!"*

I could hear voices in the parlor and I opened the door to find Mrs. Gibson and Millie sitting very calmly by the fireplace. Mrs. Gibson was reading aloud from the Bible and only paused briefly when she lifted her eyes to me,

"The Lord is my Shepherd; I shall not want.
He maketh me to lie down in green pastures:
He leadeth me beside the still waters.
He restoreth my soul:
He leadeth me in the paths of righteousness for His name' sake.
Yea, though I walk through the valley of the shadow of death,
I will fear no evil: For thou art with me.

"Mrs. Gibson, the fires! Who started the fires? Are we under Union attack?" I asked, feeling sure I would get a straight answer from her.

However, when Mrs. Gibson looked up at me, her eyes were glassy and distant like someone not of sound mind. She smiled at me and in an oddly pleasant voice said, "My dear don't you know that it is the end of the world? No need to make a fuss about it. Just come and sit down and we will all wait for Jesus together."

"No, No!" I said pulling Cindy Lou out of the chair. "We have got to work fast and get some of the valuables out of the house before the fire gets here."

Cindy Lou and Millie started to get up, but Mrs. Gibson called out to them, "Wait children the Lord is coming. Do you not want to see Jesus?"

"Yes, I do Mrs. Gibson, but not tonight!" I declared. "Now Cindy Lou, you and Millie get on your feet and help me load up the wagon. We are all going to Sandy Ridge tonight. You to, Mrs. Gibson!" I ordered.

"Cindy Lou looked at me and shouted, "Mammy?"

"Yes, Mammy!" I said. "Now get your things together, Simon will be here any minute." I turned to Mrs. Gibson, "Do you have anything special you wish to take with you? I will have Millie help you."

"Why, no child. Why should I go anywhere? If I am going to die I would just as soon do it here."

I did not have time to argue with her right then, but I was not going to leave her there. I met Simon on the porch and told him my plan. Together we hooked up the other two horses to a small wagon and loaded up a few precious items including Clarence's medical journals.

Midnight would pull Clarence's carriage and Simon would drive the wagon, Cindy Lou and Millie were ready, but Mrs. Gibson could not be persuaded to leave.

"Fine," I said and called out for Simon. "Load her up in the carriage, we are leaving now!" Simon scooped Mrs. Gibson up and threw her over his shoulder and she began kicking and screaming. Millie held the door ajar for them to pass through, but Mrs. Gibson braced her feet against the doorframe and took hold of the curtains. I was afraid I had hurt her when I forced her hands loose and took hold of her ankles. With great struggle, it had taken all four of us to get her in the carriage, but not before she had given Simon a bloody lip and ripped the front off my dress.

Cindy Lou was sitting on the screaming Mrs. Gibson as I took off down the road with Simon following. Once we were heading north out of town, I was relieved to see things seemed normal. I was fairly sure we were not being attacked now, but if this fire was an accident, I could not be sure. All I knew for sure was I wanted to go home to Sandy Ridge. I wanted to be with Papa, Mother and Mammy and I was willing to risk my life to get there.

After being on the road for just a short while, Mrs. Gibson calmed down and soon she was asleep. Cindy Lou said, *"She done and wore hers selfs out, or else she iz deads."*

We both laughed, mostly just letting off some of the tension, but not at Mrs. Gibson's expense. Out here alone in the dark, I looked back at the enormous clouds of smoke. I felt like I was reliving a dream I had not so long ago.

It was long past midnight when we arrived at Sandy Ridge. I knocked loudly at the door. Before anyone came to the door. I saw Samuel coming up from the slave quarters. He was carrying the rifle that Papa had given him.

"Samuel, it is me, Lizzie!" I shouted, afraid he would take aim at me.

"Lizzie, what da tarnation iz yous doin'outs heres, in da mid night?"

"There's been a fire in town, a terrible fire. I have got to talk to Papa." I knocked harder and called out until the door opened and Papa stood before me. I had not given thought to how I must look until I saw the look on Papa's face.

"Lizzie," he said in soft voice. "What has happened to you?"

I threw myself in his arms and collapsed. The next morning the news had spread all over South Carolina about the great fire that was burning its way through the town of Charleston. Thousands of people were homeless and left roaming the streets. Most of Charleston was destroyed; shops, factories, government buildings, banks, churches, cathedrals, theaters and hotels.

Simon told Papa he heard the fire was started by a band of rioting runaway slaves from the middle part of the state. They were supposedly armed and dangerous. Papa left mid-morning to find out the truth and to assess the damage. We were anxious to know if the Bullwinkle house and Mrs. Gibson's had survived.

Mrs. Gibson told Mother she could not remember a thing that happened the night before. Her mind was a complete blank even as to how she got to Sandy Ridge. I will always suspect she did recall, but was embarrassed at how badly she behaved.

It was late afternoon when Papa returned with the news from town. It was true most of Charleston was destroyed. Although the fire was losing ground, it was still spreading. Thankfully, as early as this morning trains were coming in with supplies and extra workers to help fight the fires. Miss Georgette's dress shop was gone as well as the Cotton Press with thousands of pounds of cotton belonging to local planters including Papa. As far as the rumored slave uprising, it appears to be unfounded at the time. A band of Negroes were seen marching through town with shovels, picks and axes, but were found out to be on a mission to help fight the fires.

Papa sat down and held his head in his hands, "I cannot believe this has happened. Dear God was the war not enough that you had to destroy us from within too? What on earth have we done to deserve all this?"

Mother walked over and put her hand on his shoulder, "Now Jacob, You cannot lose your faith over all of this. Pull yourself together and we will all get through this."

Papa stood up and glared at Mother as if he were angry with her, "You have no idea Tempie, no idea!"

Mother did not show any emotion as Papa stormed out the door. She sat down and picked up her needlework as if nothing had happened and Mrs. Gibson read from her book. I decided the both of them had truly lost their senses.

I went upstairs to write to Sallie and tell her of what had happened as well as write to Sister Irene. If God had seen reason to spare the Bullwinkle house and me, perhaps it was for the sake of the children. I would go to New York as a soldier of faith.

I finished my letters and got up to look out the window. I could see a huge cloud of smoke rising from the back of the fields. In horror, I ran downstairs calling out to everyone, "The fields are on fire!"

Mother raised her head to say, "Yes, your father set the fires."

"Why?" I screamed at her trying to get some kind of reaction.

"Something he said he had to do. Go ask him dear, he is in his study," she said and looked back down at her handwork.

I walked down the hall, feeling angry with Mother. I was beginning to detest this new personality of hers.

I found Papa sitting quietly at his desk looking out the window at the fire.

"Papa, what is happening?" I asked almost not wanting to know the answer.

"Lizzie, the Union has already taken over Beaufort and a good part of the waterways. If those Bastards come through here, they will take everything they can get their hands on. They will sell our Negroes and Cotton for a big fat profit, while the blockage is preventing me from making one red penny. I have hired out most of the Negroes to work on the railways and it is for damn sure I would rather sit here and watch my cotton burn than see the Yankees take it!"

CHAPTER 21

Hell's Window

January 9, 1862
New York Park Hotel

Dear Sallie,

I am very glad to hear your Christmas holiday was pleasant. We understood why you did not come to Sandy Ridge. Believe me Dear Sister, you did not miss much. Mother is physically well, but her mind is as cold as stone. I am not sure to the cause of her indifference, but she is becoming more withdrawn with every passing day. Papa is very unhappy too and I am not sure if it is all to do with Mother. He says if this war goes on much longer, he is sure to get called up. I heard him tell Mr. Jones he felt he ought to sign up anyway. Perhaps you did not know, but Mr. Jones has since left to join up. Samuel is in charge of overseeing what is left of the Negroes. Papa hired out most of the males to work on the railways.

I was most thankful the Bullwinkle house was spared from the great fire as well as many of the other houses on my street. I am staying in town most of the time now and it was my suggestion that Mrs. Jones and little Ladybug move in with Mother and Papa while Mr. Jones is away.

I have been busy with all the projects I have in place.

The Medical Clinic and the duties of the house are nearly a full time job. Yet, I am also helping with the relief efforts for the victims of the fire, which is why I have resorted to working on Sundays at the Soldiers Aid.

Have you heard from Mrs. Cuthbert in Beaufort? You do know that all the white people fled from Beaufort just as soon as Federal troops took over the forts. Some came to Charleston, but I hear a good part of them left the state altogether. The newspapers say the Yankees are making themselves at home down there and living it up in Southern style. They have even sent for their wives and children. I say it is a disgrace.

Now for my news from New York. I hope you will forgive me for the length of this letter, but there is so much to speak of, none of which is too pleasurable. I am so homesick I could cry and I still have seven more days before I will be leaving. I spend nearly every evening alone in this awful hotel. I am freezing as I write to you now, the service is poor and the staff workers are rude and indifferent to your needs. The window from my highrise apartment I have very appropriately named "Hell's Window," for it is from this great vantage point that I look upon this city of wickedness.

All this being said, I am holding up well even though I have lost a few pounds since my arrival. Fear not, I am not ill, but the food I find mostly unfit to eat.

I think you will find this rather amusing. When the nuns came to Charleston, arrangements were made for them to overnight at my home before we left to go to New York. When we first met, they looked at me as if they were very disturbed. I was afraid they were not pleased with the accommodations or disapproved of staying in a household managed by slaves.

The next morning, I was already dressed to leave when Sister Irene came to speak with me. She told me they had

227

decided my appearance would attract far too much attention; however, they had a solution. When I stepped on the train, I was dressed in the holy habit and white coif of the sisterhood. It is not so becoming, but I admit it does not attract much attention. Since I have been here, they insist I wear the attire on every outing. I am becoming dreadfully tired of this plainer.

Sallie, one visit here is enough to last me a lifetime. You have never seen the likes of such filth in all your life. Tall buildings stacked to the sky with thousands of people living in just one city block. The rat-infested streets are lined with piles of garbage and sewage. The stench makes me so nauseous that I am relieved to stay inside as much as possible.

The cobblestone streets are busy twenty-four hours a day and are badly in need of repair, with large cracks that are packed with trash and horse manure. Chickens, cats, pigs and dogs roam the streets and vile stagnated water backs up in the courtyards.

People are in every spot you look, many of them German and Irish immigrants living on the streets or in the shabbiest dwellings. It is a heartbreaking sight to see how many children are abandoned and living in conditions not fit for animals. Not only are the children mistreated but the horses are badly abused and sickly. They soon die and the carcasses are left on the street to rot. Just yesterday, I saw a group of children climbing up and down and playing on a dead horse.

Maybe the miserable conditions here have contributed to such immoral trades such as gambling, prostitution and drunkenness. Sister Irene says there are rapes, robberies and murders here nightly, but few are ever arrested for the crimes. Not only are the people vulnerable to such crimes, but disease spreads rapidly under an unsanitary environment. Presently there is an outbreak of cholera and tuberculosis.

Overflowing public water closets are less than five feet from household wells. I have even witnessed ladies tossing out chamber pots filled with night soil onto the sidewalks.

I have a grim view of this city, although Sister Irene explained to me that the privileged enjoy immensely the theaters, restaurants and luxurious hotels. Even with her suggestions, I think I shall not return to experience them. I now understand how much work there is to accomplish in this world for the sake of children.

Tomorrow, at last, I am to meet with Dr. Holloway. I am very hopeful that it will have a favorable outcome. Therefore, I will close for now and try to get some rest before my big day tomorrow.

With all my love,
Lizzie

I was to meet with Sister Irene and Dr. Holloway for lunch downstairs in the hotel restaurant. I debated on adorning myself again in the nun's attire, but this time I decided it would be more appropriate to represent myself honestly and I would feel more confident in my gray traveling suit.

I was not convinced of the safety of the hotel's new Otis elevator. I suppose New York has many lazy people. I took the steps and it was shortly before noon when I walked in the café. I asked the waiter to seat me at a table for three by the window. It was a nice sunny day and I thought I might take advantage of a little warmth. The room was empty except for a man sitting in the back corner and a dark skinned Negro woman sitting alone at a table by the door. The waiter poured my tea as I observed the well-dressed Negro woman elegantly drinking tea and reading her newspaper. I fleetingly gave thought to this oddity, but it was nearly half passed the hour and Sister and Dr. Holloway were late.

When I finished my tea, I asked the waiter to check with the hotel concierge to see if there were any messages for me. While waiting for him to return I saw Sister Irene come through the door.

I lifted my hand, but she walked in the opposite direction. Feeling that she had not seen me I stood up to be more visible. I was puzzled to see her stop to speak to the Negro woman. I was still standing as the Negro woman and Sister Irene walked over to my table.

"Miss Sanders, this is Dr. Holloway," Sister Irene said with a smile, knowing she had completely caught me off guard.

"Nice to meet you, Miss Sanders," the Negro woman said extending a clean white gloved hand to me.

"Pleased I am sure," I returned. At that moment, I could have been knocked over with a feather. Not only was Dr. Frances Holloway a woman, she was a Negro.

Sister Irene took a seat first and Dr. Holloway and I followed suit. She raised her hand to the waiter and he came running with the teapot and three menus. As we placed our orders, I was impressed by the way Dr. Holloway conducted herself. Her manners and speech were altogether sophisticated and if not for her outward appearance, I would have sworn I was lunching with a Southern Belle.

Sister Irene encouraged Dr. Holloway to speak on her qualifications. With confidence, but without arrogance, Dr. Holloway began to give me her background. "Miss Sanders, I apologize for the shock we may have inflicted upon you. Sister Irene was afraid that prejudices would have stood in the way of us meeting had you known of my sex or race beforehand. I understand I am not what you expected and my existence is inconceivable to you. Let me assure you, Miss Sanders, that women are going to reach equality to men and I believe education is our key to success. In England where I attended medical school there are many such as myself. Sadly, the number of Negro women with degrees is still a rarity."

I was enthralled by her words and Sister Irene looked at me and nodded her head, as if to say "I told you so." Whether she came to Charleston or not, I just had to know more about her. I ate in silence for a few minutes as I tried to find the proper words to address her.

When I began to speak my words came out all wrong, "Dr. Holloway, how did you do this? I mean, who do you feel has influenced your career? "

Dr. Holloway looked at me for a minute; her sparkling eyes were as dark as coal and her skin nearly a match. Even with her African features she was quite a handsome woman with a pleasing smile, "Miss Sanders, let us let down our guard and talk as one friend to another. Do not be afraid of insulting me; thick skin comes with the territory. May I call you Lizzie?" she asked.

"Of course," I said. I suddenly realized there was a warmness about her that gave me the feeling I had known her all my life.

"Well, you may call me Fannie," she said and took a sip of her tea. She set the cup down slowly on the table and paused for a moment, appearing to be admiring its rose pattern.

When she lifted her head to speak, her eyes were watery as if something sad had invaded her thoughts. "Lizzie, you and I are more alike than you might think. I am not, nor have my family ever been slaves. My father was a free man of color and owned a sugar cane plantation in Louisiana. Now, for something that might surprise you even more, we also owned slaves. When my mother died, my Father sent me to Massachusetts to live with my aunt who called herself a nurse. She had no formal medical training, only a great desire to help the suffering of all classes of people. I too shared her compassion and worked along side her to learn her trade. When I was eighteen, I was hired as a nurse to work for a doctor in Boston. He recognized I was eager to learn. I confided in him I would like to be a doctor. He wrote a letter of recommendation to a women's college in London, where I was accepted. While I was away at school, my father got sick and lost the plantation. I have not been back to Louisiana since he died."

She pushed her teacup away, folded her arms on the table, leaned forward and raised her eyebrows waiting for my response. A million thoughts were running through my mind. She certainly was qualified and her motives seemed pure, but would Charleston accept a Negro woman doctor? Disregarding my hesitations, I told her about my plan and she listened intently and asked questions on certain points. She did not flinch as I explained the terms would be room and board only, but there was the potential to build a successful practice.

Sister Irene told Dr. Holloway about Charleston and described the Bullwinkle home as charming and spacious. She hoped the Bullwinkle Clinic would work with the orphan train program to pre-qualify families who are interested in adoptions.

Fannie shook her head as if she agreed, "Well Lizzie, as you know, I have nothing to lose here. As I see it, you have everything to gain. I am not naive to the fact that we will have our work cut out from day one. I am well aware the southern whites will not readily accept me. However, I believe all things happen under the watchful eye of God and I am sure we have not been brought together by mere chance. Nothing has come easy for me. My success has come through hard work, a humble heart and a willingness to prove myself to others. Lastly, remember I told you I had thick skin."

"Well, is it a deal ladies?" Sister Irene asked, looking at me and then to Fannie.

I felt pressured and wished that somehow I could talk to Papa before I gave my answer.

However, I heard Fannie say, "Yes!"

"Yes!" flowed out of my mouth as well.

The next couple of days seemed to fly by. Fannie and I spent almost every moment together talking and planning the clinic. I was glad for the time I had spent studying Clarence's medical journals and I could see Fannie and Clarence were of like minds.

My last night in the hotel I wrote home only to say I would be returning on Friday, January 17th, with Dr. Holloway. She had proven to be an amazing woman and I would let her prove herself to Charleston.

Again, the nuns would travel back with us to Charleston and I would masquerade as one of them. I was more upset than

Fannie was over the seating arrangements. Hers would be in the service car with the slaves.

We were due into Charleston around three o'clock in the afternoon. For the last couple of hours I watched a slow peppering of snow falling on the landscape. When we arrived at Charleston, the ground was already covered. I saw Simon bundled up and waiting for us in the carriage. I was thankful he had the foresight to find out our arrival time

It was here that I was to say my good-byes to the sisters; they would be traveling on to Savannah. I gathered my belongings and waited in the back of the train to reunite with Fannie.

"I did not expect to see snow here. I thought we had left it behind us," Fannie said as she pulled a funny little wool hat with a bright colored feather down on her head.

"Snow is not a common sight for Charleston, but not as uncommon as seeing the likes of you," I replied, teasing her.

We both were laughing when Simon approached me regarding my luggage. He barely looked over at Fannie and asked the whereabouts of Dr. Holloway. I was feeling playful and said, "Oh the doctor is coming, this is Fannie."

"Oh, alright, nice to meet you Miss Fannie, you must be the nurse," Simon innocently assumed.

Fannie caught on to my game and covered her mouth to hide her laughter. Simon loaded our luggage and we headed to the house. I was reconnected with the horror of the night of the fire with every block we traveled. There were some efforts here and there of reconstruction and several plots looked to have newly laid foundations.

Cindy Lou met us at the door and looked on with wonderment at Dr. Holloway. I still made no effort to explain. I instructed Simon and Millie to take Fannie's things up to the second floor bedroom across from mine. The two of them went upstairs whispering.

Fannie said the house was lovely and could not wait to see the clinic. I took her straight away to Clarence's office and we closed the door. We had been so caught up in our orientation that we forgot the time. It was seven o'clock and we had not eaten a bite since late morning.

Millie prepared something for dinner and we sat down together to eat. I told Cindy Lou we would take our coffee and pie in the parlor. Although not one word was said to me about our new houseguest, it was without doubt that plenty was said behind closed doors.

The next morning, bright and early, Fannie and I went back down the hall to start to work. I was only beginning to see the depth of her knowledge. I watched as she precisely organized the medicines and compounds. She was sitting at the desk with her feet propped up engrossed in one of Clarence's journals when Simon walked in the door. Before she could get her feet off the desk, Papa walked in behind him. Both men looked shocked to see her reclined back and me on the floor sorting a sack of herbs.

"Lizzie?" Papa said, almost in an angry tone.

I jumped to my feet and dusted off the front of my dress and Fannie slowly lowered her thick little feet off the desk. "Oh, Papa it is good to see you," I said, and gave him a big hug.

"I came by hoping to speak to the doctor on your Mother's behalf, but Simon tells me he has not arrived," Papa said in a serious tone.

"What is the matter with Mother?" I asked and looked at Fannie who had now regained her professional appearance.

"She has a chest cold which has lingered on far too long. Mammy fears possible pneumonia," Papa said, with great concern.

"Pneumonia?" Fannie asked, making her the center of attention.

Papa looked irritated at her interference and turned to speak to me directly, "Perhaps not, but I think I will ride over to Summerville to speak to the doctor there.

"No need to do that Papa," I said, now realizing it was time to reveal the truth.

"Dr. Holloway, I would like you to meet my father, Jacob Sanders," I said, going over to stand beside Fannie.

Simon gasped as Fannie walked over and extended her hand to Papa. He did not accept her hand and turned to walk out of the room. "Lizzie! I will see you in the parlor."

I turned to offer an apology to Fannie, but she only smiled and said, "Remember I have thick skin, my friend."

Papa was pacing the floor in the parlor and had lit a cigar; he rarely smokes in the house. When I walked in the room, he looked at me and took a long draw on his cigar. I was wishing I had some brandy to offer him, or for that matter, myself.

"My dear girl, have you lost your mind? What on earth were you thinking and furthermore whose idea was it to pull such a stunt as this?" Papa asked. Then he sat down firmly in the rocker making it bounce on the floor.

"Sister Irene, sir," I said, trying to watch my tone.

"Well, now I know why I am not Catholic! I sent you to New York in what I thought were good hands, thinking that some good might come out of it. Now you come home with this voodoo priestess!"

"Papa, I am prepared for this challenge and I assure you I have not acted without reason or in haste. Dr. Frances Holloway is a free colored woman and graduated from the Bedford College for Women in London, England. With honors I might add, she has come highly recommend by not only the nuns but her peers as well."

"Well, it sounds like you are sold on this Darkie, but your Mother needs a real doctor, a white man. So, before I waste more time on this foolishness, I am off to Summerville!"

Simon heard the whole thing and was standing in the hall with Papa's hat and coat. He attempted to help Papa with his coat and hat, but he jerked them out of his hand and stomped to the door. He opened the door and turned back to me, "We will talk later, Theodosia Elizabeth Sanders!"

"Oh, Theodosia Elizabeth," Fannie said sticking her head out from around the corner. "Daddy is not happy."

"No, Daddy is not happy," I said, and turned to see her and Simon laughing at me.

"Well, we just have to see if we can change Daddy's mind, won't we," I said, looking at the two of them acting like old friends.

I did not hear from Papa or Mother for nearly a week and I felt it was reason to be concerned. On Wednesday, I asked Simon to drive me to Sandy Ridge. As we were preparing to leave, Fannie came out dressed in her funny little hat and carrying her medical bag.

"I will go with you. If the doctor in Summerville was not able to help your Mother, perhaps your father will reconsider. I have found people not so hard headed when they are desperate. If all is well, I will just wait in the carriage with Simon."

Who was I to disagree with a woman whose mind was already made up? Doctor or not, she was a real friend if she would agree to be in the company of my father after the way he treated her. When we arrived at Sandy Ridge, Simon secured the carriage to the back of the house as not to be visible by the windows. I was glad the weather was mild if they were to wait outside. I got out and went to the door alone.

Mammy came to the door and nearly pulled me inside the house, *"Lord Child, I'z sho glad yous come. Yo Mama ain't doin' no good at 'tal. Dat doctor done send over his medince and been down here two time, but she ain't takin' to none of it,"* Mammy pulled out a rag to blow her nose, but I did not wait to hear more and took off upstairs to Mother's room.

"Mother, it's me Lizzie," I said, kneeling down by her bed.

She opened her eyes partly and raised her hand to touch mine. I brushed the hair from her face and she smiled. Her head was wet and her face was nearly transparent except for flushed red patches on her cheeks. Mother squeezed my hand and tried to sit up in bed, "Lizzie," she said, in a deathly voice.

I turned around to see Papa standing behind me, "Papa please let Dr. Holloway at least come in and see if she can help. Please Papa, for my sake."

Papa nodded and I got up to go for Fannie, but first I caught hold of his hand before I opened the door. I was in such a hurry I almost fell over Mammy coming up the stairs.

When Fannie saw me, she jumped out of the carriage without asking any questions and followed me into the house. Papa opened the door and stepped aside to let Fannie through. "Miss...Dr. Holloway, I don't know what to say," Papa said looking at her very humbly.

"Well then say nothing, my friend," Fannie replied. She patted him on the back and gave him a warm smile. "Now, take me to my patient, this is not a time to dilly-dally around."

Papa led her upstairs. At Fannie's request, he tried to tell us what treatment the other doctor had administered. Papa's voice was trembling as he spoke, "First we were giving her quinine and chest dressings of mustard plaster. When that gave no relief, the doctor came and gave her an inhalant of ether. He told us to keep a window cracked to allow clean pure air in the room at all times. She is steadily getting worse. He says we should just try to keep her comfortable and left us a bottle of laudanum.

"He expects her to die," Fannie said rather bluntly. "And he should because he is killing her!"

I looked directly at Fannie, "Can you save her?"

"If she is not already in the grave there is always hope," she replied and opened the bedroom door.

Mammy looked shocked when we came in with Fannie, but stepped back to let her approach Mother. Papa and I stood at the back of the room holding hands.

"Mrs. Sanders, can you hear me?" Fannie asked. I did not hear Mother reply, but she must have because Fannie said, "Very good. I am Dr. Holloway. Together we can conquer this monster, but I am going to need you to put your faith in me and your trust in the good Lord. Can you do that?"

This time I heard her try to speak, but it was more of a death rattle.

"Lizzie, go and close that window right this minute and you, kind lady, bring two kettles of boiling water," she said looking at Mammy. "Mr. Sanders, we need to heat this room up as hot as Hell's fire. Go tell your man to bring up more firewood and about twenty bricks. Lizzie you are in charge of bringing me a stack of wool blankets and flannel sheets."

No one questioned her orders. We just obeyed. I ran into all the bedrooms and pulled the blankets and sheets right off the beds. When I came back, Fannie had her ear to Mother's chest listening to her breath. We wrapped Mother up tightly in the blankets. I stood back to watch Fannie finish her examination. First, she examined Mother's tongue and asked her to spit on a white cloth. I gasped when I saw the thick rusty spot on the cloth. I knew by reading the medical books, Fannie was concerned about Mother's blood when she pulled her eyelids down and checked her fingernails. Lastly, she parted Mothers lips and put several drops in her mouth from a small brown bottle.

When Mammy came back with two kettles of boiling water, Fannie moved the bedside tables as close to the head of the bed and possible. She cleared them off and Mammy set the steaming pots on each side of the bed. Fannie put several drops of oil into each and within seconds, the room smelled of wintergreen or perhaps eucalyptus. The fire was blazing now; Fannie heated the bricks and placed them next to Mother on top of the blankets. Within just a few minutes Mother was asleep and Fannie made a motion for us to follow her outside in the hall.

She lowered her voice to speak, "We are all going to have to work at this hot and heavy around the clock if we are to sweat this infection out of her lungs. Here is what is to be done. The room is to remain hot, free of drafts and the steam pots going at all times. Mammy, you are to see she gets a cup of hot milk with 2 tablespoons of beef broth and 1 tablespoon of whiskey every 2 hours. Once she awakes, I will start the steam baths and clearing of the lungs."

When Mother had rested and drunk the milk, the bathing tub was brought into the room and set down by the fire. To the steamy tub of water Fannie added salt, mustard and soda. It took Fannie and Mammy both to help me get Mother undressed and into the bath. Fannie said she was to be vigorously massaged while in the hot water. Afterwards a chest lotion of lard and winterberry was to be applied. We lifted her up and wrapped her wet skin in a flannel sheet, put her back in bed, covered her with the wool blankets and hot bricks. Fannie gave her a few drops of medicine and we let her rest a while with the steamy eucalyptus pots filling the air.

In less than forty-five minutes Mother began to cough as though she was choking to death. Fannie was asleep slumped over in a chair by the fireplace. When she heard Mother, she jumped up and ordered Mammy to bring the chamber pot.

"What is happening?" I asked, afraid Mother was dying

"Lizzie, help me turn her over on her belly," Fannie said as she climbed up in the bed with Mother. I stood back and watched as Fannie began to beat on Mother's back with her fist. "Cough, Mrs. Sanders and when the infection boils up spit it into the pot," she said to Mother who could barely hold her head over the side of the bed.

The treatment seemed rather barbaric, but I did not interfere. I felt my stomach churning when the thick yellow liquid splattered with blood hit the bottom of the pot. I was forced to run out of the room. Fannie insisted everyone that entered Mother's room tie a cloth over their nose and mouth and wash their hands with lye soap. In addition, bedside tables were washed down with a germicide of vinegar and water. Even her sheets and clothing were to be washed in boiling water. This was to be our routine for the next seven days. Simon brought Fannie fresh clothing, and she bedded down on the floor outside Mother's room.

On the fourth day of treatment, Mother sat up in bed and ate solid foods. The sixth day she was walking and two weeks later she was able to make her first trip into town where she was greeted warmly at Society Hall.

News spread quickly of Mother's miraculous cure and her Negro woman doctor who saved her life. One by one, the people came to the Bullwinkle Clinic. Yes, it is true; God does work in the most mysterious ways.

CHAPTER 22

Spring of 1862

I walked the same route as I had for the past two months. The trees were budding and birds were happily singing. The joy they felt was not mine. As the war campaigns continued, staggering numbers of wounded and sick soldiers were pouring into Charleston. In addition to running the clinic, Fannie and I were recruited to work at the hospitals. Fannie was a good teacher and it amazed me how much I had learned just by watching her. I still flinched at the sight of blood, but I could change a bandage almost as well as she could. In time, I would become almost immune to the soldier's misery and could perform my duties without the slightest faintness of heart.

It was while I was working at the hospital I first saw him. He was on a mission of concern for the safety of Sullivan's Island and Fort Pulaski. The minute he entered the room I recognized him as a man who commanded respect; yet there was nothing about him arrogant or intimidating. His face was perfectly proportioned and his gray hair and beard were neatly trimmed. He stood about 6 feet tall and carried himself with grace and ease. He was well received by all the soldiers and his visit seemed to give them encouragement and a purpose to their suffering.

He made his rounds and was leaving, but he unintentionally passed over a young soldier I was attending. The boy, who had been badly wounded, told me he wanted very much to meet Lee. I found myself running after the General in hopes of retrieving him before he got out of sight. When I told General Lee about the boy, he followed me back to his bedside. He knelt down on one knee so the boy could plainly see him. When he spoke, his voice was as soft as velvet. I will never forget the tenderness I saw in his dark keen eyes that day. *I knew without doubt that Robert E. Lee was no ordinary man; he was born to be a leader and destined to be a hero.*

After General Lee left, I discovered a button had popped off his uniform. I picked up the button and showed it to the young soldier. He took it in his hand and clasped his fingers around it as if it were a precious jewel. For the rest of the afternoon, I sat on the little metal stool next to soldier John, wiping his brow and reading to him from the Bible.

Toward nightfall, he asked if I would sing to him. "What shall I sing?" I asked.

"How's 'bout Dixie, if you knows it," he rattled in a low watery voice.

"Of course," I said and I began to sing softly. The other men in the bunks lying next to him quickly detected my song, first one and then others began to sing along. Soldier John smiled, closed his eyes and the button he had so cherished fell to the floor. I picked up the button and slipped it into my apron pocket.

That night going home Fannie told me, "The first one is the hardest. After about a dozen or more, you'll get numb." She put her arm around me and we walked home in silence. Millie had supper waiting, but I was not to eat. I wanted to be alone and went straight to my room. I took the button out of my pocket, held it in my hand, and wept for the death of soldier John.

The days were finding us working long hours. Simon handled the bookkeeping and the accounts receivable; what there were of them. I was proud to say Millie and Cindy Lou both had become good nurses. The days of sitting in the parlor and watching people go by were long gone. By the time my day was over, I was too tired to eat and fell asleep in my clothes.

On the rare days I did not work, I worked on scrapbooking. My newspaper stack was piled high from January to June. I was too busy living history to record it. I no longer saw my scrapbooking as a pastime or a pleasant hobby, but as a living eyewitness account for future generations, should there be a future generation. Millie and Cindy Lou often helped clip the headlines,

February 6, 1862: Ulysses Grant and the Union troops seize Fort Henry.

Lincoln comes to Grant's defense despite rumors of drunkenness, which is said to have resulted in Grant's falling of his horse. His own men are calling for his removal, but Lincoln is quoted as saying, "I can't spare this man, he fights!"

February 20, 1862: President Lincoln's son dies of typhoid fever. Ten-year-old William (Willie) Lincoln dies after ninety hours of suffering."

February 22, 1862: Union forces occupy Nashville, Tennessee.

Thomas (Stonewall) Jackson in Shenandoah Valley.

March 6, 1862: Lincoln plans to free slaves and reimburse their owners in Union Border States.

March 11, 1862: Lincoln removes General George (Little Mac) McClellan.

March 13, 1862: General Robert E. Lee assigned as military advisor to President Davis.

April 6-7, 1862: Battle of Shiloh, Tennessee is a blood bath! Over 20,000 causalities, wounded and missing. Union claims Victory.

April 16, 1862: Confederate Congress passed the Conscription Act! All white males ages 18-35 are required to serve for three years.

Two North Carolina Cities, Newbern and Camden have fallen under control of the Union.

New Orleans surrenders to Union. General Benjamin Butler's troops now occupy the South's largest city.

Sparks began to fly when the news spread of the unmerciful treatment the people of New Orleans were receiving from General Butler and his troops. People were outraged to hear citizens were being robbed and forced to turn over their homes to Federal officers. Women were afraid to leave their houses and rumors spread of the uncivilized behavior of drunken Yankee soldiers taken up with Negro prostitutes. Our General Beauregard was outraged with General Butler's threat to arrest the women citizens as common prostitutes should they insult or show contempt to any of his soldiers. In no time, General Butler earned his name as 'Beast Butler.' He had become the dictator of New Orleans. He even resorted to hanging local men who cut down the US flag or would not swear allegiance to the Union.

In May, just right out in the Charleston harbor Robert Smalls led other slaves in the overtaking of a steamship and turning it over to the Union. Needless to say, we were all afraid of what might happen next.

Dear Lord,
    Show mercy on us. We are falling prey to the enemy. If this be the end, then help me to be strong and offer up what I have to serve you.
    St. Luke 12:35: Let your lions be girded about and your lights burning.

Sometimes, I ask myself, why we take things as a surprise when, if we had been looking ahead, we could plainly have seen it was inevitable. Such was the case, when we learned Ransom and Joel had been conscripted into the Army. Ransom with the

42nd Regiment of North Carolina, Company H and Joel with the 5th Regiment of North Carolina, Company E.

Papa actually received Joel's letter ahead of Sallie's breaking the news on both accounts. Joel offered up his house to us as a place of refuge, if at any point Charleston should be invaded. He sold most of his horses to the military. He kept one to take with him and the others were placed in the custody of a neighbor.

Monday, June 2, 1862

Fannie and I had just gotten home from working at the hospital, when Papa knocked at the door. I was prepared to see the delivery boy with supplies, but not Papa.

Just as unprepared as I was to see him, he was shocked at my appearance. I invited him to the parlor, where Fannie and I were indulging in a glass of sherry. It was becoming our daily habit and served to help us recuperate after the days at the hospital.

When Papa entered the room, Fannie stood up to leave. "No, you don't have to leave on my account" Papa said and took a seat.

I noticed Papa's eyes were still on my bloody apron. I took it off, folded it quickly and tucked it under my chair, "Well, to what do we owe this pleasure?"

"I have a letter here from your sister, with news you might need to know. In fact I would also like Dr. Holloway's input on this matter as well." He removed the letter from its sleeve and began to read.

"*My dearest family,*

I am writing to you today with good news and bad news. I will first warm your heart with the good news I am with child again. I have written Ransom and he is happy, but he fears he may not be home for the birth of the baby. He signed up for just 12 months, but now it looks like they will have three more years.

I was thankful, up until now, he has been nearby in Salisbury working as a prison guard. Now he writes his company will be detached to Camp Ashby, near Lynchburg, Virginia to guard prisoners captured by Stonewall's troops.

Mr. Huneycutt had to close the store. No use keeping the doors open if you have nothing to sell. Even what he could manage to get in, the price was so high folks could not pay it. We put us in a real pretty garden. The tomatoes and beans are coming off now and soon we will be getting potatoes and corn. All us women got together last week and canned us up a bunch. Harper planted enough of black-eyed peas to feed all the pigs and cows and he said we can eat them too if we have to. I hope ya'll have got a nice garden too. It takes a plenty to feed all the mouths at Sandy Ridge.

Now for the more distressing news. As you know Joel and Ransom are in separate units, but their paths have crossed and they regularly exchange letters. Joel Simpson's regiment was present at the battle of Williamsburg. Ransom received no correspondence from Joel thereafter. He wrote his commanding officer on the whereabouts of his friend. He was to receive a letter back stating Joel had been wounded and captured. He is being held at Fort Delaware prison.

As to the nature of the wound, a source tells Ransom that Joel was shot in the foot, which prevented him from escaping with the others. I hope his injuries are mild in nature. It is the prison that is a great concern. They say they are not fit for man nor rodent. The dark filthy condition renders the men subject to lice and parasites, resulting in Typhus or Jail Fever. I have read where many of the men are dying before they can be exchanged or released. We will all have to pray he can maintain his health.

I have heard from Thomas and he is well, but he says food and medical supplies are thin. Measles, yellow fever, pneumonia, typhoid are all feared. However, he says they all suffer from what he calls "quick step," which I learned is the loosening of the bowels.

245

Before I close I must tell you little Minerva is learning to walk and is babbling all sorts of funny little sounds. As to TJ, she is practically a little lady and is as pretty as our dear Annabelle. I do wish you could see them both. I hope to be able to get a photograph to send to you soon. Take care and write to me just as often as you are able.

Love, Sallie."

Papa folded the letter and looked back and forth at both of us. I made an effort to bite back my tears, but the significant effect the letter had on me was obvious to both of them.

I stood up, turned my back to them and looked out the window. Papa walked over, put his arm around me, and said, "Lizzie, you don't have to suffer alone. Joel talked to me about his feelings for you. I can only assume you have feelings for him as well."

My silence was answer enough. Before anyone could say more, someone knocked on the front door. Seconds later, Simon carried in a large package, "Dr. Fannie your medicines have been delivered." Simon looked surprised to see Papa and apologized for interrupting.

"Good, thank you Simon, just set the box there by the door," Fannie said, looking at the box as if her mind were wandering. "You know something, if even one package like this could be delivered to the prisoners, hundreds of lives could be saved."

Papa and I both stopped dead and looked at her. It was one of those moments where great ideas come out of nowhere. "Fannie, how is it, you are able to get medical supplies, when the rest of the South has been cut off?"

"Easy, I have the supplies sent to Sister Irene and she, in turn, sends them to me in a package marked *Bibles*," Fannie replied.

"Can you get more?" Papa asked, as the wheels began to turn.

"I suppose so, as long as supplies are available and the mail is still running," she said, now seemly catching on to the idea.

246

"Fannie, is it not true the nuns would be sympathetic to the suffering of all men, Yankees and Southerners alike?" Papa probed deeper.

Before Fannie could answer, I shouted out, "yes! Furthermore, the nuns could easily be granted safe passage in and out of all the prison camps. With all the clothes they wear, they could personally carry in enough medical supplies to sustain a whole prison camp."

"Lizzie, do you really think you can convince them to reduce themselves to being common smugglers?" Fannie asked.

"I don't think I can, I must convince them, and I will!" Hearing my own words, I felt empowered by a force greater than myself.

Papa left that day with the mind set to call together the "Masons." He hoped to organize a secret mission to deliver supplies directly to the Confederate encampments. He agreed it could be dangerous. Yet, he reminded me the Masons have their connections. The next morning, I sent my letter off to Sister Irene.

June 3, 1862

My dearest Sister Irene,

First, I want to tell you what a blessing Dr. Holloway has been, not only to myself, but also, to the people of Charleston. She has proven not only to be a good doctor, but a good friend as well. I will forever be grateful to you for making our acquaintance.

However, the reason for my letter is to ask for your help once more. I hope that God will open your heart as you read my words and lead you to make a decision that is pleasing in his eyes.

I am sure I do not have to tell you of the suffering our soldiers are enduring. Young men from both the North and South are sick and dying everyday. Sadly, many of them could be saved if medical supplies were available. Fannie and I have both been working at the hospital here. I have seen first hand the miracles of modern medicines.

247

Although the number of soldiers suffering on the bat-
tlefields and in the hospitals are alarming, there are also
thousands more who are suffering alone in dark, filthy
conditions without food, medical supplies or even paper
to write a farewell to their mothers. I am speaking of the
horrors of the prison camps.

With the help of the Sisterhood, I believe we can find a
way to help these men rotting away behind closed doors.
Your arrangement with Fannie is working wonderfully. I
dare speak of it in detail, for fear this letter might fall in
the wrong hands. If that same plan could be extended
upon, I have reason to believe that I can make excellent
use of more "Bibles".

As for the prison camps, never have there been more
souls begging to hear the gospel. I am sure the Sisters
would not be denied safe passage in and out of the prison
camps. I can only imagine how the Nuns' hearts will beat
tucked under those flowing robes, knowing they carry the
gift of salvation. I am sure God will reward them for sav-
ing so many men.

I believe this ministry could be extended to all prison
camps both in the North and in the South. Foremost of
concern for me is a man by the name of Joel Simpson
who is being held at Fort Delaware prison.

I hope you will adopt my plan and we can work
together on this great mission.

Please return your thoughts as soon as possible.

Sincerely,
Miss Elizabeth Sanders

With the letter sent, Fannie took the initiative to request a
large shipment to be delivered to the Nuns. We could only hope
they would be cooperative and forward it to us. Two days later,
Papa returned saying he was successful in rounding up a number

of older men who were willing to help deliver the medical supplies. He would not tell the names of the men, the routes or dates of the missions. All I knew was they had organized into groups and were hoping to make delivers across the Carolinas and Virginia. Papa explained to me if any information would leak out, it could endanger the missions, as well as the lives of the men. I was not to speak to Mother; he would talk to her if he felt it necessary. He cautioned Fannie and I to be careful of what we did and who might overhear us speaking. As to whether he would take part himself in any of these missions, he would not comment. "It is going to take a lot of hands working together in silence to pull these missions off," Papa said. "We must tread lightly to ensure all who are involved are trustworthy. The Nuns go without question and I have little doubt of the honesty of the men. Still, there is another source, which was strongly suggested at our meeting. Frankly, I think we would be taking a big risk and nothing could be further removed from the Nuns than the likes of Miss Lucy's girls."

"The Miss Lucy's girls?" I asked, almost shocked.

"Yes," Papa said. "Those kind of girls go in and out of the encampments without question. Even if the Yankees stopped them, it would be clear what the nature of their business was with the soldiers. The men say, Miss Lucy can be trusted, but to this I am not so sure."

Fannie had been listening quietly to what Papa said, but at last, she spoke up.

"I am familiar with these ladies. In New York, I was the doctor for such an establishment. I suggest Lizzie and I approach this Miss Lucy under the pretense of taking up medical care of her girls. From that angle we could determine if this is an avenue to consider."

Papa looked at Fannie and smiled, "Once again, Dr. Holloway, I am astonished by your wit."

That was it. For the next couple of weeks we tried to put the mission out of our minds while waiting for the packages to be delivered. My dream of the children's clinic had practically been abandoned. Fannie and I both were spending the majority of our time at the hospital.

Clarence's bank account was shrinking under the collapsing economy and we were spending more at the clinic than we were generating. Mr. Caldwell at the bank felt things would turn around after the war, but that end was nowhere in sight. I had taken Papa's advice and invested Aunt Sara's money in privateering. At first, the Seagull was bringing in profits, but now hardly any of the ships could get past the blockade. I was beginning to worry over the household expenses and the cost of medical supplies. I had not mentioned this to anyone, not even Papa.

Wednesday June 25, 1862

My fears for Joel's safe return were expanded with every newspaper I read. I had made up my mind to write again to Sister Irene, if there was no word from her by the end of the week. When Papa showed up with the following letter from Thomas, we all knew action had to be taken as soon as possible.

Dear Mr. Sanders,

I hope all of you are doing are well. As I am writing this letter, my company is now just north of Richmond. We have not long left the area around Chickahominy River where we got into terrible rain. For days, we marched through nothing but mud and swamps. Most of us were plum give out by the time we came up on the Yankees at Fair Oaks Station and Seven Pines.

We still gave them a hell of a fight and it looked like we were going to whip them until they managed to get their reinforcements across the river. I am still not sure who can claim this a victory. All I know it was just one bloody muddy sight too sickening to describe.

I was sure I would be kilt and if I had not had a clear mind about me, I would not be writing this letter. A can-

non ball came hurling by and hit the tree next to me. A big limb broke off and knocked me out. When I came to, the guns were quiet. Lying on top of me was another North Carolina boy, who had been kilt. Just as I lifted my head, I saw the Union soldiers coming through and checking over the dead. I knew if they found me alive, they would kill me or take me prisoner. I reached up to the body laying over me, covered my hand in blood and spread it over my chest and face. I closed my eyes and prayed they would take me for dead. I must have laid there for a couple of hours. When they all were gone, I got up and took off running until I joined up with my company again.

I am sure by the time you get this letter, you would have heard that General Johnston was wounded and General Robert E. Lee is now the commander-in-chief. I think he is going to do us good.

Now here is the real reason I am writing to you. After a fellow sees all this, he knows it is not likely he will be so lucky the next time. Sure enough come, one of them bullets has my name on it. I don't mind so much for myself. I reckon if there is a heaven, I will see Annabelle up there. It is TJ that I worry for. Please promise me that if I don't get back home, you will see to her for me. Well, I will close now; they are calling for us to move on. Say a prayer for me sometimes.

Yours truly,
Thomas

After Papa read the letter, Fannie spoke up, "Those boys tromping through all those swamps are going be subject to malaria, yellow fever and who knows what. If they don't have medical supplies, in no time they will be dropping like flies."

"Well, maybe that is better than the hell some of them are going through!" Papa said, with an angry rise in his voice.

"Then we will just have to pray the packages are delivered to us!" I said, and closing my eyes and lowering my head. Papa and Fannie followed my lead and prayed. At first, I did not open my eyes when I heard a knock. As it grew louder, I realized someone was knocking on the front door. It was the delivery boy, "Miss Sanders, I have ten big packages for you. Where do you want me to put them?"

I did not even answer the boy, but called back into the parlor, "God has answered our prayers."

We all ran out and helped the boy bring in the packages and set them in the hall. Papa gave the boy a two-dollar tip. The boy's eyes lit up as he took the money, "This is my lucky day! I sure hope you folks get another delivery tomorrow!"

We carried the crates back to the clinic. When I opened the first box, I found a letter addressed to me from Sister Irene and I read it aloud to Papa and Fannie.

Friday, June 20, 1862

Dear Miss Sanders,

Again, I apologize for my delay. I admit your call for so many Bibles was at first overwhelming. However, after carefully reviewing the great crisis at hand, we have voted to help you in your mission. I wrote to several other convents and they have agreed on their own accord to partake in this mission as well.

I received a letter today from Sister Maria in Delaware. She and two others Sisters have personally visited Fort Delaware prison. She reported that your Mr. Joel Simpson is well. He and the other soldiers who were being held there were grateful to receive the Bibles. Please tell Fannie to order more Bibles for our missions.

Yours in faith and love for our Lord and Savior,
Sister Irene Maloney

"Well, I suppose we need to get to work on labeling all these medications, Fannie announced. "Lizzie, I think it is time we pay Miss Lucy a visit."

Fannie was already working on separating the bottles when Papa called me out in the hall to speak to me alone, "Mr. Jones is on his way home, seems he got wounded and lost a couple of fingers. Even though it is not a serious injury, a man can't shoot a gun without his trigger finger. When Mr. Jones comes back, I am thinking of taking your Mother up to North Carolina. I think it would be good for her and she could help when the new baby arrives. What do you think, Lizzie?"

Yes, I think she would like being there with the children," I said, looking at him suspiciously. Even though I agreed with him, he was not fooling me. I knew he was trying to get her out of the way so he can go on those missions. Papa said he would let me know when he would be taking her. He grabbed his hat and wasted no time leaving. I was sure he was off to meet with his contacts and plan out their routes.

After Papa left, I wrote a quick note to Miss Lucy. I walked out in the hall and called for Simon. "Do you know where Miss Lucy's place is?" I asked Simon.

Simon looked at me oddly and said, "I might, I mean, I do. Now, Miss Lizzie, just because I know where she keeps her girls, doesn't mean I have ever been there," he said, looking over his shoulder for Millie.

Fannie and I laughed at how he suddenly took a very nervous demeanor. "I am not asking **have** you been there," I said, clarifying my inquiry. "I just need you to take this note to her and wait for her reply." Simon made off with the note, without saying another word.

"Looks like someone has a guilty conscience," Fannie whispered as she watched Simon go out the door.

Regardless whether Simon was guilty of being a customer at Miss Lucy's or not, he made quick work of returning with her reply. Simon handed me the note and I studied the fancy penmanship on the cover. The fine linen stationary reeked of perfume or was it Simon I smelled?

Dear Miss Lizzie,

I find it strange that you have contacted me on the behalf of Dr. Holloway. I myself have been meaning to inquire about her services. I feel a woman doctor would be more sensitive to my ladies needs. So, yes indeed to your proposal. At this time, the ladies are all due their annual physicals.

The house is free of guest on Sundays. This was the day the doctor from Summerville chose to do his examinations. I think you will find this to your liking as well. I can have them all bathed and ready to receive you as early as this Sunday, July 5th. My little night owls are late morning sleepers and around the noon hour would suit us best.

Please let me know if this proves agreeable.

Sincerely,
Miss Lucille McGill

After breakfast on Sunday, Fannie packed her medical bag. When I came downstairs she and Cindy Lou were patiently waiting for me in the hall.

Walking in a whorehouse might have been old hat for Fannie and as for Cindy Lou, she was clueless. I, on the other hand, was uneasy. Simon drove down the rear alley and let us off at the back door. Fannie gave the doorknocker a firm rap and an old Negro woman in maid's attire opened the door. From the moment I stepped in the back door, I would have known where I was, even with my eyes closed. The sweet aroma of perfume in the air was the same perfume on Miss Lucy's stationery.

We had arrived a little early and we followed the maid down the hall to a lavishly decorated sitting room. The dark velvet curtains were drawn tightly and the room was dimly lit. In the corner I eyed a well stocked bar with assortments of liquors and wines. I was thinking I could use a nip myself, to settle my nerves.

The center court of the room was bare and rows of red velvet chairs were lined up against the walls. Although the house looked clean, the layers of perfume and cigar smoke made me think of it as dirty. I reluctantly chose a seat. I sat across from the piano and looked up to see a large painting of a beautiful, but very scantily dressed woman. I walked over to examine the painting a little closer and I was sure it was Miss Lucy. It was signed Mr. Devoe. I smiled, thinking of that odd little man painting Miss Lucy. Maybe this was the reason he was in such a hurry to leave after painting Mother, he had this job waiting for him.

I was disturbed from my thoughts, when I heard voices coming from the side hall. I turned to see a young woman with bed hair, wearing only a thin nightdress. She was leaning against an open door kissing a man. Before the man turned to go down the hall, he gave her a little pop on the rear. She was still giggling until she saw Miss Lucy coming up the hall. The man nodded at Miss Lucy, but she did not smile. Her eyes were focused on the young woman ahead. I turned my back to them as not to appear to be spying. I could only hear them whispering, but I knew Miss Lucy was angry. I heard a door shut and Miss Lucy entered the room in a gracious fashion. Her tall, thin figure glided across the floor and collapsed gracefully on a small settee. Her blonde hair hung in curls in the back, but was coiffured high on top. I assumed the aqua colored gown she was wearing was a street dress, but it looked more like a dressing robe. She arranged the folds of silk around her and lifted her painted lips and spoke, "Good morning ladies, it is nice to see you." If she had been angry before, there was not a hint of bitterness in her voice now. Her words were soft as butter, making me think of her entrance as a well-rehearsed performance.

Fannie made her a proposition and Miss Lucy accepted it without batting an eye.

Then she led us to a second floor bedroom, which had been prepared for our examinations. The bed was made with fresh white sheets, but no pillows or blankets. As I looked around the room, I saw two basins of water sitting on the dresser. In the middle of the room sat a bare table and two straight chairs. The only light in the room was a tall floor lamp standing at the foot of the bed. Miss Lucy explained this was how the previous doctor instructed her to set up the room. Fannie looked around and shook her head, "I think this will do fine, but I will need to open those windows."

"Yes, of course," said Miss Lucy. "I will give you time to set up before I start sending them in." Miss Lucy left the room and closed the door softly behind her.

It had been determined before we left home, that I would take the medical notes and Cindy Lou would be Dr. Holloway's assistant. Fannie warned the girls may speak vulgarly and she briefed us on the nature of the examinations. I felt I was prepared.

The first one that came in the room was a thick looking young woman, who was called, "Bunny." I strongly expected that was not her real name, but I wrote it down anyway. She was not at all attractive and when she removed her clothing, she was less. She knew the routine, plopped down on the bed, and spread her legs. I knew now why Fannie had insisted the window be open. Fannie talked to the woman about hygiene and gave her medicine and a cream to apply to her underside. When she told the girl, she was not to assume her work for two weeks, the girl got cross, "Two weeks! *Why, Miss Lucy will kick me outs in the streets fer then.*"

The next five girls also proved to be suffering from the "personal disease" as Fannie called it. Two of the girls were feverish, possible measles, one was pregnant and almost all of them had pubic lice. The last to come up for an examination was a frail looking young girl who looked to be way under age for this type work. She spoke very little, but I briefly detected an Irish dialect. Fannie asked her to undress and she was very shy about doing so. When she exposed herself, she had a number of large bruises across her backside. Fannie looked at me and I could tell this was out of the ordinary.

"How old are you?" Fannie asked.

"The girl returned, *"seventeen, almost eighteen."*

Fannie came back at her again, "I ask you again, how old are you?"

"Fourteen, nearly fifteen," she responded this time lowering her pretty little head.

"Now, I want to know how long you have been working here?" Fannie insisted.

"Miss Lucy took me in after me Pa died. I's only been heres a couple of weeks," she said. She looked at me and suddenly I felt sick to my stomach. I knew those dark eyes; she was the little Irish girl I had given my cloak to the night of the homespun party.

"How did you get these bruises?" Fannie asked.

It was a long time before she spoke, *"Me falls down the stairs."*

"Stairs my ass! This is a disgrace and there should be law against this kind of thing!" Fannie raged.

The girl who told us her name was Molly was examined and found to be one of the few who were not infested or infected. Fannie inquired, "Have you had men in your bed?"

"Only one man so far, but whens me could not do his work he gots real mad and Miss Lucy had to gives the gentleman backs the money."

"That was no gentleman, my little Lass, no gentleman hit's a woman." Fannie said, helping the girl off the bed. "Here is what I need you to do. Go and pack your personal belongings. Do not stop to speak to anyone and come back down to this room as quickly as possible." Molly looked as though she might have hesitations. Fannie took Molly's face in both her hands, "Do I make myself clear?"

"Yes, Ma'am," Molly said and hurried out the door.

Fannie instructed Cindy Lou to empty the basins of water and we gathered our things to leave. Shortly, Molly returned carrying only a paper sack and wearing the cloak I had given her. We went downstairs to look for Miss Lucy. Across from the large sitting room, we saw Miss Lucy in her office. She was sitting at a

257

French style desk and having a conversation with a gray haired woman. Both of the women were smoking a pipe and an open bottle of whiskey sat on the desk. I could hear them laughing and talking as we approached the room.

Suddenly I was in shock. The second woman was Miss Georgette. Fannie told us to take a seat and wait for her. Then she walked in front of the door to present herself to Miss Lucy. "All done?" Miss Lucy called out.

"Yes indeed, we are completely finished," Fannie's cheery tone was phony.

"Well, I will leave you two ladies to settle up," Miss Georgette said, without the slightest hint of a French accent. She walked out of the room without poise. I was sure she had been drinking and now her natural state was revealed.

She passed through the room, but I was not going to let her go without noticing me. "Miss Georgette," I spoke up. She turned looking shocked to see me.

"Oh my dear Miss Sanders, how are you? She gushed with a French accent, pulling herself back into character.

"Just fine and you?" I replied.

"Oh, best as can be expected, for a woman who lost everything in the fire." she said, awkwardly. "Thanks to the good nature of Lucille, I have a roof over my head. She keeps me busy enough with her clothes, but now I have her entire staff to dress. Please tell your Mother if she needs any work done, I am happy to make house calls."

"Oh, yes of course, we will certainly keep that in mind," I said knowing I was lying.

She left the room and I turned my ear to listen to Fannie and Miss Lucy talking in the next room.

"Well, Dr. Holloway this has turned out to be a bit more costly than we discussed," Miss Lucy said in a stern tone.

"My dear Miss Lucy, I had no way of knowing I would find your girls health so neglected. The cost of the medications alone would justify my fees."

"I see," Miss Lucy, said counting out the money and handing it over to Fannie.

Once she had the money in her hand, Fannie began, "Furthermore Miss Lucy, here is the list of the girls that have infections, I think it is all but two. They cannot be permitted to work until they are clear. Otherwise, your men will be leaving here with more than a just a calling card.

"Dr. Holloway, are you asking me to retire my most popular girls for two weeks? I can hardly afford to do this, especially in these difficult times. It is out of the question!" Miss Lucy declared.

"Suit yourself, but once words gets out, your girls are rotten, not a man in this town will step foot in this establishment. I can also, assure you, your troubles will be double fold, if the women in this community find out you are working girls as young as fourteen.

"Oh, I see. I suppose you want me to pay you to keep your mouth shut," Miss Lucy said lowering her voice.

"Not exactly. My concern is for the girls, especially Molly. I could be persuaded to keep my mouth shut as long as you agree to take my terms. First, you start taking responsibility for your girls' health. Second, I am taking Molly with me, and I had better not ever hear of you working a girl under the age of seventeen. Do we have a bargain, Miss Lucy?" Miss Lucy nodded her head, to agree. Fannie turned not saying a word and went straight out the back door; we followed.

Simon was waiting out back and all four of us got in the carriage. Simon looked over at Molly, but did not ask questions. Fannie threw her head back and started laughing. I looked at her and I laughed too. "I was wonderful, if I do say so myself," she chuckled.

"I figured we deserved to get paid enough to make this trip worth our while." Then she leaned over and whispered in my ear, "Especially since we have another mouth to feed."

Cindy Lou was stroking something against her face. "What do you have there?" I asked.

"One of dem' girls gave me dis fancy hankie, it iz so soft," she said admiring it.

"Well throw it out the window! No telling what you might catch from that thing!" Fannie said.

Cindy Lou dropped her hand out the window, but unknowing to us, she slipped the handkerchief back down the front of her dress.

Dear Lord,

I am thankful this day is over. I have seen things today I hope to never witness again. I know you have sent Molly to us for a reason. Yet, with another person under my roof, I fear even more for my financial stability. I pray that you will provide for us. Please give me the faith to trust in you, and the strength to overcome my fears. Protect my family and those that are in my keeping. Oh mighty God, I know war is not of your liking, surely goodness will come to us soon.

Amen

CHAPTER 23

"Steel Magnolia."

Molly settled in quite well and was thankful to be rescued. She was a smart young lady and more than willing to earn her keep. Fannie had taken her under her wing and hoped she might follow in her footsteps. Cindy Lou was a little jealous, even though I think she understood. I often felt sorry for Cindy Lou. She had such a kind heart, but she would never rise above her lot in life. As hard as we tried, she could not grasp the concept of reading or writing.

One thing we learned about our visit with Miss Lucy, she was not entirely honest. Papa agreed and we dismissed the possibility of including her on the missions. Surprisingly enough, two weeks to the day after our visit at Miss Lucy's, a note smelling of perfume arrived for Fannie.

Dear Dr. Holloway,

I have followed your instructions to the letter and I am happy to say, my girls appear to be in fine form. It is my hope; you will consider a follow up visit to determine if they are healthy enough to resume their careers. In addition, if we can settle on the terms, I would like to employ you for monthly follow-ups. Hopefully, we can insure these issues do not reoccur.

Sincerely,
Miss Lucille McGill

Fannie was pleased with the possibility of a steady income, even though she had no idea our funds were dwindling. Fannie sent word she would perform the exams on Sunday. Millie and Cindy Lou went with her on that visit and all visits thereafter. I never returned to Miss Lucy's.

That week Papa sent a message asking Cindy Lou and I to come and help Mother pack her things to go to North Carolina. I made the decision to leave Cindy Lou at Sandy Ridge with Mammy. I did not tell her it was a permanent arrangement. Now that we had Molly, we had little need for her. Cindy Lou was better suited for plantation work. Besides, that would mean one less mouth for me to feed.

It was Thursday before I could free myself of my duties and leave for Sandy Ridge. When we arrived, I was shocked to see how pale and thin Mother looked. Even more alarming was the fact that Papa and Mother would be leaving for North Carolina the very next morning. It wasn't like Papa not to have given me more notice.

I planned to discuss my finances with Papa and hopefully get a positive update on the Seagull, which we both had invested handsomely. However, the opportunity did not arise. Papa was preoccupied most of the day with Mr. Jones. Later in the afternoon, a couple of men arrived and he spent the rest of the evening with them.

Ladybug was now staying in my room, so we shared my bed. She was growing up to be a lovely young girl. The next morning there was barely enough time for good-byes before Mother and Papa left to catch their train.

Mammy and I stood on the porch as they drove away. In the still of the morning, we could hear a lone dove calling across the meadow. *"Here's dat? It be a bad omen, Miss Lizzie. It'z sho feels like the end of the world to me,"* Mammy wiped her eyes on her apron and went inside. How true that statement would soon be for Mammy.

I spent one more night at Sandy Ridge. Papa's actions were suspicious and I was not surprised to find this letter when I unpacked my bag.

August 6, 1862

My dearest Lizzie,

In time, I hope you will forgive me for leaving in such haste. I think you will find this letter to be self-explanatory.

Lincoln has signed an agreement for a prison exchange. Whether he holds true to his agreement remains to be seen. However, if this blessing comes to pass, thousands of men will be in desperate need of medical supplies once they are released. I have volunteered to travel with a group of men to make deliveries at the encampments. In addition to the medical supplies, we will provide them with food and warm clothing.

I am leaving Sandy Ridge in the capable hands of Mr. Jones until I return. I believe him to be a good and trustworthy man. I have instructed him if he has any questions or concerns that you are to have the final word.

As to when I will return, I expect to be gone until around Christmas time. I did not tell your Mother as I saw no need to worry her. She has not been well and I am sure this would set her back. I will write to you often and enclose a letter for you mother. I would like you to forward my letter to her with Charleston post. Please don't think me dishonest. It is all in her best interest.

Lizzie, I know much has been laid upon your tender shoulders. If it were in my power to change it, I would gladly lay down my life. Sadly, it is not. I must trust God will bring us through this and happier days will soon be here. I want you to know I am so very proud of you and your sacrifices have not gone unnoticed by me.

You have proven to be a true 'Steel Magnolia,' strong as steel with your roots planted deep in the Southern Soil. Remember to always bend with the wind. Although time may weather you, you will always be my beautiful Magnolia.

With all my love and devotion,

Papa

I could have easily thrown myself on my bed and wept for hours after reading Papa's letter. Yet, it occurred to me I was the only one left to hold Sandy Ridge together. I had to be the rock and for Papa's sake; I was not going to crumble.

The following week we were worried when our long over-due medical shipment from New York did not arrive. Fannie sent all the medical supplies, but the bare bones, with Papa and his men. She was sure we could replenish our stock.

My worries came to the surface when Fannie received a letter from Sister Irene, informing us that my check had not cleared the bank and therefore they were unable to purchase the supplies. After Fannie read the letter, she turned and looked at me. I could not tell if she was angry or concerned.

"Fannie, I am sure this is a misunderstanding. I will go to the bank tomorrow," I said, trying to buy myself some time. Time for what, I was not sure. Perhaps, my ship would come in. My highest hopes were on the Seagull now.

The next morning I went to the bank. Mr. Caldwell confirmed my fears. Unless my stocks went up soon, I was at risk of losing everything. Stocks going up right in the middle of a war was not likely to happen. He then made me a scandalous offer to buy the house, which I quickly refused. "Well," he said, "I have little more to offer you, unless you have funds set aside for a rainy day. Perhaps, you have undertaken too much, my dear. In my opinion, women have never been good at managing money. I suggest you go home, speak to your father and we will talk again soon."

With that being said, he got up and opened the door, so much as saying, "Get out!"

He stood at the door with a little smirk on his face, as I made my exit. I was sure somehow, he had taken advantage of me and my money. Just how, I was not sure; but I aimed to find out.

I left there and went straight home to sort through my books. Fannie met me at the door with a letter from the doctor in Summerville. She began reading the letter, but asked me to sit down first.

Dear Dr. Holloway,

I regret to inform you there has been an outbreak of smallpox here in Summerville. I am warning you of such, for it is sure to spread your way.

With no medication, I am presently forced to make my own vaccines. However, I do not need to tell you the risk this involves and many of my patients strongly object.

I heard you have connections and may be able to obtain some of the new vaccine. I would be greatly appreciative if you could assist me in anyway. It is my desire to help all my patients, especially our dear daughter of sixteen, whose life is hanging on by a thread.

If you have nothing to offer but your prayers, they are appreciated.

Sincerely,
Dr. Oliver Simpson

Fannie walked over and closed the door so the servants could not hear her. "Lizzie, I sent most all the vaccine I had with your father. I have only enough here for five people. We need to make a decision here. If and when smallpox spreads to Charleston, we are going to need a whole lot more than this. Whites have some immunity to the disease, but I have seen smallpox wipe out a city's entire Negro population. Now for the hard question, who gets the vaccine? There are five of us here, six counting Cindy Lou." Fannie took a step back and looked at me.

"What of the doctor's daughter?" I asked.

"Here is what Dr. Simpson does not understand, the vaccine is a preventive. Once the disease takes hold, there is very little evidence that it will do any good. It is possible, but odds are it would be a waste," Fannie explained.

I quickly made my reply, "Well, we certainly can not risk you getting sick. We will need you too much. Poor little Molly is so frail, she would die for sure. If Millie is working with you, she will be subject to the infection. So, that leaves me, Simon or

Cindy Lou. Since I am white, I will be the one to take the chance. It only makes sense," I said, lowering my voice.

"Don't be ridiculous, we need you too. My suggestion is to leave Cindy Lou at Sandy Ridge. Make certain the slaves are quarantined with no visitors in and out. They should be safe until we can work out something to get more medicine."

"Yes, I suppose that sounds reasonable," I said.

"Go round up the rest and I will prepare the vaccines, she said. "There is no time to waste." She turned quickly and left me standing alone in the Parlor.

Now, I would have to find someway to get the money for more medicine. If worse came to worse, we could all go to Sandy Ridge, but this was greater than losing a house.

I found Simon in the garden and Molly and Millie in the kitchen. I think Molly was more afraid of the needle than getting smallpox.

That night I made a decision. In the morning I would go to Sandy Ridge and take some of the gold Papa had hidden. If Papa was here, I feel sure he would make that decision.

It was around noon the next day when I got to Sandy Ridge. I walked through the house and I did not see anyone. I assumed I would find Mammy in the kitchen, but instead I found Mrs. Jones and Ladybug preparing lunch. "Where is Mammy?" I asked.

At first Mrs. Jones did not answer, "Lizzie, she is sick; they all are sick. First it was Cindy Lou, then a couple more. Mammy made some kind of medicine out of white clay and some of them were getting better. Then we heard this morning that Mammy was down too.

"Have you seen them? I cried out to her in anger.

"No, but my Tom has, he says we best not go nowhere near any of them. They are covered up with spots and burning up with fever."

"Damn," I said, not caring that Ladybug heard me swearing. I could hear Mrs. Jones calling to me as I took off toward the slave quarters. I first went to Mammy's cabin. I knocked, but no one came to the door. I opened the door and went inside. Mammy was lying on a cot on the floor and Cindy Lou was lying in the bed.

"Lizzie, what are you doing here?" Cindy Lou said in a weak voice. Mammy looked up but, she did not speak.

I learned over Mammy and took her hand, "Mammy, it is me, Lizzie."

She tried to speak, but her mouth was swollen and blistered.

"Mammy, you just hold on, I am going to get Dr. Holloway. She will know what to do."

I went to get some fresh water and when I got back Cindy Lou sat up in bed to speak, *"I be som' bet'r todays, Miss Lizzie. Mammy iz whos I worrys over."*

"Me too, Cindy Lou," I said, looking her right in the eyes. Suddenly, I saw something around her neck, it was the handkerchief that she had found at Miss Lucy's.

"Cindy Lou! Dr. Fannie told you to throw that handkerchief away." I screamed, thinking it might to be blame for all of this.

Cindy Lou started to cry, *"I sos sorry, It was just sos purtty. Heres you can have itz, Miss Lizzie."*

"No, you keep it. It is alright, Cindy Lou." I said, knowing she did not have a clue what she may have done.

I found Harriett and told her to sit with Mammy until I came back with the doctor. She did not like it, but I told her I would tan the living daylights out of her if she didn't.

I walked across the meadow and down to the duck pond. I sat down on the bench and scanned the landscape. I did not see a soul. I took a small hammer out of my bag and opened the door like Papa showed me. I dropped the ladder down to the pit and lit a candle. I opened a box in the back, where I found several small sacks of gold. Quickly, I filled my bag and climbed back to the surface. I had just hammered down the nails and moved the bench back in place, when I saw Mr. Jones riding up. I quickly sat down.

"Miss Lizzie, Rose told me you were here. What are you doing out here?" he asked.

I had to stop and think. What was I doing out there? "I came out to pray a spell before I went back in town. It is so peaceful out here," I said, watching him carefully to see if he bought my story.

"Yes, you got that right. It sure is a shame all the coloreds are taken to their beds. If there is one thing I am afraid of, it's the Pox. I reckon, we will be burying them all soon and if you don't stay away from around there, we will be burying you too!"

"Thank you," I said, even though I thought his remark was very insensitive.

I left and went directly to the bank and asked to speak to Mr. Caldwell. He kept me waiting for over an hour. Once I produced the gold, he was back to his old pleasant ways. He made me an offer, but I declined. He was almost foaming at the mouth when I told him I was going to take all my banking down the street. Mr. Caldwell may have done me in once, but I was not about to pick up that rattlesnake again.

After I completed my business, I wired the money to Sister Irene for the medicines. I returned home to tell Fannie what was happening with the slaves. Without a word, she went to pack her bag. I sat down in the hall and realized it was the first time I sat down all day. Fannie came back and ordered me to eat before we left.

It was dark by the time we got back to Sandy Ridge. It felt strange that I should knock on my own front door, instead of using my key. Mrs. Jones opened the door and looked surprised to see us. I told her Fannie and I were here to treat the slaves. Mr. Jones came from upstairs wearing what I was sure was Papa's smoking Jacket. "Lizzie, you and your medicine woman might as well go back home. They already buried a couple of them this afternoon and the rest of them got one foot in the grave."

"Who did they bury?" I asked, feeling put off again by his insensitive tone.

"I don't know them darkies' names. I think one of them was that big one that used to try to oversee the others."

"Samuel, Samuel's dead?"

"Yep, I think that is right," he said and turned to go back upstairs.

His attitude made me want to run up behind him and give him a good swift kick in the rear. How dare him. This was my house and he was treating me and my friend like we were not welcome. I will see he is fired when Papa gets back, or maybe I will do it myself before many more days.

Fannie and I went first to see Mammy and Cindy Lou. Mammy was now in the bed and Cindy Lou was tending to her. Harriett was nowhere in sight. I would address that later, but for now, my concern was Mammy.

Fannie made it her business to exam Cindy Lou first, although it was clear Mammy was the one who needed immediate attention. "Lizzie, go get those blankets off that woman and get her some fresh water," Fannie ordered.

I did not question, but did the work. Mammy shivered when I lifted up the blanket and her body smelled of urine. She was always thin and boney, but now her teeth looked like they might break through her tightly drawn face.

Out of the corner of my eye, I saw Fannie take a long needle and Cindy Lou started crying. "Hush up!" Fannie whispered to her. "You have got to do this and I don't want to hear another sound come out of your mouth."

It was a sickening sight as Fannie began to drawn yellowish fluid out of the crusty and decayed sores on Cindy Lou's arms. I turned my head to keep from losing what little food I had in my belly. Fannie continued her work long after she had turned Cindy Lou loose.

Once she had created her vaccine she turned to Mammy. As she examined her, I knew. I recognized that look in Fannie's eyes all to well. It was a death sentence. I tried not to cry and took Mammy's hand. Fannie gave Mammy the first vaccine and she did not flinch. I suspected Fannie gave it to her for my sake. She already said it would do little good once the infection had set in. Then she gave her some drops and a large dose of laudanum.

We wrapped Mammy in a cool damp blanket in hopes of bringing down the fever. I took up a little cane bottom stool and sat next to her. "Mammy, this is Lizzie. Can you hear me?" I asked in a calm low voice. Her eyes opened and she looked at me; she did not answer, but squeezed my hand.

Once Fannie treated all the Negroes, she went inside to speak to Mr. Jones. I stayed by Mammy's side. When Fannie came back, she was noticeably angry. Apparently Mr. Jones had refused to take medicine coming from some darkie. She said if he wanted to die, so be it. She was concerned for the child and the woman.

Most of the night Mammy and Cindy Lou slept. Fannie leaned a chair against the wall and I sat by Mammy's side all night. About two o'clock in the morning a rat ran across Fannie's shoe causing her to jump up and knock over a small table. The commotion woke Mammy up. Mammy tried to sit up in the bed and I propped her head up with a pillow. Her glassy eyes were open wide. Then, I stood up so she could clearly see my face.

"She looked at me and tried to smile, *"My name is Victoria."*

"Victoria?" I asked, realizing I never even knew her name.

"Yes, dat's right. My Mammy called me Vicki, but Papa jus' called me Vick," she answered in an amazing clear tone.

She reached out her arm and I thought she was reaching for me, but instead her eyes were staring off in the dark. *"Lizzie, whos is all dem folks standing all arounds yous?"*

I felt a strange sensation as if someone was breathing down my neck and turned around, but Fannie had stepped out and Cindy Lou was asleep. "It is just me Mammy."

"Oh, I see dem clear now. Angels, da come fer me," Her face was glowing and there was not a hint of sorrow or pain in her eyes. Very peacefully she closed her eyes, and gave my hand a little squeeze. Her last words were, *"You's remember me, girl."*

She was gone. I had watched my Mammy leave this world. I could have cried, but there were no tears in my heart. I had seen the angels come and take her to heaven. She would suffer no more and she was free. I will forever be honored to have witnessed her passing.

After the passing, I walked out of the cabin and into the moonlight, Fannie was sitting on the porch steps and I sat down beside her. "She's gone isn't she?" she asked, and put her arm around my shoulder. She said nothing more, but it was enough. Suddenly we saw a shooting star cross the sky. "There she goes." Fannie whispered.

At daylight, Fannie woke Cindy Lou and took her outside the cabin before she told her Mammy had died. Now we had the unpleasant task of burying Mammy. Who would do the task was the next question. Papa had hired most of the men to work on the railroads. Samuel was dead, and the rest were sick. I would have to rely on Mr. Jones.

I went to the front door and knocked, but the only sound I could hear was the barn door flapping. I knocked again, surely they were not still sleeping. I used my key and went inside. The house was dark and I could not even smell a fire. I called out, but there was no answer. I ran upstairs. There was no one there, the wardrobes were standing open and all their personal belongings were gone. I quickly ran downstairs and out to the barn. Papa's carriage and a pair of horses were missing. The thought ran though my mind, perhaps they went on trip, but where? My next thought found me running toward the duck pond, screaming out loud. "Please God don't let it be!"

As I got closer to the gazebo, I slowed down, there was no need to run any longer. I could see the bench turned over and the trap door standing wide open. My knees went weak and my body collapsed to the ground. The hot August sun was beating down on me like rays from hell. I literally had to drag my body off the ground and up to the gazebo. I climbed down the ladder. Just as I suspected, all the valuables were gone. Only the food and water remained. At least that was something. When Mr. Jones saw me that day it must had aroused his suspicions enough that he discovered my secret. Whatever would I tell Papa.

271

With nothing left to lose, I decided to tell Fannie. She insisted I go to the authorities, even though we knew it would do little good. First, I stopped at the kitchen hoping to find something to eat. There was only a half loaf of bread. I broke it in three pieces for Cindy Lou, Fannie and myself.

While I was in town, I picked up Simon and was able to hire a couple of Negroes to help bury Mammy. Unfortunately they had more work to do, Cato and four more Negroes died, leaving only Cindy Lou and Harriet. We stayed for a couple of days to secure the house. I had no choice but to take Cindy Lou and Harriet back with us. Now I had two more mouths to feed.

When we got back into town, there was a letter from Papa. He said their first mission was successful. Perhaps the best news, Papa had seen Joel! He had been released from prison and was returned to his unit. Papa said he was doing well and he sent his best to me.

Before retiring that night, I read through my stack of newspapers and clipped a few headline.

There is panic over Union troops advancing toward Charleston.

Robert E. Lee, now commander and chief, was feared by some to be too shy for battle. He showed the enemy his other side after leading an aggressive 7 day attack against Union forces. Although causalities were high, General McClellan withdraws and Richmond is safe!

General Nathan Bedford Forrest Confederate Cavalry takes Murfreesboro, Tennessee and prevents Union advancements by destroying the railroad tracks.

CHAPTER 24

Edmond Cook

The second Battle of Manassas brought the news of heavy casualties, but shallow in comparison to some 13,000 killed in the Battle of Sharpsburg, Maryland. Hardly a family in the South was untouched by the loss of a loved one.

Some said the war would never end, but you had only to work one day in the hospital to know different. With the numbers killed, wounded or sick soon there would be no one left standing on either side. Over the last year, I had seen more death than any woman should see in a lifetime. Strange thing about death. Some of the men took it screaming, cursing, crying or calling out for their mothers. Others took it as peaceful and natural as a summer sunset.

In late September there were more fears of slave uprisings when news spread that Lincoln planned to abolish slavery.

Fannie made her views clear, "If this be for moral reason, why will his so called "Emancipation Proclamation" only apply to the Confederacy and not to the border states?" "It is clear to me, old Lincoln is not acting on the welfare of our people, but for the welfare of the Union." "Without slave labor, the South's economy would fall. A weakened nation is much easier to conquer. That old Lincoln should be tarred and feathered for what he is doing to our people. Just how does he think all the coloreds are going to survive with no money, no homes and no means of support?"

273

Yet, I personally could not blame a man, colored or white, for fighting for his freedom. I can honestly say I never met a single Yankee that would have given a slave the time of day, much less go to war and risk his life for one. On the other hand, I would have done anything to save Mammy's life had it been in my power.

The good news that Fall of 1862 was the weekly letters from Papa and Mother. The news from North Carolina was uplifting. Sallie was carrying the baby happily, the children were well and Mother was much improved. Ransom, Thomas and Joel were all still safe. I only wished I could talk to Papa, if he knew what happened, I am sure he would come straight home. The authorities were little help in apprehending Mr. Jones. As a last resort, they alerted the South Carolina State Troops. It was suggested I contract a Mr. Hayes, a known gunman, to go after Mr. Jones. His fees were high and I could not afford the upfront cost.

The bit of gold I was able to obtain before Mr. Jones proved his dishonesty was keeping my head above water at present. I was glad I took my stocks and bonds out of Mr. Caldwell's bank. I believed the new bank to be more honest. However, in order for us to survive until things improved, we were going to have to conserve.

It was an unpleasant subject, but I found it necessary to hold a meeting with my household. Simon and Fannie listened carefully as I outlined the state of our affairs. I knew them both well enough to know they were contemplating a plan. Millie understood, but whatever was to be done, she would follow Simon's lead. Molly sat quietly until I finished. Then she stood and said, *"Miss Lizzie, me's don't want to be a burden on you. I will pack me bags and goes backs to Miss Lucy. If she will have me."*

"That is not going to happen!" Fannie said, standing up and stomping her foot. "We can get through this together. I have seen hard times before and that which does not kill us makes us stronger."

"Yes, said Simon. "Certainly there are ways we can cut the budget here. Millie and I will start on a plan right away."

After our meeting, Fannie asked to speak to Simon and me in private. We walked across the hall to the parlor and I closed the door. Simon boldly suggested we sell some of the silver and valuables from the Bullwinkle estate.

"Simon, what would Clarence think of me?" I asked.

"He would think you were using your head, Miss Lizzie."

We discussed possible ways to conserve household expense, but Fannie interrupted. "Lizzie, I have a good idea Miss Lucy would buy Cindy Lou and Harriet, if you are willing to offer them at fair price," Fannie said bluntly.

Her statement took me back at bit, until I remembered her family was slave owners too. Simon looked a little uncomfortable with the announcement, but shook his head.

"Are you suggesting she would prostitute them out? Harriet is too old and Cindy Lou, well, she just would not be fitting for that kind of thing." I laughed.

"No, not at all," Fannie smiled. "Lucy had just one maid for the whole house and she recently died. Harriet and Cindy Lou could serve her well. Cindy Lou could also double as a nurse if the need arose. "Shall I mention it to her?" She looked at me intensely and waited for my reply.

"I suppose so. It sounds like the best for all concerned," I replied, clinching my jaw. "Letting go of Harriet will not be so hard, but Cindy Lou, she is Mammy's daughter. Fannie, do you think she will take care of them properly?"

"I have gotten to know her a little better," Fannie said. "She is a business woman and that much I can understand. She can be harsh, but without thick skin some of us will never survive. Lizzie, in many ways she reminds me a little of you."

"Me!" I said feeling almost insulted.

"Yes, just as beautiful and even more stubborn," Fannie smiled patting me on the back with her thick little fingers.

Simon's final suggestion was to retrieve any perishable food items left from Sandy Ridge. There might be enough to hold us over for the winter. It was an excellent idea and we arranged to go the following morning. He made his exit and Fannie followed, leaving me alone. I thought of Papa and how many times I heard him say, "It is time to put that one in my pocket." Usually when he sold off a slave, it was because they were hard to handle, not because he needed the money. I missed Papa and I needed him more.

I do not know what was more pressing on my mind. The thought of resorting to selling Clarence's valuables, selling off Cindy Lou or writing Mother. Even though, I had written Mother and Sallie often, I made no reference to Mammy's death which was two months passed. She was sure to take it hard, but the longer I waited the harder it will be for all of us. Furthermore, I would have to tell her that Papa was not here in Charleston.

I picked up my pen and began writing. I ripped up several letters and must have begun at least a half dozen times before I found the right balance of words.

October 12, 1862

Dear Mother,

I must ask that you sit yourself down before reading my letter. First, do not fear, I am well and in fine form. Yet, it is with heavy heart that I must tell you the turn of events that have happened here at Sandy Ridge. I trust you will not judge me too harshly for my delay in informing you of this news. After you read this letter you will understand the delicate circumstances I have been dealt.

First, I must betray Papa and reveal to you his secret. He has not been at Sandy Ridge since he delivered you to North Carolina. He has been on an important secret mission for the greater good of our South Land. For privacy reasons, I cannot disclose the nature of his business in a letter. Should we be speaking face to face, I would gladly do so. Per his last letter, he says he is safe and well. I can only imagine how hard this is for you. I hope you will not think ill of Papa. His intent was to shelter you from undue stress. Papa says he will be home in December. Perhaps we will be coming to North Carolina for Christmas.

The next news I must bring to you is even more distressing. You may have heard that smallpox swept through Charleston not long ago. Dr. Holloway did all she could do, but sadly it claimed the life of our dear Mammy. She died peacefully with me by her side. Furthermore, the disease took Samuel and all the slaves with the exception of Harriet and Cindy Lou. We buried them all up on the hill next to Old Wiz. It was indeed a sad day.

I am sorry that I must leave in your hands the unpleasant task of telling Violet her Mammy has gone to be with the Lord. As for Sallie, you yourself can be a better judge if she is strong enough to hear all this bad news. I know she has a lot on her mind with Ransom being gone and Thomas too. Please tell me if her baby is due in December or January.

I had no choice but to close up Sandy Ridge until Papa gets back and we can sort out what is to be done.

It is times like this that we must trust in our heavenly Father and pray for brighter days. I hope your faith will be a comfort to you as my letter comes to a close.

I will write to you often. I look forward to hearing from you and Sallie. You all are in my prayers,

With all my love,
Lizzie

I told her everything, except for the part about the gold. What good would it do to share that information with her? I sealed the envelope and was attending to addressing the cover when I was interrupted by a knock at the door. It was Dr. Walker from the hospital. He had news of a ship that exploded out in the harbor. Over a hundred men had been rescued and were badly in need of care. Fannie and I grabbed our wraps and rode with the doctor to the hospital.

The hospital was already overcrowded. Now the halls were filled with men laying on cots, blankets and some even on the bare floor. We worked all night tending to burns, cuts and those suffering from hypothermia. It was dawn before we stepped out in the fresh air to go home. Fannie suggested we just walk home; it was only a couple of blocks. I agreed. Although I was exhausted, I could use a little time to wind down.

We discussed how the whole explosion was still a mystery. We had no idea the name of the ship or if the explosion was a result of an accident or enemy attack. We assumed it was definitely military, because no private ships got past the blockades in months.

We walked in the house without speaking and went upstairs to get a couple of hours sleep. I undressed and closed the curtains. Funny how not so long ago, if I were to find myself crawling into bed at five o'clock in the morning, it was after an all night ball. This night had been far from a party.

Around eleven o'clock the next morning, I composed a letter to Miss Lucy with the offer of two house slaves, Cindy Lou and Harriet. I sent Simon to deliver my message right away. Fannie was still asleep when Simon got back; I did not wake her. I wanted to get on the road and did not bother to fuss with my hair. I threw on an old calico dress and apron. I was not looking forward to the work awaiting me at Sandy Ridge. We could have used Cindy Lou's help, but this was my first visit back to Sandy Ridge since Mammy died. I was going to have a hard enough time holding on to my own emotions.

When the carriage stopped, all looked the same, but once I opened the door, the house felt cold and dead. I sent Simon around back to the kitchen and I went upstairs. Why, I am not sure. I walked through every room, lastly my own.

"Where have you been?" the house seemed to call out to me in agony. All was still with no human sounds or smells, only the wind blowing outside the window and the woody smell of a burned out fire. Something inside me wanted to light the fire, lay down across the bed and go to sleep until the war was over. I might have done just that, but I thought about what Fannie said. She compared me to Miss Lucy. She was right; I was too stubborn to be taken down by all this. After all, I was Papa's *Steel Magnolia*.

I crawled under my bed, retrieved my little box of childhood treasures and clutched it to my breast. Even though I may never sleep under Sandy Ridge's roof again, nothing will ever take Sandy Ridge out of my heart. I walked to the door and turned for one last time to scan the room. I took the key out of my apron and locked the door behind me. I am not sure why, it just seemed like the right thing to do.

I started down the steps when I heard Simon calling. He had loaded the carriage with canned goods, salt, sugar, flour and coffee. I joined him and we both went down to the root cellar for the potatoes, apples and beets. Next, we went out to the smokehouse and took the remains. I was pleased to find enough to last us all winter. This being said, I would not take the food from the underground shelter. God only knew what remained to be seen.

Simon loaded up the last bits and I went back in the house. I emptied out the silver into my bag and picked up the family bible. I took one last look into the parlor. I thought about the day we found out Annabelle was going to have Thomas's baby. I could almost hear the echo of her crying across the hall. I wondered if she was looking down today from heaven. "Good-bye," I whispered. The joys and tears of so many years all closed behind me when I locked the door.

Although the sun was shining, it had begun to rain. It was almost like an old habit. My first thought was to run to Mammy and ask her what omen this might be. The harsh reality stabbed my heart and I sat down on the steps and wept. Simon got out the carriage and stood with his back to me. I knew in his own gentle manner he was saying he understood.

After I regained my composure, Simon helped me back in the carriage. I was thankful he was kind enough not to make conversation. It was dark when we arrived and Fannie was still at the hospital.

I slipped off my shoes, made myself a fire in the parlor, and took up the paper.

The headline read, **"Please keep our dear General Robert E. Lee in your prayers."**

Fearing for the man I had met at the hospital not long ago, I continued to read.

Faith has dealt a heavy hand to the South's most revered General. First, he was to see his son, Rob, after the battle of second Manassas so worn, ragged, and stained in red soil that did he not to recognize him. Yet, the noble General sent his son, back to duty saying, "We must all do what we can to drive those people back."

Next, as if the agony of war and it's stresses were not enough, the General was thrown from his horse, Traveler. He received injuries to both of his hands. When last seen his arm was still in a sling.

However, as the month has come to a close. General Lee received the tragic news his dear daughter, Anne, had died in North Carolina at the Warren White Sulphur Springs on Oct. 20, 1862.

I bent my head to pray and had just closed my paper when I heard a knock on the door. Simon answered and I heard a man's voice. Simon came to inform me that a Mr. Edmond Cook was here to see me. I was shocked. What could he want? "Shall I send him away, Miss Lizzie?" Simon asked, seeing I was unprepared for visitors.

"No, it must be important. I will see him in the parlor."

Simon returned shortly with Mr. Cook. "I am sorry to trouble you at this late hour, Miss Sanders. I hope you will forgive me, but Dr. Holloway assured me I would be received. When I heard one of my ships met with an accident and many of the men were injured, I set out for Charleston unprepared. Now, I am embarrassed to say I was unable to find lodging. While I was at the hospital, your kind friend suggested you might rent me a room for a couple of days." Even though he was serious, I detected a slight flirtatious smile.

"I see," I said. Hesitating, I smoothed out the front of my apron and twisted a piece of hair out of my eyes.

"Well, if you would rather not, could I possible stay in the barn until morning," he pleaded looking up at me with his clear blue eyes.

"I would not hear of putting you in the barn, Mr. Cook. These are hard times, but we have not resorted to that yet," I said trying to make light of my delayed response. "Please make yourself at home, while I have my woman prepare your room." I excused myself and sent Simon in to offer him a brandy. On my way to look for Millie, I saw Fannie returning from the hospital. "Are we the boarding house now?" I whispered to her.

She giggled and pulled me down the hall to speak to me, "Well, why not, he is willing to pay and he is not bad to look at either. If you are not interested in him, I might try for him myself," she teased.

"You are too much, Frances Holloway, too much."

"I will flip you for him," she said taking a coin out of her pocket. "Heads you win and tails I lose." She flipped the coin and said, "Well, heads you win."

Simon took care of our houseguest and I went to bed. I was almost asleep when I thought of what Fannie had said, heads you win and tails I lose. I lay there in the dark alone laughing. It felt good to have something to laugh about again.

The next morning before I dressed, I thought of how dreadful I must have looked last night when Mr. Cook saw me. I slipped on my blue print dress with the white collar and arranged my hair becomingly. Simon passed me in the hall and turned around twice to look at me. When I walked in the kitchen, Fannie and Millie were having coffee. "Mighty pretty dress to go to work in the hospital, Miss Lizzie," Fannie said poking Millie.

"Well, I felt since we had a house guest, I should at least try to look presentable," I said calmly.

"Oh, yes of course," Millie said trying not to laugh.

"Especially if the guest happens to be a handsome young gentlemen," Fannie joked. They were still having their fun when

Mr. Cook entered the room. Their voices cut off in midstream making it obvious they were talking about him.

"Can a fellow get a cup of coffee in this fine establishment?" He asked looking at us suspiciously.

"Millie!" I said, trying to break her from staring. She responded at once and served Mr. Cook a cup of coffee.

"Just like my Momma always said, "When folks are talking about you, they are letting another poor soul rest." Edmond said looking intensely at Fannie.

To this remark, Fannie only said, "Maybe so?" She then announced she was late and made a quick exit.

Edmond turned to me and asked could he trouble me for transportation. He explained he had an important meeting with Mr. Tudor this morning. Before I could answer, he added, "better still, perhaps you would do me the honor of joining me. Following my meeting, we could lunch at the Mills Hotel."

Surely, Mr. Cook knew it was not altogether proper for a woman to go traipsing all over town with a strange man. I stumbled with my words, explaining I would be busting in unannounced on the Tudors. Edmond insisted that my surprise visit would be a delight and certainly not an intrusion. Simon sealed the deal with his comment, "Miss Lizzie, you best take this gentleman up on his offer. A little break will do you good. Too much work is going to make you old before your time."

"Yes, indeed. I can almost see the wrinkles in your forehead now," Millie said trying to encourage me.

"Well, then it is settled. Shall we depart in about a half hour?" Edmond asked, but it was more like telling me.

"I suppose," I said feeling apprehensive. I could not help but wonder what Mother would think. Well, that was in the old days. Much has changed in the last year. Now, I have no one to answer to but God and myself.

Edmond took one more bite of his eggs, wiped his mouth with his napkin and jumped to his feet. "I will see you downstairs shortly."

Simon and Millie were silent until he left the room. I pretended to eat to avoid their eye contact. Simon started laughing and Millie joined him.

"Simon!" I must ask that you not poke fun at me. Mr. Cook is here on war business and I must be obligated to help. Now go and get the carriage ready!"

"Yes, Ma'am," he said still in a teasing tone. He left the room whistling and Millie began to gather up the dishes.

I went across the hall to wait for Edmond. I could possibly take Cindy Lou with us, but her silliness is somewhat of a nuisances. Whether it was proper or not, we would go alone to visit Mr. Tudor.

Oddly, it did not seem strange at all when Edmond helped me in the carriage and went around to take the seat next to me. Cindy Lou, Millie and Simon all stood on the porch and watched us leave. I almost felt like a new bride riding away on a honeymoon. Thanks be to God that Edmond could not read my mind or could he? He flashed a white pearly smile at me and gave me a little wink as we pulled out on the main street.

The conversation was pleasant and I found Mr. Cook's adventurous stories to be quiet entertaining. In contrast I was afraid he would think me a bore, so I said little.

When we arrived at the Tudors, Edmond said he would go to the door and announce us. I could hear him addressing someone at the door, but I could not see to whom he was speaking. Feeling self-conscious sitting alone in the carriage, I pulled out my mirror to check my appearance. In the reflection, I could see a man and woman walking up behind me and I quickly stuffed the mirror back in my purse.

Edmond returned with Mr. Tudor in tow and opened the carriage door to allow me to escape. Mr. Tudor extended his hand and I stepped out of the carriage, as the two men smiled at me admiringly. I had no sooner put a boot on the ground when I heard a familiar voice. "Lizzie, is it you?" I turned to see Verina and her husband walking up to us. We made all the polite gestures and they escorted us in the house.

Verina pulled me close to her, "Let's go out on the porch while the men have their meeting."

I took a seat overlooking the courtyard and she excused herself. Within minutes she returned with a ginger colored woman carrying a tray of refreshments. Verina's family seemed to be fairing quite well. There was not a hint of a war recession and the gardens were just as lovely as the last time I was here. I took notice of the silk dress she was wearing. It was lovely even though it was an enormous size. Her protruding middle made me question whether she was pleasingly plump or expecting a baby.

"Go ahead and ask," she laughed. "I am not just fat. We are expecting our first child round about the first of December."

"Congratulations, I am sure you are both thrilled."

"Now, Lizzie. Do tell, are there wedding bells in your future?" she leaned forward, whispering with a smirk.

"Someday perhaps, but I have no plans for such at the present." I answered.

"Well, I assumed you driving up all alone with such a handsome man as the likes of Mr. Cook, you might be telling us all something."

"Well, my dear Verina. I hate to burst your bubble, but Mr. Cook and I have a business arrangement. There is nothing romantic about our acquaintance."

"I am sorry to hear that darling. Perhaps you might change your mind. After all, men are not just falling off the trees after you get past twenty and one. I am sure glad I got my husband when I did," Vernia said taking a bite of a sugar cookie. She continued to rattle on having no perceptions that she was insulting me.

At last, I ended the conversation with, "I don't think I shall ever marry. I am more the independent type."

I thought we were speaking in private, until I heard a man's voice.

"Now, won't that be a crime to see a belle like you whither up like an old maid?" Edmond said coming around from behind my chair.

I was at a loss for words and he knew it. Mr. Tudor heard too and started to laugh, yet Edmond's expression remained serious. Verina was not about to let this interruption distract her from eating the last of the sugar cookies.

Edmond cut our visit short explaining we had plans for lunch. I was glad to be back on the road. The conversation was easy and in no time we arrived at the Mills Hotel. During the meal, he wanted to know all about me, my family and Sandy Ridge. His eyes never left my face when I told him about the night of the great fire. His questions were almost prying about how I acquired the Bullwinkle estate. Yet, his eyes sparkled as I told him how I loved to ride Midnight down by the old mill and spend the afternoon fishing down at the pond.

"You know, Lizzie. I would love to see your Sandy Ridge. It sounds wonderful. Perhaps we could ride out and take a picnic." Edmond looked at me hopefully.

"I think that would be nice," I responded.

"Then, there's no better time than tomorrow morning." Edmond replied.

"Tomorrow?" I asked.

"Why not?" he asked, taunting me with a mischievous smile on his face.

"Alright, providing all is well at home. I will have Millie pack us a lunch and you will see our Sandy Ridge," I said accepting his dare.

I felt alive; he made me feel alive. The war, Papa being gone, worries over Mother and the lost gold, seemed to be someone else's concern that afternoon.

CHAPTER 25

No Remorse

The next morning I was up bright and early. I instructed Millie to bring my breakfast to my room, which must have sent up a red flag to Fannie.

I slipped on a fresh calico dress and was in the process of pinning up my hair when Fannie knocked at the door. I opened the door and without saying a word, went back to my dressing table.

"So, you are not going to the hospital again today I take it," she pried.

"Nope," I said clinching a few hair pins in my teeth. I continued arranging my hair. In the mirror I watched her pacing the room. I tried not to laugh.

She went to the window and pulled back the curtain. "Well, would you lookie out here. Mr. Edmond has pulled your carriage right up to the front door. You don't reckon he is fixin' to steal your rig do you?"

"You never can tell what a body is up to these days. I best go down right now and see to it," I said, slipping on my jacket. Fannie stood in front of the door with her hands on her hips trying to block the door. I laughed at her and gently pushed her aside.

"Ain't you the high and mighty one this morning, Miss Lizzie." I heard Fannie call out to me as I hurried down the stairs.

Edmond looked pleased to see me and helped me in the carriage. Before we pulled off, I looked up to see Fannie standing at the window. I waved and she blew me a kiss. My heart was warm this morning. Fannie was not just my friend, we were as close as sisters.

It was a splendid morning. The birds singing and the warm Autumn sun were the perfect backdrop for a romantic day. It was obvious to both of us there was romance in the air. I suppose in a finer time before the war, I would have been far more reserved. I would have teased the poor man half to death, but today it seemed a waste of precious time. Perhaps I was not the belle I used to be.

Being with Edmond was comfortable, there was no need to pretend with our feelings. So, when he reached for my hand as we headed out of town, I did not pull away. I smiled.

Edmond's companionship was the healing I had so longed for. I was totally infatuated with him; I wanted to know everything about this mystery man. Where did he come from? Who was his family? What were his hopes and dreams? Most of all what were his feelings for me?

When we arrived at Sandy Ridge, he stopped the carriage midway up the drive and scanned over the property with admiring eyes. "Your father is a fine man. No man builds a home like this unless he is driven by love. Love for his country, love for his family and love for his creator."

His words filled my eyes with tears. "Yes, my father is the finest," I said. "He is driven by love."

"How could he feel otherwise, looking into the face of an angel like you?" Edmond responded softly. His eyes were directly on my face. I did not turn my head, but allowed myself to sink deeper into the river of his blue eyes. If he had kissed me, I would have welcomed it. His face suddenly became serious and he jumped out of the carriage.

"Let's take a look at the barn," Edmond said as he helped me to my feet.

As we walked across the field. I thought of Joel. Would he be happy to know I was here with Edmond? I almost felt as if I were betraying him. Yet, he told me to fall in love and today perhaps I will follow his instructions.

Edmond and I walked into the barn and looked around. It was empty. For conversation, I leaned up against the wall and began to tell him about the rainy day I was thrown from my horse. He listened attentively as I explained it was Samuel who pulled me out from under the horse, saving my life.

"Where is this Samuel now?" he asked.

"Dead...They are all dead," my voice dropped off. "Seems like everything I love is slowly being taken away."

Edmond gathered my hands in his, but I turned my head and stared out across the duck pond. "Happier days are sure to come. You must trust this Lizzie. " Then he pulled me closer to embrace me against his chest. "Lizzie, look at me," he said sweetly.

I turned my head to his and he lifted my chin, lowered his lips to mine, and kissed me. It was only the second time I had ever been kissed like that. Once by my beloved Joel and now by Edmond. I was glad I had the previous experience, for this time it did not feel awkward or unexpected, it was natural. Edmond was eager for my kiss and I became aware of the splintery barn wall as his body pressed against mine. There was no one to oversee or call a stop to our passion. Yet, as if an alarm had been sounded, Edmond gently released me.

I could have acted shy or coy, but it was not how I felt. Instead, it was as if a sea of laughter had filled my body with renewed energy. I took off running across the field and Edmond followed. I did not stop until I reached the old oak tree down by the pond. I collapsed on the soft green grass, laughing and gasping for air. Edmond fell down beside me and we lay looking at the sky together.

Strange how it was that day, there were no need for words. Just being there together was enough. After a little while, Edmond helped me to my feet and we toured the house and the property. I showed him every room in the house with the exception of my room. When we passed the door, he turned the handle,

I was glad it was locked. I was not ready to reveal everything to Edmond, at least not now.

Edmond and I returned home just before dark. I left Edmond with a brandy and went upstairs to freshen up. When I returned, it was almost like magic. A candle light dinner was waiting for us in the dining room. I would have thought the house was empty if it had not been for the faint sounds of footsteps in the hall.

After our meal, we retired to the parlor to relax and sit by the fire. Edmond began a conversation about why he was released from the military. I hoped he would clarify some things in my mind. However, around eight o'clock Simon knocked. He set a tray on the table with a bottle of sherry and two glasses. Next, he presented Mr. Edmond with a letter that was delivered earlier.

My mind flashed back to the day Mammy brought the sherry into the parlor after the letter came telling us Annabelle had died. I closed my eyes and prayed.

Simon poured the wine and Edmond opened the letter. "I trust the news is not unfavorable," I questioned.

"No, actually it is good news, but I am afraid it requires my immediate attention. Sorry, my dear, but I must retreat to compose a response," Edmond explained. Without hesitation, Edmond jumped to his feet, walked across the room and kissed me quickly on the lips. "Good night sweetheart," he said.

Once the door closed, Simon started giggling.

"Something funny that I am not aware of?" I asked angrily.

"No, No, just amusing," he said and made a quick exit.

Suddenly I realized I was exhausted and this would be a good time to write to Sallie. I did so wish to tell someone about Edmond. My new romance would surely be welcomed news in midst of all this unpleasantry.

October 20, 1862

Dearest Sallie,

   A greeting from Charleston and indeed it is greetings. My last letter found only bad news, but this letter I write with excitement and hope in my heart. I do not know exactly how to begin, so I must just spring it upon you. I think I may be in love. I do not believe you have met him, but Mother and Father have. You may tell Mother a teeny bit about this, but most of my letter is just between you and me. If the romance flowers soon you may tell more!

Not long ago, I met the handsome Lieutenant Edmond Cook at the rail station and then again, briefly at Verina Tudor's wedding. I found him fascinating, but I was with Clarence and nothing came of our meeting. Then as a result of an extraordinary coincidence, our paths crossed again. Perhaps, it may be divine providence. The Lord does work in mysterious ways.

He is witty and devilishly handsome. He says he attended the College of Charleston, and I am sure he must be from an outstanding family. I do know that he was released from military after being wounded in the leg. Sadly, he walks with a limp, but he is sturdy and healthy otherwise. He is in Charleston at present on secret business of the government. I am sure he will tell me more once our confidence has been sealed. Furthermore, dear sister he is staying under my roof as a houseguest. I can almost imagine the joy of having my own husband, as I am sure you have experienced first hand. To the latter I suggest you not inform Mother. She will most likely disapprove.

I have not heard from Papa this week. I am not worried. These days the post is always delayed. I trust that your baby carrying is coming along well and that little Minerva will not be too jealous of the newcomer. I was so happy to hear that Mother is feeling better.

With this newfound happiness in my heart, I can now see past the gloom and into the future. I know that God will deliver us soon and blessings are sure to follow.

> Give my love to Mother, Minerva and TJ,
>
> Lizzie.

PS: I will write soon with more on my love story, should it develop. Cross your fingers!

The next morning, I was to find Edmond had borrowed a horse and left to go to the hospital. I would have gladly attended him, but I had to assume it was personal in nature. Simon said Edmond was due back by lunch, so I instructed Millie to set out a nice lunch on the upstairs veranda providing the weather was not too cool.

Edmond was back before noon and we would have enjoyed a delightful lunch had I not learned he was leaving that very evening. My heart was broken and I could not detain my despair. I left the table and retreated to my room as soon as he announced his news. Edmond called my name as I walked up the steps, but I had nothing to remark.

I intended to lock myself up in my room until he departed, but Edmond was not to have it that way. He followed me upstairs and knocked on my door. I lay across the bed and looked up at the ceiling, he knocked harder and at last, he called out, "Dammit, Lizzie open this door."

At that, I jumped to my feet and threw open the door. "Mr. Cook, how dare you speak to me in that manner in my own home!" I declared.

"You listen to me Miss Lizzie. Hear me loud and clear, I-love-you!" he shouted loud enough for the whole household to hear.

I slowly moved away from the door and he stepped inside. He took me in his arms and kissed my tear stained face. "I will be back and we shall set about making plans for the future. Do you hear me?" he said in a loud whisper.

"Yes," I am not hard of hearing, Edmond," I said, smiling up at him.

"Lizzie, from the first time I saw you at the train station, I have dreamed of finding you in my arms. So, come hell or high water, I am not about to let you go."

My knees felt weak from all the excitement and slowly I dropped down on the floor. Edmond sat down beside me, collected me in his arms and kissed me. I had forgotten the door was open until I heard Cindy Lou in the hall.

"Cuse me, Miss Lizzie, I's gots a note from Miss Lucy fer yous," she said holding her head down looking embarrassed to have walked in on us.

Edmond jumped to his feet and helped me up. "Mr. Cook was just leaving," I said, taking the note from her hand.

"Well excuse me ladies, I will go pack my bags." Edmond kissed my hand gently and promised he would not leave without saying goodbye.

Cindy Lou scrambled out the door and I sat down to read the note.

Dear Miss Lizzie,

I am in receipt of your offer to purchase two house slaves. I apologize for my delayed response. I must say in all honesty, owning slaves has never been an ambition of mine. I cannot wholeheartedly embrace slavery, as I believe that we as woman are enslaved by our own mere existence. However, your offer was most generous and I am in need of domestic help. I am also not blind to the necessity of ones need to sell off assets during these most difficult times. Therefore, I will accept your offer to purchase the following, a young girl, Cindy Lou and the middle age woman, Harriett.

You may deliver them at your earliest.

Sincerely,
Miss Lucille McGill

I completely forgot about this offer. In fact, I had not given a concern for my finances since Edmond arrived. Strange how your priorities can change, once love is in the mix. Now, this brought me back to reality.

I found Fannie in the clinic and told her I had received an answer from Miss Lucy. She said, the sooner the better, before

292

Miss Lucy changes her mind. She left to break the news to both Harriet and Cindy Lou.

Edmond met me downstairs. I wanted very much to drive him to the station, but Edmond felt it would be easier if Simon took him. Cindy Lou and Harriet were packed and waiting on the front step. Simon would drop off Edmond at the station and deliver them on the same mission.

Harriet stepped up in the carriage without expression, but Cindy Lou held on to me with a display of emotion. I tried to comfort her explaining I would visit with her often. I knew this was a lie. I had no intentions of gracing the door of Miss Lucy's.

Edmond tried to look distracted by walking off toward the garden. When they were all loaded up, I watched until the carriage was out of sight.

I had neglected my hospital duties and today was as good as any to offer up my services. I changed my clothes and walked to the hospital. When Fannie saw me, she smiled, "hello stranger, welcome back to my world." She patted me on the shoulder and said there was a fresh load just came in from a battle in Beaufort County just north of Yemassee. I nodded and went off to do my duty.

Luckily, we were relieved about suppertime. Fannie and I walked out the back door. She stopped on the porch, reached in her pocket, pulled out a small white pipe and lit it. I suspected she used tobacco, but this was the first time I had seen this display. "No secrets here with me," she said taking a draw of her pipe. "How's about you?" she asked.

"Nothing much to tell, as of yet," I said trying to be honest. "Edmond has left."

"That bastard!" Fannie said under her breath. "Just like a man, wine you and dine you and then drop you like a hot potato. That is the very reason I ain't got one. If you ask me they are not good for nothing but filling up your belly with babies."

"Fannie!" he is coming back. "He says he loves me," I answered defending Edmond.

"Well, that's what they all say, my dear. For your sake Lizzie, I hope you are right. She put out her pipe and studied my face for a second. "Let's go home," she announced. "Tomorrow is another day."

She took off walking, leaving me to follow. It was almost dark when we turned in the driveway, I could see someone sitting on the porch steps. As we got closer, the figure began to wave and jump up and down.

"Oh my God, it is Cindy Lou! She has run away!" Fannie shouted.

"Cindy Lou why in tarnation did you run off like this? Miss Lucy is liable to tan your hide and I don't blame her!" I said grabbing hold of her shoulders and giving her good shake. Still she just kept looking at me with a silly grin on her face. When I let go of her she pointed to a letter pinned to her jacket, with my name written on it. In shock, I open the envelope and read,

My darling Lizzie,

I know these are difficult times, but I could not leave knowing you have been forced to part with a treasure such as Cindy Lou. I persuaded the dear Miss Lucy to sell her back to me. Please accept her as the first of many gifts I hope to shower you with when I return.

Love always,
Edmond

Cindy Lou threw her arms around me and knocked off my bonnet, *"I's still yours Miss Lizzie. We wills always be together now!"*

Fannie laughed and we went inside. Cindy Lou ran down the hall, upsetting a little table. In just the nick of time, I lunged forward and caught the oil lamp before it splattered on the floor. "And this is a good thing?" Fannie teased as she walked up the stairs.

Over the next couple of weeks, I continued my work at the hospital. It was still as stressful as before, but now I had hope and the days did not seem as long and treacherous.

Papa wrote and said their supplies were running out and this next mission would be his last. His plans were to be home as early as Thanksgiving. Mother wrote to me the very night Sallie told her about Edmond. She cautioned me to take it easy until Papa got back, but she was excited in the prospects of having such a handsome new son-in-law.

The letters Edmond sent were full of promise. With each letter, he revealed more about himself and his feeling for me.

November 14, 1862

My darling,

Every morning I find I am lonelier than the one before. How is it I have lived thirty-two years and was content to rise on my own? Now, I find all that I do is long to be with you. I can scarcely wait to see your sweet face again and to kiss those dear and tender lips. Please pardon me, but sweetheart, the thoughts of how much I desire you overtakes me with great passion. I warn you that I may not be able to detain myself next time I see your fine form.

I have been a loner most of my life, but I am ready for all this to change. My Mother died when I was just twelve years old. Papa was a wealthy attorney and in less than a year, he married a widowed woman with three young girls. She never took a shine to me and Papa sent me off to military school. I never saw my father again; he died not long after that. He was a fair man and left his new wife the house and a reasonable allowance. However, much to her displeasure, he left me the bulk of his estate.

So, at the age of thirteen, I found myself on my own. I continued my education at the military academy and then went on to study law in Charleston. I would have entered into politics, but the war broke out and I joined the military.

I am not sure if it was fortune or my misfortune, but the first battle I was to partake in; a cannon ball exploded filling my right leg with metal. The wound cost me about three months in the hospital and left me unable to sit in the saddle for any extended length of time. My commanding officer said he had no choice but to discharge me. You see, this is why I much prefer the carriage to the saddle. The doctors said I was lucky to be alive. Darling since I have met you, I am sure I am the luckiest man on earth.

For now, I have partnered myself with other concerned businessmen in an effort to help save our South. I wish I could tell you more, but it is unsafe to discuss such things. Besides, I do not wish to burden you with more than you already have suffered.

Enough of all this. Know that I think of you every day and just as soon as I can arrange my affairs, I will be back to see you again. I know it is too soon to talk about a future together. Yet, I see no reason to deny my feelings. I confess I am head over heels in love with you. I think you are fond of me too, but perhaps it is just wishful thinking.

Please write to me as often as you possibly can. I beg for long and intimate letters. Spare not a single detail of your health, daily life and all that you dare to share of your most personal desires.

With my deepest devotion,
Edmond

The coming weeks found me looking up the road for Papa. According to his last letter, he was due home any day. I could hardly wait to tell him about Edmond. What a glorious Thanksgiving it will be to have Edmond and Papa both at the dinner table. Yet, that week I did not receive a letter from Papa, I could only assume he was busy on his way home.

Today I had a visitor. As soon as I opened the door I recognized him as one of Papa's associates. I opened the door widely and bid him in, hoping he had news of Papa. It took only minutes to see the man's face was downtrodden and his heart was heavy as he began to speak.

I thought I might faint as the blood rushed to my face. I called for Simon to bring me a glass of water and sat down just inside the foyer. The gentleman who introduced himself as Ralph Ern was indeed with Papa on the mission. He did not sit, but stood bracing himself against the door facing. Simon must have alerted the others and soon the whole household was standing behind me in the hall.

"Miss Sanders, I am sorry to tell you this," the man said, accepting a glass of water from Simon.

"Papa, is he alright? Where is he?" I begged the man to continue.

"I wish I could say. You see, our last mission was an arrangement to meet a Mr. Joel Simpson and drop off our remaining supplies. After our rendezvous with Mr. Simpson, all seemed well until shots broke out and a band of Yankees came out of nowhere. Some of our men were wounded and I saw another take a bullet right in the head. We all took off running in all directions. Last I saw of your father he had climbed on the back of the horse with Joel and the Yankees were hot on their trail. I hope they made it back to camp safety, but I fear they were captured," he said and slowly dropped down in the chair next to me.

"Captured? Papa is a civilian; they can't possibly take him prisoner!" I stood up and focused my anger at the man.

"Them damn Yankees don't play by nobody's rules. It is hard to say what they might do," he replied.

Fannie jumped forward and took hold of me before I could slap the man. "Lizzie, you get a hold of yourself now. The gentleman has had a hard enough time. You can not take this out on him!" she said squeezing my arm tightly.

I went limp and she let go of me. "I am sorry," I said.

"All understood, Miss Lizzie," he said standing up and taking hold of my hand. "I reckon we will hear something soon. You have to trust there are a lot of good men out there trying to get to the bottom of this. Don't you give up hope now; we will find your Father and that Mr. Joel too. I will be in touch just as soon as we hear something," he said. He tipped his hat to all of us and let himself out.

I looked across the room at my household family and I knew they too were feeling my pain. Fannie reached for me and I pulled away. I did not want sympathy I wanted answers. How could any of them understand? It was my Father, and only I knew how special he was.

I needed to escape and I needed to be alone. I instructed Millie to pack me a basket of food, plenty enough to last for a couple of days. There was a brief debate about my safety and welfare, but I was going to Sandy Ridge.

I don't know what I expected to find at Sandy Ridge; I just had to be there. I rode as fast as I could, never taking mind or lifting my hand to anyone I passed on the road. Sandy Ridge was the only place on earth I wanted to be.

When I arrived, I unlocked the door with my key. I dropped my bag on the floor and set the basket of food on the hall table. Something inside made me scream out, "Hello, Hello! Only silence fell around me. Dammit, why don't you answer me! Why did you let him leave? Why didn't you bolt your doors and keep us all here forever?" Speaking to the house showed no logic. Yet, my anger was beyond logic. I ran my hand over the dusty table and sat down in one of Mother's French chairs. I realized this old house's silence was as good an answer as anyone could offer.

I cannot say how many hours passed. I had been weeping so long my belly was aching and my eyes were sore and swollen. The evening sun crept into the house. Its sunny fingers reached up to the chandelier causing tiny little rainbows to dance on the wall in front of me. I watched until the room grew dim and they disappeared. I felt as if I too, was slowly disappearing in the shadows.

"Dear God," I prayed. "I can't do this anymore on my own. If you are listening and if anything in my life has ever been pleasing to your eyes, help me now. I have no one to turn to except you. I am too weak to walk and I am overcome by my fears and sorrows. Dear Lord in heaven above, please direct me and I will follow."

I sat there in a ball with my head on my knees. The crying left me within moments after my prayer. I felt a shiver down my spine as if someone was breathing down my neck. Amazingly, the hall suddenly seemed crowded as if God had sent a multitude of angels to comfort me. I am not sure if I stood or I was lifted up, I was no longer afraid, just hungry and sleepy. I walked over, opened the basket, and ate a piece of cheese and a small loaf of bread. I was completely at ease. I did not even bother to secure the door, went upstairs, and slept peacefully all night.

The next two days I spent tidying up Sandy Ridge. I worked from sunup to sundown, dusting and cleaning around the house. I wintered Papa's rose garden. I had watched him all my life and I knew what he would have done.

On the third evening, I realized I was out of food. Even though I was not ready to go back to town, this would have to be my last night here. It was a cool evening; still I wanted to look out across the garden. I took my food and a bit of wine out on the lower porch. Suddenly I realized it was Thanksgiving.

Dear God, Please have mercy on me. I beg of you to send me an omen, just a tiny sign to let me know if Papa is alive.

I looked over the garden one last time. Just a year ago, the plantation was alive. Now there was not a single sound of human existence. I felt like the last human on earth. Just as I started to go inside, I noticed something glowing. I wrapped my shawl around my shoulders and slowly walked over to investigate. I was amazed to discover one lone yellow rose in bloom. I lowered my head to inhale its fragrance. "Thank you Lord," I shouted up to the heavens. The yellow rose was Papa's favorite. Yes, he was alive and somewhere out there he was thinking of me too.

I lit a lamp by the door and made my way upstairs. It was just after eight o'clock when I blew out the light and climbed in bed. I barely drifted off to sleep when I was awakened by a noise. I jumped to my feet and looked out the window. I could see nothing except it had begun to rain. Assuming it was the storm that awoke me, I lay back down.

An hour or so later, I was awakened again. This time I was certain I heard footsteps downstairs. I did not dare light my lamp or make a sound. Very carefully, I arose and slipped my hand in the drawer for my pistol.

I could hear the intruder's footsteps in the hall. From underneath the door, I could see the flickering of his lamp. I was debating hiding under the bed or calling out, "Get out or I'll shoot." My heart was beating so loudly, I could not tell if the footsteps were getting closer.

"Lizzie, where are you?" a voice called out. I recognized the voice. It was Edmond. I jumped to my feet, opened the door, and found him standing before me.

"Thank God you are alright," he said, taking me up in his arms. He pushed me away so he could look into my face and asked, "Are you all alright?"

I shook my head, "Yes, but you almost gave me a heart attack, sneaking in on me like that." I said taking a deep breath.

"Better me than that band of Yankees I saw down the road. Lizzie, have you seen them?"

"No, there has not been a soul here, except me," I replied

"Lizzie, you are telling me that nobody has been here and there are no slaves on this property?" he asked.

"No, Edmond, I told you the slaves are all gone and I have been alone here for three days. Why do you question me?"

"We will talk about it in the morning, but for now I need to get you back in bed before you catch cold."

He lifted me off my feet and carried me back to bed. He threw on a few logs on the fire and the room lit up. "I'll just sit over here until morning and then you and I will have a little talk about your running away like this."

I was not sure what to say. I only knew I wanted to be close to Edmond.

"No Edmond, please come and lie next to me," I said softly.

"Lizzie, don't you think…," he said slowly rising from the chair.

"I don't want to think, I have had way too much of that lately," I said and turned back the covers.

Edmond smiled at me and lay down next to me, remaining in control with his feet on the floor. He kissed me and I opened my lips. I heard him moan softly as his hands stroked over my soft cotton nightgown. He was aware it was the only thing between us. It felt good to be in Edmond's arms. The rain pounded against the window as our passion grew. I unbuttoned his shirt and laid my head on his bare chest. I could feel his hands underneath my gown. He kissed my lips and buried his head into my neck until his lips reached my breast. I was the receiver and Edmond was the giver. There was no right or wrong there alone in the moonlight. Too much was already lost and no one knew what tomorrow would bring. That night, I was to find the act of love making not awkward or strange, but a new beginning of things I never knew.

Morning came and it was still raining. Edmond was still sleeping and I took care not to wake him as I slipped out of bed. I walked across the hall and stepped out on the balcony in the rain. I found myself crying, not because I was sorry for what happened, but because I felt no remorse. When I turned to see Edmond standing at the door, my wet cotton gown was transparent.

"Lizzie what on earth are you doing out here?" he asked, pulling me inside.

"Mother was wrong, there are some sins even a *Carolina Rain* can't wash away."

CHAPTER 26

December 1862

The line was crossed and Edmond and I now were lovers. For the sake of such we stayed at Sandy Ridge for three more days.

I discovered much about Edmond those few days. My most important discovery was that he needed me as much as I needed him. Not just to satisfy the flesh, but to heal his wounded soul. I learned how deeply he had been hurt by his mother's death and then his father's rejection. He had no one to share his life with; his dreams, his hopes and his fears. He was tender and gentle and wanted only to love and to be loved.

Edmond was so different than the first impression I had of him that day at the train station. Even though he appeared to be a ladies' man, nothing could be further from the truth.

Those days together were like a forbidden romance novel. We shared long walks in the brisk country air, afternoons reading to each other by the fire and passionate nights in each other's arms.

On the morning we were preparing to leave, I found myself wishing we could stay there forever; however, I knew reality was waiting for us. It was all too true, the South was falling around us and Papa was missing.

I told Edmond I had instructed Simon to come for me at once if any news arrived about Papa. Still, I was surprised he had not come out to check on me before now. Edmond laughed, "I think he knows you are in good hands. I told him I would be back right away if something was wrong. If not, I might just stay until you run me off."

"Oh, I see," I said smiling. "So you came with intentions of having your way with me? Now the whole world will know the likes of my kind. Well, to tell you the truth, I do not care what anyone thinks. Let those without sin cast the first stone."

"Judge not, and you will not be judged; condemn not, and you will not be condemned; forgive, and you will be forgiven. Luke 6:37," Edmond quoted.

"Thank you and well put, darling," I said, feeling surprised by his Biblical knowledge.

Edmond said he was concerned about the security of the valuables in the house. He suggested I take Mother's portrait back to town with me and anything else that might be irreplaceable. As for the rest of the valuables, he wanted to know if I knew of a safe place to hide them. I hesitated, thinking of Papa coming home and finding a bare house, but better shocked than robbed. I decided to tell Edmond about the secret chamber.

It took several hours to clear out a portion of the valuables and load them in the chamber. It was almost noon. We both were starving, but there was nothing left to eat.

We tied Edmond's horse to the back of the carriage so we could ride back to town together. After we had been on the road for a while, Edmond pulled over to the side.

"Lizzie, I have something to tell you. I purposely withheld this information until we left Sandy Ridge."

My heart skipped a beat and a million thoughts flew through my head at once.

This had to be bad news; perhaps he is going to tell me he is married or is leaving and not coming back. "Edmond, I have been honest with you about my feelings. I don't know if I can bear to hear you have been dishonest with me,"

"Lizzie, this has nothing to do with us. I just did not want you to be frightened. You remember I told you I saw a band of

Yankees on the way to your house. Well, there is more to the story. Let me explain, I was coming around the ridge when I saw their camp through the trees. I figured I should see what they were up to, so I tied off my horse and slipped through the woods. From the ledge, I had a bird's eye view of their camp and could hear every word. Two men rode up. Apparently they were sent out as scouts. Both men looked shook up and one said he would never go back to that Sandy Ridge for no amount of gold. The other man said something strange had taken place there. They heard the house was vacant and not a single slave was left at Sandy Ridge. They figured it would be easy pickings, until they got closer to the gate. They were surprised to see four big Negroes standing guard armed with axes and farm tools. Knowing they would play hell to get past them, they went around and came up on the house from the back. Just as they stepped on the porch, an old black woman came running out after them with a butcher knife. One of the men opened fire and the bullets went straight through her."

"Edmond," I gasped. "That sounds like Mammy, but Mammy is dead. So, are Samuel and all the other slaves. Yet, I did hear something that sounded like a gun shot. I resolved it was just the wind or thunder, until now. You don't suppose…"

"I don't know, Lizzie, but it sure sounds like someone or something was looking after you."

"We rode in silence for the longest time and finally Edmond said, "Maybe it was not Sandy Ridge they visited."

"Maybe it *was* just thunder," I responded. Yet, just what happened that night, we would never know.

When we arrived back at the house, I stood out in the drive while Edmond unloaded the carriage. I looked up at the house and saw the curtains pull back in Fannie's room. She was staring down at me and I waved sheepishly. The curtains closed and she disappeared. What would she say to me? Was she waiting to scold me? I was sure my entire household, even Cindy Lou, knew I had been alone with Edmond at Sandy Ridge.

The front door opened and Simon greeted us with a big smile, just like this was an every day occurrence. "Welcome home, Miss Lizzie. I trust you and Mr. Cook had a nice visit in the country."

"Yes, Simon we did." I replied.

"The best," Edmond said and winked at me.

When we opened the front door, I could smell fresh baked bread. I walked back to the kitchen, "Hello Miss Lizzie," Millie smiled.

Cindy Lou came bursting through the door and gave me a big hug, *"Miss Lizzie, I was scared yous wuz gone for goods."*

Millie prepared a plate of food for Edmond and me. We were just finishing our meal when Fannie walked in. She was dressed in a fresh clean dress and her hair was arranged nicely.

"Hello, my friend, good to see you," I said speaking up first.

"Good day to you too," she said looking at me with great suspicion. She fixed herself a small plate of food and covered it with a cloth. "I will be in the clinic today, Lizzie. I have a few patients due in this afternoon, but I would like to speak to you first."

I looked at Edmond and he nodded. I folded my napkin and followed her to the clinic. She closed the door behind us, set her food on the desk, and began eating.

"So, Lizzie, what do you wish for me to assume? I am a woman of the world. I am not so dense as to believe that nothing happened between you and Edmond after all this time. Mind me; I am not here to judge. I personally would not have missed the opportunity, especially in these dreary times. I am only prying because I have your best interest at heart. Will you listen to me?" she asked.

"I am listening," I answered her. There was no need to say more.

"First let's tend to your physical health. Slip off your dress and let me exam you, she said wiping her hands and slipping on her apron.

I raised my eyebrows to question her, but she stopped me before I could say a word. "Are you listening to me or not? It is your choice," she said.

306

I nodded and started to unbutton my dress. After her exam she reported all looked fine, but she would like a follow up exam in two weeks. I knew full well what she was looking for. It was degrading and I felt almost like one of Miss Lucy's girls.

Then she gave me a bottle of drops, which she claimed would induce my monthly. Hopefully it would eliminate the chance of pregnancy. She said it might cause cramping for a couple of days, but I would be fine. She also filled my head with more information than I wished to hear about how to prevent pregnancy in the future. "Lizzie, you will have to discuss these things with Edmond if you plan to continue a relationship with him. It is neither the time nor place for you or anyone else to be having a baby. Promise me you will or I will!" she said looking at me sternly.

"Alright Fannie, I will, I will," I said, but I was not sure I would. After my episode with Fannie, I was on my way upstairs when Millie said there was someone here to see me. I was hoping it was news about Papa. I was disappointed to see Mrs. Gibson from next-door sitting in the foyer with a little cup of sugar.

"Here dear, I have been meaning to return this to you for the longest time," she said standing up to hand me the little cup. This allowed her a view of the hallway behind me. "Have you been well?" she asked sweetly. "I have not seen you out and about for the last couple of days."

"Yes, I have been fine. Thank you, Mrs. Gibson." I said, taking the cup of sugar from her. In days gone by, I would have been gracious and not accepted the sugar, but these days it was welcomed. I had been drinking weak coffee and tea for months without a speck of sugar. As hard as sugar was to come by, she must really want some gossip to give up even a thimble full.

"I was just wondering when I saw the gentleman bring you home today, if you had been in the hospital or off visiting sick family," she said as she stepped closer to take up my hand.

"No, Mrs. Gibson...I have been..." I was trying to explain, when Edmond walked up and interrupted.

"Miss Lizzie has been away on important business," he announced. Then he leaned forward and whispered to Mrs. Gibson, "Can you keep a secret?"

"Oh, yes indeed, I won't tell a soul," Mrs. Gibson said feeling extremely flattered.

Edmond winked at me and he folded his arm around Mrs. Gibson and led her out the front door. I could hear him winding her a story and she was all ears. "Tonight?" she asked.

I went upstairs and instructed Millie to tell Edmond I would be resting. In reality, I knew I had to write Sallie and Mother a letter and it was not going to be easy to tell them about Papa. I went to my desk to gather my pen and paper. I looked out my window to see Edmond riding down the drive. He must have something to take care of, I thought. I spread out across my bed, but after only writing a few lines I fell asleep.

I was alarmed to see it was five o'clock in the afternoon when Millie woke me. She was smiling and said she had prepared a tub for me to bathe. "That sounds nice, Millie," I replied, finding this an unexpected pleasure.

She rolled the tub in and poured some rose oil in the hot water. "Where did you get that?" I asked.

"Mr. Edmond sent it up to you," she said, not looking up at me.

I undressed and slipped into the steamy water. It felt wonderful. Shortly she returned with my blue dress, freshly pressed. She laid it out on the bed for me. "Mr. Edmond asked if would you do him the pleasure of wearing this one. It is his favorite."

I finished my bath, dressed and walked out into the hall. Before going downstairs I paused to see Millie putting fresh sheets on the bed in Edmond's room. The table was set beautifully and I smelled dinner cooking. I walked into the kitchen and found a nice piece of beef cooking on the hearth. "Where did this come from?" I asked, Cindy Lou.

"Mr. Edmond," she said, stirring the pot and avoiding eye contact with me.

"Next, I went looking for Edmond. The house was quiet as I walk down the hall.

I called out but no one answered. The parlor door was closed and I opened the door.

Much to my surprise I saw Edmond dressed as though he was going to ball. "Where are you going?" I asked.

"I hope no where, my darling," he said and stood up and took my hand.

He dropped down on his knees and looked me in the eye. "Lizzie, will you marry me?"

"Well, I can't make a discussion like this on my own. What about Papa and Mother?" I answered, feeling overwhelmed.

"Lizzie, they are not here. It is only you and I. Do you not think you are old enough to know what is best for you?" he said standing to his feet.

"Yes," I answered

"Do you love me?" he asked.

"Yes," I said again.

"Then again I ask, will you marry me?"

"Yes," I answered for the third time.

"Wait here," he said and ran out of the room. Within minutes, he returned with the whole household, Mrs. Gibson and Mr. Shive the Minster from Calvary. Mrs. Gibson was smiling as if she would burst, hurried herself over to the piano and began to play the wedding march.

"Edmond," I whispered. "Now?"

"Why not?" he said and took up my arm.

We were married, that day on December 3, 1862 at seven o'clock in the evening.

CHAPTER 27

Mrs. Cook

It was going to take some time getting used to being called Mrs. Cook. Edmond said he liked the sound of it and insisted the household address me as such.

The evening following the wedding, I finally sat down and wrote my long dreaded letter to Mother. I would not tell her everything. With Sallie's baby being due any day, I saw no need to put more stress on them. Hopefully Papa would be home soon and the worry would all be for nothing.

December 4, 1862

Dear Mother,

I hope this letter finds all of you in good health. I know you have been waiting to hear from Papa. I regret telling you I do not have the best of news to share. Mr. Ralf Ern visited with me before Thanksgiving to inform me Papa was with Joel Simpson and had been detained. I know this is distressing, but with any luck he will be home soon. As soon as I hear more, I will try to send a telegram. At the very least, I will write to you immediately.

Mother, I have some good news to share with you. I hope you will find it good news. Edmond Cook and I are married. I know you are shocked, but I need not tell you how lonely I have been. We all know these are dreadful times we are living. I just did not see the sense in waiting when who knows what tomorrow might bring. I hope you will forgive me, as you always do for my forthright behavior. Papa will be surprised too, but when he sees what a good choice I made, he will be happy for me.

Edmond and I are as happy as we can be under the circumstances of war and family being separated. I want you to meet him as soon as possible; I know you will love him.

I have been on pins and needles waiting to hear about Sallie's baby. I wish I could be there to see this one born too. Please tell her she is in my prayers and let me know as soon as the baby is born.

Edmond and I will not be able to go on a honeymoon, which is understandable.

For now, we will be staying between the Bullwinkle Estate and Sandy Ridge. He says when the war is over he will take me to England and Paris.

Love to all my North Carolina family,
Mrs. Edmond Cook

It was half past nine when I sealed my envelope. I turned to see my handsome husband with his shirt undone standing in the doorway. "Are you ready to turn in?" he asked.

"Yes dear I will be right up," I replied. I laughed to myself thinking about what Sallie said after her honeymoon, "Men never tire of the experience." No Sister Sallie, they do not. They certainly do not. I was still laughing when I slipped under the sheets next to Edmond.

The weeks before Christmas Edmond was busy catching up on his work and answering letters. At least twice a week his affairs took him into town and I went with him. I spent those days taking care of my household shopping. Edmond was most gracious and encouraged me to be thrifty, but assured me there was no reason to do without.

The merchants were delighted to see me coming to buy what little they had to offer. Often on those days, Edmond would surprise me with something special like a little bottle of French perfume or an Irish linen handkerchief. I would scold him as I found myself feeling guilty. In a time when so many were doing without, he should not spoil me so. He would just laugh and say, "It is my job."

We were all better off since Edmond came in our lives. My fears of losing the Bullwinkle estate were calmed and my bank accounts were not dwindling away so quickly.

It was decided we would not exchange Christmas gifts. Just being together was enough. I did send a package to North Carolina. Edmond feared the package might not be delivered. I took his advice in not sending anything too dear. I made Mother and Sallie both a scarf and TJ and Minerva a little rag doll. I enclosed a tin type that Edmond and I made together. I hoped it would cheer Mother to see our photo. Lastly, I sent a package of assorted garden seeds. I only wished I had news of Papa to send.

When I went to the post office to mail the package to North Carolina, I was to find a letter addressed to Mrs. Edmond Cook, in Sallie's hand.

December 12, 1862

Dear Sister,

It is with happy heart that I write to you this morning. I do not know which to brag on first, my sister with the handsome new husband or my little son, Noah Wesley. Yes, Lizzie, we have a new member in the family. A big 8-pound boy. He has blue eyes and a head full of red hair.

I must tell you about the day Noah was born. Early that morning, Mother left me briefly to take some corn meal to Mrs. Huneycutt. I laid Minerva (who calls herself, "Nerva" and now we all do.) on a blanket in the hall to play. Shortly she began screaming. I ran to see what was wrong and saw a man's shadow at the door. I was scared to death because we had heard there were Yankees in the area. Through the curtain, I could only tell that the man was tall with a beard. Next, I heard a familiar voice call out, "Sallie."

You can never measure my shock to open the door and see my own darling husband standing there before me, thin as a rail and frozen to the core. At once, I bid him in by the fire and stirred up a pot of stew. I found out his regiment was camped nearby and he had permission to come home for one night. I was much relieved he had not slipped off. We heard Mrs. Hinson's son deserted from his regiment and when the troops caught up with him, they gave him 39 lashes across his bare back. I suppose it was necessary to set an example, although it seemed awfully harsh. If all the soldiers took off, our cause will all be in vain.

The excitement was great for me in my delicate condition and by the time Mother got back, I was in labor. Ransom did not get much rest that night, but we both felt it was God's blessing he was there to see our baby boy born.

The next morning, Ransom's entire regiment came to collect him. Ransom invited Colonel Gibbs and several other officers in to see his new baby boy. Mother and Violet fed them as much as we were able. They took refreshment from our well before they marched off.

Oh, I have also heard from Thomas. In his letter, he said he shot a man and killed him outright. Here is the story in brief. For three nights in a row, the man taking his turn to stand night guard was found dead the next morning with his throat cut. When it came Thomas's turn, he made sure he did not fall asleep for one second and kept a keen eye open at all times. In the wee hours of the night, he saw a wild hog out in the field. He decided to shoot it for meat and when he went to retrieve it, he discovered it was not a hog at all. It was a Yankee covered in a pig's hide. He has since been promoted to first sergeant and thinks he is fitted for military life.

With Christmas near, it will be a sad time. We have organized prayer meetings for all the soldiers and Papa and Joel are at the top of our list.

I close now, to take care of my new bundle of joy. I miss you greatly and wish you much happiness with your new husband.

With my deepest affection and love,
Your sister, Sallie

Edmond and I planned to spend Christmas and New Year's at the Bullwinkle house. Although the social season would not include parties, there would be a few gatherings and church services. In fact, Edmond encouraged me to host a small gathering for a few neighbors and friends to maintain some sense of normalcy in our chaotic world. Besides, he said it was high time we were introduced to society as husband and wife. Unfortunately, we knew it would spoil some of the old ladies' fun once they found out we were not living together in sin.

It sounded like a delight, but I was concerned over what to serve. Edmond told me not to worry. There would be flour and sugar for cakes and cookies and he even promised enough whiskey for a nice hot punch.

Edmond made good on his promise and on Christmas Eve, we had a house full of happy guests. All seemed grateful for the invite, as this was the only party they would be attending this season.

For the first time I asked Edmond, "Darling, how are you able to buy such coveted items, while the rest of the town does without?"

Edmond did not respond for a second and I could see he was choosing his words carefully. "Why just look at me, I am a lucky man. I am married to the sweetest most beautiful woman in the world."

"Edmond, please don't think that I am ungrateful, but there are things I do not understand," I said, looking at him more seriously.

"Well, I suppose you have found me out, I am a privateer," he said laughing.

"Well, I am the Swedish opera singer, Jenny Lind," I teased back. Edmond was full of himself. One thing I had learned, it was sometimes hard to get a straight answer out of him. I decided when he was ready to tell me, he would.

Christmas morning, Edmond knocked on the door and offered me a cup of fresh brewed coffee. Not a weakened down or twice brewed cup, but a fresh and full-bodied cup of coffee. I sat up in bed to accept it. I held it under my nose to take in its aroma. I took a sip. I had almost forgotten what a good cup of coffee tasted like. "Edmond, this is heavenly," I said appreciatively.

"Get dressed dear, breakfast is waiting. No, just throw on your dressing robe and come downstairs with me."

I started to resist, but he tossed the robe my way and I obeyed. As soon as we got downstairs, I could smell hot cakes and bacon cooking. "Oh my," I declared as I stepped in the kitchen. It had been a long time since I had tasted a strip of bacon.

Millie was wearing a new red apron with lace trim and Simon was sporting a new silk vest. I looked at Edmond in disbelief. "Two lumps or one, my dear?" he asked holding the sugar tongs over my cup.

Before I could ask questions, Cindy Lou came in wearing a new shawl. Lastly, Fannie arrived in a new felt hat with a peacock feather. "Edmond, somehow all of this has your name on it." I said looking at him in question.

"What makes you think that?" he asked, teasing me.

"A little birdie told me so," I replied.

"Well, my little chickadee, I have something for you too."

"Edmond, we said we were not going to exchange Christmas gifts," I said, feeling heartbroken that I had nothing for him.

"Yes, I agreed that *we* would not exchange Christmas gifts, but, I did not agree not to *give* gifts," Edmond said, pleased he had mis-led me. "Lizzie, sit down and eat your breakfast before it gets cold."

Just as I sat down, I saw a piece of paper in my seat. I picked it up and read it.

It was a bill of sale for fifty slaves. "Edmond! Is this what I think it is?

"Yes, it is, and they are all for Sandy Ridge. By the time your father gets back, we are going to have Sandy Ridge up and running again."

"Edmond, have you lost your mind? This is an impossible task. We couldn't get a thimble full of cotton through the blockade if we hid it in my shoe."

"No one is more aware of that than me," he said, taking my hand. "Listen to me, if this war goes on much longer it will be all we can do to survive. No one is going to give a damn about cotton when their bellies are aching for lack of food. Someone has to be cocked and ready to feed the masses. I am proposing that Sandy Ridge step up to that challenge. I am talking about provision crops, like corn, okra, field peas, peanuts, potatoes. If it can be eaten, I say we grow it."

I was stunned. "Edmond, what you say makes sense, but how can we possibly afford to start over in this economy? Slaves cost money to keep up and the cost of planting is not free."

"Lizzie, I did not dream this up just last night. There are other businessmen of like mind, who are willing to invest in this endeavor with us. I am asking you to trust me. Have I let you down so far?"

"Edmond, I do trust you, but I don't want to do anything to put Sandy Ridge in jeopardy. Even if, God forbid, Papa never comes home, Sandy Ridge is what he has worked for all his life."

"I understand completely, Lizzie. I would like nothing more than to wait until your father is home. However, this is not all about us. We must act now if we are to put food on southern tables."

"It will be a lot of work and I am not sure I can manage," I said, feeling the tears coming to my eyes. "It is Mother that comes to my mind. All her years of record keeping, sleepless nights and worries, no wonder her nerves suffered."

"Lizzie, it will not be like that. At no time will I place a single demand on your shoulders. My only desire is for your happiness and well-being. I want a wife, not a business partner."

"Very well, Edmond. I put my fate in your hands."

I was not sure how much Fannie had overheard. She walked over and sat next to me, looking as if she was examining me through my clothes.

"Feeling alright, Miss Lizzie?" she asked.

"Never better, Fannie," I replied.

CHAPTER 28

Overwhelming News

The new slaves were due to be delivered by the end of February. The cabins were in need of repair and there were no supplies or food on the premises. Papa had sold all the livestock and we would need to purchase at least a half a dozen mules.

Edmond wanted to get the slaves established into their routine before we moved back to Sandy Ridge. Edmond placed an ad in the paper for workers. With jobs being scarce and money tighter, soon he had all the help he could use.

By the end of February Edmond established a routine of leaving early to go to the shipyard and then to Sandy Ridge. Very rarely would he be home before dark and some nights he stayed over. If he came home, he would stay up to the wee hours of the morning writing letters to his business partners. I appreciated his ambition, but there were more important things in life than money. Me for instance.

I was seeing less and less of Edmond and slowly sinking into despair. I could barely claim to be married except for the nights Edmond and I shared a bed. Although I was glad to have his attention, it sickened me to think that possibly that was all I was good for.

I found myself fantasizing about being married to Joel, living in North Carolina, sitting on the porch with Sallie and taking afternoon rides over the rolling hills.

The last couple of months were like a whirlwind and I allowed myself to be completely wrapped up in Edmond. I escaped reality and rarely read a newspaper. I no longer went to the hospital and most days I spent alone.

Papa said my scrapbooking was important work; yet, I had completely neglected it. I had the brief idea Edmond would be interested in my scrapbooks, but he was always too tired. I wondered if he was too tired to look at my books or tired of me.

I made up my mind not to disappoint Papa and have my scrapbook updated when he returned. I collected all the dated newspapers and sent Simon out for more. It was a rude awakening back to reality.

The "Cotton Famine"
The effects of the war and the lack of cotton are felt far and wide. England's factories are forced to close down. Same true in Yankee land. Unemployment at all time high.

December 11, 1862, *Union troops take over Fredericksburg and chase the Confederates up into the hills. The town is reported to be destroyed. Federal troops confiscate valuables and burn homes. Abe Lincoln reports he believes the war will be over soon.*

December 13, 1862 Union soldiers sitting ducks for General Lee's riflemen.
When Federal troops attacked the Confederate troops on the hills of Fredericksburg, the day turned into a horrendous slaughter and a grand victory for the Confederates.

Dec 20-1862 General Nathan Bedford Forrest Raids continue.
His troops have successfully destroyed Federal railways and bridges. They have confiscated much needed supplies, guns and ammunition. Last reported General Forrest had taken over 1,400 Yankee prisoners.

Edmond seemed to turn a blind eye to my expenses at the Bullwinkle home. Fannie gave what she could and I dipped into my bank account for the balance. I found myself questioning Edmond's character and worrying about the security of Sandy Ridge. Most of the decisions were made without my knowledge or consent.

He put up fences to separate the slave quarters from the main house; it was a safety issue. It had never been necessary before, but he claimed the Negroes could not be trusted now days. Perhaps the most alarming news was he hired a man to live in the old farmhouse as an overseer. I knew too well the trouble that could bring. Edmond was not interested in my input.

I thought about writing to Mother about the mess I was in; but it would do no good. I needed Papa. He would know if this was all on the up and up.

April, 1863

Edmond claimed it would be only be a couple of weeks before we were ready to move back in the house. He was more like his old self again; which was a great relief to me. I felt ashamed of myself, thinking I had misjudged my dear husband.

The stress of the winter had taken a toll on me and Fannie was concerned. I assured her it was nothing that the fresh county air would not cure. A couple of days at Sandy Ridge and I would be good as new.

On the evening of April 5th, Edmond came home early and announced he was expecting Mr. Tudor, Mr. Caldwell from the bank and two other men. When the men arrived, I was surprised to see Ralf Ern the gentleman who had informed me Papa was missing. I was curious what this meeting was all about, especially why Mr. Caldwell and Mr. Ern were here. Was it Edmond's secret business or news about Papa? Yet, it would not be polite for a woman to ask questions. I excused myself to go upstairs.

319

Even though I knew it was dishonest to eavesdrop, I felt entitled. Instead of going upstairs, I slipped inside the coat closet in the hall. In one of Clarence's diaries, I read where he hid in that same closet as a child. He was right. Through the cracks in the wall you could see what was going on and hear as well as if you were in the room.

Mr. Tudor spoke first, "Now Edmond, I understand what you are trying to do. I am sure I speak for all of us, but you are taking a big risk here. If Mr. Sanders were here, he would tell you the same thing. Under different circumstances, you might be able to trust those men, but you cannot trust anyone during war times. Even if they are true Southern sympathizers, Lincoln will have them arrested. "

Then Mr. Caldwell took the floor, "Gentleman, we must consider the monetary effects of Edmond's proposal. It cost money to send those ships out. The ship could be confiscated and the whole crew captured. What do you say to those odds?"

"Mr. Caldwell," Mr. Ern interrupted. "We are all concerned about our finances, but it is a man's life we are talking about. He is our good friend and a fellow Mason."

"It is a dangerous plan destined to fail," Mr. Caldwell declared. "Union vessels are thick as thieves along our waterways. Even if we could get one of our ships out, it would certainly be a suicide mission. Who's to say they will even make the trade once our ship gets on enemy soil. I don't like this double dealing!"

Now Edmond, who sat in the corner not saying a word, entered into the conversation, "Actually Gentleman, everything would be done at sea. I know the Captain personally and he is a man of his word. He is only interested in medical supplies for his crews, not our little endeavors. Once the goods are delivered, he will give the orders to release Mr. Sanders and the other men from Fort Delaware."

Edmond stood in the middle of the room with his hands on his hips waiting for a response. Finally, the heavyset man sitting next to the door stood up, "Who is going to foot the bill for all of this? Surely, you don't expect us to do it."

Edmond smiled and cleared his throat, "Here is the beauty of this deal, the Yankees have already paid for the medical supplies; they just don't know it."

"I am all ears," Mr. Tudor said.

"Well," said Edmond. "Last month, the *Seagull* was lucky enough to overtake a Yankee clipper and guess what was aboard?"

"Medical supplies?" asked Mr. Ern.

"That's right," said Edmond with a smirk.

"You devil," laughed Mr. Tudor.

"I can tell you this much, we will all have hell to pay if we are found out. Lincoln will send his troops right up to our front doors and carry us away to prison too!" said, Mr. Caldwell.

Mr. Ern, sitting on the edge of his chair and noticeably angry turned to Mr. Caldwell, "John, the reason you are not for this plan is because there is no money in it for you. I have known you for twenty years and I have never seen you do one thing that did not pad your own pocket."

"Is that so, Ralf?" Mr. Caldwell announced. "Well, in that case you won't take offense when I say, Count me out! Furthermore, if anything happens to the ship, then you boys better be prepared to come up with the cash for my part of the investment."

Mr. Caldwell grabbed his hat, shoved it on his head and left slamming the door behind him. The jar caused the closet door to fling open and he saw me standing in the closet in full bloom. "Mrs. Sanders...Cook, why don't you just go in and join your husband and his band of crooks."

Mr. Caldwell said no more and slammed the front door in the same fashion as the parlor door. I was afraid I would be discovered, but Edmond resumed the conversation and I quietly closed the door to the closet.

"It is just as well he pulls out, he is a horse's ass to deal with," said Mr. Ern.

"As soon as we have the capital, I say we buy him out. I just hope he does not rat us out before," says the other man.

"There is just one more issue, Edmond," Mr. Tudor spoke up. "We must have a captain and a crew. The crew will not have to know the nature of the mission, but the Captain will have to know."

"I thought about that already; I will go," Edmond said. "It is the only way we can assure the mission is kept secret."

"What will you tell the Misses?" Mr. Tudor asked.

"I'll think of something. I'm not the kind of man that thinks a woman needs to know everything, if you know what I mean," he said slyly.

"Indeed I do, my friend," Mr. Tudor replied to receive a roar of laughter.

I could tell the meeting was about to adjourn. I slipped out of the closet to go upstairs. It was a lot to think about. Edmond had known all long that Papa was being held at Fort Delaware. They mentioned the other men; was Joel one of the others? How much more did Edmond keep from me was the question?

I decided to wait and see what Edmond would tell me. I readied myself for bed; it was after midnight before Edmond slipped in beside me.

The next morning when I woke up, Edmond was gone. The minute my feet hit the floor, I realized I did not feel well. I went downstairs to the kitchen; Fannie was eating a bowl of grits. Millie set a bowl in front of me and the first bite made me ill. I ran out to the courtyard and emptied my stomach. Afterwards, I was so weak Fannie had to help me back inside.

"Let's take a look at you," Fannie said taking me to the clinic. I was not much for it, but I was too sick to resist. After her exam, she gave me some bicarbonate soda and told me to lie down for a while. She sat down at her desk in the other room, and I must have drifted off to sleep. When I woke, I felt fine. I was just dressing myself when Cindy Lou burst in the door to speak to Fannie. "*Dr. Fannie, here iz you's check from Miss Lucy's. I sees Mr. Edmond again, comin' rights out de back door.*"

"No you did not, you are mistaken," Fannie said firmly.

"*I did toos,*" declared Cindy Lou

322

I walked in the room buttoning up my blouse and Cindy Lou looked my way.

"*No's iz must bes som'body eles, da's right Dr. Fannie, not Mr. Edmond.*"

"Cindy Lou!" I shouted. "Did you or did you *not* see Edmond at Miss Lucy's?"

Cindy Lou dropped her head and did not answer. I walked over and took her face in my hands, "Answer me!"

"Yes, Miss Lizzie," she said and ran out of the room.

"That's it; I am going to Sandy Ridge right this minute and confront him. If he would rather spend his nights at Miss Lucy's, then that is where he better start hanging his hat!"

Fannie ran behind, telling me to wait and calm down first. It was not wise to light a fuse without having all the details. "I have details, more than you know!" I said.

"Alright, at least let me go with you," she begged.

"Fine, I could use a witness, tell Simon to bring my carriage around." I went upstairs combed my hair and washed my face.

It was just the first of April, but already it was hot and humid. I must have eaten something that did not agree with me and the bumpy road was making me feel nauseous again. When we arrived at Sandy Ridge, I was amazed to see Negroes in the fields and crops knee high. There were a couple of slaves in the barn working on a new plow, two large mules in the pasture and chickens fluttering around in the courtyard. It was as if someone lived here again, just not me.

I got out of the carriage and I felt faint. I felt like I was losing control of everything. Fannie took my arm and we went to the door. At once the door opened and a gray haired Negro man introduced himself as Grover. "*Good morn'n ladies, may I hep' you,*" he said looking at us as if were just visitors.

"Yes, you may!" I said loudly. "I am Mrs. Cook and I came to see my husband."

"*Well, com' right on in; Is will sho' yous to da study,*" he said, leading the way.

"I know the way, thank you," I said and pulled away from him.

Edmond heard the commotions and came out of Papa's study looking bewildered. "Lizzie, what in the world is wrong?"

Suddenly the room began to spin and the next thing I knew I was lying on the sofa in the parlor. When I opened my eyes, Fannie was putting a cold cloth on my head and Edmond was holding my hand.

Once I regained my wits, I jerked my hand back and sat up. "I want you to know Edmond Cook; I will not have you make a fool of me. Apparently, when I thought you were working, you were out carousing around with the likes of Miss Lucy's sort."

Much to my astonishment Edmond and Fannie were now laughing.

"Wait here, Lizzie," Edmond said and left the room.

Fannie turned her back to me and I stood up and straightened out my skirt. I could not believe that both of them would mock me so. Edmond returned carrying a large bundle in his arms. "Darling, I think when you see what I have, you will understand my visits to Miss Lucy's." He held up a beautiful tea dress. "Miss Georgette had all your measurements and I wanted you to have something nice for our open house."

"Open house, new dress?" I said softly. Feeling light headed again I sat down.

Fannie turned back around and said, "Well, I hope that thing can be let out, because Mrs. Cook's waistline is surely going to be expanding."

"Fannie, how rude, it will fit perfectly," I said at her unexpected comment.

She started laughing, "Maybe so, but you will be the first woman I've known to carry a baby and still have a twenty-two inch waist."

"A baby, Lizzie, this is the first I have heard of this," Edmond said.

"This is the first I knew of it also," I replied, looking at Fannie who was laughing.

"This is wonderful news my dear," Edmond said taking me up in his arms. "I planned to have an open house and surprise you once the work was all done here," Edmond said smiling. "But now, it is Fannie that has given us the biggest surprise. Are you happy dear?" he asked.

"Of course," I answered, but secretly I was not sure.

"Girl or boy?" he said, looking at me intensely.

Fannie spoke up, "Maybe one of each."

"Stay the night, both of you," Edmond encouraged. "I will have Nina make us a nice dinner; then I'll give you the grand tour."

We did stay. It was nice to be back at home and Fannie enjoyed the break. Edmond was most attentive and everything seemed as it should. Only I knew the closet walls were full of secrets.

Early on the morning of April 7th, we left to go back into town. It had been raining the night before, the roads were muddy, and the sky was hazy. I was glad Edmond was driving.

As soon as we arrived in town, we were aware something had or was happening. There was smoke out over Fort Sumter and the stores were all closed. Virtually the streets were evacuated. Edmond drove us straight to the house.

Simon met us at the door, "The Harbor had been attacked by Union ironclad warships. The bombing was over in less than two hours and their ships never penetrated our first line of defense. All the fleets have retreated, one in sinking condition and the others heavily damaged."

"Casualties?" asked Fannie.

"Five killed and eight wounded is what the newspaper said," replied Simon.

"What have you heard of damages to the shipyards?" asked Edmond.

"Nothing sir," Simon answered.

Simon started to take hold of the horse, but Edmond stopped him. Leave it be, I will need to go into town."

"I suppose I should go to the hospital and see if they need my help," Fannie added.

I was instructed to lock the doors and stay inside. Edmond did not feel I was in danger, but no use taking chances. For the rest of the afternoon I was alone again with my thoughts. Papa was alive; I knew that for sure now. The thought of Papa or Joel in a prison camp was horrifying. I heard the terror stories of how hundreds of men were packed in those camps fighting to stay alive. All I could do was pray,

Dear Lord,

    Please have mercy on this miserable country. For many it has become a living hell. Please hear my prayers. Shelter my father and all the others imprisoned by their enemies. Open the door for their escape and safe passage home. I am but a pebble on the beach in comparison to others in such great need. Therefore, I will not ask for myself, but for the child I carry. Please let this war be over soon. Amen.

When Edmond came home, we spoke only briefly. Mr. Ern was with him and he announced others would be joining them. I had learned by observations of his behavior, there was something wrong. The men went in the parlor and I went across the hall to the dining room. I sat down by the window and opened a book. From my seat I could plainly see who came into the parlor.

First, Simon answered the door to Mr. Tudor and the heavy-set man.

Then the last to arrive was Mr. Caldwell. He angrily came into the house spilling arrogances. Even so, Simon was polite and took his hat. Mr. Caldwell started toward the parlor, but first jerked the closet door open. I put my hand over my mouth to keep from laughing; he had expected to see me in the closet again.

I waited until the meeting began and again I slipped into the closet. I rather liked being a spy; I only wished it were under more pleasant circumstances.

"Well, gentleman," Mr. Caldwell began. "The *Seagull* is no more. If any of you would have listened to me, she would be safe today. I pleaded with you to harbor her in Wilmington. You all knew Charleston was likely to be attacked. So not only has your little rescue mission been called off, so has the future of our financial investment.

"Mr. Caldwell, you are just the man I like to run into in times of despair. You always have the most comforting words," Mr. Ern replied sarcastically.

"Gentleman!" Edmond said, calling the meeting to order. "Let us not be petty, but deal with the issues at hand. The *Seagull* is not destroyed. True, it was caught in the crossfire and it will need some repair. As we speak I have some men assessing the damage."

"Well, you can bet your bottom dollar I will not spend one cent for the repairs," Mr. Caldwell said.

"One thousand dollars!" came from a voice in the corner. It was the heavyset man. "Mr. Caldwell, this is my offer to buy you out!"

"Are you joking? I have twice that much invested," Mr. Caldwell said angrily.

"Take it or leave it," the man replied.

The room was hush quiet until Edmond started laughing, "Mr. Caldwell, even rats know when to leave a sinking ship."

"Be in my office in the morning with the money and I will sign the papers." With this, Mr. Caldwell stormed out slamming the door behind him. This time, I held on tight to the closet door. Simon had heard the uproar and met him at the door with his hat.

To my surprise, Edmond immediately opened the parlor door and invited the other men out on the porch for refreshments. I was trapped. "Lizzie," he called. "Lizzie."

Simon appeared. "Where is Lizzie?" Edmond asked.

"Don't know Sir, perhaps upstairs," he answered.

"Simon, ask Millie to fix something for my friends and serve it on the porch," Edmond said, giving up hope of finding me.

I listened carefully until I heard them leave. Suddenly the closet door was jerked opened, "You can come out now, Miss Lizzie," Simon said laughing.

CHAPTER 29

Sleeping With the Enemy

Edmond's good humor was brief and he was back in his old solemn mood.

We were living comfortably at Sandy Ridge just like the Tudor's with not a hint of war recession. There was coffee and sugar in the pantry. Even with flour up to thirty-five dollars a barrel, we had plenty.

On Saturdays, we came into town, but left as soon as church services were over on Sunday. On one of those Saturdays I persuaded Edmond to take me to a benefit concert.

Halfway through the show, a man I did not know came and tapped Edmond on the shoulder. He excused himself. When he returned, he said he was tired and wished to go home.

I had reason to suspect he was not well. He awoke in the middle of the night, profusely sweating and his limp was progressively getting worse. I didn't dare make mention of it to him.

On Sundays, Edmond offered up excuses for not attending church. He was tired, had letters to write or didn't like the preacher. I was forced to go alone and deal with the questions. By May, they had stopped asking about Edmond.

On Sunday May 24th, I came home from church and found Edmond and Fannie in the clinic. They did not hear me come in and I stood by the door and listened.

"Edmond, you are going to have to take care of that leg. This is the third time I have removed shrapnel and before long, it might be the whole leg. You need to stay off that leg, if you ever expect it to heal. I told you this heat is not good for infection and what do you do? You keep on pushing it to the limit," Fannie said in a motherly tone.

"I will do better. This time I promise to take your medicine, Fannie. It is just that I have too many irons in the fire. I have to keep one step ahead of the poker," he said, and jumped off the table.

I did not try to hide and they both knew I overheard. My face flushed and I felt a fury of anger toward both of them. Fannie knew more about Edmond than I did. "Wait Lizzie," Fannie called out as I went upstairs to lie down.

It was later in the afternoon when Fannie came in to wake me. She informed me Edmond went back to Sandy Ridge alone. He claimed he was worried over my health and asked Fannie to watch over me. He would be back on Saturday. It sounded reasonable, but I was in favor of thinking differently. Edmond did not want me in the way. It was his Sandy Ridge now. I was even beginning to think he seized the opportunity from the beginning. I was vulnerable prey for his charms with Papa gone. It was a frightening thought. I wanted to tell Fannie about my devious husband, but I needed more facts. It was time I did some detective work.

The next morning I went to see Mr. Caldwell on the pretense I would consider banking with him again. I alluded to him I had a rather large sum of money to deposit. He at once was my friend again. I knew he had answers for me if I could retrieve them. "Mr. Caldwell, I know I can trust you. You are a smart businessman and we can talk frankly, can we not?"

"Oh yes, Miss Sanders! Forgive me, Mrs. Cook."

"It is no secret to you how I have come by this money," I said, winking at him.

"Certainly not, among the elite business set your husband is a respected privateer. In fact, I too have invested in a few of his endeavors. We need not say more," he said, handing me a stack of papers to sign.

"Thank you, Mr. Caldwell, I will review them. However, until we speak again, I trust you will not discuss our little meeting with my husband."

He kissed my hand, "Of course, I would not think of it. Let me say again, Mrs. Cook, how nice it is to see you again. May I ask when the little one is due?"

I dropped my hand to my middle and smiled, but gave no answer. I suddenly realized it was noticeable I was going to have a baby.

I now knew for sure, Edmond's good fortune was not due to just hard work. He or we were living high on the hog off stolen goods. I could only pray it was at the Union's expense and not the Confederacy's. Something told me the door swung both ways. One thing was clear, in my present condition I could not afford to confront him.

I went over in my head all day what I would say to Fannie. I did not want to turn her against Edmond because, after all, we both needed him.

That evening when she came home, she looked tired. I asked if she was up to some conversation, "Always with you my friend," she answered, trying to smile.

After dinner we went in the parlor and I closed the door. "Fannie, in the time we have known each other, I have come to trust you like a sister. I feel I can tell you anything and you will listen without judgment or conviction."

"It goes without saying, my dear, and I feel the same about you," Fannie said, looking a little defensive.

"I need your advice. It is about Edmond. I am afraid he is not the man we thought. Fannie, I am sure you have noticed the change in him. He has never discussed business or finances with me. He claimed it was not good to clutter up a woman's head with such matters. Now, I am certain he is hiding things from me. All his mail is sent to a private postbox and he keeps his papers and correspondences locked up. My suspicion grew when he held a meeting here; I hid in the closet to listen."

"Wait," Fannie stopped me. "You hid in the closet in your own house?"

"Never mind that, Fannie. It is what I found out that is shocking. Edmond knows where my father is. Papa is being held at Fort Delaware prison camp. Apparently, Edmond was attempting to arrange to have Papa and some of the other men released in exchange for medical supplies.

"And what's the problem with that?" Fannie asked.

"Fannie, the medical supplies were stolen from a Union ship, by one of Edmond's own ships."

"Are you saying Edmond is a privateer?" Fannie asked.

"Yes, and apparently not just on a small scale. From the sound of things, he is involved in plenty of double-dealing."

"Lizzie, do you know what this could mean. If Edmond is caught by either side and is found to be a traitor, they will string him up by his neck and everything you own could be confiscated."

I started to cry and even though Fannie realized she had spoken in haste she continued. "We can work through this, but we are going to have to break up this elephant in small pieces if we are going to eat the whole thing. Do you have any idea where Edmond may have those medical supplies hidden?"

"No, but I would guess somewhere on the property," I said, as the wheels began to turn. "Fannie! Good Lord in heaven, the duck pond. Edmond knows about the chamber!"

"If you are right, we could steal the medical supplies back; send them to Sister Irene and employ the nuns to deliver them to Fort Delaware. Perhaps we can still arrange an exchange. Have you written to your father?"

"No, I have not even considered it," I answered.

"Well, I suggest you do so, there is hope a letter would reach him. In the meantime, keep your eyes and ears open. At our first opportunity, we will look for those medical supplies."

That night I composed a letter to Papa,

My dearest Papa,

I pray this letter reaches you. I have only recently learned of your whereabouts. I want you to know you are in my prayers and on my mind every waking moment. So much has happened here, but please do not worry for us. All of us are healthy and as well as can be expected. Sallie has a new baby boy, Noah Wesley.

Fannie and I are trying to arrange for some of the nuns to bring "Bibles" into the camp where you are being held. I will keep writing you, even if I do not get a response. If you are able to get a letter out, please tell me first and foremost if you are well and second is Joel Simpson with you.

With all my love, Lizzie

The next morning I went to the post office to mail the letter. I asked the clerk if there was any mail for me. After a few minutes, he returned with a letter from Sallie. "Oh, Mrs. Cook, do you want to pick up your husband's mail while you are here?" he asked.

"Yes," I answered quickly, but feeling a little dishonest. I thanked the man and stuffed the letters in my bag. I made quick work of getting home to look over Edmond's mail. The first letter I untied from the bundle was from Philadelphia and the sender was Idora Cook. I sat down in the hall and was just about to open the letter when Fannie walked in the door. She saw I was shaking and asked what was wrong. I told her I had Edmond's mail.

"Good work," she said. "Here give it to me." I followed her into the kitchen where she skillfully steamed open the envelope, so it could be resealed. Together we read the letter.

My dearest Eddie,

It was good to hear from you. I am happy to hear you are assigned to details in Charleston. I was unaware the Union had taken over the city. Not saying much for me, I don't read the papers much anymore, only bad news. Besides, I need new glasses. Your father is getting along well after his stroke, although I am afraid he will never be able to walk again without assistance.

I think when you come home, he will be willing to settle with you the old disputes. Men do tend to mellow in their old age. If you ask me, it is a bad idea for father and son to partner in business. Money can separate the best of families.

I told Anne Jane you were promoted to Captain and she was very impressed. She is still not married. Although I told her just the other day that my Edmond was not the marrying kind, I still think she will wait you out.

Jack and Carl are enlisted, but they are just privates. Try not to rub it in too much when you get home. You know they are jealous of you. Everyone knows you are my favorite and rightfully so.

Well, I will close for now. Please don't keep your poor old mother waiting so long for your next letter.

With all my love, Mother

I closed the letter and carefully placed it back in the envelope, "What kind of man am I married to?" I asked in disbelief. "Fannie, he claimed he was from Savannah and had no living family. I felt sorry for him and now apparently he is a damn Yankee and a lying one at that. What have I done, Fannie?" I cried out hysterically.

"Lizzie, you have done nothing that any other woman would not have done; you fell in love with a man. How were you to know, or any of us to know, he was not what he appeared to be? You have to go about this logically. If not, you stand to lose a lot more than your pride. I would suggest you act as if nothing is wrong until we can work out a plan. I hope that will include getting your father home. Can you promise me that, Lizzie?" she asked, kissing my trembling hand.

"It will be the hardest thing I have ever done. Fannie, how can I sleep in that man's bed after this? If I do, I suppose that makes me no better than him."

"You won't have to," Fannie smiled.

"I will Fannie, he will expect it," I looked at her, puzzled.

"You are forgetting I am your doctor. Due to complications, you are now unable to perform your wifely duties. In fact, I am recommending separate rooms altogether. I will tell him myself and save you the trouble."

I looked through the balance of the letters, but I did not open another. Nothing could be more of a shock. Fannie suggested we go for a ride and I agreed.

That night when I blew out the light, I was reminded of Sallie's letter. Quickly I lit the lamp and took out the letter.

Dearest Sister,

Mother and I are so thrilled to hear you and Edmond are going to have a baby. Children make a home and you will be a good mother. It is wonderful that Edmond has taken over the management of Sandy Ridge in Papa's absence. It is not just any man who would so dutifully take on such a financial responsibility. You must be so proud to have such a kindhearted husband. I intend to tell him myself when we at last meet.

There is no easy way to break this news; we have heard from Papa! A letter came from Delaware where he is being held captive. He said up until now he has not been allowed to write. It seems he has befriended one of the colored guards who sent out the letter on his behalf. More good news, Joel Simpson is also with him. I am not sure how much he could say in his letter, but he claims they both are well. He said if we write to him, Washington, the colored guard, will do his best to see he gets the letters. Mother is much relieved that he is alive, but we all know prison camps are the poorest of living.

Ransom says to tell you hello. He is in Wilmington or somewhere in the vicinity, last we heard. The winter was hard on him and now the heat is just as awful.

I suppose you knew we had to close the store. We took out what supplies were left for our three families, but I am afraid that too is thinning out. Thank you very much for the garden seeds; Mother and I put in a nice little garden and it is coming on.

Harper and Violet are still with us, but I almost wish they were not. It is hard to provide for so many people. We are raising chickens and a few hogs. As long as the Yankees don't come through here, I expect we can hold on.

I am lucky I paid off the farm with the money I got from Aunt Sara. I dare not complain of potato soup when there are others much worse off.

I suppose you heard what happened at Chancellorsville. Even though it was a great victory for the South and many are calling it General Lee's perfect battle, it was darkened by the mortal wounding of our "Stonewall" Jackson.

Thomas sent a letter; his regiment, the 14th North Carolina was there the night it happened. Jackson was scouting ahead to determine the feasibility of a night attack on May 2nd. When they came riding back, they were mistaken for Union cavalry. The 18th North Carolina regiment was given orders to open fire.

Stonewall was shot three times and his horse took off wildly after the ambush. When they carried him back to camp, many of the men were seen openly weeping. After his arm was amputated, pneumonia set in and Jackson died on May 10th.

Thomas said the men are losing their morale for war. For some, the despair is worse than death.

Mother is well and she says she is becoming a regular farmwoman. I am sure Papa will be glad to see her, even *though he will be sad to see her hair has turned gray. She is still beautiful, just like you my dear sister. I only wish I could see her in a pretty dress once in awhile. I guess we all wish for better times. All of us women are sick to death of this war.*

Take care of you and your little bun in the oven. Please write to me soon,

Love, Sallie

PS: I have enclosed a newspaper clipping for your scrapbook,

Salisbury has witnessed today one of the gayest and liveliest scenes of the age. About 12 o'clock, a rumor was afloat; the wives of several soldiers now in the war intended to make a dash on some flour and other necessities of life belonging to certain gentlemen, who the ladies termed "speculators."

They alleged they were entirely out of provisions and unable to give the enormous prices now asked, but were willing to give government prices. About 2 o'clock they met, 50 or 75 in number, with axes and hatchets, and proceeded to the depot of the North Carolina Central Road.

The excited women said they were in search of flour, which they learned had been stored there by a certain speculator. A rush was made and they went in, the women reportedly hauled off ten barrels of flour.

—Salisbury Daily Carolina Watchman, 23 March, 1863

I blew out the light. Here I lie in comfort and ease, while Sallie and Mother are in dire need. The thought came to me; Edmond is playing me for a fool. Turn about is fair play. I will play Fannie's game, at least until Papa gets home. Surely I can humble him to allow me to send money to Sallie and Mother. Yes, Mr. Cook, this is war, and you ain't seen nothing yet.

CHAPTER 30

The Lord Taketh and

The Lord Giveth

When Edmond came back for me on Saturday, Fannie told him I was suffering from "Gaffeur." I was not to be disturbed in any way during my pregnancy as it would be harmful to the baby and me. Edmond bought it hook, line and sinker.

Later I asked Fannie, "Exactly what is "Gaffeur?"

"French for fool, because that is exactly what he is," Fannie laughed.

With my new condition, Fannie suggested I stay with her at the Bullwinkle house. Edmond showed no signs of disapproval and it was agreed. At least this would give us time to plan.

June 25, 1863

There was news of an outbreak of cholera in Charleston. It was suspected the waterways had become contaminated from sick soldiers dumping sewage. This did present a problem and it was too great of a risk for me to stay in the city. Therefore, Fannie took me to Sandy Ridge.

Fannie came at least twice a week to visit, bringing me my mail and newspapers for my scrapbooks. Every visit, we were waiting for an opportunity to search for the medical supplies. Unfortunately, we were always under Edmond's watchful eye as if he knew we were up to something.

We had all been optimistic after Fredericksburg and Chancellorsville, but General Lee's invasion of the North was not so successful. The Union had taken over parts of Virginia, Tennessee and portions of the coast. Our fears heightened as Federal troops steadily pushed further south.

Danger was everywhere. Fannie said Charleston's streets were not safe for her, let alone for a white woman. Everyone was talking about the uprisings and runaway slaves.

Now, it was not just Edmond who bolted doors and put up gates. I felt cut off from the rest of the world, fearing Yankees or a band of angry Negroes with torches would descend upon us at any moment.

The newspaper clippings were becoming more upsetting. The Union was burning and destroying homes and towns. Women and children were forced to take to the woods or caves to forage for themselves. Horror stories of our soldiers starving to death in the trenches, eating shoe leather, horses and rats.

Edmond's good luck was running out too. We had substitutes for almost everything and substitutes for the substitutes. It was a wise idea of Edmond's to raise provision crops, yet not a morsel would be sold for profit. It was just July and with fifty some slaves, we were quickly consuming all we were raising. At this rate, there would be nothing left to put up for winter. Salt was so scarce we boiled the boards in the meat house hoping to produce enough salt to preserve a few hogs.

Fannie had written to Sister Irene about the possible exchange. Fannie encouraged me to continue writing to Papa. I wrote to Papa every week. I spared no details. I wanted him to be prepared when he came home. Somehow, I just knew he was getting my letters.

On one of Fannie's visits, she brought me a present. It was a beautiful little curly haired puppy. I had not had a dog since I was a child and I found this new friend a great comfort. I named him "Rebel." Edmond was not fond of the dog, nor the dog of him.

July 1863

Newspaper clippings:

Independence Day brings tears for the South after two great battles are lost.

July 1-3 The Battle of Gettysburg, Pennsylvania, is a major Union victory.

July 4, 1863 Vicksburg, Mississippi surrenders to General Grant's forces.

Is the Confederacy doomed? With the Mississippi River cut off and the great loss of men at Gettysburg.

July 7, 1863 Washington holds a delayed Independence celebration. It was a great sight to behold with soldiers and bands marching up Pennsylvania Avenue. When they reached the White House, President Lincoln gave a speech to the crowd.

After the news that the war was not going well for the South, Edmond went into town almost daily. I was happy for him to be gone. My only concern was being alone. Although I had servants, none of them were like Mammy. Nina was the house servant. She and her husband, Grover, lived on the third floor. She was not overly attentive or kind. She did what I asked, but always with a slight hint of defiance. I could have fallen dead on the floor and she would have just stepped over me. Maybe it was a sign of the times, but all these new slaves were distant and cold. They seemed to be walking around in some sort of trance with faces like the living dead.

August 1863

On Sunday, August 1st, Fannie came to visit. When Edmond saw her arrive, he went to the door himself. I was now well into my sixth month and suffering greatly from the heat. My expanding waistline made it difficult for me to venture up and down the stairs. Fannie and I usually took our visits on the upstairs porch or in my room.

I felt like a prisoner having not set foot off Sandy Ridge since Fannie delivered me here in June. It was just as well, as all my clothes were so ill fitting. I had no one to sew for me and I resorted to wearing a nightgown most days.

I heard Edmond ask to speak to Fannie in the study. I was worried, until Fannie came in my room smiling. "Good news Edmond is leaving on business and will be gone for at least a month."

"Where is he going?" I asked, realizing I really did not care.

"I didn't ask, I just agreed to come and stay with you until he returned," she said flopping down on the bed beside me.

"When is he leaving?" I asked.

"Tomorrow or maybe today, if I can get back with my things in time."

"Go on! Get out of here!" I teased.

"I will my friend, but first I have a letter from Sister Irene.

I took the letter over to my desk by the light of the window.

Dear Dr. Holloway,

I am sorry to hear about Miss Sander's father. I have seen that prison with my own eyes and it is not for the faint of heart.

I am sorry for my delayed response, but I have just received your letter. I have been on retreat due to the numbers of riots and violent disturbances here in New York City. Lincoln's authorization to draft all men between the ages of 18-35 was not accepted well here. The working class does not want to serve in the military and there was strong objection to the provisions allowing wealthy men to send a substitute or pay a fee to be exempted. The streets have been filled with armed mobs and numerous buildings have been destroyed. Sadly, many Negroes have been murdered and orphanages have been burned.

I will write at once to the Sisters in Delaware and request they visit the prison. I must warn you, even for us, things are much more difficult. However, I give my word to do all I can. Once the "Bibles" arrive, I will address that issue as well.

Yours in faith and love for our Lord and Savior,
Sister Irene Maloney
The New York Children's Society

"Fannie, she called me Miss Sanders; she has no idea I am married. What would she think if she knew I was in such a mess?" I asked, handing her the letter.

"No, I left that detail out. I must go now. I will let Edmond know I will be back before sundown."

Fannie was good for her word; she was back before sundown and she brought Cindy Lou to stay as well.

The next morning I walked with Fannie and Cindy Lou down to the duck pond to search the chamber. I was not able, nor would I fit, through the door, so they went down without me. Just as I expected, they found the medical supplies, along with a purse of jewels, a small bag of gold and a few silver coins.

"Shall we take it all?" Fannie called up.

"Let's not press our luck, hopefully he won't miss the medical supplies. Leave the purse for now." I watched them climb back up the ladder and wondered if I had made a wise decision.

Those weeks flew by and for the first time I was looking forward to the arrival of my baby.

September 1863

The afternoon of September 15th, Fannie and I went for a short walk. I was not much up to it, but she insisted it was good for me. When we returned, we saw Edmond's horse. "Well, the devil has returned," Fannie groaned and took hold of my arm.

We walked in the house together. Trying to show some excitement that my husband had returned, I kissed him on the cheek.

"Save it, dear, until you have something more to offer and by

341

the looks of you that might not be in my lifetime," Edmond acted as if he was joking, but he was not. Then without saying a word more, he got up and went out to the barn.

"I hate that man, Fannie!"

"Not as much as I do," Fannie remarked. As soon as this baby is born, we are going to get rid of him, even if we have to kill him," she teased.

When Edmond came back in the house he announced, "Well, Dr. Fannie. I had Grover pull your rig around front. Daylight is burning."

I started to speak my mind, but Fannie grabbed my arm and we went upstairs to pack her things. She promised to be back in a day or two to check on me.

"Don't take Cindy Lou. Edmond does not know she is here and he will not even notice her," I pleaded.

I was right, he never mentioned Cindy Lou even though she was staying in the room with me. To pass the time, I took up the notion to resume efforts to teach her to read. I was pleased she was showing progress.

Edmond came and went as he pleased. Sometimes it was just day trips, but often he was gone for a day or two. Upon returning from one such trip, he carelessly left a letter lying on the hall table. I seized the opportunity and opened the envelope. There was no return address or letter inside, just two articles from a Yankee newspaper with handwritten notes.

Privateers or Pirates?
They have got to be stopped!

IS This You, Edmond Cook?

Rebel spies hung June 9, 1863

REmember, WiLLiams AnD PEterS

Edmond became increasingly more nervous, carried a gun at all times, and slept fully dressed in the study. It may not have made sense to the household, but for a man who was trying to save his neck, it made perfect sense.

On Monday, October 6th, Edmond came in and demanded I sign some papers. I refused, insisting I must read them first. He towered over my chair and his anger overtook him. Drops of sweat dripped off his brow on to my face. He was no longer handsome to me with bags under his eyes and stinking breath. For the first time I was afraid he would strike me. I made an attempt to lift myself out of the chair, but he pushed me back down.

"What good are you to me anyway?" he said, pointing a dirty finger at me. "I can take care of this myself."

I felt the tears come to my eyes. I did not care what he thought of me, but he was right. What good was I to anyone? He stormed out of the room with his papers. Rebel was sleeping at the top of the stairs and growled as he approached. Edmond raised his leg to kick him, "Edmond, No!" I cried. My words were in vain and with one hard thrust, Rebel lay at the bottom of the stairs.

"Who's your master now?" Edmond gloated as he stepped over him at the bottom of the steps.

I called for Cindy Lou at the top of my voice, but there was no answer. I was halfway down the steps when the front door opened, it was Fannie. She saw Rebel lying in a heap and knelt down beside him. By the time I got to the bottom I could hear him whimpering. Fannie lifted him up and carried him to the dining room table. His eyes never left my face as Fannie's hands examined him. "Lizzie, he will be all right, but I think his leg is broken. I can splint it." She left and came back with her medical bag and proceeded to make a cast for Rebel.

Edmond showed up in time to see Fannie finishing her work. Fannie went straight up to him, "Edmond, I need to know what happened to this dog?"

"You don't need to know anything except I am telling you to get your black ass out of my house!" he shouted angrily.

"Your house?" she asked.

344

"You heard me," he said, looking pleased. He leaned toward me and planted a kiss on my cheek, "Ain't that right, sweetheart?" Then in a degrading manner, he took hold of my head and nodded it up and down to make me agree.

Fannie stood tight with her hands on her hips.

"Go now before I shoot you for trespassing," Edmond laughed, pulling a small pistol out of his pocket.

"Edmond!" I screamed, holding on to my belly. He looked at both of us for a moment and slipped the gun back in his pocket. I took hold of Fannie's arm and started walking toward the door.

"Edmond Cook, if you so much as lay a hand on Lizzie or that dog again, you will have me to deal with," she shouted back as we left the room.

Fannie and I walked out on the porch and she handed me a small package, "Here, this is for your birthday."

I undid the package to find a lovely family bible. "Thank you! It is beautiful, just like Mother's. I suppose soon I will have a birth to record too," I whispered, staring off in the distance.

"Of course you will," Fannie said patting me on the back.

I tried to cheer up and convince her I would be all right. She promised to be back the next day. I laughed at her joke telling me she would have her pistol next time, too. Although, I suspected if she had one, it would not be a joke.

I sat down on the steps and watched her steer the carriage out the drive. I was twenty-one years old that day. Oh how my heart yearned for the days when I was just a little girl growing up here without a care in the world. I bowed my head and prayed,

Dear Lord,
Please forgive me of my many sins and help me to be strong. Give me faith in knowing the child I carry will be a great blessing to us all. Amen.

"Speak to me Lord," I prayed, opening the Bible and allowing the pages to open up at free will.

"The wolf shall dwell with the lamb and the leopard shall lie down with the young goat, and the calf and the lion and the fattened calf together and a little child shall lead them."

Sunday November 1, 1863

On Fannie's last exam, she warned me the baby was due any day. I was alone in my room when I heard Cindy Lou scream. I lifted myself up and managed to make my way downstairs. I could hear noise coming from Papa's study. I pushed the door open to find Edmond lying across Cindy Lou on the floor. Her blouse was torn and her skirt was raised.

Neither one of them saw me. All I could think of was I had to stop this. I took hold of the fire poker and the months of anger came down with a mighty blow to Edmond's head. He stopped moving and Cindy Lou crawled out from underneath him.

I took hold of her arm, "We have got to get out of here!"

"Rebel!" I cried out at the top of my lungs, "Here boy, here!" He did not show. We had no time to waste; we ran to the barn. I could hardly breathe, but together we managed to hook up the horses. Cindy helped me in the carriage and Rebel came from behind and leaped in next to me. "Good boy, now let's get the hell out of here!"

Once we were a good distance from the house, I regained my voice, "Cindy Lou, you must promise me you will not say a word about this to anyone."

"Yes'um, I do's. Nev'r a word," Cindy Lou promised.

When we arrived at the Bullwinkle house, I could barely walk. My heavy belly was throbbing and the pain was wrenching. Simon met us at the door and helped me into the clinic. "Where is Fannie?" I asked.

"She is at the hospital," Simon replied nervously.

"Please go get her; I need her." I cried.

Simon called for Millie, but it was Molly who came to the door.

"Millie is not here; she went with Fannie to the hospital," she answered. Molly, seeing me sweating and gasping for air asked," Miss Lizzie is the baby coming?"

346

"I suspect so," were the only words I could speak.

Simon left in a dead run to go for Fannie. The pains were getting more intense and I collapsed to the floor. Molly knelt down beside me and with amazingly skilled hands she examined me, "Cindy Lou, help me get her over on the table," she called out. "The baby is crowning."

Cindy Lou gasped.

"I don't think Fannie will make it back in time; we are going to have to deliver this baby ourselves," Molly said calmly.

"We ain't never...," Cindy Lou started, but Molly's little hand was over her mouth before she could finish her sentence.

I was not resentful of the pain. I deserved whatever God brought upon me. As the labor intensified, I found myself hovering over my own body, looking down at the three of us. I could hear moaning, but I was not sure if it was my voice. I felt as if I was in the space between the living and dead. I heard Annabelle laughing and Mammy calling my name. I was brought back to consciousness when a vision of Edmond's angry face flashed before me. I screamed.

"Push Lizzie, push!" Molly was saying.

All was quiet for a moment and I felt a gush of relief. Within seconds, I heard the voice of my newborn child.

"A girl," Molly said, placing the tiny new soul in my arms. With wide-open eyes, she looked upon my face. She knew me and I knew her. The bond was made. Sunday was a fine day to be born.

Some hours later, I awoke to find Fannie sitting by my side. "What will you name her?" she asked tenderly.

"Victoria, it was Mammy's name," I muttered and drifted back to sleep.

Between nursing and recovering, it was not until the next afternoon before I was strong enough to talk to Fannie. I was afraid as soon as Edmond recovered he would come looking for me.

After hearing what happened Fannie said, "It is over Lizzie. No matter what; you have got to get rid of him. Do you know an attorney you can trust?" she asked, but before I could answer, Millie knocked on the door and asked to speak to Fannie.

"I'll be right back," she promised.

Judging by the sun, it was several hours before she came back. She was carrying Victoria who was eager to nurse. Once my motherly duty was completed, Molly came for the baby. Fannie sat quietly staring out the window.

"Fannie, what is wrong?" I asked.

"Edmond is dead," she said softly.

I bit my lip, "I killed him?"

"Yes, I would say so," she said, rather matter of fact. "The overseer found him lying on the floor in the study. It was the sheriff who came to break the news."

"Do they know?" I asked, starting to cry.

"Absolutely not! I told him you have just given birth after being in labor since early yesterday morning. He was satisfied with my explanation. To buy us a little time, I said it would be best to wait until you were a little stronger to break the news."

"Fannie, this is all so much. First, I was guilty of sins of the flesh, but now I am a cold-hearted murderer. May God have mercy on my miserable soul. I wish I had never laid eyes on that man's face."

"Do you Lizzie? Then what of Victoria?"

"Yes, some good has come out of all this and she is perfectly innocent. I hope the day never comes when I have to tell her what happened."

"You are as pure as the driven snow and no one will ever prove differently. Now, you just have to play the part of the grieving widow until this blows over. I will go into town tomorrow on your behalf and make arrangements to have him buried. Once you are on your feet, the only fitting thing to do is to have a nice graveside memorial service.

Tuesday November 3, 1863

When Fannie came back from the undertaker, she made the announcement to the household Edmond had been killed. Cindy Lou's mouth was sealed and a wreath was hung on the door. By afternoon, the news was all over town.

The Charleston Post

 A graveside memorial service was held today for a Charleston businessman, Mr. Edmond Cook, who was mysteriously murdered at the country home of his wife, the former Miss Theodosia Elizabeth Sanders. Only a small group of friends and neighbors attended the service. His wife, unable to stand for the service was seated in a carriage. It was a mournful site seeing the beautiful young widow sitting by the wayside holding the couple's newly born child.

 It was Fannie's idea to set me aside in the carriage with the baby. She was right; it removed me from all suspicions. No one dared question me about Edmond's death.

 The next morning I wrote a letter to Mother and Sallie. Fannie agreed we should send a letter to Edmond's mother. She wrote the letter as his doctor and made no mention of a wife or baby. Afterwards, we recorded the events in my new bible.

Victoria Frances Cook, born Sunday, November 1, 1863
Edmond Stanhope Cook, died Sunday, November 1, 1863
Underneath Edmond's name, I wrote:
'The Lord taketh and the Lord giveth"

CHAPTER 31

You Owe Me Nothing

After Edmond's death, there was a steady stream of visitors, leaving small gifts and parcels of food. A widow was not expected to receive visitors for the first month and Fannie politely turned them all away. It was important that I follow all the rules of etiquette down to the very last thread. We certainly did not want to raise a single eyebrow. However, when Mr. Ern claimed it was important he speak to me, I agreed to see him.

Dressed in a robe with my hair hanging lose, I met him in the parlor. My appearance must have made an impression on him, "Mrs. Cook, you look, I mean I can see how hard all this has been on you."

"Yes, it is all quiet a shock," I said mournfully.

"Lizzie, with your permission, I would like to speak to you like a father. Jacob and I have been friends for a long time. I feel he would approve of me stepping in on his behalf. Can we speak frankly?" he asked, looking at me tenderly.

"Go ahead, Mr. Ern; speak what is on your mind." I was careful not to make unnecessary comments.

"When Edmond first came to us with his grandiose ideas, we all bought into them, including your father. It appeared his privateering ventures were a smart investment and an opportunity to help the South. Our ship was named the "Seagull" and it was profitable. Soon after that, your father and I left to go on the missions.

Once I returned, I discovered Edmond brought on more investors. We now owned a small interest in a whole fleet of ships. When Edmond came into town, I met with him. I planned to ask for a buyout for your father and myself, but he assured me we would all be rich men soon. There is no polite way to say this; but the only one getting rich was Edmond. Furthermore, we heard rumors of our ships ambushing Confederate supply ships. We were afraid he was selling goods to whomever could pay the highest price, North or South. Lizzie, these cargos were not just tea or sugar, but guns and ammunition too. This was far more than any of us bargained for and we wanted out. None of us wanted to wind up in prison or, forgive me for saying this, like your husband.

"Mr. Ern, you don't have to apologize. I will be honest with you; Edmond was not the man I thought he was. Just like you, I wanted out. However, when I found out I was expecting a baby, I was trapped." I could say nothing more. I held my head down and struggled to contain myself as the long awaited tears began to flow.

"Lizzie, I am so sorry. I know you have suffered and I wish this were the end of it. Yet, I am afraid there is more I need to tell you," he tried to continue, but I interrupted him.

"If you are going to tell me about Papa, I know. I made my own investigations. Fannie and I have contacted the Nuns and sent them the stolen medical supplies. They have agreed to try to negotiate an exchange for Papa and Joel's release.

He stood up, walked across the room, and took up my hand, "Excellent. You are as clever as your father!"

"Well, let us just pray he is home soon," I said, standing up, thinking this would end our visit.

"Lizzie, please let me take up a bit more of your time. There is more urgent business. Do you know where Edmond kept his records and documents?"

"Nothing here, he kept those things locked up in Papa's study," I answered, suddenly realizing the danger we all might be in.

"We have got to destroy them. If they are found, it could cost you Sandy Ridge. Then he cleared his throat and dropped his voice to a whisper, "And all of us might wind up at the end of a rope."

I felt my knees start to buckle and he helped me back to my seat. "I understand, but as you can see I am not able to take care of such a chore. Maybe next week," I said doubtfully.

"Lizzie, will you trust me? Give me the keys to Sandy Ridge and I will search the house over and burn any incriminating evidence."

"Yes, but there is the overseer. He is suspicious too. I saw him and Edmond unloading a wagon of weapons just a few weeks ago. The new slaves are not the most agreeable lot and you may be in danger if you go alone. I will send Simon with you, he can be trusted."

"Thank you, I can leave immediately if it is agreeable," he announced, picking up his hat.

"I will call for Simon and you can brief him along the way."

Mr. Ern returned and reported he was met with opposition by the overseer at Sandy Ridge. The man was staying in the main house and refused to let him in the house. Not wishing to create more suspicion, Mr. Ern left without a fight.

"Mr. Ern, I am going to write a personal letter to that man, demanding he give you complete access to the house and property. Furthermore, I am demanding he vacate the premises at once," I said, outraged. "Does this man think he has squatter's rights to my house?"

"No Lizzie, I would not think so. Perhaps he was trying to protect the house until he received orders from you. If I were you, I would first ask him nicely," he coached.

"You know we can not afford to get the sheriff involved in this."

"Wisely put," I said, reconsidering.

I composed a polite letter,

Dear Sir,

I am grateful for your precautions since my husband's death. However, Mr. Ern has my full permission to enter the house at will. He will be staying at Sandy Ridge and taking up office in my father's study. I am sure you under-

stand the urgency to settle up some estate matters.
Therefore, you may return to your home, in receipt of this
note.

Thank you for your coorporation,

I pondered how to sign my name. Lizzie sounded too girlish, since I was married. Legally I was still Mrs. Cook, whether I liked it or not. I decided I would sign my name simply, *Elizabeth Sanders Cook*, without Miss or Mrs.

Mr. Ern read over the letter and nodded. He agreed to return to Sandy Ridge in the morning. He was a widower with no children and said he would stay at Sandy Ridge as long as I needed him to. "Before I leave, there will not be a trace that Edmond Cook ever lived there."

I walked him to the door and before I thought, I gave him a kiss on the cheek. He looked at me appreciatively, "You're a good girl, Lizzie."

I smiled and stood on the stoop long enough to watch him climb up on his horse and ride away. He was like Papa; they shared the same gentle nature. Suddenly, I realized summer had passed and the front porch was covered with brightly colored leaves. I was reminded of how Annabelle used to love to collect the leaves. The trees' glow only meant their beautiful leaves were slowly dying. I would have Millie sweep them up in the morning. In my twenty-one years, I had seen enough of dying.

Victoria was a joyous addition to our household, but I admit I was thankful for all the helpful hands eager to hold, rock and diaper. Even Simon was happy to take his turn rocking my pretty little angel. She was a good baby, rarely fussy and most of all she had a healthy appetite.

Nursing an infant, I was to discover, was a full time job. Fannie worried between the rations on food and nursing my health would suffer. She tortured me with terrible tasting tonics, bitter tinctures and herbal teas. She insisted I coat my nipples with honey and lastly, to regain my figure, I was to trot up and down the stairs at least a dozen times each day. The latter she enforced strictly, saying I would thank her someday. I was not so sure, my figure was the least of my concern these days.

Several days passed and Mr. Ern had not returned. I could only assume he was successful. I was unable to follow up what was happening, nor did I want to trust anyone else. It was too cold to venture out with a newborn, so I was homebound.

I was nursing little Victoria eight to twelve times a day, which left only a window of no more than two hours for myself. Fannie had introduced me to a breast pump, which I found painful and produced little results.

Sunday, November 29th was exactly one month since Edmond died. Society now expected me to make my first church appearance as the grieving widow. Fannie kept the baby and Molly accompanied me. I was in mourning with a full-length weeping veil and a black dress. I knew I would have to get used to this dull heavy bombazine material, for a widow remained in deep mourning for at least one year and one day.

The first time I tried to fit in my dress, I was amazed; Fannie's stair climbing ritual had paid off. The problem I quickly discovered was my tightly laced corset against my engorged breast caused leakage. Fannie fit me with a set of peculiar glass breast shields. They were designed to fit over the nipple and collect the milk, uncomfortable, but undetectable through my clothing. Strange, what secrets lie upon a woman's bosom.

When we first stepped out of the carriage at the church it occurred to me, I would be entering the church carrying a great sin in my heart. I hesitated before we entered, wondering if God would strike me dead as I passed through his holy doors. Once inside, even through my veil, I could see them staring at me. Molly took me by the arm and like a bride led me down the aisle. I could hear their whispers as I passed by. I was thankful for the veil. I closed my guilty eyes, bowed my head and in my thoughts I prayed,

Dear Lord, I am not worthy of being in your home. I am a sinner and no better than the lowest. I pray through your grace and understanding, I will find forgiveness. You

alone know my true heart. I was only trying to right a
wrong, not end a man's life. Please do not let my sins bleed
upon my dear little child; she is innocent. I pray that you
watch over my father, he is a good and righteous man.

I did not hear the service nor stand for the singing. It was not because I was unable, but because I was overcome by the glory of the Lord. I felt his presence and he was with me. I could feel his arms around me and his tender lips upon my cheek. How sweet redemption, how sweet Thou holy name!

"Lizzie, are you alright?" Molly whispered.

"Yes, Molly, I am perfectly at peace." I said, giving her hand a squeeze.

The minister was giving the final prayers and I looked up to see his face. I watched his lips and without warning he said, "He hears you in Delaware."

Molly said, "Amen." She took my hand and we walked to the carriage without being stopped.

I ran the words over in my head, "Molly what was the last words the minister said?

"In Jesus' name, Amen. Why?" she questioned.

"Nothing about Delaware?" I asked.

"No, Lizzie, are you sure you are feeling all right."

"Yes little one, I am better than all right and God is good!"

The moment I walked in the house I went straight up to my room and wrote to Papa. I knew without question, my letter would be answered.

The Lord is my Shepherd. Yea though I walk through the
shadows of death, I will fear no evil."

I felt blessed that day. I knew I could face anything now. God had heard my prayers; he had not forsaken me.

That very evening, we were awakened from a dead sleep just after midnight by a loud noise. At first, I was unsure what the origin of the noise could be. I met the others in the hall and we quickly determined it was someone pounding madly on the front door. Simon started to the door and I cautioned him, "Wait, let me get my pistol. It is far too dangerous to extend an open door to any one these days, let alone in the middle of the night!"

Before, I could return, the knocking stopped and was exchanged by an earsplitting whistle. I carefully dropped to my knees, lifted the edge of the curtain and looked out. It was a full moon and I could plainly identify the man as the overseer from Sandy Ridge.

I ordered Simon to open the door, still keeping my hand on my pistol.

Once the door opened the man exclaimed, "Sandy Ridge is on fire!"

"What has happened?" I asked, pushing Simon aside.

"Don't know that man of your'n has been a been a burnin' rounds back. I spect he left some embers smoldering and when the wind got up the sparks set sail and caught the house. Most of the slaves took off runnin' in the woods, but a few stayed to haul water, but it ain't looking good, I can tell you, that right now," he said and wiped his brow.

"Simon, go find the sheriff and tell him to round up some of the men from the fire department and tell them to send the wagon out right away!" I screamed out hysterically. Simon took off in a dead run upstairs to get dressed.

"Hold on," the overseer called out. *"Ain't no need to do that. I done and been by the sheriff's house first. I'm headin' backs there right now to meet them."*

"I am going with you!" I said, clearly not thinking of Victoria.

Fannie reached for me, ""Don't be foolish Lizzie. There is nothing you can do, let Simon go with the man."

"Yes, let me go," Simon insisted. "I'll be your eyes and ears and report back to you in full detail."

"We sure enough can use ever hand we can get. Better take your own horse, no telling' how long this thing is goin' take," the overseer said, turning to go out the door.

"Wait!" I called out after him, "Was Mr. Ern in the house?"

"Don't know Ma'am," he said riding off.

Simon left and Millie put on a pot of roasted acorns for coffee. We had not had real coffee in so long; I had forgotten what it tasted like. None of us could go back to sleep. Victoria was crying and Molly ran upstairs for her. I sat down at the foot of steps and took my baby to my breast. Fannie sat next to me. My tears fell on Victoria's sweet little face. Fannie took out her handkerchief and gently wiped them away.

Everyone tried to go about their normal household activities as if the great disaster was not happening. Fannie did not go to the hospital. Around two o'clock the sheriff knocked. I held my breath and stayed seated, allowing Millie to answer the door. She showed him into the parlor where Fannie and I sat.

He was covered in soot and refused to sit, "We did all we could, but the house could not be saved. By the time we got there the fire had already spread to the slave quarters and the fields were blazing. There is still a crew out there trying to round up the Negroes and load up the wagons with anything that is worth salvaging.

"What of Mr. Ern?" I said, almost afraid to ask.

"He will be all right, pretty shaken up, but he will be fine," he answered. "Your man will be along shortly to give you the details. I reckon when we finish up, they will head over here with the wagons."

"Thank you," I said calmly.

"Oh, Mrs. Cook, the old farmhouse is intact and the barn seems to be saved. That's something anyway," he said, looking for my reaction.

"Yes, just like it stood thirty years ago," I replied.

"Well, I will get back over there now," he nodded and Millie let him out.

"What can I say, my friend?" Fannie asked.

"Say nothing. It was the Lord's will. I suppose Sandy Ridge was so full of sorrowful memories that it took a fire to destroy them. I will shed no more tears for lumber and bricks."

One lone wagon arrived around four o'clock with Simon following behind. I told Simon to unload the charred cargo in the barn. I would deal with the remains when I was able.

Once the chore was done, Simon came in the parlor where I sat reading the Bible. His clothes were too soiled and blackened to sit on the furniture. He sat down one the floor in front of me.

It was a few minutes before he spoke. "Miss Lizzie, it is all gone. Such a sad thing I have witnessed. The slaves have all run off, except for three, who are housing in the barn. The overseer said he would stay as long as you needed him. He expected something needed to be done with the mules and the livestock."

"Thank you, Simon," I said, suddenly realizing the bond I had with this ebony man. "I love you Simon; I love you all. One day, I will repay you for your kindness," I said, looking at him tenderly.

"You owe me nothing," he said, raising his weary body off the floor.

CHAPTER 32

A New Beginning

Tuesday, December 1, 1863

Mr. Ern's visit was tearful and heartbreaking. Even though he was willing to take full responsibility for the incident, he recalled some suspicious activity around the plantation the day the house was burned. A party of four or five men rode up around noon, looking for Edmond. When he told them Mr. Cook had been killed, they did not believe him and refused to leave. After he produced the newspaper with Edmond's obituary notice the men reluctantly left. A couple of hours later, two of them came back in a wagon. They did not come to the main house, but went directly to the overseer's residence. Later they were seen down at the barn loading up several large crates. He did not give this information to the authorities, fearing it might lead to a trail of some of Edmond's double-dealing.

Mr. Ern believed it to be a great mystery. How could a small paper fire on a cold damp ground ignite a whole house? Before he left that day, he promised to take me to the site on Thursday. He would be by to pick me up around 10 am.

My desire to go to Sandy Ridge was the initiative I needed to master the dreaded breast pump. My success, a nippled bottle and a little goat's milk was accepted without delay by my little Victoria.

Fannie agreed to go with us. When Mr. Ern arrived, we were waiting. It was a cold and bleak day, even though the sun was making a feeble attempt to shine.

Mr. Ern gave a vivid description of the damages, but nothing could have prepared me emotionally when we arrived.

The carriage stopped and I slowly got out. The visions of my childhood flashed through my mind. I could see Lottie and me, climbing down the old magnolia tree. There was Mammy coming up from the slave quarters with that prize rooster stuck under her arm. Running across the meadow hand in hand were Annabelle and Thomas. Bent down on one knee was Papa in the rose garden, waving up to Mother rocking on the front porch. Lastly, I smiled remembering on the day the Huneycutts arrived on Sallie's wedding day.

In the whispering breeze, I could almost detect the soft lyrical songs of the slaves and the smell of meat roasting on Christmas day. They were all gone, their joys, their tears, gone up in a puff of smoke. Now with Sandy Ridge buried in the dirt, there was no evidence that they ever existed.

Who will know about the night Edmond and I spent here wrapped up in love, or the painful days he slowly broke my heart? Who will know what happened the night I fled from here. I will know, it is burned in my memory as black as the lumber at my feet.

The three of us walked the vacant site in silence. Mr. Ern sat down in a broken down chair, which I sadly recognized as one of Mother's French chairs. "This is all my fault," he cried out in despair.

"No Mr. Ern, you are not responsible for this, no one is at fault, not even Edmond," God has set this land free to rebirth a new generation. Far be it for us, to question God's ways. Now, let's go home." There was nothing left to say; I walked slowly back to the carriage and climbed in on my own.

Fannie tried to force a little conversation on the way home, but it was mostly one sided. I sat quietly looking out the window, haunted with the memories of this day. Just one year ago. December 3, 1862, Edmond and I were married.

Thursday December 24, 1863

Victoria was sleeping in her cradle. For some time, I sat quietly next to her listening to the soft puffs of air escaping her rosebud lips. How dear she was to me. All my suffering was not in vain, she had become the purpose of my very existence.

After a bit, I sat down at my desk to write Papa. I now spoke to him in a manner one speaks to God; I poured out my soul, my desires, confessed my sins and begged for his forgiveness. Just as we live in faith that God hears our prayers, I lived in faith that Papa was receiving my letters. I told him Edmond had been killed, but it was too risky to say more in a letter. Someday, I will tell him the whole story.

I sealed my letter and turned to look out the window, but winter's icy fingerprints blurred my glass. With the corner of my worn shawl, I cleared a peephole. I saw a few people bundled up making their way down the street. Perhaps they were some of the lucky ones with families and friends to share Christmas cheer. Yet, for most of us, a least one seat would be empty at our table.

Before the war, the streets would have been buzzing with men, women and children, carrying packages, singing carols and ringing bells. Now the only bell ringing was one from a small church in the distance. Its melody sad and mournful seemed to call out,

> *Ding dong, how sad our song,*
> *Ding dong, so much is wrong*
> *Ding, dong, it won't be long,*
> *Ding dong, before all is gone.*

From my window, it barely looked like Christmas. Only a few scattered houses adorned their doors or burned candles in the windows. Yet, what would our homesick soldiers give to sit their weary bodies next to the home fires? I doubt they would give a damn if there were festive decorations or packages under the tree. We had all come to realize the season was not about what you had, but who you had.

I closed my eyes, prayed for my family, and thanked God for my acquired family at the Bullwinkle house. Before closing the curtain, I reflected back on my trip to New York City, "Hell's window," I called it. Would my beloved Charleston follow suit?

We all tried to keep our spirits high. Although baby Victoria had no mind to know it was Christmas, this was her first. It should be special, no matter how modest it might be. Simon brought in a small tree and we decked it with decorations we found in the attic. He managed to catch a nice mess of fish, shrimp and crabs for our supper. Fish, grits and corn muffins would be a most satisfying meal for Christmas Eve.

The only Christmas gift I purchased was a small bag of tobacco for Fannie. She knew I did not approve of her pipe smoking, but who was I to disapprove of anything these days. I had gifts for the rest, but they were all handmade. I sent a card to Sallie and Mother. Even if we could have afforded gifts, the postage was too expensive.

We just returned from church services and Millie was preparing our feast when there was a sudden knock on the door. Simon opened the door with caution to a man in long dark trench coat. "Bullwinkle house?" he asked. "I got three travelers here to drop off. Where do you want their bags? "

I listened quietly, hearing Simon was unable to reason with the man. I came to the door, "You must be lost sir, this is a private residence, not a hotel."

"Nope, got the directions right," he said. "Now, who is going to pay my taxi fee?"

"I will," a woman's voice called out in the dark.

I could see two women emerging from the carriage, their heads were covered and I could not make out their faces.

"My good man, could you help us please," this time the voice seemed vaguely familiar.

The man on the porch left his post and went back to the carriage. It appeared they were helping a feeble traveler to the ground. Once the man was upright, the woman approached the door. My knees went weak when I saw her face.

"Sister Irene!" I cried out in disbelief. I opened the door wide and embraced her as if she were my own mother.

"My dear Lizzie," she said. "I have brought someone to see you."

I looked out to see the driver and the other nun assisting a man to the door.

I did not recognize him, "Lizzie," he called out in a trembling voice. "I am home."

At once, I ran out in the drive. I threw my arms around the frail and weak body of my dear sweet Papa. The commotion brought the whole household out on the porch, while Fannie stood in the doorway, holding Victoria in her arms.

"Come in and warm yourself," I said, helping Papa into the house.

He caught hold of the hall table as we entered. "I want to see this baby."

Fannie smiled and turned Victoria's blanket back for her grandfather to lay his eyes on her sweet face. "She looks like her mother," he said, tenderly.

"Sister Irene, how ever can I thank you?" I asked.

"It is Sister Mary who you must thank," she answered, stepping back to put the older lady in my view. In contrast to Sister Irene, she was dwarf in appearance. I reached for her tiny little hand, which was boney and frail, but instead she reached up to embrace me. I was almost afraid her miniature size body would collapse under the pressure.

"How in the world did a little thing like you accomplish such a feat?" I asked.

"Don't let her size mislead you," Papa said. "She could put any General to shame," to his own joke he started laughing, which brought on a chest rattling cough.

"Jacob, I warned you this trip would be hard on you," Sister Mary said sternly. Then without asking, she pulled up a chair and demanded he take a seat.

"See what I mean," he said, turning to wink at me.

"Your father would be dead if it were not for me. He is as stubborn as a mule. Good thing he was as healthy as one before he came down with pneumonia," Sister Mary said, patting Papa on the back. "When your crates of medications were delivered to our Abby, the Sisters and I went right over to the prison camp. Finding the living conditions appalling, I demanded to see the officer in charge. As it turned out, I knew him and his well-to-do

Catholic family. It is a long story, but let's just say I put the fear of God in him," she said, looking pleased.

"Lizzie," Sister Irene interrupted. "Can you put us up for a couple of days before we head back north?"

"Of course and please join us for supper," I said, and gestured toward the dining room. We went into dinner and Millie served up what we had. They seemed pleased, although Papa did not eat much. As the night progressed, he was noticeably getting wearier.

"Papa, where is Joel?" I asked, almost afraid to hear the answer.

"Joel faired better than me," when we were released, he was sent back to his unit.

There was one more question I wanted to ask Papa, "Did you get all of my letters?" I asked.

"I suppose so, the last one I received was about your husband's death," he answered.

I tried hard not to show my emotions, "There is so much we have to talk about Papa, but it can all wait until you have had a good night's sleep."

I dreaded the task that lay ahead of me. I would have to tell Papa about Sandy Ridge. Millie took our guests upstairs and in short order the household was quiet.

I wrote a letter to Mother and Sallie and if possible, I would send them a telegram. It was truly a miracle Papa was home. Suddenly, my joy faded. This was not his home; Sandy Ridge was his home. He would never go home again.

Friday December 25, 1863

It was Christmas morning and our household was up long before our guests. Fannie managed to locate a small bag of real coffee. Breakfast was fish again and we had a few fresh eggs and enough flour for a pan of biscuits. Fannie and I took our coffee in the parlor, "Does he know about Sandy Ridge?" she asked.

Before I could answer, a voice came from behind, "Know what about Sandy Ridge?" Papa asked. I turned to find him looking stronger and more refreshed than the night before.

Fannie looked at me and said, "Let me tell him."

"Mr. Sanders, come in and have a seat," she said pulling out a chair.

Papa followed her instructions and sat down. In less than two sentences she did the deed. I expected him to cry or rant and rave, but he just sat quietly looking at the floor.

"Well, this makes my decision all the easier." he began. "When one door closes another one opens. Maybe this is the Lord's way of saying it is time to move on.

"Papa don't talk this way; you can always stay here," I said, trying to ease his suffering.

"Lizzie, hear me out. It was never Sandy Ridge that kept me here; it was our way of life, family and friends. This war is going to be over soon, and from what I have seen the South will not be victorious. Our life as we know it has ended. We all must learn to live by new rules. The grand days are over and our stories will soon fill nothing but the pages of history."

"Papa, we can rebuild Sandy Ridge. You did it once you can do it again," I pleaded.

"My dear, that was a long time ago when cotton was king. Now there is a new age dawning of modern machines and factories. We have got to look to the future if we are to survive. I am going back to North Carolina. Lizzie, I want you and Victoria to go with me."

"But Papa, I have the Bullwinkle house, the clinic," I said, standing up and looking around the room.

"Lizzie, I know my words have just been dumped at your feet like a pot of hot water. I have not made this decision in haste; I have heard and seen the ins and outs of this war. Now that the North has control of most of the railways and waterways, nothing is going to stop General Sherman from pushing his way further south. Lincoln wants this war over and if it means burning every house and building, or killing every man or woman that stands in their way, they will do it. Lizzie, you have not seen the horrors I have seen and from here on out it is only going to get worse. Charleston is a prime target and as a single white woman, it will not be safe for you to remain."

"I can take care of myself. I have proved that Papa," I said and turned to Fannie for encouragement.

"Yes, you have, but now you have Victoria to consider. She has no father, what if she is to lose her mother too? Lizzie, in North Carolina both of you will be out of the line of fire."

"Fannie, I can't leave you here. What about Simon, Millie, Cindy Lou and Molly?"

"Listen, Lizzie," Fannie said, standing up and stroking my head. "He is right; you have to think of Victoria."

Sister Irene knocked softly at the door, "I am sorry to over-hear, but perhaps I can help. Lizzie, the young girl Molly, Sister Mary and I will take her back to the abbey with us. Fannie has highly recommended that she be sent to London to study medicine. If she is willing we will do what we can for her."

"This is all so sudden. When are you leaving?" I asked, Papa.

"Today the stations are closed because of the holidays, it will be Monday before I can start to make arrangements and hope-fully *we* can leave as early as Wednesday.

"I will need to think about this, but for now I have so much to tell you."

"Ain't none of it too pretty, Mr. Sanders," Fannie teased. "Except that little baby of hers. Well, if you good people will excuse me, I think I will make the rounds at the hospital. Those boys can use some cheering up on this Christmas Day. Besides, a couple of them are sweet on me. I might just have to marry one of them if you go to North Carolina, Lizzie," she said bluntly.

Papa laughed, "Is she joking?"

"That's my Fannie," I smiled. "You never know with her. She tells it as she sees it, without the least concern what anyone else will think of her. She is her own woman and a better friend I shall never find. I don't know what I will do without her."

Saturday December 26, 1863

Papa and I visited Sandy Ridge together. His mood was somber but not completely despaired. He eyed over the property as if he was a spectator planning a purchase. I followed him up to the top of the ridge. His hollow eyes fixed in the distance filled with tears. "Sandy Ridge," he recalled. "It is hard to believe it has been thirty years since your mother and I first stood up here on this ridge." For a moment, he reminded me of a bird preparing for flight as his silver hair blew in the wind.

We walked past the barn and down by the duck pond. He picked up a few pecans and cracked them together. Then we walked down to the old farmhouse and he spoke to the overseer who informed us he would be leaving by the first of the year.

After all was said and done, we walked hand and hand back to the carriage. Before he stepped up in the carriage, he took one last look, "You know Lizzie, this worthless six hundred acres of crawling timbers and soggy soil sure has served me well. I have no regrets, no regrets at all."

Sunday December 27, 1863

Papa and I attended church service. He was happy to see his old friends again. Mr. Ern was tearful when he shook Papa's hand. They agreed to meet on Monday.

Monday December 28, 1863

Papa said that he would have to know my answer today. I dropped him off to see Mr. Ern. After his visit, I would take him to the bank and then the train station. He would have to know the number of tickets to buy.

I went to the bank and spoke to Mr. Caldwell, then to the see Attorney Winslow. I made my decision. Papa and I went to the train station. We spent the balance of the day sorting through the remains of Sandy Ridge stored in the barn.

Tuesday December 29, 1863

As soon as I finished nursing, I asked to see Molly in the parlor. I told that her I felt it was in her best interest to go with the Nuns.

When Fannie came home, we had dinner as usual, but afterwards I called them all into the parlor. Papa sat down next to me. They all looked up at me like children waiting to be scolded.

I collected my thoughts and I was ready to reveal my decision, "As you all know the war is not going well for the South. No one can predict what the future will hold, but we must safe guard ourselves as best we can. My first concern is for Victoria and second to my family. When I say family, I don't just mean my birth family, but each one of you as well. Here in this house, it is not just a roof we share, but one heart. We have cried and laughed together, but most of all we have learned to survive together. We will always have a common bond, love," my voice began to tremble. I looked at Fannie and she was shaking her head to encourage me to go on.

I took an envelope out of my pocket, "Simon, Millie, please accept this certificate from me as a token of my appreciation for devotion and service."

Simon slowly opened the envelope and as he read his bottom lip began to tremble, "The Negro man, known as "Simon" and his wife known as "Millie" belonging to "Theodosia Elizabeth Sanders Cook, are hereafter to be know as "Simon Sanders and Millie Sanders." Furthermore, they are both to be known to all men as free, not held under bond by no man or master other than God Almighty."

"Miss Lizzie, we are proud to have your name," Millie said.

"Simon, as a free man, you will need a home of your own and a little land to farm. My father and I have decided to deed the farmhouse and nine acres of land to you. May God bless you both."

"Fannie, my dearest friend," I said, trying hard to keep my voice steady. "It is my wish that the Bullwinkle Clinic, the house and its belongings be deeded to you. My hope and desire is that you will continue the work we have begun."

Fannie was openly weeping, "Lizzie, you can count on me. But, only if you promise to visit and think of this always as our home."

"I promise," I said, standing up to embrace her.

Everyone began to talk at will and suddenly I realized I had forgotten Cindy Lou who was sitting quietly on the piano bench.

"Cindy Lou," I called out. Do you remember when Edmond bought you back from Miss Lucy? The first words you said to me were, *we will always be together now.*

Well, Papa and I have three tickets to North Carolina, and one of them is yours. Pack your bags. We leave tomorrow on the 937 train at half past ten.

Wednesday December 30, 1863

With my decision to go to North Carolina, I would shed the mourning dress. It was time to bury the dead and turn toward the living.

We left that morning; me in my blue dress, Papa by my side, and lastly Cindy Lou traveling as the baby's nurse.

We settled down in our seats, Papa took up his newspaper and Cindy Lou and Victoria soon drifted off to sleep. I was reminded of the unopened letter from Sallie and a small package Fannie had stuffed in my purse as we were leaving. I opened Sallie's letter first.

Dear Lizzie,

I received a letter from Joel; he has been released from prison. Forgive me for my quick hand, but I wanted to forward his message to you as soon as possible:

"Tell Lizzie the key to my home is underneath the second step in a small metal can. My horses are staying at the farm across the road. I am sure they are as lonely as I am. News from the hospital in Black Mountain, Amanda has passed away."

Next, I opened the package revealing the purse Edmond hid in the chamber. I carefully looked inside at the contents. It was all there, the jewels, the bit of gold and silver. There was a note from Fannie inside,

Dear Lizzie,

Sorry I did not obey you that day. As you can see, I took the purse. Good luck my friend, Love, Fannie

The engine roared and I looked out the window and watched Charleston slowly fade away in the mist. The past has all been written and the book is closed. Now I must look to the future for a new story, a new beginning, *beyond Sandy Ridge.*